FARE FORWARD

FARE FORWARD

A NOVEL BY
WENDY DUBOW POLINS

Hamilton Hall Press

Boston

FOR RICHARD,
YOU HAVE MY HEART

ACKNOWLEDGEMENTS

My profound thanks to everyone who helped make this book a reality.

To all my first readers who cheered me: Mary Lee Broder, Mim Cohen, Laura Donald, Rachelle Kagan Dubow, Rhonda Gilberg, Beth Gold, Jane Goldstein, Holly Bienenstock-Grainer, Elizabeth Greif, Elaine Harris, Miriam Harris, David Judson, Alice Leidner, Susan Levy, Renee Nadel, Marjorie Patkin, Phyllis Patkin, Amy Pliner, Richard Polins, Sophie Polins, Jordan Rodman, Glen Sears, Robyn Stavis, Susan Feinberg Stelk, and, especially, Laurie Judson.

To the artists, architects, teachers, and scientists who have brought light into my world: Jerrilynn Dodds, Wallace Gray, Baruch HaLevi, Steven Holl, Paola Iacucci, Layah Lipsker, Bernard Tschumi, Barry Ulanov, and Mark Wigley. And to the ones whose words and actions live inside my heart, Albert Einstein, T.S. Eliot, Louis Kahn, and Mark Rothko.

To my own students, who have so much to teach me.

To the incredibly supportive and vital community of writers at Grub Street in Boston, thank you for being there.

Alan Lightman at MIT, who inspired parts of this work with his writings on Albert Einstein and his own unique accomplishments in science and the humanities.

To my classmates and alma mater, Columbia University, for providing such a rich source of material for the novel and the amazing, life-altering experiences I had there as an undergraduate and student in the Graduate School of Architecture.

To the amazing city of Boston and the beautiful North Shore of Massachusetts that inspired so many scenes in the novel: MIT; the beaches, dunes, and marshes of Gloucester; the Leonard P. Zakim Bunker Hill Bridge; and the Museum of Science. I never take for granted that I live here.

To Joyce Colahan and everyone at DE in Marblehead.

To my Los Angeles connection: Heidi Levitt, for her enthusiasm and vision, and the people at Landscape Entertainment for encouraging me to push the story farther.

My editors, Stuart Horwitz and Karen Byrne, of *BookArchitecture* for their razor-sharp eyes; my amazing copyeditor, Heather Grant Murray, who "fixed" everything; and my brilliant cover designer, Sarah Bishins of SarahBdesign; and the graphic designers at *A Life in Print*, for their beautiful work inside and out.

This novel could never have been written or completed without the generous assistance of all of you and many others who I cannot mention but who shared their knowledge, support, and expertise.

To my devoted family: my siblings; parents; grandparents; and especially, my darling daughters, Sophie and Rosie, and my husband and partner, Richard. Thank you for riding this wave with me, through the highs and lows, and loving me fiercely through it all.

And, finally, to those in my life who have shown me through their own example that life is not about finding yourself; it's about creating yourself, making a difference, and giving back—thank you for giving me something to strive for every day.

Wendy Dubow Polins, March 2011

A NOTE

In this novel, I have been inspired by the many and sometimes inconsistent theoretical ideas that are offered in physics, literature, and ancient mystical texts. Some of the ideas and theories have been proven, while others remain in the realm of possibility and belief. I have not attempted a scientist's or historian's standard of completeness or accuracy because this would have moved very far away from the intent of the story. In any exploration into the unknown, we must often take a leap of faith.

It is important to stress that this story is fiction. While a number of the characters who appear in this novel are based on historical figures and many of the areas described do exist, certain physical characteristics may have been altered or augmented. Specifically, the reliefs discussed at the Cathedral Church of Saint John the Divine do not exist there. Dates have been changed and portraits of the characters who appear are fictional as are the conversations, events, and journeys undertaken.

— *Wendy Dubow Polins*

What we call the beginning is often the end
And to make an end is to make a beginning.

T.S. Eliot, "*Little Gidding,*"
No. 4 of Four Quartets, stanza V

While time is withdrawn, consider the future
And the past with an equal mind.

Not fare well,
But fare forward, voyagers.

T.S. Eliot, "*The Dry Savages,*"
No. 3 of Four Quartets, stanza III

GABRIELLA

THE ICE COLD surrounds me and, finally, I let go.

Salt water rushes into my lungs, and its weight pulls me down, deeper—into the infinite blue space. The crushing pain is gone because I've left my heart behind, and, this time, I'm not afraid, because I know he's with me.

I need to remember. The way our bodies would meet in the dark, and in the light, floating in the moving tide of our pleasure. The *worlds* between us melting.

I know that I could paint his words with my brush, draw the shape of his breath with my pen, and sculpt the meaning of his thoughts into stone. But I understand that it cannot be—so I choose this. I'm tired of searching and trying to understand. Instead I let go to the powerful force and become one with the sea.

I won't live in this world without him; I know there's another way. Maybe this is it.

1

SOPHIE

JUDEAN DESERT, 1943

"YOUR EYES WILL adjust to the darkness," the soft voice says.
I had wandered away from the group and into the silence of the cave to find a few moments of solitude. A quiet that only the desert could provide. The darkness is a welcome relief from the extreme daytime heat that burns my skin and the powerful sunlight that shines down on this small, sacred piece of earth. I need to clarify the strange sensation, the one I never seem able to explain—the feeling that I've been here before.

"Yes," I respond cautiously to the reassurance and point my voice in its direction.

I'm aware of his presence as he follows me into the bell-shaped space of the cave. The cistern, as it is called, where light bends its way into an opening that reveals a small patch of blue sky. There is something about this place and something about him. It all seems oddly familiar.

In the last few days, I seemed to be drawn to him. I recognized the warmth in his words and the slight unidentifiable accent, even a hint of humor at my expense. We had been introduced at orientation a few weeks before and were told he was a special guest—not part of our academic team from the American university. His presence was a mystery, and I noticed how he was constantly accompanied by an armed driver and an assistant, all dressed in formal military gear too hot for the desert.

I watched as he would walk through the large tent that contained the findings of our research: mesh screens, small trowels, and brushes all carefully laid out on tables. These were the tools with which we would slowly separate layers of dirt from any small treasures that waited to be catalogued in the arduous system prescribed by the High Commission on Antiquities and Archaeology. He would carefully inspect the log, where every finding was meticulously recorded, to see whether we had uncovered the elusive evidence, often with a cup of tea in his hand and a slight smile on his lips. The formality of the English traditions were familiar to me from years of travel with my family. Crisp, white linen, crystal, and china seemed incongruous in this desert setting where, under the flapping wings of the tent, everything became covered with a fine film of desert dust.

He moved with elegance and conversed easily in French, English, German, and Hebrew. As he sat at the long table where our food was served by the young Turkish chef, I wondered who he was and noticed his patient manner—whether talking with the British High Commissioner or a simple server. Like the archaeological findings here, there was something different about him: *timeless.*

"This site has been marked by the British Archaeological Commission's Department of Antiquities as a protected area." The formality of our introduction on the first day matched the seriousness of the team leader's words. "These caves and their contents are evidence of a people's desperate effort to survive—ultimately unsuccessful."

I tried to break down what he was saying, the overwhelming implications of where we were, the crushing history, and my own certainty of who had been in this very place, particularly during the time of Herod. These caves were where ancient mystics had found refuge, fleeing for their lives and their beliefs as they recorded words onto sacred scrolls. They were searching, looking for answers to the most profound questions about the nature of the universe. The legend was that the ancient scrolls contained the secrets of how to harness divine energy through mystical traditions and practices, the key to the elusive elements of creation.

But I knew why *I* was here.

These texts were the source of my bedtime stories: tales of an angel who visited Abraham and gave him answers to the many questions about the world, understood through words and numbers outlined in the Book of Creation. Ideas that were at the heart of mysticism and studied by my parents and grandparents and the many generations who came before them. This was what we were looking for, clues to that world.

Their *secrets*—and mine.

I turn slowly and look at the remarkable face, the kind that I would have wished to paint. It is hard to determine his age as he stands and takes me in. Even in the faint light I can see the intensity of the light eyes, the way they turn up, framed by dark wavy hair, and their remarkable color: green.

"The power to choose your fate—like the men, women, and children who hid here, facing the mighty Roman Empire. But you know this don't you?" He smiles as he says the words, seeming to enjoy his own personal secret.

I drop my backpack onto the ground and watch the small cloud of dust it makes as it lands in the sand. It is good to have it off my shoulder, its heaviness a reminder of the objects I cannot seem to separate from—my paints, brushes, small pieces of paper, and my diary—so that I can be ready to record impressions and feelings, as I hoped there was a way to capture the strange spiritual essence of this place in two dimensions. I look up at him and take a moment to understand how I might respond to the personal nature of what he has said. I seem to have lost my place and realize that after the many days of watching him, we are now quite alone. He is answering questions that I did not remember speaking out loud, things I had only wondered about in silence.

"It has not been determined exactly which people were here," I start to respond but I'm not sure what to say.

"The ones writing the ancient texts, searching for answers."

I continue, "Yes, well, we really haven't found conclusively yet who occupied this place and exactly what they were doing. I mean this area has been accessible to many and most recently to the Bedouin tribes. So, the Art History Department in our university has several theories."

I try to say it with authority. I want to fill my words with a confidence and challenge that I do not feel.

He watches as I shift my weight back and forth, taking in everything I am saying. "And what is it exactly that you believe?" I see the floating dust dance behind his shoulders and give shape to the light.

"I'm simply interested in the archaeological aspect of this dig. Uncovering layers of the past. Finding things. I want to learn about a civilization that no longer exists. Like piecing together clues from a mystery. A puzzle," I answer.

It sounds so trite and impersonal to minimize why I am here into this small, inaccurate sentence, so very far from the truth. If anything it was quite the opposite. I was returning to a place that had shaped the lives of generations of family who had come before me, my own ancestors, some of whom I knew had occupied these very caves, searching for the answers that he was alluding to.

He looks right at me as if he knows the lie in what I have said, forgiving its necessity. Understanding why.

I can hear voices coming from outside the cave and realize that the others have begun to gather and prepare for the ride back to Jerusalem. The light coming from above has changed to an orange color, and we need to hurry to be out of this zone by the mandated curfew imposed by the British, before sunset turns into the blackest darkness of the desert, a velvet sky filled with stars.

"I need to go. I think we need to get back now," I say but don't mean it.

As my eyes meet his, I know that I want to talk more. There is something fascinating about him—the way he seems to anticipate my thoughts and the things he said about this place. Yet I push past him, down and out into the late-afternoon sun.

"Sophie! There you are!" a friend shouts as I run back to join the group. I am relieved to be outside of the cave, meeting up with the other students at the end of the long day. My head is hurting, in that way it often does: when I have the dreams.

When I see things.

"Are you all right?" another friend asks me.

I realize that I have knelt down and am squeezing my temples together, trying to push away the dreaded, familiar sensation.

"Yes, yes I'm fine. I just was talking to—" I stand up and realize that he has disappeared.

"Who?"

"Actually, I don't know his name."

I squint my eyes in the direction of the narrow road that follows the edge of the salted sea toward Jerusalem. As I turn back around to gather my belongings, I notice the sun completing its western arc, disappearing behind the iconic mountains of the Judean desert.

2

JERUSALEM

"IT'S SO BLOODY COLD when the sun goes down."

I pull the inadequate sweater around my shoulders and try to straighten my dress and backpack at the same time. The hot days in the desert are always followed by a seemingly impossible drop of temperature, when the stars come out to light our way. I had fallen asleep on the ride back up to Jerusalem, exhausted from the day's activities and emotions. I stumble out of the vehicle onto the plaza in front of the Grand Hotel. I feel chilled and want only a warm bath and bed—but that, I know, is impossible. I have less than an hour to get ready for the evening and I need to navigate past the crowds of people in the lobby.

"Come, join all of us for dinner?" a friend asks me.

"I'm sorry but I can't." I hate myself for turning down another invitation. "My parents have just arrived from the Far East. I haven't seen them in months but I promise, another time." I hope that my constant refusals will not be misinterpreted as disinterest. "They sent a telegram; their ship will be into port in Haifa. Today."

"Righhhht." My friend raises her eyebrows as she stretches out the word, nodding her head as she remembers who I am, my family name.

"They are traveling with *him*, aren't they?"

"Yes," I answer softly, wondering exactly how everyone seems to know the private details of my life—things I have never spoken of to the other students.

A large crowd is gathering in the hotel, and it seems to be a curious mix of locals, press, foreigners, and the ever-present military. The desert light and quiet has given way to a new energy, and I am in no mood to navigate the crush. I only want to think back to the cave and the conversation with the fascinating stranger.

"Looks like his contingent has already arrived. Sophie, look!"

I remember suddenly where I am and why. Everywhere are signs of celebration. There is loud music and food being passed on silver trays by white-gloved waiters. A festive atmosphere of jubilation animates the usually reserved hotel, the fortress on the hill that overlooks the Old City: a witness of time.

"The Nobel Prize! 1921—that's when it happened!" I hear an awestruck man behind me say.

I stand on my tip toes and try to see a clear path through the lobby. Any hopes I had of stealing through the space and up the grand staircase quickly evaporate.

"I'll see you tomorrow," I say to my friends as I back away from the group and consider my few limited options for escape.

"Good-bye, Sophie."

I know there is a back staircase and I press out through the crowd, against the magnetic tide drawing everyone toward the middle of the room to see the small, white-haired man. I need to hurry, to prepare for the reunion with my parents and the evening ahead. What we have all been waiting for: the chance to meet Albert Einstein.

"The Jerusalem air agrees with you; we've missed you terribly."

I am folded into my father's embrace, the warmth of my mother's arms are behind me as I inhale her familiar scent. It is so good to be with them. Their eyes sweep over me as they look for any changes—those that would be visible. I try to stand up straighter, hoping that the way I feel on the inside, touched by the amazing spiritual energy I feel in this place, will somehow be reflected in my face. Within an hour, we are catching up on

8

everything that has taken place in the last few months: my academic life and their trip to the Far East. We walk the short distance from the hotel to the elegant house where the party is being held, and I stop in front of the tall iron gate, stunned by the location and the amazing view of the Old City below.

As we approach, I notice the torches that line the path to the entry, and the yellow glow cast on the stone walls. This is Jerusalem stone, the golden-white limestone that covers every surface and wall of the city below, much of which was built by Suleiman the Magnificent in the 15th century. I know that generations have come here and passed through the ancient gates. People from all over the world, from every major religion, all on very different pilgrimages, but all looking for answers to their prayers.

Voyagers.

"Come inside. The host of the party is a friend of ours. Someone quite interesting." I feel my mother squeeze my hand in encouragement, as if she senses my hesitation.

"I wish we could just be together tonight as a family, Mother. I'm not really in the mood to socialize. I mean, it feels like forever since we've been alone."

She takes a deep breath before she answers me. Her eyes seem to soften with the familiarity of the circumstance, my hesitancy to partake in these types of situations. "Tonight is special, Sophie. I promise. You won't be disappointed. After all, you never know who you might meet." Behind the lighthearted words is a seriousness I don't expect.

The large wooden doors of the home swing open, and we are swept into a grand room. The back wall is composed of tall arched windows that frame views of Jerusalem's Old City. Everywhere I look are paintings by artists that I have only seen before in museums. My parents introduce me to their colleagues, many of whom have traveled to the Far East with their entourage: artists, scientists, and academics who had collected money for the establishment of the university in Jerusalem. I politely answer questions about my activities on the archaeological dig, the findings in our cave, and the strict restrictions of the British Department of Antiquities. Yet, I try to focus, to push away the strange, wonderful, familiar recognition. Like the sensation I experienced earlier in the cave with the stranger. The feeling that

I have been here before.

The room suddenly becomes quiet as a wave of electricity passes through the crowd.

"Sophie, look—it's *him*. Einstein."

He is smaller than I expected, recognizable by the shock of white hair and mustache. I realize the great scientist is preparing to speak.

"Welcome, all of you. I appreciate you gathering here tonight at this beautiful home." His words are heavily wrapped in the distinctive German accent. "I want to thank Dr. Landsman for his hospitality." He turns and raises his glass to someone behind him, hidden by the many people standing in front of me.

I want to know who is fortunate enough to live in this place, in the company of all the art I have been admiring. The host.

"Many of you have come here tonight to celebrate the honor I received of the Nobel Prize. But tonight is not about past accomplishments, it is about the future."

Everyone in the room strains to catch each word the great man speaks.

"I consider this one of the greatest days of my life. Today I have been made happy by the sight of this people learning to recognize themselves as a force in the world. This is a great age, the age of liberation, and with it the growth of the university here. In the search for knowledge, we must learn about more than mathematical formulas. We must understand people, how we treat each other. This is how we will understand this world and perhaps others. Through words, thoughts, science, and art. Astronomy, action, and energy—we will prove that everything is connected. "

People are listening, nodding, stunned at the truth they feel in his words, acknowledging the dream that is about to be realized. I recognize something else, however. Albert Einstein is identifying the key concepts of the secret mystical tradition my grandparents had taught me.

The fundamental recognition that everything is connected.

I suddenly feel dizzy, overwhelmed, and I need air. With everyone listening to him continue, I know I can escape unseen and am drawn out the doors onto a large stone terrace that overlooks the city. The scientist's words float through my head.

I breathe in the cool, dry air in the garden that is filled with ancient olive trees and roses. My hand skims the surface of their twisted trunks as I walk through them. I feel the night air as it circles around me. I'm drawn to the edge of the tree-lined space, bordered by an ancient stone wall that provides a perfect vantage point to view the Old City below. I sit down at a small table and close my eyes.

It is so quiet that I can hear the wind.

Then, voices, low at first then louder.

"He's going to do it, isn't he? Reveal the proof of the ports? He's been waiting for twenty years."

"He will not; he cannot. He has *agreed,* Sydney, the world is not ready yet."

There is a powerful urgency in the first voice, a concern that frightens me. The other voice sounds strangely familiar. It's that unidentifiable accent. I look carefully but can barely make out the two forms as they walk through the trees back toward the house, away from where I am trying to conceal myself. I catch fragments of what they are saying.

"Yes, I understand, Dr. Landsman."

"Good, Sydney. It is critical that you do. It has been decided."

I try not to breathe, in or out.

I am aware of the crushed stone beneath my feet and am afraid to move. Even though I don't understand why, I can sense the importance of what I overheard. I exhale slowly, realizing that I have been holding my breath and search for a way out of the garden. I can see a long, narrow stairway that leads back up to the party, but it is too well lit, and I know returning this way is no longer an option. I try instead to move in silence to a path cloaked in darkness created by the shadows of the house. I carefully place each foot down with a softness that defies my mass and step deeper into the shadows. Finally, I find a door that leads into the lower level of the building.

As I enter, I feel that I can touch time, the centuries upon which this city is built. A place where the ruins of one generation form the foundation for the next. I am led forward by a familiar feeling I don't stop to question. I seem to know where I am and where I'm going. I climb up a small staircase, move down a narrow hallway, and try to find my way back to the party. I realize that I've found a private wing of the home, it is dark and still, but the sounds of the party are getting louder. This must be the way back; I'm almost there.

Einstein's words flow through my head.

"We will understand the world . . . through words, thoughts, science, and art. We will prove that everything is connected."

There is something about what he said. I know that I have been told these very things many times before. The pounding in my head returns, and I force my palms up into my temples. I try to push away the pressure, the sensation that seems to always come before. Then I stop. I have to bend over and wait for the pain to pass.

Suddenly, I know that I am not alone.

"Sophie."

It's the voice. The one I had overheard in the garden and earlier in the day—in the cave. The unmistakeable eyes, looking at me with an amusement and interest I can't explain. As if he had been expecting me.

"I'm sorry, I was outside. I needed some air. The garden is so beautiful." The words are falling out of my mouth. "I just was trying to get back to the party and to my parents."

I turn my face away, afraid to meet his eyes. My arms wrap across my chest as I grab onto my shoulders and try to prevent myself from shaking, cover my pounding heart. He reaches his hand out toward me.

"I'm so glad you found my garden; I knew you would like it. Come with me."

I follow him down the narrow hallway, which is lit by the moonlight. I marvel at the strange coincidences of the day and, now, seeing him again in this place. *One, two, three, four*, I count as I try to distract myself and steady my breathing.

"We didn't finish our talk earlier today. In the cave."

"Yes, I'm sorry that I ran out." I do not continue. I realize that I have no explanation that makes any sense.

We stand together in a small room filled with books, a large wooden desk, and art. He turns away, and I quickly look around at more of the paintings by artists I recognize. All the questions I had not had a chance to ask him earlier begin to enter my head. Who he is, how he knows my name, his presence on the archaeological dig and, especially, how he is connected to Einstein.

I walk over to look at a large painting on the wall. It is all grays and blacks, different than the others in the room but interesting. Modern.

"You like my paintings?"

I turn around to face him. I want to be the one asking the questions. "Of course, everything here is incredible, beautiful. So this is your home?"

"When I'm in Jerusalem. I travel . . . a great deal." His voice drops down. "Please." He lifts his hand and waves to the space as he invites my inspection.

I walk around the room and look at everything: photographs, ceramics, and the many shelves filled with books, every subject, many languages. I realize that he has been watching me.

"Tell me, the archaeology, you seem somewhat disappointed with the lack of findings on the dig. Are you not?" he asks.

"No. I didn't really know what to expect. I mean, I was hoping to find something. A connection to—" He waits for me to finish, but again, I seem to be uncharacteristically at a loss for words. "I don't know, we haven't found many answers."

"Well, I have something for you. A gift." He reaches into a drawer in his desk then raises his hand out to me. I watch as his fingers slowly uncurl and reveal a small disk. "Come."

I take a step toward him and reach out to touch the inside of his palm and take what he offers. My eyes scan the surface of the small object. I see the lines that create seven spaces, the faint ancient letters and shapes. The rough, uneven surface polished in places from touch and time.

"What is it?"

"Look closer." I hear the smile in his voice.

"A Roman coin?"

I turn the uneven charm over and examine the strange symbols. But as I hear the words come out of my mouth, I realize that I know the answer. What I hold is an amulet. A secret charm believed to contain energy, even mystical power, part of the legend of Kabbalah. None had been found on the archaeological dig, and I catch my breath as I look at every detail.

13

My hand carefully cups the coin, protecting the energy I can feel coming from its surface. I know that I am taking my place in a long line of others who have held the amulet in this very way. Yet, more than that, I see it being passed on to those who will come after me, searching for answers to similar questions.

The sounds of the party filter back into the room, reminding me of the strange day and events. I look up at him and see that he is smiling at me.

"Thank you so much, Mr.—"I want to say his name but I realize that we have not been introduced.

"Benjamin Landsman. Very pleased to meet you, Sophie."

"Well, yes, Mr. Landsman. I really do need to get back. Thank you again—for this."

I want to hurry. I know that my parents will be wondering where I have been and I need a few moments alone to think about what has just happened. I want to try to put all the pieces together—who he is, his beautiful home, and what the discussion I overheard could possibly mean. As I reach the doorway of the room, I stop and turn around to make sure I have not imagined it all and I see him looking at me. I raise my hand in the beginning of a farewell, unable to speak. He says what I hoped to hear.

"We will see each other again."

His words are filled with promise.

My parents seem older. Changed by time or perhaps by the shifting lens of my own eye. These last few months as I searched in the caves of Judea, I found time to think about myself and my family. I had even seen very clear images of my future, the premonitions that were always accompanied by the familiar sensations. The silence and energy of the desert lit places within me that had been dark and undiscovered.

My own archaeology.

I seem to love my parents more and understand them better. What they have given me, what I have inherited, and, more, what is to come. As

I approach them, I see that they are talking to a young man about my age. My father's hand rests on his shoulder, and my mother's head inclines toward his, taking in his words. I have come from behind and don't want to catch them off guard. My hand reaches into the bent shape of my mother's elbow as the familiar softness of her form welcomes my fingers. My other hand covers the treasure in my pocket.

"Mother, I'm so sorry. I—"

She turns slowly to greet me. "Where have you been? Come here; I want to introduce you to someone."

I recognize the moment with shock. I have seen it before; in a dream, a premonition. I know what is about to occur, what it means and, more importantly, I know who he is.

"I want to introduce you to Sydney Vogel. He was traveling on our ship, with Professor Einstein."

As his eyes lock onto mine, I am sure. I can feel it in my heart.

I know this is the face I will look into for the rest of my life.

3

GABRIELLA

FIFTY YEARS LATER
GLOUCESTER, MA, 1993

"I SAID NO, SYDNEY—NO!"

I open my eyes as quickly as I can because it is happening, again—the voices, the arguments, the strange meetings that happen at the house, the ones late at night that I pretend to be unaware of. I strain to hear fragments of what they are saying.

"Once again, they are reorganizing and have new leadership."

"The world will soon find out that their deaths were not an accident, that it was murder, who they really are. I'm telling you, it cannot be revealed!"

"You're *wrong*. We've worked our whole lives for this moment, we can't keep the findings a secret any longer."

"No. The information must be kept hidden. We have sworn an oath to protect the secret, as so many before us have. It has been decided."

I hear a crash, something being thrown against the wall in a room several floors below mine, and I sit up in bed. I have that familiar feeling, not only from what they are saying but the clear images about the past and future, connected to the people downstairs.

An intersection of time and worlds.

I try to come back to where I am, into the present and the dark room. I see my books, toys, and the shells we have collected together on the beach, each one a shape and color that touches something in me. They are all here, and so am I, safe in my room at the beach. Tucked into bed, I hear my friends Emily and Lily breathing, their soft sounds of sleep confirming that I was awake. I cross my hands over my eyes as I press them down hard into my forehead and try to push away the pain, the feeling that always comes before—what I see. When I know what is going to happen. I need to separate, close myself off. I don't want to let the images in.

I had decided that things were going to be *different* now.

"You are ready to understand," my grandmother, Sophie, had said, "what we share. It's our special gift, our connection to the future—and past. Come here, Gabriella." I had felt her soft lips on the top of my head. "Always remember that you're different." Her arms circled around me as we rocked back and forth. "Very few people have this ability. It means you are very, very special; I promise you." She smiled. "You'll see."

That was why it happened; this was her promise. But I didn't want it. I didn't want to be special, or different.

The waves crash on the beach below my window, and I climb out of bed. I want to see the movement that makes the sound, connect back to something reliable—the rhythm of the sea. I can still feel the icy cold water we play in during the summer days, the way it stings my ankles and makes my skin tingle. I look over at my friends, Emily and Lily, as they sleep peacefully. They were tired from another summer day together running up and down the beach, looking for crabs, building sandcastles, and throwing our small bodies against the tide. Trusting, knowing that the waves will always carry us back into shore. I treasured my summers with them, away from my other world, the life my parents had chosen to lead in the ancient mystical city so far away.

"Look at this!" Emily had screamed in joy earlier that day as I spread large splashes of color on the blank canvas in my grandmother's painting studio. "Look what Gabriella is making!"

Lily's red hair caught the light as she danced to the music, turning up the volume when no one was looking. We inhaled the scent of the sweet sticks that burned all around us, casting flickering shadows around the room.

"We're creating magic." Our hands would clench together in the small circle our bodies made. "We'll be best friends, forever—always together." I remember how I looked into their eyes, wanting it to be true.

"Gabriella, maybe this time you can stay here? Go to school with us instead of so far away?"

I wanted to; I wondered how I could make time stretch on without an end. I loved them both so much, but there was something about Lily. She was different. I knew that she could really see me. I wanted to test the limits of what I might reveal to her. She would often come and find me seated against the wall, my eyes focused on a pattern of clouds in the sky or the paper on which I was drawing shapes and lines.

Separate.

"It's okay, Gabriella," she would say and put her arms around me, "you can tell me what you see." She knew something. She was connected to the deep dark place inside of me. I wanted to tell her, but I couldn't.

"Maybe next time, Lily," I had said.

This night, there is an urgency to the voices with my grandfather that I haven't heard before. A tone of fear in their words. I feel like I can't breathe and want to go out onto the roof. I pad over to the small door in the slanted walls of the attic bedroom and push it open. I feel the cold wind as it pulls me out into the night. I bend down and crawl carefully, gripping the safe spots my grandmother had shown me. I reach the little ledge where we would sit for hours together and I see her staring out at the sea. I try to be quiet, I don't want to make any sudden movements that might frighten her.

"Is that you, Gabriella?" she asks rhetorically. My grandmother turns and smiles at me. She reaches her arm out to make the perfect small space I fit into.

"I thought you were downstairs, with *them*," I say.

"No, silly, let them argue amongst themselves."

I know she is trying to reassure me. She was the only one who understood. I lean into her safety and pull my nightgown tighter around my legs, not letting the cold late August air in. This is our secret space on the roof of the house, built for those who wait for the ships to return from sea.

As they look out into time.

"It's starting to happen when I'm awake. I thought they were dreams but they're not. They're something else, something very real."

"I know." She wraps her arms over mine as she exhales slowly, preparing herself for whatever I will say. "Tell me, Gabriella. Tell me what you saw this time."

4

I TELL HER OF this night's dreams, some I have seen many times before and some that are new. I describe the sensation of the icy grip of the ocean pulling me down into its inescapable depths, the feeling of my feet walking on a flat-topped mountain under a star-filled night, and the skyline I see of a beautiful city with thousands of lights in its towers before it disappears into darkness. I tell her how I can clearly hear the sound of chanting voices twisted by the rounded walls of a dark cave in a far away place. Even the remarkable green eyes of a stranger and how he looked at me, but mostly what it felt like to be near him.

"Wait—" My grandmother stops me. We are interrupted as I realize that the voices from the meeting have emerged from the house and into the night. I hear car doors slamming and the familiar sound of tires on the crushed-shell stone of our driveway.

"Benjamin, stop! When will you be back?" My grandfather's voice sounds uncharacteristically desperate as he says the strangely familiar name, "Benjamin!"

I feel every muscle in my body tense and turn to look at my grandmother, afraid to ask the question.

"What's going on? Who is that?"

She looks at me then smiles, recognizing something in my words but doesn't answer my question.

"I see so much of myself in you." She squeezes her arms tighter around my small frame.

I wanted to see it too. What she could see in me.

"Who are these people? Is Papa in danger?"

"Shhh, so many questions. I promise you; he will be fine. Please don't worry, Gabriella—not about this." She looks away.

"Emily and Lily, they . . . they ask me questions. They want to know what happens to me. But I can't tell them that I see things sometimes. What I described to you tonight and so much more. It's as if I know what's going to happen next, even before it happens."

"You might be able to tell them one day, to trust that they love you and will understand."

I wanted to talk about it, to try to understand what it was and what it meant. "I know I'm different. We are, right?"

"Gabriella, there are things that we are each given. This is not something you choose. It's simply a part of who you are. It makes up all the beautiful pieces of you." She turns my face toward her, and behind the encouragement I can see the sadness in her eyes. "I know this is difficult and frightening, but I promise you—it can be wonderful, too. You are connected to so much that has come before and, also, to what will be. As you get older, you will learn how to use this power. It will provide many of the answers you are looking for. Until then, I am here to help you."

"Sometimes I don't know what's real and what's not."

"You will know; you'll see. You have already learned so much—how to choose and what to believe."

I push myself back into her, closer. I know she is telling me things that are important, as if they are in anticipation of what is to come.

"I'm not sure I understand."

"You need to live your life, Gabriella. Just *live*."

"Those people who were here tonight. Are they trying to warn Papa? Is it his work?"

"Remember, things are not always what they seem." She points to a star in the night sky. "There will always be light in the darkness, if you know where to look."

"What do you mean?"

"Sometimes what seems to be an ending is really a beginning.

Promise me that you will remember that. Promise me? And also what I said about finding the love that was made for you."

She had never spoken to me about that kind of love.

"Grandma Sophie, I'm only eleven."

"I know." She smiles.

I want to tell her that I don't want to go away, so far from this place, as the summer draws to a close. That I worry that she and my grandfather and the magic of Gloucester cease to exist when I am not here. But I fight back the tears, trying not to let my own selfish sadness ruin the last days of our summer together. She presses her arms into me tightly, as if she is transferring something into me: strength, courage, filling me for the future.

"Can't I stay here with you? Go to school with Emily and Lily? I don't ever want to lose you; I don't want to go back."

"You won't ever lose me, Gabriella, and you will have so much."

"How do you know?"

"It's time to go to sleep now." I notice the white light the moon makes on the ocean, like a path to infinity. "Good-bye, my beautiful child, may all your dreams come true."

I stop and look back at her and wait for her to speak, to correct her mistake, to say something—to realize.

"You mean *good night* right? Not good-bye."

"Yes, of course, good night."

She has always given me so much and tonight, I know, she is preparing me for everything ahead. Giving me her blessing as if she had to do it now, as if her words were not a mistake at all.

As if *I* was not the one who would run out of time.

5

I LIE IN BED and stare at the ceiling.

I try to listen to the sea, the rhythmic pounding of waves on the shore, but instead hear my grandmother's reluctant steps down the staircase. I imagine where she is as she carefully holds the banister and walks by framed pictures of the many years of play at this beach, documents of lives well lived. I hear the sounds the house makes along her path, through the main hallway and into the room where my grandfather always stands behind his desk. I go to sit at the top of the stairs and listen, finding comfort in the familiar voice of the architecture, out of sight where I can easily hear their conversation. I have done this many times before because, so often, they were talking about me.

"It's absurd, Sydney—this has really gone too far."

"Nonsense. We thought that this was the generation where it would be revealed."

"You are not an army for God!"

My grandfather laughs as he exhales slowly. The worn leather chair behind his desk creaks loudly as he spins away from her accusing voice.

"We are not going to discuss this again, Sophie. It is done."

"Sydney, for thousands of years the information has remained hidden. Concealed. Others before you understood and made that choice."

Silence.

"We have the proof . . . of the connection. Traditional science can no longer provide the answers that will satisfy those who—" My grandfather is cut off by my grandmother.

"This is not about science or even faith. It's all about money and fame and their own ideas about immortality. One alone. *One* would be motivation enough, but together they form an irresistible platform on which some of your colleagues' research rests. Einstein understood didn't he, Sydney? Darwin, Newton, and so many before."

"Sophie, Einstein believed simply that religion would be made more profound by science. Darwin offered evolution—no God, no moral code."

"Just what Hitler used to justify his actions."

"Do NOT say that name in this house!"

"It's true, though, isn't it? In his twisted logic, Hitler used the idea of evolution as justification for the 'master race.'"

"There are rules in the universe, *order,* despite what some have been able to do."

"Order? And rules, Sydney? Enforced by whom?"

"I don't have the answer."

"Tell me, why is he back now?"

"Benjamin?"

"Yes, there must be a reason—it's not about Gabriella is it?"

"We made a deal, Sophie. He promised me. If I agreed to keep my proof secret, he would stay away from her, from Gabriella that is. He would allow her to live her life in this world without his intrusions."

"Don't be absurd, Sydney! He can make no such promise. No one person can stand against the force of fate and the inevitable. If, in fact, they are meant to be together then it will be as it must."

Were they speaking about *me?*

"We learned the same thing fifty years ago, didn't we?"

I can feel the space between them and close my eyes to soak in the momentary tenderness of her voice. I remembered the story of how they met on a magical night in Jerusalem so many years before.

"It's too dangerous, Sophie. You of all people know better than anyone. We have control, we can choose! Change our fate."

"I was with her before, on the roof. She *knows,* Sydney. She is becoming aware that she has the gift. Things are happening to her, and she wants explanations. She clearly possesses the abilities—and she's the only one I've seen it in. She has been born into this family for a reason. I am convinced of it. It is as Benjamin said."

I strain to hear everything they are saying. I want to run away but am too afraid to miss any of the shocking information.

"It does not have to be this way!" The rage in my grandfather's voice frightens me.

"What has happened to you, Sydney? You've changed, lost your belief. Your desire to pursue the truth at any cost. You've become like the others. Accepting the rules imposed by those who came before, who are guided by fear and uncertainty. That was never you."

"This is so much bigger than just us, than simply what I might want. You see—"

"You're a *scientist!*" My grandmother yells, interrupting. "You've devoted your life to uncovering the mysteries of this world and everything in it. If you've found the connection, the link through the barrier of this world to beyond, then—"

"I have always aligned myself with the ones who did not believe, who needed irrefutable proof of the existence of something other than what we can touch and see and feel. The search for something beyond this life has never been considered scientific, yet we now have the ability to prove that it is. You see, Sophie, it's all so clear. The answer has been in front of us all along. Doggedly pursued by those who claim that nothing else matters. Nothing but discovering the Truth. Their god is science."

"You were always one of them."

"Ironic isn't it," he laughs.

"When will you decide, Sydney?"

"Perhaps it's simply enough to know. To finally have the proof that there is so much more beyond this world."

"That's the question you've been trying to answer your whole life." My grandmother's voice is low.

"*This* is the world we live in and must protect," he says.

"And what about Gabriella?"

27

The sound of my name sends chills down my spine.

"She will be kept safe, Sophie. I have seen to it."

6

AND THEN, A FEW days later, I know my childhood is over.
The terrifying and powerful ability I have to see things before they happen, shows me. I see the unthinkable: that I would lose one of the few relationships that filled the dark, quiet spaces of my life.

I can't understand where the beginning will be in this ending.

The summer is drawing to a close, and Lily, Emily, and I run along the dusk-lit streets, holding hands. My feet hurt, wounded by the new shoes I had insisted were comfortable enough for our last summer adventure together before I need to go back, so far away. I hoped their shining promise would bring the same qualities to my new beginning. Fall, cold and fresh, was ready to wipe away the heat of summer with opportunity and change.

We are almost home, the last light of day casts a deep orange fire across the beach. We kick through the leaves, breathless and laughing, as we race to see which of us would reach our imaginary finish lines first. We have our new books, sharpened pencils, and paper waiting to be filled. Our days' treasures from the hunt, placed safely in bags that swing around our small frames.

Endless possibilities lie ahead.

My perceptions shift when the sounds of our laughter become low echoes in my head, thoughts with sonorous vibrations. It feels as if we are moving in slow motion. Slow, slower. Sound and action twist together, backward, forward, flashing before my eyes. It is that feeling, the one I don't understand, but this time it is a terrifying realization of impending doom. I can feel my body electrify, an immeasurable amount of energy with no place for discharge. The droning sound gets louder—thunderous, deafening, painful—and I reach up to hold my hands on either side of my head. I try desperately to stop it, what I see happening to Lily.

Just at the moment the last of the day's light slips away and darkness envelopes us, two beams of light come around the corner and shine directly on our moving frames, freezing Lily's beautiful smile in an expression of abandon and joy.

It is too fast.

Screeching tires, lights, wind, speed, and combustion as time and energy merge and explode into our space on the sidewalk. I try to scream but I trip and fall to the ground.

"NO! Lily! No!"

Does she hear me? Did she hear it too? I pull myself up and turn to look at her, but she is twirling in a dance move we had learned earlier that week. Emily is hunched over, laughing. I try to cry out as the reality of what is about to occur flashes before my eyes. Sometimes vague or unclear, this time I understand the impending horror with perfect clarity as my ability to see into the future tortures me with a vision I don't want but cannot control.

"NO!!!!!" I scream as I turn around and see the car.

It rounds the corner too quickly. It loses control.

I lunge for Lily's beautiful frame as she jumps up to reach a tree's red limb, hair dancing around her head, smiling and unafraid. Right before the car crushes her body, our eyes meet. In the unspoken exchange is an acceptance as she realizes it is too late to escape, and I helplessly submit to the finality of our last childhood moment together.

7

TWELVE YEARS LATER
GLOUCESTER, MA — AUGUST 2005

THE PATH TO THE beach never changes.

The timeless beauty of this place slows my heartbeat and steadies my breathing. I feel calm, energized as my feet push through the deep sand. The sea air fills my lungs and paints circles around my face as it catches my hair in a swirling dance. The wind speaks to me, silent echoes of recognition.

You are not alone, Gabriella. I am with you.

I hear my grandmother's words, the ones she whispered into my heart. It is always like this, the connection to her. On this beach path that I have traveled so many times, the sea and wind meet me with open arms, acknowledging my return, a union of flesh and limbs, breath, wind, sand and sea.

"Yes," I breathe softly.

The grasses bow in a rhythmic wave of greeting as the water shimmers from the early-morning light.

Winking.

This beach was my summer. It held so many memories of time with Emily and Lily, my grandparents, and the beautiful town of Gloucester. I remembered the many nights we spent as children lying on the beach together looking up at the dark sky, counting the shooting stars and tracing their momentary arc. I knew their life continued well beyond our line of sight. It made me think about what we can see and feel and touch—and what we cannot. What comes before and what comes after, our endless search for answers and the drive to explore and understand everything.

The beach, the house, and my family history were an open book, waiting for us to discover the many mysteries they contained.

"Wow, look at this one, Gabriella!"

I remembered clearly the day Emily had held up a small yellowed photograph in a tarnished silver frame of a distinguished looking couple leaning against a ship's railing. They smiled into the camera with a fierce pride and independence.

"Emily, *please,* put that down," I had begged her. "We're not supposed to touch things in her studio."

I hadn't wanted to cross the line into my grandmother's private world. There was so much that I couldn't understand, the many treasured objects that I knew had been carried across the barren landscape of Eastern Europe, things that contained the vibrations of a lost world. Evidence of a life of struggle and oppression from which my family had emerged. Yet, these were the adventures of our summers in Gloucester, and we took our charge to uncover the secrets around us very seriously. Detectives we were— determined to understand it all.

The powerful memories flood my mind.

"You are welcome, children, to explore whatever you want when you are here. I have no secrets from you." My grandmother had swept into the room and saw Emily holding the photograph. She seemed pleased with our inquiry. "You like that picture? That was taken in 1943. Such an incredible time, the beginning of everything for me."

She had walked over and picked it up, smiling at a private memory as she closed her eyes.

"Who are they?" Emily's impatience broke the silence.

She turned and faced the three of us, knowing how much we loved her stories.

"Those people are Gabriella's *great* grandparents." She placed the frame back down on the windowsill. "My parents. They were traveling on a ship with Albert Einstein, on his way back from Japan. It was very exciting you know. He won a very special award. The *Nobel* Prize."

She emphasized the word Nobel, and I thought I was the only other one in the room who knew what it meant.

"My Papa is going to get one too." I directed the comment at my friends who immediately nodded in agreement.

My grandmother laughed and said, "I don't know about that, sweetheart."

"Where was the picture taken?" Lily asked.

"At the Port of Haifa, in Israel. Well, it was called Palestine in those days. That was how people traveled, on big beautiful steamships. It took a long time to go places."

"Isn't Haifa near where you live during the year, Gabriella? Near *Zzzfat* or however you say it?" Emily exaggerated the word.

My grandmother was lost in her memory and continued, "And then my parents traveled to Jerusalem where I joined them."

"You were there too?" Lily asked.

"Yes, and I met Professor Einstein and some other *fascinating* people." She turned away from us momentarily when she spoke, as if she didn't want us to see something in her eyes. "But most important, that's when I met your grandfather."

"Yes, my Papa knew Albert Einstein, the famous scientist. He is brilliant like him." I was so proud.

"We know who he is, Gabriella." Emily glared at me.

"Well, I love your stories, Grandma Sophie," Lily had continued, looking around the room, inspecting everything. "You always teach us so much."

The collection of possessions reflected the very mixed class of Eastern European aristocracy, farmers, and Jewish intellectuals we had descended from. This blended background explained my physical appearance—and my temper. The "Russian peasant princess," my grandfather liked to call me.

Gloucester was so different from where we had come from. At its heart a small village, this northeastern cape of Massachusetts was primarily inhabited by blue-collar workers and fishermen. However, there was another side to this place. It was home to many artists, writers, and thinkers and fostered a rich history of invention. There was a romance about this town that inspired so much creativity, its fragmented beauty continuous through all seasons. Our home in Gloucester had always been a gathering place for artists and writers, and I could feel the power of those who had been in these rooms. Of their minds.

"This painting is beautiful." Lily had pointed to a painting that hung near a chair on the wall in the studio. "Squares, but soft, glowing—what squares would look like in heaven," she said, her face lit with excitement, "or if Gabriella painted it."

"No." My grandmother smiled. "That is quite a compliment, but that is a painting by a famous artist named Mark Rothko. Now *he* was really something." She pushed up the sleeves of her flowing caftan as if just thinking about the painter raised her body temperature. Her hands smoothed the hair down and away from her face as her eyes closed in a dramatic gesture. "He loved to remind your grandfather that what really matters is the way we feel, the emotion in our lives. This he wanted to express with color, scale, and the simplest of forms. Rectangles! He used to say 'there is no such thing as a good painting about nothing!'"

She shook her head at the genius of the simple statement and continued, "He wanted to question the physics, the science of your grandfather, 'so complicated' he used to say. But you see, they were all looking for answers—just in different mediums. Physics or art, it doesn't really matter, right? We are all searching for something."

She stopped and knelt down to look at the three of us, her captivated audience. "Your lives should also be about ideas. Creating things. Decide what you want to change and how you think the world should be."

This was how I grew up in this place: talking, dancing, kissing, questioning, laughing, and always, always creating. These were the beautiful memories that returned whenever I came here, and I would let myself live in them, especially when I was alone on the beach. But so many years had passed and everything had changed—Lily's accident, my parents' and the recent death of my grandmother, even my grandfather's retirement. Leaving me to navigate graduate school in New York with Emily as we prepared to fulfill a lifelong dream of living in the city together.

I strip off my torn sweatpants and zip up the insulated top that so many of the surfers wear: a treasured necessity to protect against the frigid, biting waters and the shifting tides brought by the New England fall. The changing temperatures are no deterrent for the hypnotic and magnetic quality the sea has on me.

I walk with my eyes closed toward the water. The first wave kisses my toes as if to beckon entry into this world below. I inhale sharply at the tingling pain of the ice cold water and the sudden shift in perception. I know that even though the sun still rises high in the sky, the tides are moving into the currents of fall and winter and the waters have come from distant places. Carrying messages.

I enter the surf with confidence drawn from years of play on this shore. As I submerge below the surface, the chains of gravity are released, and the compass of tides guide my movement. My hair becomes weightless, circling my head and covering my eyes. I lose the sounds of the world above as the wind, sea gulls, and waves disappear and are replaced by my own internal rhythms. I hear the beating of my heart, the sensation of blood as it courses through my veins and pounds in my ears, my body cushioned by the mass of salt water. Floating and suspended in time.

But this time, there is something else. Something new.

I try to control the images, the unclear premonition, the recent dreams of these waters betraying my memories of the safety of this place. I feel it, the powerful danger, twisting and pulling me down into the sea. I want to escape the image of myself gasping for air, the sensation my mind creates as the burning rush of water enters into my lungs. The terrifying feeling of the power of the current, twisting and throwing my form around, claiming my body to the deep cold depth. I shoot up out of the icy water and explode back into the atmosphere. Proving to myself that I do have control as I push away the dark thoughts. They have no place in this ritual end-of-summer swim that marks my new beginning.

Trust that in the end, you can find a beginning.

This was one of the last things my grandmother had said to me before she was gone. She had asked me to promise her that I wouldn't forget: our gift she had called it. I could see it in her, she knew her future and she was not afraid. She had smiled and held me tightly as she said good-bye, promising that things were going to happen as they were meant to, as they needed to. The many things made clear right before the last time she went away.

When she never came back.

I push back against the powerful force of the undertow and out of the sea, wrap myself in the towel that has been warmed by the sun, and turn around to face the horizon. I will take this moment with me, the sense of endless possibility and promise. The feeling that I am standing on the threshold of everything that awaits.

8

" TEDDY!"
My beautiful golden retriever bounds over the dunes and tries to reach the water. "No, Ted." I grab his collar. "You're not swimming today, let's get back to the house." I notice the unmarked black vans that line the driveway. "You are wild today; what's going on?"

He prances madly around me and wags his tail as if he understands. I stop and tighten the towel around my body as I suddenly feel cold and frightened. Something was wrong, the energy had shifted.

"And be careful with that ladder!" I can barely hear Maggie's authoritative voice coming from the house over the howling wind. "We just had all the shingles repaired."

I pull open the screen door. "Maggie, where are you?" I try to keep my voice calm and not betray my rising anxiety, praying that my instincts are wrong.

"There you are!" Maggie had worked for my grandparents since before I was born. She reaches out and pulls me toward her, practically knocking the air out of me. She joyfully shouts, falling over herself in the exuberant realization that I am not an apparition but actually standing in front of her. I feel the strength and warmth of her arms as they wrap me in her bear hug. The delicious perfume of onions and fresh basil present on her skin has always reminded me of home. "Another summer, another year gone by." She shakes her head in disbelief. "Just look at you."

"I know, Maggie."

"My little pet, starting architecture school already or as we like to call it archi*torture?*" She looks me over with suspicion and a raised eyebrow, unsure whether I am beginning the most exciting phase of my life or some sort of sentence in a prison. She circles behind me, looking for some telltale sign of distress. A reason to call the whole thing off.

"Who are these people?" I ask and try to shift her focus.

"I hear you get no sleep, no fun. They work you so hard there—for what?" She clucks disapprovingly, not understanding why I seem to be submitting to this strange form of tortuous education when the guest house and studio await. She wraps her arms around me again, and I soak in her familiarity and the connection to my past.

"It's okay." I try to gently pry myself out of her bear hug. "I'll be fine. Remember, we've been planning this for years."

Her eyes lock onto my wet bathing suit.

"What is it?" I can see she is trying to decide what to say but I feel the need to explain the obvious. "I just went for a swim." Teddy wags his tail in agreement.

I look at her and cross my arms over my chest, hoping she won't notice the sand and salt water that both Teddy and I drip onto her clean floors.

"I asked you *not* to do that, go there I mean, without someone with you, watching. You know, Gabriella, the tide is so dangerous."

"But." I'm surprised by this sudden change of heart. The beach house was a place where I could do whatever I wanted. "I always swim alone."

"Well it's not a good idea. Anymore."

She seems nervous, more agitated than I have seen her in a while. She wipes a tear quickly from her eye with a handkerchief that she pulls out of her dress and wrings her hands in a nervous habit I have seen many times before, and I know I need to change the subject. Unfortunately, the next one is no better.

"What's going on?"

Out the window I see a team of men fanning out across the property, up into the trees and surrounding the house. Teddy hasn't stopped barking at their unusual presence on the property. Maggie fixes her hair with one hand as she clears her throat and stands as straight as possible.

"Oh, it's nothing, dear, just updating the alarm."

"Don't be ridiculous, they're *everywhere*. All over the property."

Maggie pats the invisible perspiration off her brow. I know she is buying time as she avoids the question. Then there is banging.

"For God's sake," she mutters under her breath as she strides over to the front door to face a strange man. "Yes?" She seems so small next to him, but I know she would protect this house—and everything in it—with her life.

"Excuse me, Ma'am. We need to get access to the house now, the safe room."

"I just wish this wasn't necessary," she says softly, to herself. "Follow me. This way."

"Maggie?" I ask. "Where are you taking him?"

"Wait here!" She points her finger at me.

I take two steps back, stunned by the intensity of her words.

I return to the window and I hope the men might have disappeared while my back was turned, but there seems to be even more of them.

"There we go." She returns after a few minutes with a new conviction in her voice. "Everything is *fine*."

"What are you talking about?" I put both my hands on her shoulders as I force her to stop moving. "What is going on?"

"It's all this security." She sighs as her eyes scan the blinking lights on the new digital keypads. "It's some sort of state of the art system, very fancy, new technology, cameras, motion sensors—" She stops suddenly, probably feeling my anxiety. "Maybe it's just another one of his toys?"

"Stop it, Maggie. I'm not a baby anymore. You can't protect me from this. Look at these people outside. And what's this about a safe room?"

Despite the attempt to reassure us both, she is not convincing either one. It is the subject that lies right below the surface. The history that wraps itself like a shroud around my heart. The darkness in my life that I was always trying to escape and the terrible guilt I lived with. That I could have done more, sooner. That I might have saved them.

Paris.

It happened just five years earlier as I had begun to really comprehend the magnitude of my grandfather's work. An international authority on theoretical physics and cosmology, he traveled around the world lecturing and had a passionate and growing following of scholars who began to put forth his hypotheses. We all knew that he was at the center of a vital shift taking place in the academic community. Questioning the fundamental nature of what was true and real and what place science and religion could hold to answer questions about our world.

The possibility of our universe not being unique or alone.

I knew there were others, too, competing scientists who were looking for similar answers, the proof, sponsored by governments or other sources who wanted access to the information. The way into tunnels that might connect our world to other worlds—other universes. I was accustomed to the extreme vigilance, the security and caution that had always surrounded my grandparents' lives, but things were changing.

It was summer, and I was at Oxford taking a painting seminar before starting college there. We had planned a family reunion in Paris. My parents were coming, and my grandfather was to have presented some groundbreaking research at a meeting in Geneva. My grandmother had stayed back at the beach in Massachusetts. It was meant to have been a rare happy time together, but instead, it was a terrifying, tragic ending.

We were gathered in a small restaurant on the Left Bank celebrating when I started to feel the familiar sensations: when I knew what was going to happen.

But I didn't want it. I tried to push it away, deny the power it had over me. I rationalized that it was from the small space and cigarette smoke that I was unaccustomed to. So, I said I needed to get some air. I ran out leaving my parents and grandfather at the table as I tried to push away the feeling and understand why it was happening—what exactly the cause was. But I could not. This time, it was too powerful. Darker than anything I had ever felt before, a blackness as time slowed down: dread and fear and sadness—overwhelming, painful, paralyzing darkness.

He had come to look for me.

"Gabriella!" I heard his worried voice as my grandfather ran out of the small restaurant to find me. "There you are."

I remember how I had leaned over the stone bridge that connected the beautiful city on either side of the Seine. I looked down into the dark waters below as if the answers I was searching for might have been there, my head in my hands as I tried to slow my breathing.

"What? Oh yes, Papa. I'm so sorry. I don't feel well. It's my head and—well, it's something about this place. I wish Grandma Sophie was here, she would know what to do, she would understand."

"Understand what?"

And then, it happened.

The explosion, the fire, the suspension of time as the small restaurant we had just emerged from was engulfed in flames—with my parents inside. I could still close my eyes and feel the sensations: the extreme heat on my face, my grandfather's arms restraining me from running back into the inferno, the burning pain in my throat for days from my anguished screaming.

Maggie's soft voice pulls me back into the present.

"Gabriella?"

She looks me up and down, one eyebrow raised, as if she is trying to determine what is different. Deciding how to change the conversation that seems to be not helping either of our moods. She reaches out for my hand and holds it in hers for a moment, a sadness in her eyes as if she knows my thoughts.

"Is he in his office?" I ask, trying to force myself back and away from the memories of that time in Paris.

"Yes, as always, he's been waiting for you." She twists her hands again. "He has so much on his mind and now with you going to New York—well, he promised me he would slow down and enjoy his retirement."

"Is that what he told you, Maggie?" I try to find humor in the word retirement being used in any connection to my grandfather. "I think it's quite the opposite. You know how everything is finally coming together for him. Everything he's worked his whole life for."

The summer was filled with celebrations and dinners recognizing his retirement from Columbia University, the incredible scientific contributions he had made, and the move to MIT. We organized the files, plaques, awards, and boxes of books, many authored by him, that now lined the shelves of his Gloucester library. This was becoming his permanent home. As the time approached for my departure, I worried about how the transition would affect him. I knew he was on the verge of changing everything we take for granted about our world.

"Maggie, please don't worry so much about him."

"It's not just your grandfather, I'm worried about you, too."

I know that there is something in her words. Something else that she is not saying.

"I'm fine, silly. Never been better." I try to lighten the moment.

As I walk down the wide hallway, lined with my grandparent's art collection, I can still feel her eyes on me.

9

I PASS THE GREAT room, part of the recent addition I had designed, and marvel at the magnificent views of both the garden and ocean. The uniqueness of this opportunity—doing something for *him*—was a role reversal not lost on me. Conceived with love, I had chosen to create an axis past the living spaces that led to the library, symbolically reflecting the idea that there is a progression, a journey through his work and ideas. This was a space I hoped he would occupy for many years, a small jewel meant to be an envelope for his mind and heart.

The architectural equivalent of my arms wrapping around him.

I grab the cold doorknob pitted from the sea air and I'm surprised. I'm unaccustomed to finding the door closed. The combination of this strange occurrence and the appearance of the black vans has unnerved me enough that I practically do not recognize my own voice.

"Papa?" I open the door.

The late afternoon sun casts a golden glow of light on everything. My grandfather walks toward me, and I practically fall over as I lunge for him.

"Hello, my darling."

He takes his glasses off and looks me over as he takes in the sand, the wet hair, and other signs of my late swim. Unlike Maggie he makes no comment. And then I realize that we are not alone. I understand the strange change in energy that I had felt earlier in the house.

"Philip, you're here?" I am genuinely surprised to see him.

Brilliant and undeniably attractive, we had met in a summer painting studio at Oxford, the summer my parents died. For four years, we were inseparable. I watched in amusement as he managed an endless flirtation with what seemed like every female at Oxford—most of whom were astounded at my own lack of interest in anything more than a platonic relationship with him. Philip traveled with me to Switzerland often, meeting my grandfather at various scientific symposia, quizzing him on his work with the Supercollider, and spending hours talking into the night about physics and art. Philip had always been quite clear about his hopes for a serious relationship with me. Something I knew my grandfather endorsed.

But then *everything* changed when my parents were murdered. His British family had practically adopted me and they were a critical force for easing the difficult transition of managing my academics while dealing with the events in Paris. Our relationship was a perfect meeting of the minds—even though I knew he wanted more. Now we were about to fulfill the promise of going to architecture school together in New York.

Philip pushes himself up and out of the deep arm chair he has been sitting in. His confidence permeates the small room and he smiles that crooked grin I know so well as he slowly moves toward me.

"Gabriella."

The sound of his voice, the way he says my name brings back a thousand memories. He comes up to stand very close and reaches out, touching his fingertips to my face as he slowly kisses my cheek. I realize how I look: a combination of surprise, frustration, salt water, and sand. I wrap the towel tighter around my body to cover up the childhood bathing suit that I know is too small.

"What are you *doing* here?" I don't mean for the words to sound so angry.

It was a ridiculous question. Philip and my grandfather enjoyed an unusual yet profound connection begun years earlier. They were kindred souls, the generations that separated them in time collapsing into irrelevance.

"Gabriella, be nice." My grandfather's voice penetrates the moment and shatters the lock Philip has on my eyes. "He came to surprise you. Now that you'll be attending Columbia together, Philip has agreed to keep an eye on you for me."

I look down at his hand on my arm. I feel the possessiveness in his touch and abruptly pull it away. He knows that this gesture will anger me but he does it anyway. I want to stay separate, strong.

"Thank you, that's very— nice." The heat from the imprint of his fingers stays on my skin. "But I can take care of myself. Just fine."

"Of course you can. Yes, yes, my dear." He looks first at me then Philip, marveling at the realization of what we had hoped for so many years. He seems to be sizing me up, as if he wants to capture something, to hold a memory in his mind.

"Can we spend some time together before I leave for New York? Alone?" I look over at Philip wanting my words to hurt him just a little. "What's going on here today anyway? Why a new security system? Is there something you're not telling me?"

My grandfather waves his hand around in front of him. "It's nothing to worry about, there have been some new incidents, so we were told to install this. Completely unnecessary, we are safe here, Gabriella." He points to the room. "After all, I did have a wonderful architect."

"What do you mean, new incidents?"

"Gabriella, *please.*" He tries to calm me.

"No, tell me what you're talking about."

"It's under control. There's been some chatter on the internet picked up in the last few months, but it is being monitored very carefully. They seem to be, well, reorganizing. In response to all the press I suppose. The international excitement about our work at the Supercollider and all that." He looks right at me, as if he is deciding whether he has said too much.

I wait to steady my voice before I ask the question. "Are they the same ones, from Paris?"

The three of us stand in the small room together, the two men looking at me as I look down at the floor and hold my breath. I wait for his answer.

"Yes."

We rarely spoke about the extreme right-wing religious cult who had killed my parents. Elusive and mysteriously funded, they represented a powerful group of religious fanatics who did not want anyone disturbing the status quo. They called themselves the Divine Order. If science was about to introduce the possibility of the existence of other *dimensions,* then the Divine Order was sworn to destroy those leading the way.

"Gabriella, your grandfather is too important to be left exposed. This is all just a precaution."

I notice a brief look between them. I want to believe their reassurances.

"I'm sorry, Philip. I don't know what's the matter with me. I shouldn't have spoken to you like that before. I am really so glad to see you."

"I know you are. Besides—I'm used to it."

"Look, all I'm saying is that I don't know what either of you are up to, but you don't need to protect me. If there's anything going on, *anything* different that I need to know about, you need to tell me."

I wanted to tell them both that I could feel it, that something wasn't right, but I had promised myself that I would not acknowledge the intuition. The feelings, the premonitions, the memories—they were all back. Stronger than ever before.

"I'll see you in a few days, Gabriella." Philip takes my hands in his. "At Columbia. And don't tell me you didn't miss me—because I know you did."

My grandfather laughs and says, "You know her, Philip, there's so much in that head and heart of hers. But she would never tell."

"Yes, I did miss you, Philip." I reach out for him and hug him tightly, truly happy that he will be with me in New York. Surprising even myself.

10

I LOOK AROUND THE octagonal space of my grandfather's study. The design framed a view of the ocean in the east and the golden grasses of the marsh to the west, an almost three-hundred-and-sixty-degree view of the landscape. A perfect space to follow the tracking of the sun from early morning to its disappearance at the end of the day behind the dunes. Marking time.

"Well, here we are, finally, alone together."

"I wanted to have everything unpacked before I left, Papa."

"Never mind." He carefully steps over moving boxes that still cover the floor and pushes a button that fills the room with the soft melody of piano and violin. As I stood on the threshold of my own new adventure, I recognized the irony of his New York life ending as mine was beginning.

"I see *this* made it here safely." I point to the desk that had been given to him by Einstein. His most prized possession, it stood proudly in the center of the room.

"Witness to so much invention, a container of memory and possibility." He pats the desk.

"Memory and possibility, you always say that. Do you mean the past and the future?"

"You might say that."

"Being here with you in the *present* means everything to me. I feel so disconnected from the rest of the world, all the noise. I love it when it's just the two of us—and all the books of course." I feel sad to leave.

He turns to the shelves and raises his hand, pushing away the air. "Too many."

I look over at the shelves that hold my grandmother's things: books about art, poetry, and the mysterious tradition of Kabbalah, volumes that remained untouched on the shelves since she had died. It had been many years since the painful realization that the typical family I longed to be a part of was an impossibility. I knew there was a secret in my family, and it was the reason we had been divided.

I reach up to pull down a small volume. "May I?"

"Of course." He sighs as he looks out the window at the sea and sinks slowly into his chair. "All of this will be yours."

I try not to meet his eyes. I don't want to see the pain I hear in his words as I open up the page and see her handwriting.

Only art education can improve quality of life, understanding, and knowledge.

I read the words slowly to myself then out loud and look up at him.

"Art? Did she really believe that? What about science?" I reach out for him. "Smashing particles right?"

"We've been doing that since the 1950s, sweetheart. It's all theory, although it is now being tested by the Large Hadron Collider, the Super-collider as they call it." He smiles at me.

"I know."

"But your grandmother wanted more. She believed that art went farther—beyond merely practical needs or investigations of the mind."

"Like what?"

"The spiritual, the soul. Just like your work, Gabriella. Combining imagination and structure, I can see it in you, even now."

Hovering above the conversation was the inference, the suggestion of the connection between the different parts of my family. Those working in the field of science and others who explored the secrets of the mystical tradition we had inherited.

"Do you mean my parents? Art and science?"

"They chose to live in the ancient city of Zefat, to devote their lives to the study of mysticism. I have chosen science. But *you*, Gabriella, you are a combination of both these worlds."

I had been told this a thousand times and I was still trying to understand what it meant.

"I just want to make something. Anything."

I look away from him, the way his eyes burn into mine. The subject of my parents and what had happened was too painful to discuss.

I hold my grandmother's worn journal in my hands; the fraying edge presses against the inside of my arm. I can picture her recording her thoughts, the seeds of an idea for a future painting or poem. So many left unfinished, unrealized. I feel the obligation to continue her legacy, to make something of myself, to hear what she was whispering into my heart. I knew that she was all around me. I could feel her everywhere.

"You will not only make something, Gabriella, you will make a difference. You already have," my grandfather says the words quietly.

"How?"

"You changed my fate."

But it wasn't enough.

"I should have known, Papa. That night in Paris, I should have understood what it meant. Then I might have saved them, too."

11

THE ROOM IS SO still that the words hang between us. I can feel the cool air from the window, blowing gently over my body and I realize that I need to change the subject.

"What is this—the music? It sounds oddly familiar; I remember her playing it for me." I walk over and turn up the volume on the CD player. I say it without fear of hurting him. I want to talk about my grandmother now; how I feel her with me, loving me, encouraging and showing me that the promises she had made to me were being fulfilled. I wait for him to respond, but he ignores me. I try again. "Did you hear what I just said? I remember this."

"How could you remember such things? Please, stop this talk. We need to think about today. Not the past." He swivels his chair away, and I see the subtle rocking motion as he rhythmically moves back and forth. "Everything you've worked so hard for."

"I know she's here. They all are, they're *here*—with both of us," I say softly.

We are quiet for a few moments. I walk over and lift a heavy frame that holds a faded photograph. I inspect the smile, the wild white hair, and the signature. It occupies an important place on the desk, which holds the treasured files that contain the correspondence they had shared. I knew this relationship was the one that had directed the course of his life's work.

"She told me the story of how you met each other in Jerusalem.

At the party. And he was there too." I point at the photograph. "Einstein."

"You have quite the memory."

"It's an incredible story, when you met Grandma Sophie. The party, the house, and all the people who were there—"

He stands up out of his chair suddenly, as if what I said has knocked all the air out of him. All the color has left his face.

"Are you okay?" I approach him cautiously.

"What else did she tell you, about the *people* we met there?"

"Nothing. Just her parents and you. There must have been others at the party, but she never spoke of anyone in particular."

I wait, hoping that he'll come back to me. Back to the conversation we are having, but he is in retreat. I've hit a nerve.

"Why are you always pulling me into the past? Ghosts, Gabriella— they are just ghosts. Finish your packing for school. Go, please, let me be."

I back away from his desk, hurt by his uncharacteristic words. Clearly I had upset him. "I'm sorry, I didn't mean to bring this up." I choke back the tears. "I don't understand why we can't ever talk about her anymore?"

"Gabriella, just leave it alone."

"It was always through her eyes," I say slowly, "that I could see myself. Really understand."

"Don't do this; choose something else to think about!" he practically shouts, and I see the anger and frustration on his face.

"Yes, of course." I say. But I want to tell him that I need to choose for myself, that she would have wanted me to.

The sun shifts and a beam of light comes into the room and catches the edge of a small bronze medallion that I have always loved. I reach for it, its edges polished from years of touch, and turn it over in my hands. Slowly I look at the odd shapes and symbols on its surface, the lines that create a star and the seven spaces, ancient letters that I do not understand. Symbols of the ancient mystical tradition of my family.

"You've always loved that," I hear his voice behind me. I am embarrassed that he has caught me holding one of his precious objects and I quickly put it down.

"It's all right. Ever since you were a child, something about it has always attracted you. I want you to have it."

Removing an object from this sacred space seems wrong. I stare into his deep blue eyes and wait to see if he is going to say more, but it is as if he has stopped himself, catching a thought that he was not yet ready to reveal.

"No. I know how you feel about her things; I would never want to take it from here." I wonder in a way whether these precious feelings and vibrations even exist outside of this room.

"She found it on her first trip to Palestine—on an archaeological dig. I think it was the day we met. It was one of her most treasured possessions. Take it. She always wanted you to have it."

"I don't know."

"Gabriella, you have arrived at a time in your life that we have waited many years for. Such an adventure, such excitement awaits you. And, there is something else." He pulls several small leather books that are tied together with a ribbon out of a box. I know they are my grandmother's diaries. "I want you to have these." The authority in his voice is final. "Think of them as a good-luck charm of sorts, although you really don't need any luck."

"Of course I need luck." Help, his guidance—anything.

"I do remember one more thing that I wanted to tell you." He seems uncomfortable, yet there is an urgency and seriousness that I don't often hear in his voice. He smiles and his eyes mist.

"What is it?"

"I met your grandmother when she was exactly your age."

I stare back at him and try to meet his powerful words.

"No," I start to object. I want to clarify that this is not at all a priority, the last thing on my mind as I am going to begin school. "Papa, this is—"

"Gabriella, listen to me." He speaks with an intensity that I know requires my attention. "I know you have been too busy to notice the effect you have on people. Men, I mean. Except, of course, Philip."

My face burns as he proceeds with the topic that has previously been off limits. I had begun to notice the reaction men were having to me. My hair, which had once been characterized by its unruly, untamable craziness, now fell in soft curls around my face. My skin had an even glow and my eyes were a gray blue that matched the northern Massachusetts sea. My body was strong and lean with developed muscles from years of swimming against the current. I was tall, taller than most of the girls I knew, just like the women who had preceded me in my grandmother's family.

The summers when I would wander around our beach community barefoot and free—with only a bikini and T-shirt on, going unnoticed and happy in my solitude—seemed to have ended this past season. I thought that it was because of him, my grandfather and his *work,* the unusual presence of the world famous physicist in the small oceanfront community. But for the first time, the thought occurred to me that it might have nothing to do with him at all.

"Did you hear what I just said, about meeting your grandmother."

I turn back to him. "No, that won't happen to me. Not now."

My hand tightens unconsciously around the amulet, my special gift, the treasure from so many years ago, being given to me now as a symbol of the transition.

His past, my future.

"Take it, Gabriella, and remember that you are right."

"It's hard enough for me without her, but, you, how can you—"

"You are right to feel that those who love you are always with you."

"Papa, to see you like this, I could never imagine your life without each other. How you would go on."

"But you do, you must."

"I hope that I can find what you two had."

The right side of his wise, beautiful face begins to suggest a smile. Almost imperceptibly he raises his eyebrows, a mix of gray and brown, and smiles at his own personal secret.

"You will."

I look back at him and meet his eyes.

"I just remembered." I stop and face him. "That music. The music you were just playing." I point to the table where the stereo sits. "She told me it was composed by someone she knew very well."

He shakes his head and turns away.

"She said he was someone special, the composer, that she knew him. Do you remember now?"

"No."

But he says it too quickly. I see a flash, a room in a white stone house, a party, and a piano. A young man playing with many people listening and watching. My grandmother is looking into his remarkable green eyes, and my grandfather is looking at her.

"Actually, I might vaguely remember something, but it was such a long time ago."

"When we were on the roof together one night, Papa, she said it was the kind of thing that could make you fall in love or break your heart. I always wanted to ask her what she meant. She meant the music, right?"

"Yes, of course. The music." He looks at me for a few seconds then turns back to his reading.

As I walk slowly out of the library, I hear him behind me mutter something under his breath. It's my words "someone special," a strange irony in his voice. More than that, I feel his eyes on me, sealing the fate he seems to know awaits.

A mixture of joy and apprehension.

12

I RUN TO FIND A seat among the many students waiting for the assembly to begin. Excitement, uncertainty, and reverence for the campus fill the great open plaza of the university. We are all taking our place along a wavelike continuum that will create the history of our culture. Humbled by the traditions we were taking on, we have come from colleges all over the world. In this moment are all those who have come before and their accomplishments. I feel the endless possibility and promise that the opportunity holds. This is what fuels the burning desire in every one of us to make our mark and be different, add something new.

The dean of the Graduate School of Architecture takes his place at the podium and looks out at the expectant students.

"Welcome. You have come here to search. To begin a lifelong journey of clarification, the challenge of what your lives will mean and what you can add to the world. Each of you will conduct your own experiments and research. You should know that this is what links all of you to the past and future."

I want to answer the challenge. No longer am I merely a visitor at Columbia University walking along the uneven brick path and through the tall black iron gates, guarded regally by the frozen stone figures. As a small child I had passed by their timeless forms, courageously looking up at their beautiful, silent granite faces, seeking their distant gaze while holding the hand of my grandfather.

I look around at the great steps and plaza in the center of the campus, the trees and the historic stone buildings that line the walkway. I can feel the energy. But it is not simply from the rushing groups of people, laughing and talking animatedly. There are posters everywhere on campus of my grandfather's face, announcing his upcoming lecture at the university and the list of international awards he has recently received. His eyes always on me.

"There he is!" Emily has dragged me into the bookstore and screams as she runs over to a large table set up with a life-size cardboard figure of my grandfather.

"Look, Gabriella, doesn't he look cute?"

I run around to the other side of the nearest bookcase and try to get away from all the eyes that have turned in our direction.

"This man." Emily points to the center of his cardboard chest, talking to no one in particular. "*He* is going to show everybody. That he is right." She leans toward his flat corrugated face and puckers her lips in a kiss.

"Gabriella, where did you go? Gabriella?"

I crouch behind the books, wishing I could disappear. "Come on, Emily, please stop, honestly," I whisper loudly from behind the stacks. "Let's get out of here."

"Get used to it, sweetie. Your grandfather is about to change the way we see our world."

I hoped she was right. He had spent his entire life devoted to proving what many believed was impossible. Safe, I thought, in the confines of the academic world. Now, I had so much more to worry about. Before, I could find him in his office or study, in a controlled, protected environment. But now, he was *everywhere*: on every newsstand, bookstore, radio show, and television network, traveling around the globe. There was no more denying it. He had become an international celebrity, and the world was waiting for him to reveal the results of his life's work. I worried about the exposure, the press, and what we had discussed in his library, the threats to his safety. He had made light of it, but I knew he was determined to move forward and show the skeptics that he had not spent the last twenty years of his life moving toward the extreme fringes of the scientific community. That instead, he had found the very heart of it. His *proof.* Answering the questions that had been asked since the beginning of time.

I was glad to have Emily with me. Her plans, however, were quite different than mine.

"I'm in business school, Gabriella, remember? You're the dreamer, and I'm—well—the practical one." She winks and begins to list the many differences between her upcoming experience and mine.

The powerful history we shared was a bond that could never be broken, and Emily represented a tangible link to many critical events in the past. Including Lily and my family.

"Incredible how we're finally at the same school. We always hoped this would happen."

"When we only had the summers."

"Our summers together in Gloucester will always be a real and significant part of our lives." Emily throws her arms around my shoulders as she did whenever we talked about those days.

"I know." I could feel the emotion building in me. "I just wish Lily could be here with us. She should be here too."

"Gabriella, you saved her. You *saved* her life." She knew that I would not allow discussion of that terrible day when the car almost claimed Lily.

"I made a mistake; I waited too long. Emily, I—"

"We're not going to talk about that now, okay? Please?" Her voice is soft, gently changing the subject. "How about all this?" She points to the campus and the people all around us. She is exuberant at the thought of moving forward into our futures. "Please, stop worrying about everything. It's time to meet some new people, get invited to the best New York parties."

I roll my eyes. "That's the last thing on my mind, Emily."

"You can still design things, silly, but it's time for you to have some fun."

"Emily," I say and laugh at her single-minded focus, "you're too much."

"No, really, we've waited a long time for this."

Things seemed to be playing out as predicted. In a crazy way it was a comfort to know that she was orbiting the same campus as I was. She knew to respect the boundaries I had created around myself. It was for her own good, I remind myself. I'm like a bad luck charm when it comes to relationships.

"Hey guys, look who's here." I see one of my new roommates approaching us with a group of friends. "It's Gabriella—*Vogel.*"

I can see them all sizing me up, looking for any evidence of extra-terrestrial traits.

"Do you girls want to join us for coffee? We were just going over to the student center."

"Great idea we would love to—" Emily starts to accept the invitation.

"Not now," I cut Emily off. "I'm going to be late." I realize that I sound abrupt and try to soften my tone. "But thank you, anyway."

"We absolutely have time, Gabriella."

"No." I glare at Emily. "We don't."

"Well, we wouldn't want you to be late for your first day of classes now would we? Not the famous Dr. Vogel's granddaughter!" one of the young men says sarcastically.

"Yes, right." I force a smile. "That wouldn't be a very good idea."

He runs over to one of the many posters of my grandfather's face and tears it off the wall, pumping it up and down in his arms as if he was a political fanatic celebrating a martyr.

"Look guys, we live with a celebrity," he says to no one in particular.

"Leave her alone!" Emily says protectively.

"It's all right." I push her away from the group and turn quickly, relieved to escape the conversation. I reach out and link my arm through Emily's and I see her grinning at me.

"See, Gabriella, you're a normal student. Just like the rest of us."

"I love you, but I really have to go."

"Making new friends and everything. You're getting your life back."

"Thanks—but I never knew I'd lost it."

"You know what I mean; you've been sad for so long. But all of that's in the past. This is going to be the beginning of everything." She points to the campus. "Just like your grandmother always said."

"What?"

"She told us don't you remember? That we would go to school together in New York. Just like they all did, your grandparents and your parents. She said that it would be the beginning of everything for you. That's exactly what she said." Emily waits.

I stand very still as the memory washes over me. I realize that I hadn't thought of her words until this very moment and, in remembering, everything suddenly made sense.

"Yes, actually, now I do. I felt it at the beach the other day, and, now, I know why." Unlike my grandfather, Emily loved to talk about the past.

Her eyes fill with tears. "She said she would be with you, to always remind you of who you are, who your family is, and, especially, everything you love about this world."

"*This* world?"

Emily shrugs her shoulders, as if to indicate that she's not sure exactly what it means either. I look down at my hands held firmly in both of hers, squeeze them back tightly, and brush the hair away from her eyes.

"You're my family too, Emily."

13

How much this building has seen. Standing sentry like a parent watching its children, Hamilton Hall was the home of undergraduate life at Columbia University. I enter the great lobby, a central core filled with stairs and elevators so characteristic of the buildings of this era designed by the architects McKim, Mead and White. Often furnished with sofas and cushioned chairs, these areas became places for gatherings of students. My eyes scan the walls for announcements of interest as I distractedly climb the stairs to the classroom. I hadn't been in this building in many years and look down at the printout of my new schedule to confirm the location of my first classroom and lecture.

I ignore the strange feeling, that something feels odd. I am surprised not to see a larger crush of students heading to class. I try to focus on my destination. I know this professor, Wallace Gray. Famous for his lectures on James Joyce and T.S. Eliot, he is an old friend of my grandparents. I'm looking forward to taking something completely different from the rigors of the architecture school and seeing a familiar face, a connection to my past.

"It's poetry, Gabriella." I remember how my grandmother had introduced so many great authors to me at a young age. "It's an architecture of words. The beautiful, lyrical presence of black letters building shapes on a white page."

I run up the last flight of granite steps as my hand grazes the black iron banister of the building. Their shallow incline allows me to take two at a time. I feel the heavy book-laden backpack bouncing against my body. I round the top landing on the third floor and look down to confirm the room number once more. It is difficult to see in the dim light. The doors in the corridor are all closed, and, once again, I have the strangest feeling. That I am not in the right place.

It's too quiet.

Where *is* everybody? Why, despite all my efforts at organization and precision, was I never able to get it together right? I find the room and push the door open with more force than I intend, expecting to see a class full of students. But the space is completely empty and silent. The early-morning light pours through the arched-top windows that face the east side of the campus. The shocking stillness is in marked contrast to the bustling activity in the center of campus. I walk in slowly and drop my bag on the floor, furious with myself, as I realize without a doubt that I am in the wrong place.

"Great way to start your graduate career, Gabriella. Typical!" I say out loud.

Frustrated, I sink down into one of the wooden seats that fills the room. I put my head down and feel the heat of my breath on my arm. Yet, it's not just my breathing I notice. I have the distinct feeling that I am not alone in the room. It is a sense that I have often felt, an awareness that is always with me. I pick my head up and move the hair away from my eyes as I try to focus.

Someone is standing in front of me.

I thought I had been alone and am embarrassed at my self-deprecatory speech. He looks at me as if he finds some sort of humor in the situation.

"Hello, are you looking for something?"

His voice is beautiful, soft, unfazed. He has a slight accent that I don't recognize, different than the New York colloquial ways of speaking.

Nothing unusual about that, I *am* at Columbia University I remind myself.

"My class, my first class. Poetry with Professor Wallace Gray. I thought it was in this building, this room. I must have made a mistake."

I am still clutching my schedule.

He slips his fingers through his dark wavy hair. I see the strong curve and shape of his shoulders through the pressed oxford shirt he wears, absently tucked into his well-worn corduroys. An olive cashmere sweater is tied around his waist, and his sleeves are rolled up revealing his arms. He places his hands on his hips and looks at me, taking everything in. His gaze is clear, strong, and steady, and I think I detect a slight smile at the edge of his lips, as if he's confirming who I am. He seems to be illuminated by the light entering the room. And then, I see something incredible in his face. He is looking at me with the most beautiful green eyes I have ever seen. The whole scene is so contrary to my expectation that I am unable to string words together. I can't speak, yet cannot tear myself away from his hypnotic gaze.

"I'm *so* sorry to disturb you." I finally find words and attempt to gather up my things with a grace that I never did possess, dropping books and papers.

He watches, but doesn't say anything.

"I'm so late, I don't know what happened, there must have been a mistake on my printout." I wave the useless piece of paper in the air. "I'm usually in Avery Hall, the architecture building, I mean, most of the time so—well you know, I don't get over to this side of campus that often, anymore, since I'm not an undergraduate and I was taking an elective, sure that I had an English class in this room."

I try to balance everything I am holding and look futilely at the schedule in my hands. Stay calm, make sense. I know that I am not, so I stop talking and look up at him.

"Sorry again, for interrupting, I mean, bothering you."

And then it happens.

I am practically knocked over by it. The powerful combination of the pressure in my head and the vision—what I see. I realize that I've seen his face before. It's his eyes I recognize most, their color, and also the feeling of what it's like to be near him. It's crazy but I seem to know who he is—from a dream—a definite recurring vision I have seen many times before.

It's *him*.

He is everywhere in my memory and in my mind. I try desperately to separate what I know is real from what is not, push away the vision and stay in the present, standing in this room with him. Not in my head. But it is overwhelming—the images come one after another.

I see it all so clearly.

We are together, under a star-filled sky, walking on a flat-topped mountain in the desert, in a cave, in an ancient garden, and many other images and sensations that come at me too quickly to stop. What is it? A memory, an experience, a dream? I feel the heat of torches, the thunder of a cheering crowd, the chill of a desert night, and the feeling of him close to me. His lips and breath—on my neck, throat, the inside of my—

"Oh my God" I gasp.

The force is so powerful that I start to back slowly away from him. I don't know what else to do, so I turn and run out of the room, away from everything as quickly as possible. I descend the steps two at a time as I try to concentrate, desperately trying to clear my mind. I can't think clearly as the intensity of the moment and the exchange with him has overwhelmed my normal sense of control. As I emerge from the building, I try to understand what has just happened. I am even angrier with myself for running away and letting my vision overtake me.

I *knew* him from somewhere; he was in the very room I was looking for. I could feel a crazy sense of unexplained excitement. More than that, however, there was something unforgettable about the way he had looked at me and how it made me feel.

Ridiculous, Gabriella.

All the same, I knew that something incredible had just happened.

14

I COULDN'T GET HIM out of my mind.

The unexpected encounter with the mysterious stranger stayed with me. There was something about him, different—yet incredibly familiar. I was surprised at how just thinking about him made me feel: uncomfortable, off balance, electrified. I let myself move cautiously into the dark place in my heart—the one I never really dared to look into—and allowed the unexpected feelings to wash over me. The sensation of being near him, I wanted to hold on to the way it felt.

The phone rings loudly and breaks my reverie. It's Emily.

"Gabriella, are you getting ready for tonight? You know we can't be late and—"

"Em, it's only four thirty in the afternoon, the awards ceremony doesn't start until eight. We'll have plenty of time. I need to go do something."

"Can't it wait? What is so important?"

"I need to find a book, an out-of-print text. I thought I saw it at the little bookstore down Amsterdam. It's suggested reading and I want to find it."

"Suggested reading? Please, Gabriella. Can't you just stick to what's required, honestly."

"I won't be long. I've already missed the first class and I don't want to fall behind. Not for this."

I hear her sigh. She knows that once I make up my mind to do something there is little to be done to change it.

"Promise me you'll come straight back to get ready? This is a big night for everyone, especially your grandfather, Gabriella."

"I know; I'll be ready. I promise."

I hang up the phone and look around at the spare elegance of my room. I had come in at the beginning of the semester with a can of paint and whitewashed everything. All the furniture, walls, trim, and doors, even the old wood floor. I felt happiest in this spare environment that reminded me of the beach. I drop into the white Eames chair that was a gift from my grandparents. The appreciation of the icons of modern design was something that they began to teach me at a very young age, set by their own example.

The numbers on the digital alarm clock click into place and indicate how late it is. Like so many of those typical fall evenings in New York, the air is full with the suggestion of winter and night. As I exit my building I feel the crisp fall air sting my face as I turn down 116th Street toward Riverside Park. I treasure this piece of green at the edge of the city, the shimmering trees and the gray water of the Hudson River. The sound of sirens, horns, and diesel buses create the harmonic sounds of the city, vibrations of the power, energy, and possibility that exist here. I see people stand with arms raised, alerting the eyes of the passing taxi drivers; others walk head down, chins thrust forward with determination, purpose, and direction—going somewhere. Lives being lived, believing in the possibilities that await.

The last few days had been unsettling, yet, I felt something new. An explosion of memories and clear visions of my future, taking me somewhere, pulling me in. Especially the feeling that I had in the classroom, the stranger, and what I saw in his eyes. For the first time, even with everything in my life shifting, I feel ready.

The bookstore didn't have what I was looking for. Frustrated by the futile search, I change my direction home. I considered myself a person of consistency, a creature of habit as I attempted to find comfort in the rare constants of my life. The things I could rely on—I could count them on one hand. But instead of returning back through Riverside Park as I had come,

I choose instead the path that I had walked so many times with him.

Papa.

I feel the familiar anxiety, even guilt as I replay the conversation I had with him in his library before I left for school. The day he gave me the amulet. "You will not only make something, you will make a difference. You already have. You changed my fate."

I had shaken my head as I pushed away his words.

"I'm so sorry. I never want to hurt you."

"It should have been me, Gabriella. That bomb was meant for me. I was the one who was supposed to die."

The feeling of that day and the pain in his words lived in my heart.

Another memory stayed with me. Flying home to Boston from London at the end of my freshman year at Oxford—my first summer back since it had happened. There was one person I needed to see, someone who loved me and always understood: Lily. The taxi turned the corner, and I saw her small, familiar house. Always a welcome sight, the cozy porch, rocking chairs, and the unmistakeable long ramp, snaking its way from the front door down to the driveway. For her wheelchair.

I had run up the steps as I felt my heart pounding, excited at the idea of my surprise as my finger pushed the doorbell.

"I'll be right there." The familiar voice inside called out. I heard the sound of pots banging in the kitchen. "Oh hell, come on in. Whoever it is."

I pulled the screen door open and stepped inside.

"I'm coming, just a minute!" I heard her voice as it moved closer.

I remembered the sound, the slight creak of the wheels as she used her arms to push the chair over the uneven oak floorboards and her face as she turned the corner.

"Gabriella—it's you, what a wonderful surprise, I had no idea you were coming!"

"Lily."

I had dropped to my knees as I reached out to hug her, my arms around her waist, my head in her lap as I was overcome with emotion. I felt her hand touching my hair as she stroked my face, slowly wiping the unexpected tears away, which fell onto her frozen, immobile legs.

"Gabriella," she whispered.

"Oh, Lily, I've missed you so much. I've needed you these last months."

"I've missed you, too." She narrowed her eyes as she searched mine. "How are you doing—with everything?"

She looked at me with the purest affection I knew: gratitude, trust, happiness.

"I needed to get away from Europe, all the press, the security—so many changes since my parents died. I needed to come home to Gloucester, to a place where things are real. Like our summers together." I looked down at her paralyzed legs. "Except that everything is different."

She had smiled at what I was saying, recognizing things I had said before. My uncertainty, the doubts I had shared with her about my choices and the direction my life seemed to be moving in. I looked at my beautiful friend and remembered how our lives had changed in a fraction of a second that fall day when we were so young.

"Lily, I always think back to that day and—the car. I should have pushed you harder, farther, out of the way."

"Gabriella, you saved me, you saved my life. You changed my fate. This is the way things were meant to be. I know that. Even if we can't understand why."

I thought back to that day so many years ago, when I knew the car was going to hit her, before it happened.

"But my parents, Lily, I couldn't make it out. It was too unclear, I couldn't see things the way I did with you. I keep reliving that day, those moments. Over and over."

I felt her hands tighten on me. "Please stop doing this to yourself. That bomb had nothing to do with you. You can't always change fate, even though you changed mine. You have to trust yourself—and believe. Can you do that for me, for your grandmother?"

"I'm telling you, Lily, I don't care anymore what my grandmother called it. This gift. I can't trust it and I don't want it."

"You might one day."

I had looked down at the wheelchair, "I'm sorry, Lily. I'm so sorry. I've tried to understand how it works but I can't. It is impossible to describe or explain, even to myself." I looked away from her eyes.

"There are things that are simply beyond words. Things that are not definable. They just are. *You* taught me this, remember?"

"I taught you that?"

"Everything we learned when we were little. What your grandmother always said—that there is a bigger world that includes that which is not yet and that which might have been. Even that which might be. This is what you have always struggled with, right? Remember the poem she would read to us."

"The beginning is the end and the end is the beginning."

"Yes, that's it, Gabriella."

I remember how she had held me. So much had happened since that day three and a half years ago when *I* was the one who was broken. The irony of her comforting me.

I push harder to try and force the painful memories out of my mind as the earth revolves away from the sun, turning day into night. Security grates slam down to the ground, the shriek of the metal—then silence, locks are bolted, lights switched off, as everything slows down. I regret my decision to have come this way. It is longer, not as direct. In the distance I can see the half-built spire of the Cathedral Church of Saint John the Divine rising proudly into the gray sky. The landmark's idiosyncratic presence has drawn me in since I was a child. I loved its wounded, unfinished pride. I had been allowed to wander the nave and aisles of this Gothic structure alone, always finding new things to discover in its complex mystery.

"Go, Gabriella, explore and see what magic you will discover today in that building." My grandfather had always encouraged me.

Was he challenging a search in the building or within myself I wondered? Once again I thought of the trust he had in me, his unquestionable knowledge that I was safe. I want to celebrate him and his many accomplishments, stand next to him as he receives the recognition he deserves. I know that I need to get back to my apartment and remember my promise to Emily, to be on time for the awards ceremony at the museum for my grandfather. But the draw of the cathedral is too powerful, so I change direction and run inside.

Just for a few minutes.

15

THIS IS A PLACE where time stands still, where architecture endeavors to build a home for the spirit. Proof, that a building could be a symbol—of innovation, hope, and new ideas. A place where the eternal lived. A victory of ideas over gravity that brings space from silence, into the light.

The Cathedral Church of Saint John the Divine at the edge of Columbia's campus was an example of this. The most solid forms become skeletal; mass melts away to achieve impossible heights in a structure that seems to reach for the heavens. The quality of light was different here, broken into prisms of color as it passed through the magnificent stained-glass windows and became animated with energy. The visits I had made to the great cathedrals in Europe had shown me the power of architecture to capture, in three dimensional form, the soaring and limitless spirit of the divine. The monumentality of the space reflected the abilities of the human mind, man's way of addressing the spiritual universe, answering the challenge it posed in the only way we could. By building things.

Creating.

My eyes follow the lines of the rib vaults, and I see the precise points where the thrust of the load is met by the vertical supports. The impossible height of the nave was the innovative engineering feat that characterized the Gothic style. Colored glass, a completely non-structural material, replaced the masonry wall. It is cold and dim, but the spirit of the place is powerful, beckoning those who have entered to see what they can find. My feet pad softly on the stone floor, worn by the many who have come before me on a similar search. Another one of the many secrets of this cathedral was that it was constantly in use for performances and rehearsals, where the echoes of music replaced the faint dissonant sounds of the city beyond its walls. This drew a variety of people from the streets of the city inside as the notes answered the questions of those who listened.

I tighten the jacket around my body as my eyes adjust to the dim light. The sound of a haunting melody is being played in the small apse. The musicians are well beyond my line of sight, but I can hear the beautiful and strangely familiar music. I had occasionally stumbled upon rehearsals in the past and preferred to remain out of view, fearing that the condition of my audience would be considered trespassing on a product not yet ready for performance. I listen to the stopping and starting, the musician trying different expressions, and know I am witness to the embryonic moments of the creative process. Like the sketches undertaken before the execution of a painting, waiting to commit to canvas the final expression of an idea that has in it infinite possibilities. This is when you can see into the mind of the artist, their struggle and choices.

The music is an arrangement for strings and piano. The sounds fill the space with the hearts of those playing. I sit on a cold stone bench and listen, caught in the spell of the melody. When the music ends, I turn and walk slowly down the side aisle. My fingertips skim the surface of the carved reliefs along the wall: varied biblical scenes that depict judgement, salvation, and even the suggestion of life beyond this earth. A timeless art form that transcends any one religion, looking for answers yet questioning the nature of reality.

I stop and touch the cold stone. My fingers trace the lines of the flowing robes of a saint, the eternal smile and wings of an angel. Their unchanging forms permanently frozen in time. I can't leave without stopping to look at one of my favorite carvings in a dark corner of the nave. It is a scene from Genesis, the very act of God blowing the breath of life into man. The moment when Adam becomes a living being. This image is the essence of Kabbalah's teachings, the belief that there is an unmistakeable spark of the divine in every human being.

"The moment mankind was given a soul," a low, familiar voice says.

I spin around, stunned that I am not alone. I hadn't seen anyone else in the darkness of this part of the cathedral. The only sound had been the distant movement of chairs and voices as the rehearsal ended. Yet as I look up, I know immediately who it is.

It's him.

The man with the green eyes—from the classroom I had mistakenly entered. I remembered everything from that encounter. How he had looked right at me and how it made me feel. He has a stack of sheet music tucked easily under his arm, and I realize that he is the one who had been playing the beautiful piano melody. I try to read his expression, to look for something to interpret but find nothing.

"I, I thought I was alone, I never see anyone in here. Not anyone who I speak with that is." I feel the need to clarify.

I try to sound calm, unsure whether I am frightened by the realization that someone has been watching me or that I am happy in an unclear way that it is him. I had been unable to stop thinking about him, the mix up of my schedule, and my frustration at missing one of my first classes. He looks at me the way he did in the classroom. Pleased. As if he recognizes something in me. It's the smile that I remember and the powerful and overwhelming sensations that accompanied our first meeting. The weight of the silence between us is balanced out by the feeling that every nerve in my body is ignited by his presence.

He touches a detail on the relief we are standing in front of as he turns his face away from mine. "The energy of life being breathed into man. Do you agree?"

I feel the magnetic pull of his arm as it passes me and returns to the side of his body. He waits with what seems like amusement for my response.

"No." The words fall clumsily out of my mouth. "I have always believed in a scientific explanation." My voice trails off, dropping lower self-consciously. "Big Bang, Darwin . . ."

I try to recall my grade-school science teacher's explanation of cause and effect in the world: a justified and factual explanation for every occurrence, clearly defined within the boundaries and parameters of science and technology. Measurable, predictable. Evolution, dinosaurs—I attempt not to sound like an idiot. I try to appear calm, rational, and sure but feel so knocked off balance by him.

He smiles at me. "Really, cut and dry is it? All explainable—just that straightforward?"

That accent, the subtle melodic tone in his voice. I try to concentrate on what he is saying and ignore the slight humor he seems to find in everything I do. Everything about him is making me really uncomfortable. The way he looks at me, into me, and through me.

This is new. I am not used to answering questions in a place I had always cherished as my own private refuge, never wanting to share my solitude from the noisy streets of the city. Yet, I find myself standing with him, again. Suspended in time.

We walk toward the back of the church together, and I feel his eyes on me. He watches my reaction to the jarring sculptures of heaven, hell, and judgement. I turn slowly to him and, as our eyes meet, I realize how ridiculous I must look. I try to straighten the hat on my head, my paint splattered jeans—even the way I stand. His eyes move from my face, in a slow meaningful inspection, down to my feet and back up again. I lean over to pick up my backpack, and my grandmother's cherished book of T.S. Eliot's poems falls out and lands on the cold stone floor between us. We reach down at the same time as we both try to retrieve the slim volume.

"Ah, *Four Quartets*," he says, one eyebrow raised.

"Yes, assigned reading."

"You come to the cathedral to read in the dark?"

"No, I—"

There is no clear explanation for why I carry my grandmother's slim volume of poems everywhere with me. I step quickly away from him, reacting to the intense energy I felt as we touched. I'm relieved to have the focus move away from me. He looks intently through the text, noticing the well-worn paper and broken binding, the small papers that mark favorite passages. The many pages that are folded down.

"Wallace Gray's class right? He's quite well known for his *first* lecture. Hundreds of students show up. Isn't that so?" He smiles at me, a mischievous grin on his face. He asks these questions as if he already knows the answer.

The course was outside of my curriculum. One of the most popular and beloved on Columbia's campus. In the standing-room-only classes, Wallace Gray challenged students to find, within themselves, everything he knew they were capable of. I remembered him looking at me when I was small as he pointed his finger in a gesture of promise.

"When you're bigger, you will come read poems with me. We have much to learn from each other."

I couldn't understand what I would teach *him*. And yet, I waited for that day. To understand the beautiful ideas, the carefully chosen words. Where every one meant something. I knew that these were the poems my grandmother had loved and I wanted to understand too, what she found inside. Ideas about time, love, and the existential journey of life. I needed help in any or all of those areas.

The stranger waits for me to answer his question.

"Actually, I never made it to the first class," I continue embarrassed. "I was looking for the room when I mistakenly found you, I mean your room—office. A mix-up somehow with my schedule." I realize that I am not making any sense and am still confused by what had happened. "It's not my major, just an elective." I was becoming a babbling, incoherent imbecile in his presence.

He looks at me with his hypnotic stare. Calm and captivating. "I see. Well let's have a look at what you missed." Slowly, he begins to read.

> *While time is withdrawn*
> *consider the future and the past*
> *with an equal mind.*
> *What might have been is an abstraction*
> *Remaining a perpetual possibility*

I realize that I have no idea who he is or why, for the second time, I am encountering him in what is the most unlikely place. He closes the book and lifts his eyes to meet mine.

"Do you agree?"

"I'm not sure; we haven't discussed this yet," I say.

"But it's underlined here."

"It's not my book. I mean it wasn't; it is now, but—" I want to turn away from him but I can't.

"It's a question about destiny and whether we can change things. Fate maybe. That what did not happen might still remain possible if we could go back in time and choose differently."

I feel confused and look right at him. "Yes, well that's not possible."

I begin to feel the faint, familiar pressure in my head. Not knowing what else to do, I thrust out my hand in the most formal way I can, to introduce myself to him, officially. "I'm Gabriella Vogel." I try to steady my voice and speak calmly. "I've been coming here for many years, to the cathedral I mean. My grandfather used to teach at the university, a while ago."

Actually, he was the world renowned Professor Emeritus of Theoretical Physics and Cosmology, but that I would keep to myself. My voice trails off, and I can see that more than listening to what I am saying, he seems to be watching me again.

"And you are?" I ask.

I realize that I still know absolutely nothing about him. As usual, I am trying to conceal my discomfort and nervousness by rambling on and filling the empty space between us with words.

"Yes, I know who you are," he says. "My name is Benjamin Landsman and I am a student of your grandfather's work. I'm in New York doing some research."

I reach out to shake his hand.

He puts his hand out and takes mine then pulls it gently toward him so I have to step closer to keep my balance. He turns it over and looks first at my fingers, then the inside of my palm, slowly taking in every detail and curve, looking for something. I catch my breath at the shock of this intimate gesture. When he looks up, I feel that I need to respond to what he has said. That he *knows* who I am.

I pull my hand away from his grasp too quickly.

"Yes, well—he is very well known for his theories in physics, cosmology, and the universe," I say as I try to reconcile the fact that somehow he knows my grandfather.

I want to put the pieces together, yet I need more information. I'm beginning to feel that I can no longer trust my instincts. As if he can read the questions in my mind, he points to the big blue and silver tag on my backpack that Lily had given me in the shape of the solar system. A symbolic gift from our many trips to the Museum of Natural History. My name is emblazoned in large letters. I refused to take it off, for even though it was childish, the memory of those days was something I was not ready to let go of.

"Oh, it's hard to miss my name here." I find the opportunity to laugh for a moment and know my eyes reveal my embarrassment. Yet, I am relieved at the same time that he is not reading my mind. Or worse.

"The Museum of Natural History." He seems to find humor in something. "Now that is a very interesting place."

I bend down and try once again, as gracefully as I can, to gather up my belongings and push through the incredible energy that charges the air between us.

"Come, Gabriella." His hand reaches out to help me up.

I take it and realize how curious it is. The way he said my name, as if he has been saying it his whole life. As we turn and walk toward the back of the cathedral together, I know I need to leave the intimacy of the dark space, hurry back to get ready. But I'm not ready to walk away from him.

He points to a band of reliefs. "These reliefs have a profound power in their message. Don't you think?"

I stop to consider what he is saying as I look up at the last frieze of carvings near the door.

"I mean," he continues as he looks right at me, "these images from so many years ago reveal messages that are timeless. As if the people who made them still have a power over us. Even after they are no longer here."

People no longer here having a power over us? I know in my heart that this is true. I had experienced it; I *did* experience it all the time.

"They are proof of the force that moves through time. The soul of the artist transferred into his work," he says the words softly while looking at the art. "Maybe this gives them a reason for living?"

I think about what he just said. He waits for my reaction and turns to face me. I am so overwhelmed that I can't respond. How does he know that these are thoughts I have had many times before? The essence of what I believed to be the pinnacle of achievement for any artist. To speak eternally with complete silence, lighting the path of those who would come after.

"I'm not sure what you mean."

"Do you have things that you plan for, Gabriella, that you want to do? Dreams that keep you moving into the future?"

"Like what?" I try to collect my thoughts.

"What people want; traveling to a special place, climbing a mountain, finding everything you're looking for."

"Yes, of course."

As we stand on the threshold of the church I experience the strangest inability to tear myself away from him. I thrust my hands into the pockets of my jacket to conceal their trembling. It's late, cold, yet I'm completely intoxicated by the way he speaks, the way he looks at me. Everything about him.

"It was good to see you—again, I mean. But, I'm sorry. I just realized how late I am. I really need to go."

The words sound so small, so inappropriate in light of everything that has taken place.

How I feel.

I push the heavy bronze doors of the cathedral open as the cold night air stings my cheeks and realize that in so many ways, I have just traveled from one world to another. He is behind me, and I turn to wave goodbye and see him framed in the doorway. I notice the moonlight on his face.

"I will see you again, Gabriella." He smiles at me.

"And you?" I want to ask him the question he posed to me. "What is it that you wish for?"

He reaches out and barely touches my cheek. "I've already found it."

At a complete loss for words, I am only able to nod and turn to hurry down the steps. Running away once again, I think. As I break into a sprint up the long, dark avenue, I know he is watching me and that, somehow, the last words he said are a promise and a prayer.

16

I RUN ALL THE WAY from Amsterdam and 109th street as quickly as I can. I feel energized in a way I never have before.

I am consumed with the feelings of the unexpected encounter. I keep picturing him as he stood in the doorway of the church, the almost other-worldly light that illuminated him, and the way he looked at me. The hauntingly beautiful music is still in my ears, and I think about everything he said and what it felt like to be near him. There was something about him that struck a chord deep within me, and I was trying to understand why.

I knew that things often connected in my life, and I couldn't dismiss the coincidence of our two encounters. More than that, however, was the undeniable certainty that I had seen him before, in powerful premonitions, both in my past and future. As I try desperately to push away the sensations, I realize that something about him makes me want to see the visions more clearly and understand. But, I need everything I have in me to simply manage the *present*, and I know if I don't hurry back to get ready—there will be hell to pay. I turn down the street to continue my charge into the building, look down at my phone, and see that I have four missed calls from Emily.

I know she is wondering where I am, when we will meet, what I am planning to wear, and the other details of our evening together. I put the phone to my ear and brace myself for the verbal barrage.

"Where have you been?" Emily shouts into the phone as I round the entry past the doorman in my building, waving hello and flashing my ID card at the same time.

I press the button on the elevator keypad repeatedly. "Please hurry!" I'm exasperated and forget that I have the phone in my hand with Emily on the other end of the line.

"What? What did you say? Gabriella, what is the matter with you?"

"Oh, I'm sorry, Em. I have just had the craziest, most frustrating day!"

"Well, I was getting ready to call campus security. Honestly, Gabriella, you don't go wandering in Morningside Heights. There are so many creeps around here. What am I going to do with you—and it's only the beginning of the year!"

I listen and know she is right.

"Gabriella, are you there?"

"Yes, sorry, Em, I am trying to get upstairs to get ready. What is the plan? Where are we meeting?"

"I promised your grandfather I would get you to the museum in one piece. I'm coming to get you. With the car service.

I cringe at the thought of Emily and the driver in the dark shiny car pulling up in front of the building inhabited by graduate students. I feel the familiar anxiety as my hopes of remaining under the radar continue to disappear.

"Gabriella, can you be ready in thirty minutes?"

"I'll do my best." I stop trying to argue with her. There is no point.

"Remember how we would go to New York every summer with your grandparents? All the art galleries, Central Park, and Grand Central Station? It's been so long since we've been to the museum together. Tonight is going to be amazing."

I remembered the day last summer when the mailman rang the doorbell at the beach, proud to be part of delivering the news. The massive envelope had been ceremoniously carried into my grandfather's library by Maggie, to be opened and added to the scrapbook she created that contained the symbols of his life's successes. Seeing his name on the invitation to the National Medal of Science Awards Ceremony was further confirmation that my grandfather had always been involved in the most progressive and seminal work of his generation.

I had taken the invitation gratefully as my eyes scanned the list of other award recipients. There was a doctor whose ground-breaking work in treating HIV/AIDS had reduced the instances of death and mortality through a powdered antibiotic cocktail developed to be added to the water system. Medical breakthroughs were being acknowledged that helped make it possible for burn victims to heal with fewer scars and older people to hear more clearly, slowing down the process of aging. There were discoveries that led to new vaccines, prevention of childhood illnesses, safer food propagation, and innovations in electronics.

"I'm waiting for my trip to Sweden, Dr. Vogel, the Nobel Prize is next, right?" Maggie's eyes sparkled with promise. Sometimes I wondered what Maggie really knew about his work.

He looked up at her then at me. "Just in case either of you two think I'm retiring, I'm not."

I knew he was making a point that even though he had left Columbia he would in no way be limiting his research. I hoped he was right. I wanted him to find what he was looking for, and if that included the Nobel Prize then I wanted that for him too.

"Einstein got one," I had said in encouragement, "and he didn't have all the answers."

The fact was that I had noticed a new intensity in my grandfather's work that consumed him more fully. Although he always made time for me, I sensed a shift over the summer. An urgency to his research, as if there was a deadline that he was racing against.

"You are trying to unravel the deepest secrets of the universe aren't you, Papa?" I had asked him.

Each of the award recipients had deepened an understanding of the world and many had directly changed our lives. It was a night honoring those who had taken on the challenge to address some of the greatest problems human kind faced, the greatest mysteries. My grandfather was looking for an explanation that tied disparate and often conflicting scientific concepts together: Einstein's theories and the shocking new evidence being discovered through cutting-edge technology like the Supercollider. This was his dream.

There was also a very practical side to my grandfather, and it was probably this piece that allowed him to maintain and develop his teaching and academic career so effectively. Like nobody on the face of this earth, he understood me. Knowing my forgetfulness and disorganization when planning for these types of events, he had put Emily in charge of getting me there dressed and on time. She met her assignment with profound gratitude and grit.

"Don't forget to wear something fabulous. Remember last time? All the photographers will be there."

Right. In fact, that's exactly what had happened; I did forget. I lost track of time in the cathedral with Benjamin. I panic for a second remembering the many discussions Emily and I had about this night.

"What could be better than celebrating the achievements of brilliant people?" She could hardly contain herself. "Brains, now that's what really turns me on."

"Emily, the only reason I agreed to go to this . . . this event is because of him."

"Science and specifically physics are quite the vogue, Gabriella," she stated with conviction, "but I'm sure you haven't noticed."

"I leave these things up to you, Em. To keep me informed." I knew she wasn't listening to me.

"Young, fabulous scientists," she had continued, "are better than rock stars. Remember that."

Combine that with a black-tie soiree with food, dancing, and press, and to Emily, you had created the ultimate social opportunity. I was sure she had spent half the day preparing—I had less than thirty minutes.

I slam the door of my room behind me and try to concentrate completely on three simple goals: get in the shower; get dressed; get downstairs. I strip down and peel away the elements of my day, thanking fate for the many dinners I had accompanied my grandfather to over the last few years that would provide something appropriate in my closet. I wrap the towel haphazardly around myself and try to run around the corner and down the hall without attracting too much attention from my suite mates who are arguing loudly in the kitchen about the merits of postmodern architecture.

The hot water warms me as I wash away the uncertainty of the day. It's a relief to take this moment, to stand still. Needing every possible second to separate from the intensity and the undeniable force of energy between Benjamin and me, a sensation that I had never really felt before. I keep trying to push the image of him out of my mind—*away,* like it doesn't belong. But his face, his eyes, the velvet quality of his voice, and the way he had touched my hand, held it, and looked at it, as if confirming to himself who I was, keeps coming back to me.

He recognized something about me, in me. I was so thrown off balance by the way it made me feel.

Okay, Gabriella, try to focus.

I step out of the shower and run back to my room. I quickly towel dry my hair, pin it up in a twist, and find a dress, checking my watch one more time. I walk out of my room, hoping to escape the interested eyes of my roommates, but they immediately stop speaking when I emerge. All of them stare at me in complete silence, and I can see that they are reading the headline article about my grandfather. I had purposely not read it. I knew that it contained a detailed account not only of his work and goals, but the attempt on his life that had killed my parents in France.

"That bad?" I try to sound lighthearted and hope they won't start asking questions about what they are reading.

No response.

Finally, Daniel, one of my suite mates, speaks up.

"Gabriella, you are—"

"Yes." David seems to agree. "Wow, a dress. I wonder where you're going?"

He tries to sound cheerful as he discreetly puts down the newspaper and disguises the sympathy I can clearly see on his face. I had tried to keep the details of my personal life private but now I know they are out in the open, on the front page of the *New York Times.*

"Thanks." I try to sound polite. "I have something tonight, for my family. It's a dinner kind of thing."

"Come on, Gabriella, isn't tonight the night your grandfather is getting that award?" He holds up the cover of the *New York Times* and points to my grandfather's photograph. "Hardly a dinner."

I can tell how taken aback they are, both by the comment about the evening and my physical transformation.

"Yes, you're right, that's it." I move away toward the door. "I'll be back later; I really have to get downstairs."

I make it into the hallway as quickly as possible, then will the elevator to move faster, knowing Emily is arriving momentarily. As I emerge into the crisp night air, the large black sedan pulls up in front of the building. The driver Emily has hired gets out of the car and opens the door for me. Once safely inside the confines and privacy of the car, I exhale gratefully, lean my head back, and see Emily, with her cheerful overly made-up eyes, looking right at me, slightly shocked.

"Gabriella, you look very nice. Actually, amazing. You really should dress up more often. Isn't this fun?" She can't contain her exuberance.

"Emily, you look beautiful too."

She was, of course, ready and willing to start discussing every detail of what she was wearing, her preparations for the day, her classes, professors, and any sightings of gorgeous men. She realizes that I am not responding so she switches topics.

"And how was the rest of your crazy day? Your walk to the bookstore? Did you find what you were looking for?" she asks me breathlessly.

"What? Oh, you mean the book. No, I didn't find it. You know. The usual." I look straight ahead as I catch myself at the inaccuracy of what I am saying. The irony strikes me immediately. The *most* unusual things had happened.

"Well, I can't wait to come to your architecture review. When you have your midterms." She claps her hands together. "Those are supposed to be wild you know, Gabriella. They have food, wine, and really famous people who come and sit on the jury right? It's like a big architecture party!"

"Not really." I can't help laughing at her exuberance. "It's more like being on trial, but I like the way you see it better."

"I'm sure you'll do great. You never know who might be there and discover what an amazing architect you are." She squeezes my hand tightly.

"It's happened before you know. I've heard stories about how students are discovered at school and their whole life changes. Just like that. One minute you think you're going in one direction and then suddenly—" She stops talking.

"Gabriella, are you even listening to me?"

"Oh, I'm sorry, Emily. I've actually been thinking about this other class, you know the poetry one?"

"You mean the elective?"

"Yes, Professor Gray's class. We're reading T.S. Eliot."

"Your grandmother's favorite."

"It's interesting, Emily, he writes about time. Implying in poetry what science is saying. I see so many connections to everything, even to my grandfather's work." *And to ancient mystical ideas*, I think to myself. The expression changes on her face and I know she disapproves.

"A connection between the poem and cutting-edge physics?" She is clearly concerned.

"I don't know, Em. He implies that maybe things aren't always what they seem." I say it slowly and wait for the idea to sink in. "And that you have to feel things, even before you can try to understand them. Question what we're all looking for, what we're hoping for."

She narrows her eyes. "Gabriella! What you're looking for? What the hell does that mean anyway?"

"Sometimes I wonder, I don't know—if I'm running out of time."

"What are you talking about?"

"Like they did. My parents, my grandmother—even Lily. They all ran out of time."

"You promised me, you *promised* your grandfather." She takes my hand. "That you weren't going to worry so much about everything. Remember? No more scary stuff."

"This doesn't scare me, Emily. I need to think about these things. It's how I look at the world. I don't want to ever take things for granted."

"I know," she says, her voice softening. "You're the bravest person I know. You've been through so much. It's time. It's time for you to be happy."

She keeps talking, and I listen as I hold her hand tightly. Squeezing it in a tradition we had begun when we were young and excited about something that was about to occur. I turn my head to look out the window at the city that passes quickly in a blur of speed. But my mind is very far away, another universe away.

The excitement of the strange coincidences of my encounters with Benjamin are something that I have decided to keep to myself. Preferring to let the newness, exhilaration, and mystery of all of it play over in my mind. I know I am in uncharted territory.

"There is one more thing, Gabriella. Something I've been thinking about. *You* I mean. Always living your life as if you're waiting for something or someone. Forget the future, okay? Let's try to enjoy now. You never know what the future will bring."

"You're right."

I wasn't so sure anymore either.

17

"JESUS, WHAT THE HELL? Come on, people, move!"

The driver's head hangs out the window as he inches the car down the street. He is trying to get as close as possible to the front of the museum, but the streets are blocked off in every direction. Police cars, fire trucks, and ambulances fill the street, and the night sky is lit with flashing blue and red lights.

"I'm sorry." He is frustrated and trying to understand what is going on. "We've been at a standstill here for almost thirty minutes." He slams the car into park. "Stay here. I'll be right back. I'm gonna see if I can find out what the hell is going on. This is insane. At this rate we'll be here all night."

"Emily." I feel the heat beginning to burn down my back as my anxiety starts to rise. "Do you think this has something to do with my grandfather?"

My mind races back to the night in Paris, the explosion, the rush of sirens, the flashing lights, ambulances, and people everywhere, holding me, comforting my grandfather. The moment my life changed, in so many ways, forever.

"Gabriella, please don't worry. It's always like this, don't you remember last time?"

"Actually—no. This seems different."

I knew very well that anonymous threats had been made to the selection committee for the National Medal of Science honorees. Security had been dramatically increased in light of my grandfather's agreement to attend. I had also noticed changes in some of his habits and routines. He seemed to move with more caution, going over things, double checking. Even at the beach house, a place that had always been free from worry and the pressures of the world, a refuge of safety. The realities of the dangers of his life outside the isolated cape community were seeping into our sacred space. I could picture the black vans on the property, the men installing cameras in the trees and the day in his library where I sensed something was wrong. I had tried to explain this new caution to myself as his characteristic vigilance, but I knew there was more. Something was on his mind. I would catch him staring out the window, his brow furrowed in contemplation. He seemed different, almost distracted, and there were times I felt he wanted to tell me something. Struggling to find the moment or the right words, but then holding back.

Before I left for New York, I had found a quiet moment alone in his library at the beach house to question him as I looked for reassurance that my fears were unfounded.

"Papa, what does this mean?" I had pleaded, alarmed at the real changes he was making in his habits that went far beyond the new security system and everything we had done after that terrible night in Paris.

"There are certain people, forces who do not want me to reveal the proof of what I have been working toward. My Theory."

"I don't understand, are you telling me that you are in some sort of new danger? I thought the French, American, and Israeli governments had successfully shut down the terrorist cell. Those who set the bomb in Paris. You told me we were safe, that you were no longer at risk."

He paused for a moment, as if he was trying to decide how much to reveal to me.

"Tell me." I caught myself as I tried not to raise my voice. "What's going on? Does this have anything to do with you leaving Columbia and all the time you spend traveling now?"

"Gabriella, as you know, there have always been two theories, but at a certain moment in time, they negate each other. I have simply been looking for the missing connection. The proof that will finally allow for the legitimacy of both."

"Both theories, what do you mean both?"

"Quantum mechanics and Einstein's general relativity, one explains the very small and the other the very large." He looked at me and took my cold hands in his warm, protective grasp. I remember how he had leaned back in his worn leather chair as the sun illuminated his face, highlighting everything I loved about him.

"You see, even Einstein saw the flaw in his theory. He saw it break down and spent the last thirty years of his life trying to resolve the conflicts. He wanted the new synthesis to be called, the 'Theory of Everything.'"

We said the last words together.

"I know, the Theory of Everything. But it's crazy. Sometimes you end up creating more questions than finding answers, right?"

"That's true," he had laughed.

"Well, have you found it?"

"You will be the first to know. I promise you."

"Are you worried?" I had looked down at the floor as I asked the question, not wanting to legitimize my fears by meeting his gaze.

"No, of course not." He tried to reassure me. "I am safe. I promise you that I know exactly what I'm doing. If I'm worried, it's not about some external force, not about this anyway."

He had a way of not answering my questions, but I couldn't get it out of my mind. The possibility that someone or something he would not explain to me was hovering above our lives. That they were back.

"Gabriella!" The urgency in Emily's voice brings me back to the car and the crowds. "Here comes our driver."

"Sorry, I was just looking at all the police. I mean the security, the guards." I try to steady my voice.

The front door opens, and I am relieved to see the driver's smiling face as he slams the door behind him, buckles his seatbelt, and turns around to greet our expectant faces.

"Coast is clear, no problem. Everyone should be moving toward the front now."

"Well, tell us what you found out?" Emily didn't want to miss a thing.

"Some crazies. A bomb threat or something."

"What? Oh, I'm sure that can't be right—" Emily tries to stop him, but he continues.

"You know the New York police. They're the best. Take this stuff really serious. But they found nothin'. So you girls are good to go."

18

E MILY THROWS OPEN the car door, grabs my arm, and pulls me out. Our eyes meet as she nods to me in encouragement.

"No fear, Gabriella." She speaks my grandmother's words.

"Right."

"This night is about celebrating. Achievement, promise, and science. The accomplishments of the leaders blazing the trail."

"And my grandfather—"

"It's going to be a great night."

We make our way to the front of the line as Emily forces her way through the crowd to the VIP entrance. I can see the back of my grandfather's head in the distance, accompanied by the president of Columbia University and several other dignitaries from the city of New York.

"I see him, Gabriella. Come on!" Emily shouts as she points her finger above the heads of everyone in front of us.

He is surrounded by his personal assistants. The current lucky few graduate students whom he selected from the thousands who had applied to work with him. I am overwhelmed by the flashing lights of the press, the crush of people, and the massive tent we are entering where the reception and ceremony will be held. I try to concentrate and follow behind Emily's steady, confident lead, but my thoughts are everywhere, pulling my emotions along in their wild tow. They rush back to the night in Paris four years earlier and to the recent conversation with my grandfather about his safety.

I force myself to think about something good, wonderful—and especially to earlier in the day: Benjamin and our indescribable connection. The powerful energy I felt in the cathedral with him.

I can see him, the beauty of his face in the dim light of the nave, the music he played, the shape of his shoulders, and the way he said my name. I think of the strange recognition I had felt when his arm grazed mine and the unexplained power he seemed to have over me. I wanted him to move closer as I watched him exhale. I had looked at his mouth and imagined it on me, his hands, his face, his skin next to mine. "I am a student of your grandfather's work," he had said. Well, these days, who wasn't.

"Gabriella!" Emily pulls me in. "Are you okay, honey?"

She links her arms through mine and with the determination of an athlete completing the last leg of a race, guides us past the crush of curious onlookers, protesters, and photographers. We enter the giant white tent on the lawn outside of the museum. Its peaks point into the illuminated sky and enclose fountains, gardens, and cobblestone areas to create an otherworldly venue.

"Wow."

"Amazing isn't it?"

We both stand and take in the scene. This community of scientists seem slightly uncomfortable in their formal attire. Dressing up, moving in a world of flashing lightbulbs, if only for a night.

I look up at the glowing cube, the glass and steel architecture of the Rose Center for Earth and Space, and think this a fitting backdrop for the science awards. The event planners had brought in an array of LED lights and lasers, picking up the theme of space and planets that were rotating on a regular basis, illuminating the partygoers and attendees.

"This place is perfect for tonight," I say to no one in particular.

It's as if the venue had been chosen specifically to honor a man whose theoretical work was about the universe. The strength and power of possibility proudly reflected in the architecture of the place. I had spent countless hours as a child in the Hayden Planetarium's four-hundred-seat Space Theater, one of the world's largest virtual reality simulators, staring up at the map of billions of stars and galaxies. I could remember, when I was a little girl, the sound my shoes made on the polished floors, the faint echo as I ran from the different displays, looking for something. Clues. Answers.

"Come on, we're almost there." Emily looks quickly at me as she follows the usher who leads us to our table at the front of the room.

I can feel the many eyes on us as we hurry to the table. I recognize the burning sensation in the pit of my stomach, reminding me that I have not eaten all day and credit my dizzy and lightheaded sensation to this fact. We manage to arrive at our seats just as the lights are dimming. Our table has place cards that show me seated next to my grandfather and Emily, a few chairs down. She winks happily at me conveying her pleasure at sitting next to the two mysterious young men on either side of her.

"Brains," she mouths as she points her index finger to her own temple.

The master of ceremonies clears his throat at the podium. The lights dim.

"I would like to welcome all of you to the National Medal of Science Awards. Tonight is testimony to the creativity and vision of men and women who are not willing to simply accept the status quo. They won't rest until they have found answers to the questions that have been asked since the beginning of time. Their fearless voyage into the unknown is an attempt to ask the deepest questions that face mankind."

The silence of the room is filled by the counterpoint of the descriptions of mind-boggling achievements. There is a palpable energy to this world, driven by the force of possibility. The full glass of red wine that I clutch is helping to calm my nerves and the rocky condition of my empty stomach, as well as my keen awareness of the many eyes that are on our table and the whispering about my grandfather.

"I guess I'm next." He must have noticed that my eyes were down and lifts my chin so he can look at me.

"Yes, Papa, of course."

I want to be happy, to stay in the present and enjoy the moment, but I'm trying to push away the familiar feeling. The room starts to spin slowly and the voices from the podium seem to be deepening, slowing down.

"Are you all right?" Across the table I see Emily's concerned gaze locked on me as she mouths the question

"And finally, I would like to present our guest of honor, Dr. Sydney Vogel!"

My grandfather pushes back his chair to thundering applause, and I force myself to stand and help him navigate to the podium. The words of praise continue as does the standing ovation.

"Dr. Vogel is being honored tonight for his groundbreaking work in theoretical physics. Finding proof for the theories he has held for so many years, he has said that he will show the world the unfathomable. Make known the un-knowable. And we have no doubt that he will."

I try to concentrate on what is being said but I have the familiar and distinct feeling that I recognize. It's unmistakeable. I need to pull myself out of the dark zone and back into the present. I see my grandfather at the podium speaking, pointing his finger in the air, then smiling and pausing as everyone claps in response to what he is saying.

"So." His powerful voice has in it the seriousness with which he speaks about his research, practiced over the many years filled with valuing achievement and hard work, facing his many critics. "People have always assumed that just because we cannot see something it isn't there. We are now on the verge of proving the physics of the impossible and understanding the mind of God."

The room breaks into deafening applause as he is presented with the National Medal of Science for his expanded model of the Big Bang theory. But we all know what it really means.

He is going to prove that our universe is not alone, that other worlds exist connecting to ours through the wormholes that Einstein had first suggested.

"You only fear what you do not understand, what you cannot see. Soon we will show you—the proof!"

I am glad to have escaped the sensations I felt while he was speaking. I look across the table at Emily and see the pride, admiration, and respect on hers and everyone's faces as they stand to honor my grandfather. He looks so small standing on the podium. But, there is something else, something new in his eyes. It's a certain resolve. As if it no longer matters to him what others think. That what matters now is what he knows in his heart to be true.

What he has always known.

A cool breeze blows into the massive white tent; it circles me and stirs up the hem of my dress, pulls the hair across my face, and conceals my eyes momentarily. As I turn my head, I recognize a familiar face across the room, staring intently at me. It's the face that I could not get out of my mind. I blink and try to look out across the darkness, but when I attempt to find him again, he is gone.

"And so," my grandfather says, "I want each of you to remember that there is much light in the darkness of this world. Thank you so much for recognizing my team with this award. None of this is the work of one person. I cannot take credit without recognizing my peers and key collaborators."

He proudly names each of his research associates and assistants of the last few years. All at once, I know why I have felt the familiar sensation, the signs of my premonition. The last name he says, clearly and carefully, is Benjamin Landsman.

19

IT WAS TIME for my life to begin.

You've saved others, the voice inside of me whispered. *It's time, to save yourself.*

Being in New York felt like standing in a doorway, a threshold to a turbulent sea of energy and strength, a blended collection of human qualities—wisdom and ignorance, suffering and joy. Architecture school was everything: an attempt at victory of the spirit over the forces of gravity and greed and an opportunity to lose myself in the limitless potential of the city. Escape the ghosts of my past.

Several weeks earlier, the architecture critic had stood in front of the room. She seemed much younger than I expected given her accomplishments and dense resume. A look of sympathy was subtly evident on her face.

She read the vague program of the first assignment out loud to the eager students. "You will face the challenge of developing a poetic sensibility in the translation of your ideas into architectural composition. This time of investigation is meant to be a bridge between the realities of real-world construction, and the limitless opportunity of your own imaginations."

My heart had accelerated in response to her words. The challenge of translating abstract ideas into something that could be *built*—out of bricks and mortar, steel and stone excited me. We were chained to our desks by the magnetic draw of the work and our passionate commitment to the search for meaning and knowledge. I observed with curiosity that the pursuit of physical pleasure and sexual experimentation was often used as an antidote to the emotional stress of the studio by some of my classmates. I had chosen not to partake in the potential opportunities, but maybe it was time for change.

Try something new.

My grandfather had prepared me for everything he knew lay ahead; the challenge of the curriculum and the power of my own questioning. He had his ways of encouraging me.

"Proof." I had looked down at his finger as he pointed to the yellowed page in the autobiography of the architect Louis Kahn, several weeks before I left for New York.

"Everything must begin with poetry and end as art." He read the words then stopped and looked right into my eyes. "You see, Gabriella, this is what you are doing."

I had leaned against his desk, squinting in the faint light of his library as I attempted to read the small print above his finger.

"You are looking for meaning, searching for answers. Creating architecture that expresses the spirit of this time. It is a worthy effort, Gabriella," he had said in encouragement.

"I'm not sure where this is all going, but maybe I can find something." I hesitated. "It's how I can understand myself, by creating things."

Architecture, paintings, *garbage*—at least I was trying.

He nodded and hugged me, filling me with love and encouragement. Sent me out into the world with those words.

Typical of the architecture student's way, the real work gets done in the middle of the night. I have been in the studio for more than twelve hours and look around. The floor is littered with evidence of time spent: empty coffee cups and paper, fragments of the wood and cardboard used to build our models. It's the night before the first major midterm review and the studio is glowing, charged by the energy of those working late into the night. The activity inside the studio contrasts the stillness of the campus outside.

Avery Hall, the school's neoclassical home since 1912, acts as the late-night incubator of a diversity of possible futures. Its starkly defined symmetrical proportions communicate to the world a recognizable iconography, the old belief that the secret of architectural quality is known, universal, and endlessly repeatable. Yet, the chaotic studio spaces within bristle with new ideas. The future of architecture evolves while the world sleeps.

We each have a desk, laptop computer, printer, and pin-up board filled with images and photographs, quotations, schedules, and reminders. The essence of our lives reduced to this small area of space. A world unto itself that reveals so much about its occupant. The first day of school, I had quickly staked my claim on a desk in the rear of the studio, as far from the social hub of the room as possible—concealed, safe in the intimacy of the corner.

It had been hours since I had taken a break, and I was working on a particularly challenging aspect of the current assigned project. I can feel the reduced energy in the room as students leave for the night. A song called *Dreamer* plays through my headphones, the words are insulation from the distractions of the studio. I stare at the symphony of lines on the page before me and feel the space around me disappearing.

"Gabriella!" The voice is muted by the blasting percussion boring into my eardrums.

I know it's Philip. He made quite a splash on the campus when he arrived bringing his paintings, his guitar, and his attitude of sexual freedom and challenge to our space. I don't turn around to meet his eyes. Instead, my hand reaches up and smoothes the hair on the back of his neck, the familiar shape of the curve down to his shoulder. I loved the reckless abandon with which he lived his life and always hoped that somehow it would wash off on me.

"Let's go, kid, time to take a break. Burgers and beer at the club. We're all going. Enough torture." He squints at the overflowing basket of discarded drawings next to my desk. "It's time for something pleasurable for a change."

"What are you doing, Philip?" I feel his arms wrap around me in a bear hug as he stops to breathe me in. I loved him in so many ways—just not the way he hoped. "I'm perfectly happy right here."

"Tonight, Gabriella. Tonight—I'm going to show you something you'll never forget."

He looked at me with a smile that would have melted most women.

"Our relationship is very special to me, Philip. I'm not going to screw it up with sex."

"You can love many people; you just love them differently. That's all it's just different."

"Just *friends*, Philip," I laughed in response to his constant offers.

"You and me." He teasingly points his finger at himself slowly, puts it against his mouth in a kiss then presses its wetness back onto my lips. "You and me, Gabriella. That's never going to change."

"Stop it, Philip." I push him away, wiping my mouth with the back of my sleeve in mock disgust, laughing at his arrogance and the power of his personality. "You're shameless."

"I know—but that's what you love about me, right?"

"One of the things."

"So?"

"Platonic."

"I'll try, but you don't make it easy." He winks at me.

"I know you." I point my finger into his ribs. "What you're thinking. Don't forget—we're *way* past that." But I wondered what was wrong with me.

He looked at me and shook his head. "You're never going to change, but don't expect me to give up."

I thought back to our adventures together in Europe. We had traveled, many times, through the back roads of Wales and Scotland together, painting the landscape and exploring Roman ruins. I knew he didn't share my powerful need to understand history.

"Archaeology, Gabriella? Really. What is so *bloody* interesting? You spend your life trying to find things in the past."

"It's the foundation of the world around us."

"Well, it's time to live in the present."

"Easy for you to say."

"What is?"

"To live in the present only."

"Easier that is."

"Don't you feel your past, who you are, everywhere around you?"

"I don't know, Gabriella—"

"Like the roots of a tree, you can't see them because they're buried deep underground. But they're there. Holding you up, feeding you, giving you strength to withstand the wind, the storms, the years."

"And the future, you probably think that's somewhere in your tree too?"

"I can hear it—in the breeze that blows through the branches. The sound in the shimmer of the leaves. It's like a promise. Besides, I must have inherited it. My grandmother was an archaeologist."

"Of course she was." He rolled his eyes. "But you can't go through life only believing in music and art, poetry and—"

"And what, Philip?"

"Love."

"Why not. What else is there?"

20

WHEN WE WERE AT Oxford together, Philip and I always traveled without a map. We believed that what we might happen upon unexpectedly, where fate would lead us, would be more interesting than any plan. We found bed and breakfasts, villages, and the secrets of another world. We stayed in the same room to save money, often sleeping in one bed. I could remember many times opening my eyes to see him looking down at me. Embarrassed that I had caught him, he would quickly turn his face away.

"Philip, what is it?"

"You were dreaming, Gabriella. Saying crazy things. About Paris. Are you okay?"

"It pulls me back in, Philip. I can't get away from it." I wondered what else I had revealed.

"You can't blame yourself. You have to stop this. Please, stop torturing yourself." I could feel his power, his breath so close to me. The pounding of his heart. "We've been over this so many times. How could you have known? Nobody could have known."

It was the same conversation over and over, but now we were in New York, and I had come to my desk in the corner to find a small rose in a recycled plastic coffee cup with a card signed, *your British secret admirer.* I remember smiling at his thoughtfulness. The image of the red flower incongruous in the presence of everything else in the architecture studio.

I feel him pull me off the stool and away from my desk as he pries the pencil out of my hand. It's tempting, even for me.

"I really can't." I try not to laugh. "I still have so much work to do, get ready for tomorrow, but thanks anyway. Philip, you go." I am completely unconvincing.

"Gabriella, I am not taking no for an answer this time." He shakes his head as his long dark hair covers his eyes, the accent quite irresistible. He drops the bag that has been thrown over his shoulder until moments before. Clearly he needs both hands for something. Before I can brace myself, he grabs me under the arms and pulls me off the stool, practically throwing me over his shoulder. I feel the strength in his arms encircling my body, twisting the delicate fabric of my blouse as I try to object. I know I'm resisting with half a heart. Getting out of the studio is exactly what I need.

"Philip, no!" But it's too late.

I have been drawing and redrawing the same lines on the page—zoned out. We look at each other for a minute, and, rather than resist, I surrender.

"Nice rose." He winks at me.

We burst out of Avery Hall, past the tall granite columns, and run down the great steps of the university campus, out into the cold New York night. Our laughter pierces the silence of the darkness. We connect with a giddy mob of exhausted students, re-entering the world where time is measured in ways other than drawings completed and models built. We all feel the power of being in this place, on the cutting edge, the danger and promise of it. The lights in the other buildings are dark, all are sleeping giants, while the windows in Avery Hall glow around the clock. Time stands still in the pursuit of truth in the visual arts as we try to balance our lives and straddle the moving border between the known and unknown.

Whenever I am in a group of my peers, a self-conscious caution is always my companion. Controlling any release, protecting the parts of myself I have kept hidden for so many years. Never one to miss out on any experience of the mind, I wonder whether it is time to let myself go physically as well. I had allowed myself experimentation in the past, approaching the experience detached, with my emotions buried—safe—below a web of protection. It felt like an investigation, an experiment to be evaluated and analyzed like scientific data. Hardly inspiring.

Philip was trying, though, he was relentless.

He grabs my hand and interlaces his arm with mine. The undeniable pleasure in this intimate connection surprises me, and our eyes meet briefly, mine questioning, his smiling. He pulls his coat around my shoulders then wraps his arms around me.

Dan, another classmate, runs up to us and tries to grab me away from Philip.

"Well, well, the great Dr. Vogel's granddaughter has decided to join the regular people."

Philip shoves him away from me. This is not a connection I like to advertise.

"No way, Gabriella? Why didn't you tell me?" another girl asks, as she realizes who Dan has mentioned. "You are related to *him?*"

"Yes, he's my grandfather." I try to compose myself, not wanting my voice to betray my feelings. "He used to teach here but lives in Boston now."

As if who and where he is needs clarification. There are posters all over campus advertising his upcoming visit. I had seen many of my classmates reading the details in the article that had been circulating. In light of the massive press coverage of the recent event at the museum, everyone seems to know about my life and my grandfather's theories.

"Didn't you see Gabriella on the cover of the papers a few weeks ago with him? Their pictures were everywhere after that awards ceremony. Your grandfather is going to explain the universe. The 'Theory of Everything,' right?"

If it was possible to disappear I would have done so on the spot.

"Oh my God. Gabriella, I didn't even put it together, of course it's *you,*" she says. "You just look so different in the pictures."

Yes, I tried. Getting dressed up to attend an awards ceremony afforded me the chance to break away from my normal all-black, no-makeup look.

"Thanks." I'm trying to be gracious. "That was a big night for all of us."

"Come on, guys, leave her alone. Let's go!"

Philip saves me. We break into a run and pull away from the others; the race to get down Broadway and to the door of the club first is on.

As we approach the entrance, the powerful beat of the drum and guitar vibrate out the door. The crowded space is dark and full. Bodies press against each other. Students ready to release the stress of the week with live music, beer, and an atmosphere of suggestion and possibility. I am relieved to have an excuse to change the subject, the deafening music an opportunity to escape from the conversation and questions about my grandfather.

My other life.

It's nice to be out with a group of my peers. Not worrying about anything, as time carries us along in its crush of forward motion. Exploration, challenge, friendship, intimacy, these are the markers that highlight our lives.

It feels good to get out. I should try this more often.

21

IT WAS IN SITUATIONS like this where I was beginning to become aware of the effect I had on men. Philip's eyes move down the axis from my eyes and mouth across my blouse and down the length of my body. Taking everything in.

I observe him in a detached way; this is a power that I have not fully explored.

The lights, beer, and crush of people on the dance floor are beginning to make my head spin, compressing movement and energy. There is something in the way the music and the flashing lights are taking hold, and I need to find a chair.

"Let's sit, Philip."

I gesture back to the tables as I try to find a place far away from the large speakers. I know that he can't hear me above the blast of the band, and if he understands what I'm trying to say, he ignores me and instead, pulls me onto the dance floor. I recognize a force of intense pressure between my eyes. It's the familiar sensation, the rising feeling that always accompanies my ability. To see the future.

No. Not now, I plead silently.

I had decided that this power, this ability, this *curse* I have lived with for so long would not invade my new life in New York. With all the force of will that I can find, I try to push it away and focus instead on Philip and the music. I look up at him and his eyes meet mine. I know that his logic is distorted by fatigue and alcohol, yet he interprets this as interest and reaches out for me, wrapping his arm around my waist as he pulls me into him. I feel his hands move into the loose sleeves of my blouse and up my arms to my shoulders as the heat from his palms burns into my skin. I lean into him as we move together to the music, and my hands reach up and circle around the back of his neck. I close my eyes tightly as I push away the feeling, the powerful dark images, the familiar sensation. Instead, I try to lose myself in the moment and the feeling of being so close to him.

And then, I feel his mouth on mine. I can taste his desire, the salt of his sweat, the heat in his breath.

"Philip!" I push away from him.

The sensation pressing down in my head has become too much to bear. I need to get away from the booming speakers and the band, clear my head, get control.

"Stop! Please, I don't know what the hell I'm doing."

I push past him, overcome by a sense of dread and fear, and stagger away confused. Pulled by an overwhelming force toward a familiar girl I have seen on campus, I am seized by a gripping pain and intensification of my vision. She doesn't look up at me, but I feel it. The knowledge, the certainty, that she is in imminent danger. I can see her future.

This is crazy, I think to myself. Now I'm going crazy. The thoughts scream in my head. I look for any excuse, an explanation—anything to understand why I feel this way. Exhaustion, stress, and concern about the architecture review, which at this point is only hours away, must be the cause. But it is all happening so quickly.

I see it all. They are fighting, and she wants to get away. It's the girl, that girl. She tries to tell him that she must go, but he shouts and threatens her. She doesn't believe him. She gets up. He yells; he's filled with rage, but no one can hear him shouting; the music is too loud. As she walks away, he calls out to her, his anger uncontrollable. She doesn't see that he reaches for something. That he has a gun. He pulls it out of his pocket; his finger is on the trigger, and as she turns around to face him, there is an explosion. She falls to the ground; he cries out in anguish, and there is blood everywhere. Red blood, red flashing lights, sorrow, regret, screaming sirens, then darkness.

I need to do something, warn her somehow. *Now.* I turn back toward her table just as she pushes away. I catch her arm and she turns to face me, fear in her eyes.

"Excuse me, are you okay?"

"Get away from me!" She pulls her arm back and continues to storm away.

"I need to talk to you; I have to tell you something—it's important."

She looks at me, and I know, I remind myself, that sometimes the hardest thing and the right thing—are the same.

"What is it?"

"Your boyfriend, I know this sounds crazy, but he wants to hurt you; he has a gun."

"What? You're *crazy*—you know nothing about me, nothing about him." She tries to raise her voice over the band. "How dare you!" She doesn't want to hear anymore and she storms away. I follow her toward the bathroom as she slams the door in my face.

Crazy or not, I know that they are back, more powerful than I could ever remember. I had experienced it in the classroom with Benjamin, the beautiful images, and now—this. Something had awakened this part of me that I had put to sleep. Or maybe it was someone.

I push away, out of the club through the twisting, rhythmic bodies toward the door, leaving my bewildered classmates behind.

"Gabriella, stop! Where are you going?"

Philip runs after me, out onto Broadway, and reaches for me. "I'm so sorry, I didn't mean to upset you, I don't know what came over me."

I stop and turn to look at him. I realize that he thinks my overpowering need to leave is his fault.

"No, Philip, it's not that. Not *you*, I mean." I take his hands and hold them in reassurance. "It's my head. I, I'm just exhausted and need to go home. Get some rest before the review tomorrow."

He pauses for a moment as he tries to evaluate, to interpret this sudden excuse for departure. He doesn't believe me.

"Come on, Gabriella, it's two in the morning, no one is going to sleep before the review." His hand tightens around mine; his voice is soft.

"Please stay with me."

He stands before me, so incredibly vulnerable, offering himself in a way that I have not seen before. I want to tell him the real reason I have to get out, but I can't. I don't even understand it myself. It's something about that girl. The overwhelming sensation announces itself again as I desperately attempt to end the conversation.

"I'm going. I've got to get away from here. Now. Clear my head and shower." I try to convince myself, pull anything normal toward me.

I see the concern in his eyes as he takes another step closer. His fingers brush the side of my cheek, my mouth, and across my lips, outlining their shape with the slightest touch. His hand slowly travels down my arm and comes to rest on my waist. The index fingers of both hands circle through the belt loops on my jeans and before I can back away, he pulls me toward him and the fronts of our bodies touch.

"Philip, stop this, please."

"You're really just going to leave me here. With them?" He smiles.

I see something in his face: a truth, an affection I want—the history we've shared. We both know that the intensity of our connection is undeniable.

"Thanks, Philip, I'm flattered. Please don't think it's you, I'm just not—"

"I want to kiss you, Gabriella, *really* kiss you. Just let me. Even if you don't kiss me back. I don't care."

I step away. I can't look at him like this; I don't want to hurt him. A taxi is coming down the street, and as I raise my arm to hail it, the wind whips itself into a frenzy and pushes me over. I shudder from its impact and fall back as I lose my balance.

"Gabriella!"

I know that once again, I am trying to run away: from the girl who brought on the overwhelming premonition, from my peers, and from any chance at a normal life that I might have. Philip reaches out and catches me. As my face presses into him, I feel my tears on his skin.

"You are *not* going to be alone tonight," he says.

And then I feel myself letting go. Giving in. Losing myself and my resolve in the comfort of his words. I will take what he offers because I know that it's time. There is no choice. Things need to change.

22

I T IS LATE—OR EARLY— the middle of the night, but I can clearly see the outline of his face inches away from mine.

What am I doing here? I think.

I feel the unfamiliar pressure of the strange bed under me. This had been a bad idea. Wrong.

I should have been preparing my body and mind for the architecture review that was only a few hours away. I look at Philip as he sleeps and turn away from him knowing that my instincts had been right. I wished this had not happened and wonder once again what the hell is the matter with me. The New York night sky glows outside the windows as my mind races through the strange events of the day. The studio, the powerful premonition that I could not explain, casting its spell over everything, and, now, here with him.

I force my eyes shut. I need to think about the first project that I am presenting in the studio. A "spiritual retreat," they had called it, a "space for scientists pushing the boundaries in their fields."

The leaders and visionaries.

"We are challenging you to create with architecture an environment that will encourage that experience."

I review the purposely vague information we had been given.

Site: unspecified.

Goal: a building that could have significant impact in its physical and aesthetic presence, facilitating the need to withdraw. To search one's interior world, balancing out the opposing forces of the physical, thereby increasing the understanding of both.

I could relate. It was a challenge that reflected perfectly my own questioning.

The task the architecture critics had challenged us with seemed ironic. The subject of this first project mirrored the relationship with my grandfather and his work. Maybe it was no coincidence. My life was characterized by these strange intersections of fate, often blurring the distinction between what was real and what was not.

I thought back to the visit I had made to the Monastery of St. Catherine's in the desert when I was a little girl with my mother. Built at the base of Mount Sinai, this was believed to be the place where Moses saw the burning bush. Even though I was very young, the remarkable space and cell-like chambers had sparked my interest in architecture. I remember clearly the incredible silence of the desert, a place of contemplation and quiet. My goal was to translate these timeless concepts into a modernist design that embodied the power and efficiency of technology, clean and pure. Creating space for the mind to expand.

"Gabriella." I hear Philip's voice, soft with sleep.

He sighs and moves toward me. I feel his lips as they find the place at the top of my neck that he's uncovered and the slow concentrated movement down the chain of my vertebrae. He kisses them one at a time as his mouth claims my body. I want it to feel right. I want it to work—but it doesn't.

"Philip, stop."

I catch his hands as they wrap around me and try to pull me into him.

"Come *on*, Gabriella."

"We need to get ready, get up. The review is only—"

I try to stand and feel the fragments of pain in my head return. I reach up and force my hands on either side of my temples. It's the girl from the bar. I have a clear image of her face in a pool of blood.

"Oh my God."

"What is it?" He reaches out and pulls me toward him.

"I keep seeing this image in my mind. It's so clear. Of a girl, that girl last night at the bar. That something terrible happened to her."

He knows I have more to say.

"And, what else? What is it?"

"Philip, it's you. I need you." I search for the right words, not sure what I want to say. "To understand."

"Gabriella, you could pull my heart right out of me." He looks away.

I'm stunned, he has never been so brutally honest.

"I'm sorry."

"No, Gabriella, I'm sorry. To do this to you."

"Philip, this." I point to the bed. "This just doesn't feel right. I don't want to lose you. I can't lose you too."

"That will never happen." Then he seems to understand what I am referring to. "Gabriella, you don't think that, last night we—" He looks at me in disbelief.

"Well?"

"I told you, you could trust me." He rubs his hands all over the top of my head, turning my hair into a crazy mess.

"What?" I look at him, slightly indignant. "I'm practically naked!"

"You passed out, Gabriella, in the cab. It was a good thing we were together. I almost let you leave alone." He shakes off the memory.

"I just don't remember last night very well—" I look up at the ceiling, my knees up, hands under my chin.

"I carried you upstairs and into bed; you needed sleep."

I put my head down in submission, hiding my face and everything I am feeling.

"I did undress you, however." He winks at me.

"Oh, Philip, it's too much."

"Gabriella, what's going on? It's not like you to doubt yourself."

"It's not that, not just the studio, Philip, or even last night. It's everything else. My grandfather's work, the award, and all the press. The security threats. He's been acting different, unnerved."

"You need to talk to him, tell him how you feel. I'm sure you can talk to him about anything."

I remember the day in my grandfather's library, before I left Gloucester for New York, when he gave me the diaries and the special coin. The amulet, he had called it. I thought about the powerful energy I felt when I held it, the things I could see, the tears in his eyes and the pain on his face when I wanted to ask about my grandmother's death. There was so much I didn't know and now there was something else. The mystery of Benjamin Landsman. What he was doing with my grandfather and the bizarre coincidences of our meetings. I knew there was a significant connection between the two of them but I did not know what. My grandfather thanked him. He *knew* him.

Very well.

I lift my head up and look at Philip and see his eyes soft with concern.

"Thank you, Philip, for everything. For understanding and for always being there for me. Just don't leave me okay? Don't *ever* leave me."

He nods and pulls me toward him in a hug. "It's okay, Gabriella, I'm not going anywhere."

23

WE SIT TOGETHER IN his living room, and I watch the way his hand moves over his guitar, up and down. He closes his eyes as he sings to me. I laugh at his attempts at composition, playing the music that reminds me of our adventures through England together, distracting me from the pain in my head. Coffee is helping, and I'm starting to feel more like myself.

"It's so good to see you laughing, sometimes you worry me," he says.

The first pink light of morning makes its way into the room.

"Philip, the review."

"Your project is good, Gabriella. No, better than good. Actually, I would say you're almost cheating." He is teasing me again, and I relax into the familiar banter of our relationship.

"Is that so? How could I possibly be cheating?"

"Our project is about science and art. The questions your grandfather has spent his life pursuing. Things he told me himself. It's like you have an inside track."

I think about the many conversations we have shared, questioning what is worthy of a life's work. The journey to understand, illuminate, and find proof of the nature of the universe, its mysteries and man's place in it. The fundamental questions that are at the foundation of every great religion and scientific search.

Valuable and necessary.

"The desire to explain the world is at the core of human creativity and curiosity, Gabriella."

"I don't know, honestly. I'm just creating more questions—not finding any answers."

"Painting and architecture. The connection between the different sides of our brain, Gabriella. You'll see."

"I should have been a scientist, like him. Maybe a surgeon, cutting people up. That might have helped." I feel frustrated, anxious, exhausted.

"Come on, Gabriella, you have always pursued your own path. Not science and not the spiritual realm your parents occupied. We've talked about this many times. You're different. Not everyone has this deep desire to understand things."

"I don't want to be different, Philip." I wanted the clarity that always seemed to be outside of my grasp.

"Gabriella, just like in art, ambiguity is a good thing. It's filled with contradictions that are able to coexist. That's you, Gabriella, that's what I love about you. One of the things."

"Stop. Now." I try not to laugh.

"You're complicated, interesting, and very, uh, what's the word?" He drums his fingers on the table as he looks up at the ceiling. "Oh yeah. Delicious."

"Philip!" His attempt to cheer me up is succeeding.

"You defy description."

I can see him trying to conceal a laugh.

"Yes, well, I'm not sure you mean that as a compliment."

"Why don't you just try to live in the real world?"

I look at him and listen and wonder what it is that he sees in me.

"Why are you willing to accept me on any terms?"

"Perhaps there's a scientific explanation. Or maybe there isn't a theory for everything?"

"Very funny."

I wish I could tell him more about what was really on my mind: that the visions and premonitions were back, more clear and more powerful than ever. My secret, the one held in for so many years, the unexplainable connections that I had to certain people, was becoming more obvious. Even the sense that my parents and grandmother were often with me and watching me. I was certain now that my life was progressing along a preordained path—destination determined.

"My grandfather said he was going to find it. The answer, the Theory of Everything."

Philip knew the stories of his years with Einstein, how he had devoted his life to studying his theories on time.

"It's a certain arrogance in a way, Gabriella. The scientific community believes that everything will ultimately be explained. Imagine that! The human mind has simply not gotten there yet, they say, so that's what he is trying to find."

"Maybe he's already found the proof."

"Most people think that if we can't see it or feel it—then it cannot exist. This is what has always dominated man's limited thinking." He stands up abruptly in frustration and walks away. The sight of the practically naked, guitar slinging philosopher makes me laugh. He turns around to look at me. "What?"

"*You!* You're ridiculous that's what. Look at you!"

He holds his guitar in front of himself, mirroring Adam in the Garden of Eden when he discovers his nakedness.

"Gabriella, we are talking about physics here." He crosses his arms in mock authority as he lowers his voice to a deep baritone. "This is serious."

His attempt to distract me seems to be working, but I am worried. Furthered in great part by my grandfather's research and work, I knew that commonly held beliefs were shifting. I had been having strange unclear premonitions about my grandfather, his safety, and his future. I wondered how much more I could tell Philip.

"How is my friend Dr. Vogel, anyway?"

"Fine. He's fine, I think. In Europe again, back at the Supercollider."

Philip looks at me strangely.

I had shared some of my concerns about my grandfather's work. That he was moving toward the extreme fringes of the scientific community.

Spending his time underground, with a giant particle collider, comparing energy before a collision and after. I wish he could still be safe in his office at Columbia.

"It's incredible work—the findings of what they're doing there, I mean. They are proving that after a collision, there is *missing* energy. They just can't explain it, what happened to it. Where it went."

"You see, Gabriella, they are creating more questions than answers. Just like you."

"Well, it just shows that anything is possible. That's what I like about it."

The explanation given by scientists was that the initial matter still existed but had moved off into another dimension. It seemed insane and completely unscientific. Yet, I knew that both my grandfather's research and my family's belief in Kabbalah's mysticism shared a deep, unspoken secret. The possibility that hidden worlds may, in fact, exist is beyond our limited human senses and grasp.

"Anyway, it's all speculative, Philip, but the idea is captivating. Almost mystical," I speak the last word quietly.

"Ah yes. The great *mystical* tradition of your family. Let me see if I remember, Gabriella, something in that book you carry around with you. The one from your grandmother—about Kabbalah?" He grabs a broomstick that is leaning against the wall and pretends to be flying around. "Gabriella, the good witch."

I throw a pillow at him.

"Stop it, stop teasing me. It's not funny. I have no sense of humor right now. Be serious, Philip."

"I am being serious. No really, let me see. Where is your backpack?"

He drops the broom suddenly and runs over to the pile of my belongings, which are on the floor near the door, knowing I will try to stop him.

"Don't you dare. Philip, get away from that. It's private!"

But he is too fast. I dive for him, and we both crash onto the couch together, his arm raised in the air holding the book out of my reach. As we catch our breath, I realize how good it is to be here, laughing, conquering the fear of sharing this part of myself with someone. Beginning to trust.

"Please, Philip, be careful with that book."

I watch as he respectfully turns the pages, stopping to notice passages that have been highlighted and turned over.

"Here it is, 'Bringing light into the darkness of existence, into the world.' Isn't that the essence of Kabbalah?" He pauses and looks up at me. Then he continues reading, turning the small volume sideways. As he squints to make out what is written, I know he is reading my grandmother's notations, her thoughts and comments that fill every page. Her messages to me. *Everyone has divine energy that can be harnessed at any time. That's the greatest contribution to be made, whether in science or art. Whatever you choose G.* He stops. "Gabriella, that must mean you."

I look up at him, grateful, trying not to give myself away. This is a reminder of the many things she had written for me.

"Philip, I don't know what I'd do without you."

He comes and sits down next to me. I lean back into him as he tucks his chin over the top of my head. "You bring so much light into the world—to so many. Always remember that."

I don't want him to see the tears in my eyes, the deep emotion these words arouse in me. How I remembered her reading to me from that very book, as she taught me this concept. I miss her so much that the pain is almost unbearable. I need to find out why my grandmother's death is a subject that my grandfather will not discuss with me. And I need to remember everything she taught me about the darkness. And the light.

24

I DROP MY BAGS on the floor of the architecture studio and look down at the drawings and models that wait on my desk. I can feel the intensity, the powerful energy in the room as students rush through last preparations for the day.

"This is what we live for, right? The notorious juried critique. We'll see who survives," one of my classmates says as he sees me staring out the window.

"What? Oh sorry, I was just noticing. There seems to be a lot of activity today around campus. Police and—" I lean my head into the window and see flashing blue and red lights. "Security."

"Yeah." He shrugs his shoulders. "I'm not sure really. I never left the studio."

Philip pushes around the corner and back toward my desk. "Gabriella, what are you doing?"

"What does it *look* like I'm doing, Philip. I'm getting ready for the review. Come on, let's go downstairs. We're going to be late."

He tries to balance everything he's holding and block my exit at the same time.

"Philip, please, move over, we need to go."

"Stay here. Something crazy happened last night and—I want to find out what."

"No." I start to shake my head.

"Please, just wait here until I get back, okay?"

He turns and runs off, leaving me standing there with no explanation.

"Great." I slump facedown over my desk as I try to collect myself.

Everyone knew how important this day was. The architecture review was the foundation of our design education. In an age-old tradition, students would present their ideas in front of a panel of critics and students to be evaluated. The many sleepless nights of the past few weeks were taking their toll as we prepared to show our embryonic projects to the academic team and invited guests. Sometimes encouraging and often tortuous, a student's spirit could be destroyed by a critic's subtle look or comment. Even though Columbia encouraged experimentation and innovation, there was no certain system for success. I had serious doubts as to how the very personal interpretation of my project would be received, and I knew that I needed to prepare myself for anything.

"Hey, Gabriella, are you ready to go downstairs for the review?"

It's David, another student from my studio section.

"Yes, I'll be right there. I told Philip I would wait for him."

The way he looks at me makes me blush. He had been out with the group last night and had seen Philip and I leaving together. I feel the need to explain. "I wasn't feeling well last night, David. Just exhausted I guess, so Philip helped me get home. He's an old friend of mine."

"Hey it's all right, *whatever.* I mean, given the insanity of what happened last night on Broadway, I'm just happy to see that you're okay." He shakes his head at the disturbing memory.

"What are you talking about?"

"You and Philip ran out together. Nobody got to see you, to say good-bye. We tried to call, but you weren't answering your phone."

I look down. "Oh, sorry, my phone was—"

"Anyway, they had to block off the street in every direction. I have never seen so many police cars and fire trucks, and we couldn't get out of the club until about an hour ago. You know—being questioned by the police and the detectives."

"Police?"

But I knew what it was. It was the sensation from last night, my premonition.

"Kind of cool," he continues and points at the uniformed men outside the window. "Being questioned by the cops. Living in New York, I guess it comes with the territory. I'm from a small place on the West Coast and we never— "

I have no stomach for small talk and am beginning to feel the familiar sensation, when things around me start to slow down, decelerate. I open my mouth and somehow try to form the question I'm afraid to ask.

"David, please tell me. What are you talking about?"

But, I know what he is going to say.

"Gabriella, there was a *murder* last night. A girl who had been at the club on Broadway. She was a student here at the university." I look at him and feel like I'm going to pass out. "Gabriella, what's the matter?"

"I, I just don't feel well. How do you know?"

I feel crazy. Insane. Things are once again whirling out of control. The space and security of this piece of my new life is being invaded by my abilities of the past. Ghosts. I am afraid to hear what he will say next as I know he will confirm what I sensed all along.

"It was the girl who had been sitting right near us. She had an argument with her boyfriend, and, well, he shot her as she left the club."

I realize why I had felt the way I did the night before. The intense headache, knowing and seeing so clearly what was, without a doubt, about to occur. The future.

"Gabriella." He reaches out to steady me. "Let me get you some water."

"No, thank you, I'm all right. I'll be fine," I say, trying to convince myself, forcing my thoughts back to the studio and the day ahead.

"Are you sure?" *He* certainly is not.

I nod. I want a few moments alone.

"Do you need help getting downstairs? The reviews are starting and they just pinned up the order. We can go down together and—"

"David, what the hell is going on?" Philip bursts back into the bay where my desk is and shoves him away from me.

"Stop, Philip! David was just telling me what happened last night." I force a tight smile as I look up at him and say through clenched teeth,

"The murder?"

"Get away from her!"

"Hey, what's the big deal, man?" David picks up his drawings, pushes past Philip, and glares at him. "I'll see you downstairs, Gabriella."

I try to find something to say as I watch him storm away. I turn to face the windows and take a deep breath, wrap my arms around my body. My back is to Philip because I don't want him to see my eyes. The grip of his fingers squeeze into my arm as he turns me around.

"We need to talk." His jaw is set as he says the words.

I want to get away from everything I am feeling, the wild thoughts that race through my mind. And I know how. It's a skill I have perfected from years of dealing with these situations.

"Not now, Philip." I try to think of something, anything I can say. But I see the look on his face. "Really, I'm fine." I'm trying to convince myself. I'm going to *make* it that way. I pull my arm out of his grasp and look again at his distraught face. I need to find a way to lighten the moment.

"Come on, you look like you've seen a ghost."

"Gabriella." He's very serious. "*You're* the one who saw the ghost. You're going to have to tell me what this is about. What the hell is going on with you. How you *knew.*"

"No, Philip." I gather my drawings and models, forcing the memory of last night as far out of my mind as possible. I need to brace myself for the day ahead. "This review is important. Let's go."

I ignore his question and the pleading in his eyes.

25

A SINGLE ROW OF black chairs is lined up at the front of the room, facing the boards and tables where the students pin up drawings and place models. Testament to the star quality of the new dean of the school, an illustrious group of jurors has been invited, and the anticipation in the room is palpable.

"One of the perks of going to Columbia," the admissions officer had said. "World-class city attracts world-class talent."

I see the dean, smiling and talking, as he makes introductions and sweeps around the room, clearly enjoying the moment. Originally from Switzerland, his success in socializing was notorious and he used it well for both himself and the school. He had recently completed a controversial park outside of Paris, and championed the belief in taking risks. We loved his passion, his unequivocal belief that Beauty alone could save the world.

I recognize several well-known New York architects and watch as they evaluate the first few projects that are pinned up on the boards—and each other. The guests, studio critics, and two invited luminaries from the scientific world would form the review board. They were chosen for their ability to lend insight into the nature of the projects being presented. Everyone has arrived except for one of the scientists.

Sunlight pours through the large pyramidal skylight that anchors the central atrium. The walls are hung with contemporary art and photographs of projects from alumni who have gone on to distinguished careers. It is an honor to have the chance to present in this space as the openness on all sides lends a sense of drama and importance to the occasion. Caterers have set up a spread of baked goods and fruit, which remains untouched, and lots of coffee. The students cluster around the back of the room, a tentative and exhausted composition, as we wait.

I can feel the excitement, the fear, which intensifies the energy in the room.

"Gabriella, you're going third." I jump as Suzanne, a classmate throws her arms around me, clarifying the order of the juried review.

"Thanks, that's good, I guess." I try to sound optimistic, forcing my thoughts away from the discussion upstairs.

Just then I see Emily arrive. She is breathless, fresh, and colorful in comparison to the head-to-toe black uniform worn by the architecture students.

"Gabriella! This is so exciting. I hope I didn't miss anything!" She runs over to give me a hug, then without letting go, takes a small step back to pause and look at me.

"What is it?"

"You don't look so good, honey. Are you okay?"

"Of course, Em, I'm fine. Everything is *fine*. I just didn't get much sleep last night. You know getting ready for—this." My hand fans across the room.

"Of course, yes; that explains it. Oh there's Philip! I haven't seen him in ages."

He strides over to greet her. "Emily." He pours on the charm.

"Hi, Philip, so great to see you again. Is New York treating you well?"

"Couldn't be better."

"Well, I can't wait to see how this review thing works."

"Em, if you don't mind." I try to separate my two friends. "Please go sit down. Get some coffee. I need to pin up my stuff."

"No problem." She leans into him, two people aligned for my benefit. "And, Philip, could you please do me a favor? Keep your eye on Gabriella."

"That's really not necessary, Emily." I kiss her on the cheek and give her a quick hug, then point her toward the seats.

The program, the *Design of a Spiritual Retreat for Scientists,* was remarkably similar to many things in my own life. I had spent hours over the last few weeks discussing my design ideas with my grandfather. Even though he was traveling, we spoke frequently. I remember sitting at my desk in the studio and looking out at the campus. I held the receiver to my ear and listened to his voice.

"Papa, where are you? On the other side of the world again?"

"Almost. Actually, I'm *inside* the world."

"Near Geneva right? Back at the Supercollider."

"Yes, under the surface of the earth."

"I wish you were here, in New York. You would understand the nature of this project, the challenge of a spiritual retreat for scientists. I mean, do these places even exist?"

"I'm at one right now."

"I can't do it."

"Of course you can, you *already* have. My beautiful library in Gloucester. Besides, this is an ironic opportunity for you, to design a place for the souls and minds of members of the scientific community."

"Those like you, Papa, who I admire most."

"And?"

"The project is completely consuming all of my waking and, of late, sleeping hours. I have had many dreams about it."

"Tell me." I heard him sigh.

"I can't explain it; I guess it's how my mind works, in three dimensions. As if I was there, actually walking through the space. But I could never tell that to the critics. They would laugh me out of the room."

Yet I had dreamed this space, seeing a perfect vision of what I wanted my project to look like.

"You are like your grandmother," he had said, "living so much of her life through her dreams."

"Sometimes I look in the mirror and I barely recognize myself."

"Nonsense."

"No really, there is something different. I'm changing in ways I didn't expect."

"Well, my dear, things don't always turn out as you expect them to."

"I know—"

"Maybe better. Things might turn out better than you could have even imagined."

That comment stayed with me.

26

OUR ARCHITECTURE critic stands at the front of the room. Introductions are made and she explains the charge given to the students so that all those present would understand the scope of work. The visiting critics and guest jurors listen, and the reviews begin. The first student is often the sacrificial lamb as the invited guests try to evaluate the level of the student's presentation and understand the intricacies of the challenge. I feel uncharacteristically drained and am not in the mood to defend my work, especially to describe its very illusory inspiration.

"We asked the students, in thinking about this project, to question everything. How we perceive ourselves and our place on Earth at this moment in time. What can modern architecture learn from the art and science of the past? And most importantly, how can we look at the world in an original way. Add something new."

The first two students take their turns in front of the jury. They painstakingly present their projects, showing drawings and models as they point to their work and answer questions, challenges, inferences. Each review takes over forty-five minutes, and I realize that with ten students in the group, we are going to be here all day. I try to listen to the exchanges and comments, which end with somewhat disastrous results for the students.

Just what I expected.

"What a bitch," Meghan complains as she drops dejectedly down into the chair next to me. "That critic thinks she can rip into us. Did you hear what she said? That this could never be built? She hasn't been out of school that long herself."

"When your father is one of the most prolific real estate developers in the United States, you can open your own firm, design, and start building," someone responds to her as the student group huddles together, trying to gain support from our shared misery.

"Well, she's also amazingly talented," I add, hoping to channel some good karma my way by saying something nice about her.

"And my own critic." Josh looks over at the panel of jurors, disbelief on his face. "Yesterday he loved my project, then today, he didn't defend me at all. I hate going at the beginning of the day." He holds his head in his hands.

Exhaustion and defeat. A rough combination.

"Well, it's only the beginning of the semester, so take it in stride," Suzanne says cheerily. She is lucky enough to have drawn the spot to present last. Usually a good omen as the critics have run out of criticism and are ready to end.

I knew I was next and could see that the panel had replenished their coffee and were ready for me to present my project. I take a deep breath and look out at the jury, my classmates, and the other guests in the room. Philip slowly nods his head to indicate that I should begin, encouragement in his eyes.

"My name is Gabriella Vogel, and this is my project for the scientist's retreat," I begin, my voice low.

I turn around to look at everything pinned up on the wall behind me, making sure it's all still there. I stand before the carefully constructed models and large drawings, assembled through a digital collage of images and text, then overdrawn by hand. Quite miraculous, given my distractions of late.

"Our task was to create a space for scientists pushing the boundaries of what is known. These are the people who are looking beyond commonly accepted theories and laws. We were asked—what would encourage their research? I chose to investigate the internal spirit of the occupant. A space that changes the experience of time. Lit from above, with constantly evolving light and shadow, altering perspective. This is what could encourage creativity. Invention."

I pause to catch my breath and gauge a reaction from the jury. They look straight ahead as they take in what I'm saying, matching the model and drawings meant to accompany my words. Their eyes move from the table to the wall then back to me.

Nothing. No response, no questions. Silence.

I continue and answer some initial questions about the process. I describe, in detail, the shape of the glass roof and the interior two-story wall that would act as a giant screen, a large surface on which shadows would be cast, creating a theatre of darks and lights. A living, breathing chiaroscuro. Seating areas would encourage quiet contemplation, using monastic ideas of silence and solitude for introspection. The only light entering would come from above, providing views of the sky, passing clouds and stars. All of this is linked together by an enormous glass staircase that ascends through the space. I purposely try to avoid any statements that much of the vision for the design had come to me in a very specific and vivid dream.

"It is meant to encourage the varied experiences of the passage of time, the elements that make up reality. I think—I believe, that is—that this is what science is trying to explain."

I want the work to stand on its own. In the painting studios, we had always been taught that the work needed to speak for itself. To deliver a powerful message through the complex interplay of form, color, and scale, without any specific explanation from the artist. Sometimes, there is no place for words.

"Is this what you think, Miss—"

"Vogel." My critic helps the guest juror finish his sentence.

A panel of jurors were like sharks in the water. They could sense blood or any weak link made evident by the slightest hesitation of the presenter. They immediately found mine.

"This is very interesting," he continues, his words loaded with sarcasm, "but I fail to see how your forms are connected to the objective of the program. It is such an abstract premise—really impossible, actually. You describe something that is not there. What you call the 'elements that make up reality,' this is *not* architecture. I just can't see it."

"Well." I try to control my frustration and speak calmly. "That's the point isn't it?"

As I turn my back to the panel to point out a detail on a drawing, I catch Emily's worried face watching me defend myself from the continuing verbal attack. I try to collect my thoughts when I hear greetings being exchanged among the panel and the movement of chairs. I realize that the missing critic has arrived.

Great, another voice. And this one late.

"I want to introduce our guest," I hear the dean say. "A fantastic mind and brilliant physicist—working on some secret research aren't you?" Everyone laughs at the absurd comment. "Yes, well, we are certainly fortunate that you happen to be in New York today. As fate would have it."

"Yes, fate indeed," the voice says.

I know who it is, without a doubt. I can feel him. I turn slowly around and look up.

It's Benjamin.

27

O UR EYES MEET FOR a fraction of a second, but it is unmistakable. Recognition passes between us, and I notice the subtle acknowledgement, the intensity of his eyes as they meet mine.

"Thank you, please continue." He quickly looks away and gestures his greeting to the other critics. The power of his presence commands the attention of everyone in the room. He walks around my models, inspecting them before he sits down. "I have been standing in the back for a while. Listening. I didn't want to interrupt. This is quite an interesting project."

He is magnificent. It's that voice, the accent that I can't quite identify. Sitting here with the other critics and students as if he doesn't belong to this space or this time. Everyone stares at him. His amazing youth defies all expectation of what a world-famous physicist would look like. Slowly, like waters that have been disturbed by a foreign body, the energy of the group shifts and then settles to accommodate his arrival.

Everyone in the space turns back to me.

"Gabriella?" My critic encourages me to continue.

"Yes, well, it's a very personal interpretation of the project." I try to pull myself together. I look up at my drawings, pinned to the wall to find safety in my own work, attempt to steady my breathing and the subtle trembling of my hands. I know that what I have designed has come from a deep part of my unconscious. That it's impossible to explain.

"Gabriella, this is a good start." My critic speaks finally, sounding encouraging.

I see Benjamin and the intense way he takes in my work. His eyes are locked onto my drawings as he sits with his arms folded across his chest, the slightest smile on his face.

"But do continue your investigation into this *invention* you seem to be pursuing," she continues.

I nod automatically, doing anything to expedite the end of the discussion, to allow myself away from the front of the room, back to my seat. But, she is not finished. Clearly, she plans to use my review to make a point. I brace myself for what is coming next.

"May I remind *all* of you that this is graduate school. While exploring abstract and poetic ideas about space is important, we do need to shift into the real world. That, in case you've forgotten, would be things like gravity, friction, and a variety of other laws of physics that apply to buildings."

Everyone snickers.

"Ms. Vogel is pursuing a joint degree," my critic continues as she turns to the rest of the jurors.

I cringe as this unnecessary piece of information is shared.

"Really?" Dean Zumi finally speaks up.

"In the Master of Fine Arts Program. A *painter* aren't you?" She looks at me with a smirk on her face. "It is highly unusual to attempt to do both at the same time."

I have not taken a breath. My classmates were well aware of the recent sale of several paintings at a gallery in SoHo thanks to a collage of newspaper clippings near the entry to the studio noting any publicity about faculty, students, and alumni. I can't understand why this information has any relevance to the review and desperately try to find a way to disappear.

"Amazingly *ambeeshious* of you," Dean Zumi states sarcastically as he laughs. "We pride ourselves on how we push our students to their absolute maximum, with barely enough time to sleep or do anything other than architecture. I think you might be the first to attempt this." He turns to the group with a wry smile. Clearly, he is pleased with his own humor at my expense.

"I think her work is strengthened by the clear evidence of the other creative pursuits she has undertaken." It's Benjamin, stopping the momentum of the attack as he continues, "It is clear that Ms. Vogel's work is a reflection of some very deep creative forces, even those surfacing from her unconscious. Perhaps a source that is not understandable, even to herself?"

As I hear him, I think I feel the floor shifting under me. I back up slowly, to lean against the wall. I need to use its force to hold me up, to steady myself. How could he have known that this, in fact, is exactly what had occurred? That I had thought the very words he was saying.

"In many cases, physical science has been built upon the ruins of our spiritual nature. In our rage for technology, we ourselves have become machines. Through this we have destroyed our spirit or our soul, as some might say."

A hush has come over the room.

"Quite interesting, Dr. Landsman."

"Her work, I believe, is an attempt to connect to a part of her inner creativity. Looking for a new way of saying things. Appropriate don't you think? Given that science itself is looking for new things to say." He turns and looks directly at the panel of jurors as his hand points to my drawings on the wall. "After all, was that not the intent of this project?"

I glance at the jurors as I stand motionless in the front of the room.

My classmates, Emily, and everyone else are trying to absorb everything that he has just said about my project. About me. The incredibly accurate and personal nature of his words. I finally get to sit down and will the day to move forward more quickly as the other students in my group present their projects, some with more success than others. I have other things on my mind. Whoever he is, I need to find out why he keeps appearing in my life and everything else about him: the undeniable power of the magnetic draw I feel to him. I try to formulate a plan of how I will be able to speak to Benjamin.

Alone.

28

THE LIGHT HAS TRANSITIONED throughout the day, animating the forms of the skylight as the sun completes its arc above our building. I can hear the subtle buzzing of the fluorescent fixtures. One thing I know for certain, I have been waiting for the chance to find Benjamin and speak to him. It's an opportunity that I will not let slip away.

I stand alone in the room that contains the echoes of emotions and energy that suffused it all day. A war zone of paper, coffee cups, notes, and chairs, everything shifted out of alignment. I need to take time to understand everything that has happened, what it means, and what I'm going to *do*. As I mechanically unpin my drawings from the wall I hear a discussion outside the room.

I would recognize that voice anywhere, anytime in my life.

I turn around and run out the door as Benjamin and the dean walk out of Avery Hall and into the cold night. Relief, happiness, and apprehension flood me at the same time as I see him and consider my options.

"Excuse me—" I hear the words come out of my mouth in disbelief. I run toward the two men as I wonder what has come over me, what the *hell* I'm doing. They turn at the same time, Dean Zumi quite surprised and Benjamin—smiling.

"Yes?" The dean turns back to Benjamin. "Ah, look who it is. The first-year dreamer, from earlier, I believe."

"I'm sorry to disturb you both. I just—" I realize that I am at a complete loss, exhibiting uncharacteristic almost desperate behavior. I have a thousand questions, yet cannot seem to formulate any intelligent or reasonable words to come out of my mouth.

"Gabriella, there you are," Benjamin says as he reaches his hand out.

"You know each other?" The dean is genuinely surprised.

"This is Gabriella Vogel. I work with her grandfather, the physicist."

Recognition flashes across his face as the dean seems to really see me for the first time.

"Well, so it *is* you. I didn't know until the other day that you were in the program. Trying to fly under the radar are you?"

"No, not at all."

"We really need to be going, Bernard." Benjamin reaches out to take the heavy backpack off my shoulder. "It was lovely spending the day here with your students and their very interesting work. I know Gabriella must be exhausted."

I nod.

"Of course." The dean seems confused as he looks first at Benjamin then back at me, clearly trying to determine what our relationship is. I am doing everything I can to keep my face still and not betray the riot of emotion I am feeling.

"Let me know when you are back in America, Benjamin, and thank you, for coming today."

"Yes, it was quite informative."

As he turns, Dean Zumi stops and looks at me once more with both eyebrows raised.

"I have to tell you, Gabriella, your grandfather is quite remarkable. A very *brave* man."

"I—yes. Thank you."

"Now I understand where you get it from." He walks away, and then Benjamin and I are alone.

I look up at him and into his eyes, at his face. I see everything. The way he looks at me, the shape of his body under the lines of his coat. The way he breathes.

"I need to speak with you." It's the only thing I can manage to say.

His eyes are intense as they search mine. He seems to be struggling with some sort of choice. A decision that he needs to make about which direction this moment will take.

Changing our fate.

"Benjamin?" I am unable to find any other words.

And then, as if fighting against a force that can no longer be suppressed, he looks at me and reaches out his open hand for mine.

"Gabriella, come with me."

29

I NEED TO REMIND myself that this is really happening. I am not in a dream but, *here,* in the world of the present. Ever since the first day of our unexpected encounter, I've wished for this moment, and, this time, the threshold between waking and sleeping, dream and reality will remain separate.

I want to learn everything about him. I watch as the color in his cheeks changes from the exertion of our walk, the way his hands move as he talks, and, mostly, how he looks at me. The sting on my cheeks is matched by the surprising fire in my body and the excitement of being with him. I have so many questions and an intense need to find answers as I try desperately to piece together the disparate elements of his appearance in my life. The undeniable knowledge that I have seen him before in my premonitions.

There was no mistaking that.

We move through the city as he asks me countless questions. He wants details, memories, and experiences—events from the past that I can barely recall. I can see, for the very first time, what might be buried deep within the layers of my heart. A glimmer of the intense emotion that has remained so closely guarded, hidden, waiting for the right moment to burst forward. Just like my grandmother had predicted.

Trust what your heart is telling you.

"Gabriella?"

I love the way he says my name.

"Yes? I'm sorry, I just realized where we are."

We have traveled across to the most western edge of the city near the river, where industrial buildings have been converted into living spaces. I can see the shape of the wind, made visible through swirling leaves, papers, and the steam rising from the subway grates. There is a rawness to this commercial part of town. Deserted—silenced by night.

He turns to face me, and I see a resolve in his eyes. Slowly he reaches his hand out, I place mine in his, and feel his fingers close. Like the steel door of a vault slamming shut. He turns and leads me up the steps to the landing of a gray, faceless building, indistinguishable from all the others on the street. "This is my home . . . when I'm in New York. Why don't you come in?"

"I don't know if I should, I mean—" I need to think clearly but am confused by the adrenaline rush of the walk and emotions brought on by him. "It's late."

He can barely suppress his smile. His eyes shine in the reflection cast by the streetlamp and the glow of the lights inside the building. Watching me seems to be some form of entertainment for him.

"Come in for a while, then I will take you back."

I think of everything I want to ask him, the questions formulated over the last several weeks, and I know that I can't run away this time. Our eyes are locked on each other as we stand in front of the building. He waits patiently.

"Yes." I look away from him for a moment and then meet his eyes. "After all, you are working with my grandfather."

"As I hoped."

I feel him reach around me to press a code on a small keypad that releases the lock on the large industrial door. As we step inside it's clear that we have entered a private residence, completely contrary to what the outside expression of the building suggests. I catch my breath at the incredible beauty of everything around me: shining stone floors, a tall glass staircase that begins where we stand but then disappears into a two-story space beyond my line of sight. Large contemporary paintings are illuminated by low-voltage lights that grow brighter as we approach, sensing our movement. Everything is made of glass or stone, and digital keypads display an array of information about the status of each room. Benjamin leans against a wall and stands with his arms crossed as he watches me take everything in.

"What is this place?" I ask.

"Please, look around."

Doors open automatically, and I feel myself drawn deeper into the amazing environment. Art and music surround me, and he watches, clearly enjoying my astonishment as I take in the visual feast, a path of discovery through the magnificent rooms. I'm amazed by the explosion of color, form, and shape in paintings I recognize from many of the well-established artists of the world. I return from my brief examination to face him, unable to find anything to say.

"You seem quite surprised, at a loss for words, perhaps?" He laughs. The formal nature of his question is something I have noticed before in his language.

"Yes, wow, thank you." I sound embarrassingly idiotic again.

Put a sentence together, Gabriella, I say to myself.

"It's so different. Beautiful," I add.

Well, that was better than my incoherent babbling, but it's the only thing that comes out of my mouth. I am trying to talk, walk, and take it all in at once. I really don't know where to look first.

He smiles to himself as he takes my coat and hangs it in a closet. I watch it disappear into the wall surface after it closes on its own. He turns around to look right at me as if he is deciding what to say. As he pushes his hair back off of his forehead, I notice his hand, the flash of his watch, the way he moves his sleeves before he folds his arms. I can feel the path my heart seems to be taking toward the magnetic draw of his.

"How long have you lived here?"

I see his hesitation. "I travel a great deal, Gabriella. I'm not in New York that often, but this is my home when I am here."

I nod, unable to coax any words out of my mouth. I feel his eyes on me, and think about what he has just said. "What exactly is it, that you do in your travels?"

He takes a step back, away from me. It's as if I have wounded him.

His eyes change, and I can see his jaw set in a resolve I have not seen before. "You, Gabriella, are a much more interesting topic." He turns his head away for a moment then moves the conversation away from the intimacy of my questions to a safer subject.

Architecture.

"This design project you are working on is quite a challenge."

I don't want to give up. I want answers from him. "How did you come to be on our jury today?"

"The dean is a friend of mine. We spent several years in Paris working together and given the scientific nature of the project, he thought I would be interested in seeing what ideas the students had."

"I see." But I can't seem to reconcile this new information. Dean Zumi and Benjamin have been together in Paris? The age difference between the two of them is too dramatic for that to be true. Benjamin must be in his early thirties, at most, and the dean was an established architect with grandchildren in the university. Another mystery. Never good at concealing my emotions, the confusion on my face betrays me.

He takes a step toward me, his eyes burn into mine. "Time is a funny thing, Gabriella. The past, present, and future are linked in more ways than people realize, but you know this."

I turn away from him, and wonder how he can know my inner thoughts, things that I have shared with no one. I feel the rushing, pounding feeling I get in my head after standing up too quickly.

"Gabriella." His words pull me back. "After being in the review all day you must be hungry." He eyes me suspiciously, a mischievous look in his eye. Something seems funny to him and he tries to conceal a smile. I have the distinct feeling that the humor is at my expense. My appetite a personal trademark.

"Starving, actually." I'm embarrassed.

He laughs and shakes his head. "I thought so. Why don't you look around, and I'll come find you. I will see if there's anything in the kitchen."

"Yes, fine."

I know that everything here is a clue, a map to the mystery of who he is. I continue to explore and am drawn to the massive glass staircase. My hand moves up the railing that is wrapped in a soft velvet slipcover, designed to protect fingers from the cold metal. I marvel at the incredible attention to detail, where every sense is considered. At the top of the staircase is a huge glass skylight. The stars and sky are framed by the structure of the glass form, a perfect composition that brings moonlight into the core of the building. The beauty that surrounds me takes my breath away.

Through a large wall of windows, I see boxwood hedges that frame a beautiful pool, casting a blue light that illuminates the terrace in an outerworldly way. Music plays through speakers hidden in the walls of every room. It sounds similar to the piano solo I remember from the cathedral. The haunting sound that had imprinted in my head, another element of the unforgettable day when I met him there. I continue to walk slowly through the spaces, trying to absorb everything I am seeing, while at the same time, feeling a sense of familiarity that is unexplainable. Suddenly I find myself facing a most unexpected sight.

It is my painting.

The one that had sold recently at the gallery in SoHo, reconfirming through the unnecessary checklist of identification that it is mine. The conversation I had with the gallery owner when he called to tell me of the sale floods my mind.

"I can't believe the piece sold so quickly after the opening," I had said, trying to absorb the large sum I would be receiving. A first for me. "Who bought it?" I asked, realizing that one of my paintings was now in the possession of someone I did not know. A strange concept—that my art could have a life of its own.

"The purchase was made through an intermediary. This particular buyer was quite insistent. He wanted to retain absolute anonymity."

30

I CAN REMEMBER FEELING shock and discomfort, uncertainty about the anonymous sale of my painting, but had been assured that this was fairly common in the art world. I accepted the gallery owner's rationale as the happiness that I had sold a piece quickly outweighed any concerns I had.

"*Bloody hell,* Gabriella," Philip had tried to reassure me at the time. "You don't need to figure everything out. Now you can join those of us not destined to be starving artists."

"Speak for yourself, Philip, I have no clue where *my* destiny is taking me."

And now here it was. In Benjamin's home.

I am so taken aback, that I am pulled into the small room where it hangs on the far wall. I move slowly, feeling that I am entering his private office. The furnishings are a mix of classics, of modern design, and beautiful antiques, icons from the last several hundred years. Dark wood shelves are covered from floor to ceiling with books, photographs, art, and leather-bound files alphabetized by geographic area.

My hand brushes along the surface of the shelves as I tilt my head to read the titles. There is an amazing combination of contemporary works and antique volumes in German, French, Italian, English, and Russian. I notice a large section in Latin: poetry, history, and—strangely—various texts on Kabbalah.

The massive glass desk at the center of the room is covered with papers of mathematical equations and several flat-screen computers. I am reminded of the day I had stumbled into his room in Hamilton Hall. I can't take my eyes away from the shapes and numbers that keep inverting and twisting into themselves across the LCD display of the computer monitors, new forms emerging and morphing from the last. These images are unlike any I have ever seen, letters and numbers arranged in strange three dimensional configurations.

I stop suddenly.

I know that I am not alone and that he has come into the room. I turn around slowly and see him leaning against the door frame.

"I saw my painting. I didn't know who had bought it. It was you."

I want to explain why I had come into his library, the force that had drawn me in. He is not angry. It's as if my standing here in this room, in his home where my painting is hanging, is the most normal thing in the world.

I try to remember to breathe. I am once again completely arrested by his presence. His easy way of standing, hands in the pockets of his pants, and his eyes as he watches me.

"Your paintings are very beautiful. I had to have this one, here, *with* me," he says but provides no explanation, no details of when or how he had bought it.

Nothing.

I choose to change the subject. To something more manageable. At least for the moment. "You have so many interesting things here, so many books." I turn away from his eyes, buying a few seconds to steady my heart. I think about the many years I have spent alone reading everything I could find, using books as my own companions—my guide. Hoping to find my answers.

"Yes, they help me understand things. Especially the way people think and look at their world. Some of the theories are quite interesting." He seems to find humor in a memory.

"Your work." I force myself to concentrate and formulate the sentence as it emerges from my mouth. "What is it that you are looking for, exactly?" I need to understand somehow who he is and how he knows my grandfather. The many emotions that are rushing through me all at once are completely disorienting.

"What everyone is trying to find answers to, Gabriella." He looks at the sky outside the window, then slowly turns back to me. "The nature of the universe."

"I know that my grandfather has been trying his entire life—with science and mathematics that is—to find the unexplainable, what he has called 'the Infinite,'" I continue cautiously. "He wants to bridge the gap, he says, between science and metaphysics."

"Your grandfather has devoted himself to an ideal, Gabriella. The belief that science can approach an explanation for the previously unexplainable."

"Yes." I say it with caution. I am still trying to reconcile the mystery of how Benjamin seems to be so intimately connected to my grandfather's thoughts and how much he knows. "His life has been consumed by the belief in his work, always searching for the things that transcend time."

"Profound understanding through scientific proof." The words Benjamin chooses sound amazingly similar to those my grandfather would have selected. A coincidence not lost on me.

"Einstein," I say quietly.

If he knows anything about my grandfather, then he must have known the intimate connection he had to Einstein. One of the pivotal relationships in his life. Benjamin pauses, as if he is trying to decide in which direction to continue. He is somber. "Einstein himself admitted the inconsistencies in time. He said that if anything could travel faster than light it would be possible to hop backward in time, Gabriella," he says this as if he had known the great scientist personally.

"So many years of research. It's incredible how he has been able to stay so focused on his goal, despite," I say and pause for a moment, "everything that has happened." My parents, my grandmother. I think about the many times I had seen him in his library, holding his head in his hands.

"He will find his answers. If he hasn't already."

I look up at Benjamin and our eyes meet.

"His critics say that he's moved to the very fringes of the scientific community, but he has never lost his faith in his ideals and his conviction, in what he believes to be true."

"His heart is enormous." Benjamin's voice is low. "Like yours."

I don't know how to respond to the intimacy of his words, the solitary mention of my heart. "My grandfather is completely fearless."

I turn away and think about him alone at the beach house, the years he has spent searching for answers.

"And you, Gabriella, what is it that *you* are afraid of?" he says the words as he approaches and turns me toward him.

"Me? I'm afraid of being nothing, doing nothing. Having my life not mean anything."

"That's impossible," he says.

"How do you know?"

"I just do."

31

I NEED TO TURN AWAY from him. Not only because of the things he is saying, but now the subtle pressure building in my head, the familiar sensation of how it always begins. And then, it happens.

I see it all so clearly. I *see* her. My grandmother. She's standing in a cave, lit from above, talking to someone about what she was looking for—answers to her questions, our family's mystical origins. But I force myself away from the vision and pick up a small frame from Benjamin's desk and say, "This looks quite old, what is it?"

"It's an archaeological site, Palestine, under the British Mandate. Some very interesting work was being done in the Judean Desert."

"My grandmother was there."

"Yes," he says so softly that I almost don't hear him, "I know."

"I don't understand, how could you know?"

"Your grandfather—" He catches himself as the words come out. "He told me." Benjamin tries to clarify. "That was when they first met."

"He told you about *that?*" I'm surprised.

"He loves to speak about his work with Einstein, their years of correspondence, and, of course, the excitement of the Nobel Prize. That time when they traveled to Jerusalem lives in all of our memories."

"I don't understand. How could you possibly . . ." My words trail off.

He turns away suddenly, caught revealing something he should not have. A truth in his words that somehow cannot be suppressed.

The silence is making me uncomfortable, so I continue, "My family, I mean my parents, used to live there. In a small town in the north. A very special, magical place but—I have not been back for many years."

He looks at me with sadness, admiration, and other things I am afraid to acknowledge. Given everything he has already revealed, I assume he knows that my parents are gone. That they too were looking for their own answers. That I had been unable to return to Zefat since the terrible incident that had taken them away from me. They had devoted their lives to the study of Kabbalah and the *Zohar,* the text at the center of the mystical writings. It seemed surreal to be standing here talking to him about the exceptionally personal intersections of my life. My grandfather's research in science and my parents' passionate commitment to understanding mysticism.

"There is an amazing connection, Gabriella, between Einstein and ancient mysticism." He looks right at me. "In the way they are both trying to understand the nature of time and man's place in the universe."

I know that these ideas are at the very core of what has consumed my grandfather.

"The line of our life, my grandfather says, traverses time and space."

"It's not only the line of our life that can live on into the future and past, but other things as well. You have experienced this, haven't you?"

"Sometimes I feel like I've already lived my whole life. Like I've done it before," I answer.

He smiles. "That's because you know how to link to a part of the world where there is infinite information." He takes a few steps toward me. "To find light in the darkness."

I am stunned by what he has just said, the words my grandmother had used so many times. I had heard enough.

"Who *are* you?" I am overwhelmed and confused. "Answer me. Please. How do you know these things about my family. About *me?*"

He spins away and stops then slams his hands against the wall. I watch as he runs both hands through his hair, places them on his waist, and turns slowly back to me. I know he is deciding what to do next. He looks down at the floor and speaks very softly. "I'm sorry, Gabriella, I should not have brought you here." He looks like he's in pain.

"What?" I start to object. "Why are you saying this? I don't understand!"

"I've tried; I wanted to stay away from you. But it's *impossible.*"

I am stunned by his words and yet, somehow, I know what he means. I feel the same way. The overwhelming powerful force between us is a fact neither of us can deny.

"It's impossible for me to stay away," he says again. "I cannot."

He walks toward me, his eyes locked on mine. My hand reaches down to hold the side of the massive glass desk to steady myself. I feel the room start to spin. All I know is that everything I am feeling is what I want. I need him, to be with him, in every way possible. The intensity of the burning desire is unlike anything I have ever experienced.

And then, I do something I have never done before. I say it.

"I want to be with you, too."

He crosses the room and stands inches away from me; the invisible energy field between us almost pushing me over. "Do you believe in the possibility that love can transcend time?" His voice is low in his throat. His eyes are intense as they search mine.

"Why are you here?" I ask.

"Gabriella—"

"What are you *doing* to me? I feel you taking me, pulling me into the past. Into my future." The insane range of emotions I am feeling has stolen my vocabulary, the rational world that I had tried to live in feels like it is slipping away. But it doesn't matter. I know that anything I would say at this moment will be completely inadequate.

Slowly, his hands reach out for my face. "We are all trying to find the things that are unchanging, Gabriella. Beyond ourselves and beyond time."

I feel his hands on the back of my neck and in my hair. As his face moves closer to mine, I inhale him; I feel the heat of his body. I want to dissolve into him.

He reaches out and pulls me in with a force I have not felt before.

"So many mysteries have lived in my heart."

"I know," he whispers.

"But you're here. It's *you.*"

The moment his lips cover mine I know I have finally found the answer. It's as if a veil of darkness is being pulled away from the shadowed spaces in my life. Everything I have gone through has prepared me for this moment. I realize in this very instant that together, with him, I am completing myself—I become whole. Without him, I would never be.

He is what I have been searching for.

I remembered the words my grandmother whispered, which I carried deep in my heart.

You will find the love that was made for you.

She knew, and, now, so did I. Changing the direction of my life, with the promise of his kiss.

32

TIME IS NOW MEASURED differently since the day of the architecture review and the incredible hours I spent with Benjamin. The walk, the dinner, and the night that I know has altered the course of my life. It is almost impossible to concentrate on my classes, yet I force myself to try, relying on the rhythm and demands of my life.

Time moves forward, marked by nature's transformation. Leaves fall and are swept away, leaving the expression of the tree's architecture. It is an explosively beautiful fall in New York, yet my mind keeps returning to him. My feet feel as if they are each planted on separate plates of the earth, riding through the seismic shifting of my moods and thoughts, and I simply can't stop thinking about him. The intimacy of our evening together and the strange feeling that, somehow, I have known him forever. Whatever equilibrium I had barely found has been completely rocked by his presence. There is a caution, even resistance, on his part and an evasiveness when describing his frequent absences and travel schedule. Yet the way I feel when he is near me is something I want.

More, always, *forever*.

Emily, ever mindful of the more public part of my life, keeps a watchful eye. The phone vibrates in my pocket, and I welcome the excuse to leave the lecture hall I'm in to get outside and talk to her. Clear my head.

I hear Emily's worried voice on the other end. "Gabriella? Hi, where are you? Are you in class? What time is he coming?"

"What?" The questions come so quickly that it takes me a moment to remember. Today is the day my grandfather will be speaking at Columbia.

She answers for me before I have a chance to put the sentence together. "Yes, at five, in the physics building, then dinner at the Faculty Club. You're going to be all right without me aren't you?"

"Yes, Em, I'll be fine."

I wonder whether Benjamin will be there. I hadn't seen him in several weeks and he had been evasive about his plans, when he would be back in New York. E-mail is not enough for me. I need to handle the intense desire I have to be near him. All the time.

I think about what he had said. "I need to leave New York for a while, to work on my research and . . . travel."

It had felt as if the walls were moving in toward me as he spoke the words, compressing my lungs. I feel frustration and lack of control over a door that has been opened to a world of emotions I had never before allowed myself to enter. I now realize the possibility that exists on the other side and I want it.

I want it all.

The flashing crosswalk sign at the street corner signals as the wind whips the leaves on the avenue into a swirling cone. I can feel the sense of anticipation as I rush to attend the lecture. This will be my opportunity to find out more about Benjamin. To share with my grandfather whatever part of it I could put into words.

"You never cease to amaze me, Papa." I had teased him on the phone about his insistence that I come to this particular talk. He would often suggest that I attend different lectures or performances around campus, monitoring the university website on my behalf.

"Well, Gabriella, I feel the same way about you . . ." His voice trailed off, and I thought I detected a change in his tone. Something that made me uncomfortable.

"Is everything okay?" I asked him. "You sound different, is something bothering you?" It was that feeling I seemed to be having more frequently.

He had brushed off my concern. "No, I'm fine but come early to the lecture. My old friend and associate Dr. Potter will be there too. You remember her don't you, Gabriella? She's been asking about you. You haven't seen her in a while."

"I know, I just thought there might be something else."

He was quiet for a moment before he answered, "Nothing, except that . . ." I heard his low laugh. "I just might not do what they expect. What they want from me, darling."

"What *they* expect, Papa? Who are you talking about?"

It had taken me a few seconds to respond, and I had heard the click of the phone. The conversation was over.

33

THE PHYSICS BUILDING stands beyond the central plaza of the campus. I run up the steps, past the iconic sculpture of Alma Mater and Low Library, and look up at the Rutherford Observatory on top of Pupin Hall. In constant use since the late 1920s, this building represented those willing to step forward into the unknown. I think about my grandfather. Unlike some premonitions I have had, which are very clear, there is a sense about his future that is vague, ominous—even frightening. Difficult to discern but extremely troubling.

The lobby is filled with energy and anticipation as the crowd presses toward a small woman. She reminds me of my grandmother. She looks out into the distance as she tries to back away from the enthusiastic barrage of questions. A woman before her time, her heart and mind was open and available. She was also one of the first women to enter the male-dominated field of astrophysics. For an instant our eyes meet, and I watch as she gracefully moves away from the crowd, toward me, and wraps her shawl tightly around her body. Seeing her in this very public setting seemed so different from how I knew her during the years of frequent collaborations with my grandfather.

"Dr. Potter." I approach her slowly as I reach my hand out toward her.

"Gabriella, how wonderful to see you."

She pulls me into her and embraces me tightly, reminding me of the days when she would always bring me a special surprise: photographs of stars, a subscription to *Scientific American* magazine, and even my own child-size telescope. She had been determined to pique my interest in the field of science.

"It's so hard to believe how much time has passed, that you're in graduate school already. It was just yesterday that you were little, running around the beach with your friends." I can tell that she is calculating how long it's been since we've last been together, noting the changes in me. "Time passes so quickly doesn't it?"

"Yes." Ironic that one of the world's experts on Einstein's theories is talking about how quickly time seems to be passing.

"And your painting?" she continues. "You have already sold several pieces I understand. I want to put my name in for one now. Yes, that would be lovely to have something of yours on my wall."

"Of course, but how do you know?"

"Your grandfather is quite proud of you." She winks at me as I absorb the notion that my grandfather has been discussing me with his colleagues. "And how is the architecture program? I'm sure you've met some fascinating people."

Would I even dare to tell her? I assume she might know Benjamin, but it's safer to talk about architecture and painting, I reason.

"School is challenging, Dr. Potter. We've been asked to look for new ways to think about the world, to watch and observe, then invent. Be the ones making change. But, I don't know." I know I sound frustrated.

"The same thing scientists are doing."

I look at her doubtfully. "Well, it's not science, but nonetheless. Creating, adding something, making a difference even if only in a small way."

"You've already begun, Gabriella," she continues. "*You* of all people know that everything is connected. Don't you remember the stories I used to tell you?"

Unlike other children, who I imagine were told fairy tales, my bedtime stories were about the magic of science, the wizard in the form of a genius named Albert Einstein, and the imaginary worlds he predicted, connected to ours by dark magic tunnels. This was the education that had lit the dark path through my childhood.

"Of course. All the amazing people . . . and Einstein."

She seems lost in her memories. "That was an incredible time for all of us, when we met him."

"I know."

She sighs, "We were so young."

Here is another powerful connection to my past.

She can see that I am trying to say something. "What is it, dear?"

"Can I ask you something?"

"Of course."

"Dr. Potter, the idea that there exist holes, I mean *bridges,* to other universes is at the center of my grandfather's research, right?"

"He is closer than he's ever been to offering proof, and yet." She twists her hands together in a nervous reflex, looking away before she continues, "I worry about what this could mean."

"For our world?" For him? I wonder. Her reaction seems to confirm my own fears and what I really want to ask her about.

"We've taken every security precaution possible. And we have been reassured, by all the governments involved, that what happened in Paris could not ever happen again."

"Paris?"

"Those people, we were assured that they were—destroyed," she says, looking into my eyes.

I try to control myself as she brings up the subject of the incident that killed my parents. I feel her hand reach out for mine.

"They murdered my family. Those, animals."

"Yes, but I fear that there may be others. As you can imagine, the information would be unprecedented. We really don't know how this knowledge would affect the course of life on our planet. Your grandfather's work raises many philosophical and ethical questions, not only scientific ones."

She stops to evaluate my reaction to the seriousness of our conversation. "Gabriella?"

"I'm fine, please continue, Dr. Potter." I encourage her.

"As an artist there is something else you probably understand.

The theoretical world that your grandfather and I have always existed in is really a world that is *invisible*. You can't see it, so, to many, it seems conceptual and abstract. But it is very real. It is the world of the intangible."

"Reality," I say.

"We must change the definition of what we expect reality to mean."

I recognize in her words very specific ideas about my own art that I know to be true. "Looking for the unexpected. Making connections," I add.

"Yes, and your grandfather's theory should be considered in the same way. It's an idea that our universe is infinite, even that there may be many universes. Some theorize that these universes exist but are impossibly far away. Too far for us to reach using any technological intelligence that we possess now."

"But a possibility? Theoretically, of course," I add.

She puts her hand on my arm. "Some, like your parents, searched for a metaphysical interpretation. But these ideas are not really considered viable by the mainstream."

"I don't understand what you mean."

"Gabriella, maybe it simply depends on what you want to believe and what you are looking for."

"Unless my grandfather is right about the—wormholes," I say cautiously.

"Exactly. A connection through the space-time network."

I want her to keep going, to continue without wondering whether I am following her accelerated line of thinking. I wait to hear anything that could connect her words to Benjamin.

"The other possibility is that these universes are similar to ours yet the laws of physics could be different there."

"The laws of physics," I repeat.

"For example the experience of *time*. Different than our universe."

"Do you mean that everything could be the same but they could be farther ahead or even behind us in time?" I ask.

"Yes, that, and also that if time moved more slowly in their universe everything would shift accordingly. They could live much longer, even age differently." She could see the look of disbelief on my face. "As you can imagine, Gabriella, this is why I worry about him and the implications of his work."

"Dr. Potter, can I ask you something? Why after spending his entire life devoted to physics, has my grandfather ended up here? Working on these theoretical problems, really mystical ones? Putting himself at the very farthest edge of the scientific community?" My voice reflects the worry and frustration that I feel. A combination of fear for his safety and the realization that with his increasing age there is an indefinite amount of time left.

"Gabriella, he has always been—"

"I want him to find it," I interrupt. "I'm sorry, Dr. Potter. I just want him to reach his goals. Whatever they are. Besides, I thought it was my parents who were the ones whose lives had been devoted to the abstract and intangible. Not my grandfather."

"Try to understand why we explore the possibility of these worlds. It's very simple, Gabriella. We believe that they may hold the secret of secrets. Answers to questions that have been asked since the beginning of time."

I know that she can read from my puzzled expression that I am not willing to allow my mind to comprehend what she is saying.

"Gabriella, we are searching for the secret of the origin of everything there is."

34

"YOU KNOW HOW MUCH time your grandfather has been spending in Switzerland, at CERN." She stops and her eyes burn into mine.

"Yes. The Supercollider."

"The Supercollider is, truly, one of the greatest scientific enterprises of all time. Think about it," she continues. "They're trying to see what our universe was like a trillionth of a second after the big bang. Recreating the same conditions as the beginning of time, 14 billion years ago."

"One of the new wonders of the modern world as it has been called," I add.

"People come from everywhere and are stunned by its size and what it stands for. On pilgrimages. Just like in ancient times. To see the potential, Gabriella, the promise and possibility it holds, to understand the nature of—"

"Existence." I finish her sentence. "They are the wizards of our time."

"Yes, proving the impossible," she says.

"He seems to be spending so much time there, especially, since my grandmother died." I catch myself when I say the last word, the wound still so fresh in my heart.

We stand together and watch as the auditorium fills to capacity. It's a mixed group of students, faculty, and unexpectedly—clergy. The press is everywhere. The perimeter and front of the room is lined with photographers, undercover police, and Columbia University security.

"We know that we are right at the edge, we are almost there. And when we find what we are looking for—the proof that is—well, many things will change."

"What do you mean?"

"Certain basic assumptions about our world and the universe. How it all started." She looks away from me as she wrings her hands. "Who knows, Gabriella, we might even rewrite Genesis."

I immediately recognize the potentially explosive nature of what she is saying. I see a new understanding of my grandfather and the passion he feels for this work. In a profound and surprising way, I even feel an understanding of myself. I now know, without a doubt, that there is a fundamental connection between the mystical tradition from which my family has come and the research in theoretical physics that my grandfather has spent his life pursuing.

For the first time, it all seems so clear and very simple.

The lifelong quest, the search that physics and mysticism share, asks the same questions: What are we made of, when was the beginning of time, and what does it all really mean? Maybe mine and my family's secret—the ability to see into the future and past—is really the ability to connect to other realities?

"Dr. Potter, you said earlier that you thought the terrorists, that they were destroyed, captured by the authorities? We were assured, even recently that they were no longer a threat. But you said there might be others?"

She looks at me, deciding how to proceed. "I don't want to be the one to tell you. I mean, your grandfather—"

"Tell me what?" I feel my skin tingling and a sick feeling in my stomach. "If there is something else, please, tell me."

"I'm sorry, Gabriella. Maybe he didn't want you to know. Two of our colleagues were attacked last week outside of Geneva. They had left the secure main compound at CERN on Thursday to inspect one of the experiments called 'Atlas,' near the town of Meyrin, right on the French-Swiss border. The Swiss military originally classified it as a kidnapping but—"

"They were *murdered?*" I knew what she was about to say.

She is trying to present the facts calmly, but I can see how upset she is as she continues, "Yes. The following day their bodies were found in an abandoned Saab outside a café. I believe it was called Café Solstice. There is some relevance to the name of the place."

"The solstice is believed to be the exact moment when the sun reverses direction. When time stands still," I say.

"An ironic reference."

"How did they die?" I try to steady my voice.

"Poison, a lethal injection. Right into their hearts." She stops and lifts her shaking hands to cover her own. "A note was found taped to the sole of one of the doctor's feet claiming that the solstice was one of the most ancient tools used so that a traveler anywhere in the world could pinpoint their exact location on the globe. I think the inference is that these scientists had lost their way." She takes a deep breath before she continues, "And another thing. This group they—they are linking themselves to the Divine Order. They are sworn to protect, what they call, the status quo."

"I've heard that name before." I turn around to look for somewhere to sit as the conversation with my grandfather and Philip in Gloucester comes back to me clearly. "Gabriella, your grandfather is too important to be left exposed. This is all just a precaution," Philip had said.

I realize she has much more to tell me.

"The Divine Order are not who you think they are. They are well-connected, heads of multinational corporations, government officials."

"But they murdered my parents!"

"That was a splinter group, a radical faction, as are the people responsible for this. The Divine Order has always welcomed a healthy debate between science and religion. They want to move our planet forward, but keep it here, of course. This latest incident is a disaster. For many people."

I see a clear flash of the scientists: their struggle for life, their screams, their bodies. I see the hooded kidnappers on their self-proclaimed holy mission as they inject the poison that stopped the scientists' hearts.

"Why, why were they killed?"

She places her arm around my shoulder as she directs me a little farther away from the noise of the room and she looks around to make sure that nobody will be able to hear what she is about to say. "Their murders were meant to be a warning."

"What? A warning?"

"You do remember what I told you don't you? If your grandfather has found the proof that we can connect to other worlds, then it is highly likely that he may have found the ultimate *time machine*. Something that has always had a full and rich life only in the world of science fiction."

"I don't understand. Are you telling me that what happened with the scientists has something to do with my grandfather?" I ask but already know it does.

"The French intelligence is suggesting links to other incidents in Rome, Jerusalem, Cairo, even right here in New York City.

"Religious centers," I say.

"And, of course, Paris," she says gently. "We believe that some of the members are themselves scientists who would want to be the first to have access to the information. To control it."

"I know that a researcher, French or maybe Algerian, was caught by the European authorities recently, trying to infiltrate CERN. Was he not accused of being a part of Al-Qaeda?"

"It is much bigger than that, Gabriella." She shakes her head. "Al-Qaeda is a localized threat compared to this. Members of the Divine Order are global. It is the ancient battle of religion and science, evolution or a greater moral force that guides the seeming randomness in the universe." She looks away in frustration.

I feel weak as I listen and put together the pieces of everything she is saying—what it means.

She continues, "Whoever understands the pathways will have unprecedented power. Clearly, there are many who would want to stand in the way of people knowing that other worlds might exist. This would change even the most basic assumptions we have about—well, about *everything*." The corners of her mouth turn down, as if she is afraid to finish her own sentence. "You see, if the secret of the pathways fell into the wrong hands—"

"Fates would change," I whisper. The words my grandfather had often said now making sense to me really for the first time.

Dr. Potter's eyes soften. "In theoretical physics we deal with possible futures all of the time. Anything can happen."

"Anything?"

"It's possible."

"But, what if," I say, knowing I sound desperate, "what if you spend your whole life looking? Looking and looking and you simply never find it?"

"Find what, dear?" she says softly with sympathy in her eyes, as if she can feel the unbearable pain, the feelings I've been trying to suppress.

"What you thought you'd find. What you wanted. What you were always promised was waiting for you. What if it's not there at all?"

"That happens."

"Yes," I say the words mechanically. "I understand."

"I'm sorry, Gabriella, to be the one telling you these things. Come, let's go inside now and hear what your grandfather has to say."

"No, Dr. Potter, you go ahead. I'll be right there." I try to fill my words with a calm I do not feel.

"Please try to understand. There has always been two opposing ways to think about science. One is that within the complicated, seemingly random workings of our world there is a larger, loving manipulative force, the other is that our universe is simply made up of matter and energy interacting in space and time."

"So you're saying that whether you believe in God or not the science is the same?"

"Gabriella, promise me that you will remember something. There are *rules* in the universe. They may be difficult for us to comprehend, but there are still rules."

As she stands up to walk away, I see the sadness in her eyes. But for the first time, I recognize something else: The road my grandfather is on is far more dangerous than I had ever imagined.

35

I HEAR THUNDEROUS APPLAUSE coming from the auditorium as the doors push open. My grandfather walks toward me, surrounded by his teaching assistants, the head of the Physics Department, and the president of the university. I notice something else this time. He is being followed closely by two men with small earpieces and stone expressions. Security.

"Gabriella!" He lights up as he sees me leaning against the wall past the large doorway. "There you are."

I hope that he hadn't noticed that I was absent from his lecture, preferring to remain on the bench as I absorbed everything Dr. Potter and I had discussed.

"Papa." I throw my arms around him. "I've really missed you."

"I've missed you too, sweetheart." I hear the surprised happiness in his voice. He takes a step back to look at me and kisses my hand. "Let's go, there is a special dinner or something at the Faculty Club in my honor." He pushes his thinning gray hair back on his head. "Imagine that."

"You don't need to be humble with me. You've been waiting your whole life for this." I link my arm through his for the walk over to 119th Street and the penthouse restaurant that overlooks the city.

"How is Philip?"

"You always like to change the subject. But, Philip is fine. Actually, he's doing well and has been quite a wonderful friend."

"I know." He winks at me. "I invited him to dinner." He sees the puzzled, almost hurt expression on my face. "What's the matter?"

"I've told you before, Philip and I are just friends."

"He sees you, Gabriella, as does Emily. You can trust them." He squeezes my hand. "Remember that."

As we walk into the main lobby together, I become concerned by the presence of the twin security detail trailing behind us.

"What is it?" he asks me.

"Must they follow us everywhere?" I turn around to stare at the oversized, incongruous men closely following my grandfather.

They try to look inconspicuous and melt into the wall they're leaning against.

"Shhh, there's nothing to worry about." He shrugs his shoulders. "They're always with me now. Whenever I'm out or traveling."

"Nothing to worry about?" I'm incredulous.

"Someone must think I'm important."

"That's not funny." I look back at them as I try to get a grip on how anxious they are making me.

"Tell me about New York," he asks, trying to distract me.

"My life feels crazy; I just don't know what's happening to me."

Actually, it was whirling out of the carefully designed parameters I had constructed. Benjamin had completely cracked the code of my security field. Easily it seemed.

"Talk to me. Dinner can wait. What is it that's bothering you?"

"It's just that—well, I don't know. I was hoping to have some time alone with you tonight."

"Of course." I can hear the hesitation in his voice. "I always have time for you, and you know you can talk to me about anything. Whatever is on your mind, Gabriella." His voice is soft.

He has opened the door, releasing the emotions I have held in for so many weeks. The fear, the questioning, the worry over him, and of course the complete and overwhelming thrill of Benjamin that I need to express. It feels like so much has happened so quickly—as if time has slowed down or sped up. However the hell Einstein would have said it.

"I met Benjamin Landsman."

He steps back from me suddenly, then shifts his body, as if he has been struck by something. He looks away and shakes his head. His reaction makes me very uncomfortable, but he does not say anything.

I continue, "you thanked him, at the awards ceremony remember? At the museum?"

He stares straight ahead. Silent.

"How long have you known him? What is he working on with you?" I ask.

He turns to look at me, his blue eyes filled with pain and something else I have never seen before. It is *fear*. Then he says the words I never expected to hear. "I asked him, I told him. To stay away from you."

He says it so quietly, that I am not sure I've heard what he said. The noise and laughter from the dining room, the clatter of dishes overpowers his words.

"What? What did you just say?"

He pauses and I know that he is struggling with what to do next. Deciding, weighing his words. Knowing the power they will have over me.

"This cannot happen," he shakes his head. "You are to stay away from him. Do you hear me, Gabriella?"

Philip has arrived and walks toward us to say hello, but I see him stop and back away as he clearly recognizes that something unusual is taking place between my grandfather and me, a conversation he wants no part of.

"What are you *talking* about?" My voice gets louder, frantic, as I struggle to keep hold of myself. I feel the panic rising, like I am losing control. I don't understand any of it.

"Gabriella, I will not allow this to happen," he says.

He turns and starts to walk away, but I grab onto his arm and pull him around to face me. I realize that people are looking at us, shocked at the escalating scene.

"Why are you saying this? Benjamin is *everything*—everything I thought you would want for me."

"NO!" he yells. "No, I will not lose you, too!"

"I don't understand."

He storms away and opens the door out onto a balcony that leads

179

to a small terrace. The sky is gray and it is cold, but we are finally alone. I follow him and try to calm myself, to slow down the words and everything that is happening.

"Papa, please tell me, why?"

"He is not for you!"

His face is red, and I see him clutch his chest. I run over and throw my arms around him and try not to dissolve into tears. We stand together for several minutes as the icy wind swirls around us, and I wait for his breathing to become more regular.

He looks out at the city. "I should have stopped her, protected her. My beautiful Sophie. I will never let it happen again. It was just a crazy, impossible dream."

"What?"

He turns back to face me and slowly reaches up to unwrap my arms from around his neck. He pushes me away and takes a step back.

I am shaking, shocked by the exchange. "I don't understand. What are you saying, Papa? I want to be with him, to find out why he has come into my life."

I reach out for his hand but he backs farther away from me.

He points his finger at me. "No, this cannot be. It can never happen."

"Why not? Please tell me why!"

His cold eyes meet mine. It's a look I have never seen before. I stand there in shock. I know there is no way I can understand, there is no precedent for this.

"I don't ever want to hear this sort of talk again from you," he says with disgust. "Do you hear me, Gabriella? No more questions!"

He turns away and walks back into the building, leaving me standing alone, tears streaming down my face. The silence of the rooftop is overwhelming. I can't bear to stand there any longer and run inside to where a stunned Philip is waiting.

"Gabriella." He reaches for me as I storm past him and down into the stairwell. "Please stop!"

I hear his terrified voice echo off the marble walls, but I ignore him and start to run. I don't know what to believe, who to trust, or what any of it means. The pain I feel is countered by one simple truth, what my heart is telling me: There is absolutely nothing that can keep me away from Benjamin.

36

I KNOW THAT I NEED to get away—from everything. The emotional roller coaster and confusion of the last few weeks has exhausted me. Even though it's pouring in New York, the forecast is sunny in Boston. It's time to get out, go back to the beach, and clear my head so I can think about something that is good: Benjamin.

I can't get him out of my mind. This is a new sensation, making me feel out of control and unable to focus on my studies, my purpose for being in New York. Or, was that my real purpose? I was beginning to wonder. Emily was hovering and had insisted I accompany her to the Upper East Side. She is trying to distract me.

"Sweetie, I know you're not telling me what's going on with you. I'm worried."

"I'm really fine, Em. I just need to get out of New York." I try to sound convincing. "I think I'm going to go home to the beach this weekend. Maggie is expecting me," I lie. Maggie has no idea I'm coming.

"Well, I'm going to go to Grand Central with you. We haven't been there in forever. Let's get a cab."

"Emily." I laugh at her. "I'm taking the subway, it's pouring out and the traffic is terrible. You sure you still want to come?"

She doesn't hesitate. "Of course, let's go."

She grabs my hand as we run toward Lexington Avenue and the subway that will take us down the East Side. I see the shape of the sign through the teeming downpour as we approach the entry and try unsuccessfully to keep my hood over my head. The rain feels good, cleansing, like it's washing away the evidence of the last few days. We jump onto the express train, and I feel the power of the subway, the speeding vehicle that hurtles through the depths of the city, as if moving through another dimension.

Ever since we were little, we had loved to travel through the dark tunnels of the city together. We would watch the blue, red, and green lights stream by, signaling our arrival into the stations. Grand Central Terminal felt like the beating heart of the city. The pent-up energy it contained drives the destinies of the voyagers who pass through the great space on their way to unknown locations. Passengers are filtered and redistributed through the tracks that act like arteries, then, shot out to the world beyond. Beloved and historic, Grand Central deserved its recognition as one of the most important landmarks in the city. This was a place where you could feel the soul of the past.

"Come on, Gabriella. We're here." Emily pulls me out of the subway and up the stairs to the main concourse.

"Look, Em." I stop and point at the famous turquoise blue ceiling of the constellations.

She cranes her head back and exhales dramatically. "I know, it's *amayyyzing* isn't it?"

"Remember when we learned the secret about it?" I ask.

The celestial mural was one of Grand Central Terminal's most remarkable features. However, there was something extraordinary that few people knew. I remembered clearly the day my grandfather had taken Emily, Lily, and me to a special observation platform where we could look down at the travelers below and up at the painted sky.

"Listen to me very carefully, children." He had waited to speak until he knew he had our undivided attention. "I have something very special to tell you."

We huddled together like a small team, waiting for him to impart one of the deepest darkest secrets of the universe.

"What is it, Dr. Vogel?"

"Look at this image." He unfolded a large photograph of a dark night sky. His finger traced the line of white dots and circles that connected shapes and created the famous images. "You see the stars on the ceiling? That is called the zodiac."

"We know that!" Emily had said with excitement as Lily and I nodded in agreement.

"Yes, my dear, but look closely at the two. Are they the same or different?"

I knew him, I knew there was a reason for this adventure.

"Different," Lily had said with certainty.

"You are right! Now tell me how."

The three of us stood there, our faces twisted in concentration. I knew what it was, I could see it clearly. Visual images were second nature to me.

"It's backward," I said softly.

"That's correct, Gabriella. It's as if we are sky voyagers, looking down at our solar system from *outside* our world. Some people think that the artist who conceived of the ceiling, Paul Helleu, made a mistake. But he did not, it was quite intentional. I want you to think about that story every time you walk through here. Promise me that."

I remembered that day so well, the time my grandfather spent explaining this mystery to us, answering our endless questions. The concept of looking down at our earth from the heavens captivated him.

"Gabriella." Emily throws her arms around me and points to the clock. "You better hurry and get the shuttle to Penn Station. You've got twenty minutes to catch your train. Have a wonderful weekend and do me a favor, please? Be careful."

"Emily, I'll see you Monday."

As I turn away from her I look up to the painted stars on the ceiling and run for the train that will take me one step closer to home. Unlike the recent exchange with my grandfather, the memory of that day was such a happy one. The captivating and oddly personal knowledge that was imparted to us by the seeker of other worlds.

37

I LOOK OUT THE WINDOW as I sit cocooned in my raincoat and hood, my hands buried deep in the pockets of my coat. I have chosen to sit in the "quiet car." No cell phones are allowed and minimal hushed conversations—anonymous and silent.

Perfect.

I see the landscape of Rhode Island roll by as we pass through. The rain streams down the window that separates the outside world from the interior space. The wet paths trace lines that jump across the surface of the glass. Earlier, when the train had passed through a tunnel, I saw my own reflection. I was jolted by what looked back at me and realized it was not my face but my grandmother's. The image in the frame on my grandfather's desk. Mine is younger and without the dark hair that was always tied up above her graceful neck in a sleek chignon, in stark contrast to the wild golden hair I would thoughtlessly twist and pin out of my way. She was from another time, an era where great care was given to appearance and propriety. My tomboyish predilection precluded that effort.

My grandparents had shared a great and enduring love affair. He spoke of her in the present tense, as if she still were with him every day. His "*beshert*" he called her. His soul mate. He believed in the fundamental concept that for every person, every soul, there is only one other that completes them. Two lost halves created for the purpose of being united, creating a divine union.

I touch my cheek and slowly move my hand down to the edge of my jaw, across and over my lips. I want to trace the path that Benjamin's breath had moved over my face. I think about his mouth; I imagine it on me. His hands, his face—all of him. It is a sensation and memory that I have played over thousands of times since that night several weeks earlier.

The rhythm of the train's pace starts to change indicating the approach to Boston's South Station. The landscape out the window is familiar yet transformed into yellow, red, and bronze by the fire of the New England fall. Golden light on the river shimmers off the glass towers. It's an amazing city. Home to so many great minds, those who are creating, inventing, and describing the world. Revealing what is locked deep in the consciousness of yet unnamed sources.

"Charlie!" I yell into my cell phone as I try to balance everything I'm carrying.

He was part of our life in Gloucester, always around to help Maggie run the house or shuttle my grandfather to the airport. I planned to use the thirty-mile drive out to the North Shore to catch up on all the local news.

"Sorry I didn't call you sooner, but I'm here. Almost at South Station."

"Well, today is your lucky day, kid, I just happen to be doing a drop off at the airport. So, I'll be right there."

"I'll be outside, the usual spot."

Twenty minutes later, I am safely buckled into his car.

I listen to him talk animatedly, describing events in Gloucester over the last few weeks. The highlights of weather and fishing. I look out the window and realize how in just a short period of time, everything seems so different, as if I am seeing things for the first time. Was it only a few months ago that my life had not included architecture school and, of course, Benjamin?

"I've been driving your grandfather back and forth a lot lately. To the airports. He's traveling all the time. Especially to Switzerland, right? I think he said Geneva?"

I could smell the sea, the sweet air blowing in through the window. It's much warmer than it was in New York, and the late fall sun warms me through the window of the car.

"It's so pretty here, Charlie, it never changes."

But he doesn't hear me. He wants to talk about my grandfather. "He loves to tell me about that thing—the Super—"

"collider?"

"Yep, that's it. Supercollider. I hear that thing is *huge*. Might even blast us into the future, right? I saw something on PBS about it. "

"Uh huh."

"Someday, it's gonna be a whole story about him you know." He turns around to look at me. His tanned arm, still dark from the summer days on the beach, draped casually over the seat. "They're all so different, those physics types who come to the house." He exhales slowly, making a slight whistling sound. "Maggie has told me about them over the years, a strange group they are." He catches himself as he clarifies. "I mean, Gabriella, *interesting,* you know how I love Dr. Vogel. No offense intended."

"Hey, don't worry about it, Charlie." I return his smile. "I hear you."

"They just kind of stick out when they're in Gloucester."

"Well, that's what I love about being home. I don't."

He laughs to himself, amused by what I have just said. "Yeah, right," I hear him say under his breath.

I think about the relationship I have with this northern cape of Massachusetts. Like the one between the earth and moon. The magnetic attraction and gravitational pull that creates the tides, fluctuating as the moon travels around the earth. The rise and fall of the world's oceans seems to mirror my own emotional state, the personal struggles I have faced, and even my desire to find the elusive understanding of my family. Now, there is something bigger than everything else: Benjamin.

38

C HARLIE TURNS OFF of Route 128 at our exit and drives along the familiar side roads toward the center of Gloucester. I feel all the tension leaving my body. As we come over the crest of the hill, the beautiful endless vista of the Atlantic Ocean comes into view. The car circles through the narrow streets and passes the iconic sculpture of the Gloucester fisherman, a memorial to the thousands of souls who lost their lives to the sea. The center of downtown is very different from the private beachfront property where our home is. Small shops, bakeries, and restaurants create a distinctive urban character, dominated by the fishing industry that is its lifeblood. Many of the houses have small white plaques with details of the sea captains or sailors who had lived there and established this outpost on the northernmost point of Cape Ann in the early 1600s. They defined so much of the economy and history of New England as many tried to build their lives in the new world. With the crush of summer tourists gone, the town returned to its true character. Generations of hard working people descended from Irish, Italian, and Portuguese immigrants.

"Charlie, have you seen the Sullivans lately? I would love to see Lily."

He looks at me in the rearview mirror, his face becomes somber.

"Of course, Gabriella, Lily is doing great. She's already the favorite teacher at the middle school. Always happy, an amazing person, given everything she has to deal with."

I called her often from New York and think about a recent conversation. The adversity she had overcome lived in me, as did the memory of how all our lives had changed in an instant when we were eleven years old. When the car had come around the corner, and I had known.

"You sound different, Gabriella, did you meet someone special?" Lily asked.

I could picture her sitting on the porch with the phone in her hand. I wondered how she could see directly into my heart. "Lily, I wish you would reconsider, come to New York. We could live together, all of us. Get the right kind of place."

"Gabriella."

"It would be as we planned. Emily, you, and me. I really need you."

"I don't need to be in New York to be *with* you, you know that."

"I know, but still."

"Tell me about school, tell me everything. Your grandfather has been written up endlessly in the papers and not just the local ones, TIME Magazine and on television, CNN, the internet. I try to keep up with him, with both of you."

"Everything is changing, Lily."

"Yes."

"Things are starting to happen," I said.

"Gabriella, you've met him. Someone wonderful, haven't you?" she asked.

"As my grandmother predicted," I continue.

"I knew you would," she says with satisfaction.

I hear the crushed-shell stones under the tires, the sound I have trained my ears for over the years. Often it signaled the return of my grandfather after a long absence of lectures and travel. Now the sound is of my return, continuing along the path that he has set out for me.

"Well, here we are, safe and sound!" Charlie puts the car in park and stops to look at the overwhelming view from this vantage point.

I press my nose to the window as I did when I was young. The blue-gray ribbon of sea extends as far as I can see. The water is still rough from the earlier storm and the white caps of the waves rise and crash down on the beach. The distinctive salt smell and the familiar sounds of seagulls and Indian summer are still in the air.

"Hey, Gabriella, I just remembered. I saw Maggie in town earlier. She said she wasn't going to be home until later. Did you tell her you were coming?"

"No, Charlie, I didn't," I answer as I open the car door and turn to face the ocean. I see the surfers who appear after every storm, looking for waves to ride into shore. I still have an hour or so before sunset and decide to find my wet suit and go down for a swim.

"Gabriella, is there anything else?" He watches me look at the surfers.

"Oh, I'm sorry, Charlie. You know, I have to say, it really seems like I've been gone a long time. Everything feels so different."

"Everything is the same around here, Gabriella." He shrugs. "Actually I think it's *you* that's different."

Our eyes meet and I remember what I wanted to say to him.

"Please, don't tell Maggie that I'm here if you see her in town later. I want to surprise her."

"No worries. I'll see you at the end of the weekend." He winks at me and puts the car in reverse. "And be careful. I know you're one of those crazies who likes to swim in the ice cold water. The undertow has been vicious lately."

"Thanks, Charlie." I give him a hug. "I'll be fine."

I slam the car door and walk up the path to the house, thinking about what he has just said about me being different, and how even he can see the amazing and complete shift in my life.

39

I DROP MY BAGS IN the front hall and look out at the timeless view of the dunes, sea, and sand. It feels so good to be away from the architecture studios, New York, and everything that has happened. This is a rare opportunity to have the house to myself.

"We on the East Coast are the guardians of the rising sun." My grandfather often reminded me.

We would watch the path it traveled until the end of the day when the shadows it cast illuminated the grasses and pond outside our windows. The back of the house that faced the ocean was carefully composed, a wall of glass designed to frame a perfect view of the sea. I walk down the long gallery toward the staircase and see the many paintings on the walls. Interspersed with well-known contemporary artists of the last hundred years are my own paintings, even ones from when I was very young.

I had pleaded with my grandmother years before. "Please, don't hang that one. It's terrible."

"Art is subjective, dear. You know that, besides I want it here, *with* me. I can see the way your mind works in the shapes and lines. I can feel your heart."

The memory stops me, the words she had spoken were the same as Benjamin's. I think about my painting in his loft and can't understand any of it: the magnetic draw I cannot deny, the terrifying reaction my grandfather had when I mentioned his name, or the reality of Benjamin's constant absence. Too many unanswered questions.

And I think of my grandmother. The many times we were on the roof under the blanket of stars. The things she would say to me.

"Your life is limitless, Gabriella."

"I don't understand."

"You can't imagine the places, the worlds out there."

"I want to."

She would look away and pull me closer.

"Why are you sad?" I had asked her.

"I wish I could be here with you, when it happens."

"When what happens?"

"Everything."

"Everything?"

"Your first real kiss, when you hold hands, when you feel the pounding inside of your heart or that it simply might stop, when you find what you're looking for."

"You will, you *will* be with me."

"Look up there, Gabriella." She pointed into the night sky. "Can you see it?"

"What?"

"Forever."

"Where?"

"All around you."

There is so little I feel sure of except for one thing. Benjamin is part of my future. I know it; I have seen it, and I am hanging on to this belief.

Trying to trust my heart.

The sun casts its last light across the grasses that shape the path to the beach. The sea breeze touches my cheek, acknowledging my return. This is the image, the sensation I hold in my mind when I am away for too long. I can conjure up the feeling of the wind on my face and the rhythmic sound of the sea, as if I was standing right there. My hand skips along the old wooden fence that is so characteristic of the New England beaches, marking the procession up then down to the sea. The dunes create a natural buffer that hides the swimmers from the road and scattered homes.

I zip up my wet suit, knowing that without it the shock of the water's temperature will be too much to bear. A tradition I try to engage in every time I return home, the swim is like the ancient ritual of immersion that centers around the idea of hope. The belief that in moving waters is the power to purify. My ancestors had performed this physical act, and I knew it was often used to represent a radical change of heart or total commitment to something. Or someone.

A group of geese sound their way in the sky above, heading south for the winter on their cyclical path. The drive from their instinct telling them exactly where to go and what to do. Lucky, to find answers that are buried deep in their DNA. No room for doubt.

I walk toward the horizon and close my eyes. The icy bite stings my ankles. I push off from the sandy bottom, and my legs float up as my body becomes horizontal. I feel the tug of the moon and the power of the tide as my body is lifted out into the sea. The sky is pink and orange, a composition of shapes created as the sun moves into the west and clings to the last moments of the day. My ears submerge below the surface and connect to the sounds of the marine world. Safe and familiar, quiet. I rest in the rocking motion of the water as it carries me away from the shore.

I want to empty my mind, to feel all these sensations, but the powerful force in my head is back. When I can *see* things, that are about the future. But this time, it's different and—amazingly—it feels wonderful. I welcome the feeling, because it's about *him*.

We are together, far away on a beach. Not Gloucester, not even on the Atlantic but somewhere else, warm and secluded. I see the water that is so blue, bluer than any I have ever seen. The soft, warm breeze blows over my body, and I touch the white-powder sand. I scoop it up and let it escape slowly through my fingers, feeling its softness. My head rests on a towel and he leans over me, blocking the light so I can look into his green eyes, impossibly close to my face. I love the way he feels.

"Gabriella," he says my name, softly, slowly.

"Yes?"

"Is this what you thought it would be like?"

My mouth covers his eyes, his cheeks, his lips. I push them open with mine as I drink him in. I want to answer his questions with my body.

"Yes, no—I hoped it would feel like this—but it's better. So much better." I pause to fill the space with words from my heart. "We are the lucky ones."

"Do you know how much I love you?"

My fingers touch the line of his brow. I lift the bottom of his soft ear and wrap my hands around the back of his neck and pull his face closer to mine.

"How do you know?" My voice is low.

"What do you mean?"

"How do you know when someone loves you, *really* loves you. For the right reasons. That you'll be loved no matter what happens?"

"You will." He leans over and whispers to me, "You already are."

I feel his breath and lips on my neck as he moves down between my breasts. My body rises to meet his mouth. Soft, warm, slow. There is no need to hurry, no rush.

We have forever.

"I don't want you to worry about anything, Gabriella. Know that I will always come back for you."

I don't want to talk. I want to feel him, all of him, everywhere.

"Yes, I know, I believe it. We'll be together. Now *kiss* me."

His eyes burn into mine. "Remember that. It's the only way."

As I reach out I feel him dissolve and slip away, my hands slice instead through icy water.

It's over. The beautiful vision, the dream of him with me. Gone. I'm alone—in the dark. Suddenly, I feel the familiar rocking motion of the water change into a twisting, pulling sensation. I have drifted much farther away from the shore than I had intended, and panic wells up inside of me as I drift farther away from where I want to be. I scan the horizon for lights. The waves grow with intensity as the incredible undertow pulls me out. I try to swim, pushing my body with every ounce of energy I have, using sheer will to force my arms through the icy water. The waves are crushing and pulling me under. Spinning and throwing me about, like one of the many lobster buoys that dot the coast. I realize that I am going nowhere; the force of nature is too powerful to overcome.

Try to stay calm, I tell myself.

I tread water and catch my breath, get my bearings, but my arms are thrashing for survival. I reach toward the surface but am repeatedly pulled down, and I submerge. I force myself back into the night sky and gasp for air and try to escape the horrifying feeling of being sucked down.

Oh my God, my mind screams in panic. My legs are numb from the cold, and I try again to gather my strength and swim, propelling my body forward. I am unwilling to accept the terrifying inevitability of what is happening. The vacuum pulls me farther into the grip of the sea. Air bubbles, floating, twisting hair, and limbs create a swirling composition of fear and wonder. Salt water rushes into my lungs and its weight carries me down, deeper, into the infinite blue space. Darkness wraps around like a thick fog as I become one with the sea. The crushing pain is gone now because I've left my heart behind.

Yet, I can feel him with me, the way our bodies would meet in the dark and in the light, floating in the moving tide of our pleasure, the worlds between us melting. I need to remember—I will always remember—everything I love about him. I know that I could paint every one of his words with my brush, draw the shape of his breath with my pen, and sculpt the meaning of his thoughts into stone. But I understand that it cannot be. I'm tired of fighting, searching, and trying to understand. Instead I let go to the powerful force and know that, no matter what happens, this is not the end.

The last conscious thought I have is the faint recognition of a strong hand pulling me up and out of the sea.

Back into the night air and this world.

40

E VEN THOUGH MY EYES are closed, I know he is with me.
I can see myself, down on the sand, lying still. I want to gasp for
the breath I thought had left me forever. But I can't. I try to answer him,
meet the sadness in his words and tell him that I am here. There is the
astonishing shock of pain and cold trying to rocket my senses back to the
world of the living. I need to be there with him, to feel him touching me,
but I know I am caught between two worlds. I need to get *back*.

"Gabriella!"

I hear my name being called. It sounds so far away.

"Please, Gabriella, please breathe!" His words break the silence,
the mystery of how I got to this cold, dark place. But, I know one thing.
He has pulled me from the waters. Saved me.

I want to get back into my body and feel the stillness of the earth
under me. I know the rocking motion and pull of the sea is far away and I
fight for my consciousness to return. I hear his voice, desperate, pleading,
and something else: The waves crashing on the beach. I recognize that I am
no longer in their grasp but safely away from their overwhelming force and
power. His weight is on me, shielding my body from the night wind, heavy
and warm. I try to form thoughts of what has happened, as flashes of memory tear through my mind.

"No! Please, come back to me. Come back," he begs.

I want to answer, to tell him that I am here with him, but I can't.

My eyes will not open. My body feels heavy, my lungs are full of water. His head moves, he listens to my chest. His mouth is on mine as he desperately tries to push the life from his body into me, the air from his own lungs filling mine.

"I won't let this happen. This will *not* happen, Gabriella—breathe, please!"

He stays over me, not giving up, forcing his breath into me as he pushes the sea out of my body. I feel oddly detached, separate, as I watch the scene. I want to go back to the other place, the beautiful warm beach. The sunshine, the white sand, my body intertwined with his. Just let me go there now away from this pain.

"Gabriella!"

And then, I am coughing. Pulling his life force into me. Taking what he offers.

Breathing.

I open my eyes and see the sky, the stars framed in the black velvet blanket that shelters our earth, and then—I see him. The beautiful face with unforgettable eyes looking down at me.

"Benjamin." The instant recognition that he has pulled me from the water all makes sense. "It's you." The words whisper out of my mouth.

He is shaking, tears of relief come down his cheeks as he hears me speak. His face is so close to mine. His hands touch my matted hair, which has been twisted by the sea. He pushes it away from my eyes and pulls himself up onto one elbow as he turns to face me.

"I can't lose you, I won't ever let you go again, Gabriella."

I am unable to move, too weak to even respond or question his words or what they mean. I close my eyes tightly in response to the crushing pain in my shoulder and ribs. I realize that my arm is twisted in an unnatural way. The sea is wild and a distant part of my consciousness acknowledges what has happened as fragments of memory crystallize. He leans in toward me, and I can hear his urgent voice as I try to focus and clear my mind.

"Look at me, Gabriella. Are you all right, can you move your arm? I need to get you inside—it's too cold here. I'm going to lift you now."

I can feel his warmth, his breath. His lips move slowly across my salted lashes and brows, down my cheeks and gently touch the surface of my lips. Despite my pain and disorientation, I recognize the crush of desire I feel. I need to know where he has been these last few weeks. I want to tell him that I have been looking for him.

Waiting.

That my life has been empty in a way I have never known before.

I had always believed, hoped, that when I met the person I was meant to love forever, my spirit would acknowledge the instant of recognition. As if programmed into the deepest part of my soul was that very moment and the promise of all that was to follow.

"Benjamin," I say so softly I can barely hear the words myself, "I've been looking for you."

With a wistfulness and melancholy that I cannot understand, he responds, "I know."

I can see in his eyes the acceptance of an inevitability that he has tried to fight against. I reach up to pull his face toward mine. The salt taste of the sea is still on my lips, mixing with what I realize are tears of gratitude and relief.

Everything in my life has prepared me for him. This is where I am destined to be. I know that I will fight with everything in me against being without him the way I had endured the last few weeks.

The stars are my witness, I have found what I've been searching for.

41

I AM IN THE PLACE between waking and dreaming, disconnected from my body yet in it. Watching and aware.

I am *alive*.

Warm in the safety of my bed, I'm surrounded by soft pillows and my feathered quilt. The cushion of the familiar mattress is a welcome comfort. Warm and stable. I feel their presence, the voices that discuss my condition, rising and falling. The first one, Maggie's, is low and concerned, the other—unforgettable. It's the voice that sounds like heaven to me.

Benjamin.

I know they are in the room, whispering and watching. They think I'm sleeping. Slowly the events of the earlier few hours start to come back to me, flashing through my memory in clear visual frames. So powerful that they overwhelm the haze created by the strong painkillers I had been given. I shift slightly in the bed and feel a dull pain. My shoulder is bandaged tightly, dislocated by the crush of the surf and the frantic effort to release myself from the grip of the undertow. I remember everything, but mostly the miraculous sensation of being pulled out, carried from the water, and Benjamin's face, his breath everywhere over me. In me.

Maggie is crying. I haven't seen her cry since my grandmother died. I want to tell her that I am here, alive. That I have been saved and that I am happier than I have ever been. But I have to keep fighting to stay conscious. My body wants only sleep, warm, protected, safe, still sleep.

"Is she all right?" It's Maggie's agonized maternal voice.

I see the blur of her face over mine. I feel the light touch of her rough hand on my cheek as I try desperately to open my eyes.

"Yes, she will be fine, remember what the doctor said. She has to recover from the shock." Benjamin's voice is calm, certain.

"I can't believe this happened, that I wasn't here to stop her." Maggie's voice is anchored with fear. She draws small circles in the floor with her pacing as her voice approaches and recedes in a pattern of worry.

"I would think there would be very little you could have done to stop Gabriella from doing what she wants." I detect admiration in his steady voice as he calms and reassures her.

"But she almost drowned!"

"She is safe now, it was an unusual current, a riptide from the storm. There is no way she could have known."

"I can't even imagine." Her voice trails off as low sobs overtake her. I can feel the tears on her face, the way she wipes them away with the handkerchief carefully stored in her pocket, dabbing her eyes. "What would have happened had you not been there, here I mean. Seen her."

"But I was," he says.

There is silence as I wait for what will come next, never expecting to hear what I do. Maggie speaks very slowly, her voice low and tense. "She warned me, her grandmother, Sophie. She *knew* this was going to happen. I begged Gabriella never to swim alone. I didn't know she was coming."

"Yes, I know."

"And you, she told me about you." Maggie's voice gets louder, and I imagine her pointing her finger at Benjamin. "That you would somehow save her, that you and Gabriella." She takes a deep breath. "She told me that you belong together. She described your face. Your eyes."

Then, there is silence, except for Maggie's quiet sobs and Benjamin's determined breathing.

"Please, stop." His voice sounds broken, weighted down with pain.

"She saw it all, she knew the future and now you're here for her aren't you? You've come for Gabriella?"

"I have already done too much damage, crossed the line. I have broken all the rules."

"What are you saying? Sophie was never wrong. She told me, she predicted you in her notes, her letters. I *have* them."

"No, I'm afraid it cannot be. Gabriella cannot live in my world."

I feel like I can't breathe, as if my lungs are filling with water again. I want to scream, to cry out. I'm not sure whether this is a dream, a figment of my imagination, or some terrible reality that I need to escape from. All I can do is listen.

Maggie's voice holds all the desperation I am feeling. "I know that you're the one. She trusted you in Switzerland. When she never came back. It was you wasn't it? You're the one who took her?"

"Yes."

"She really believed, that it would happen, that she could go through. They both did."

"He blames me."

"No, Benjamin, he blames himself and now he wants to show the world. That he's been right all along."

"It cannot be, Maggie. It won't work."

I force myself to open my eyes. To wake up. To absorb the conversation, what they are saying and everything that Maggie seems to know.

It is said that when a thirsty man is in the desert searching for water, he will hallucinate, create the object of his desire at the precise moment when he feels death upon him. The mind creates a mirage, the optical illusion caused by the reflection of light that makes objects appear distorted, closer, above or below where they exist. Was I the lost traveler who runs toward the vision and shovels sand into his mouth thinking it's water? I had been searching for what I needed to sustain me, nourish me, and help me grow into what awaited. Now in my childhood bed, with Benjamin in the room, I could feel the collision of the past with the inevitability of my future. All merging at once.

I know that I have crossed a threshold into an unknown world of possibility. This time I'm not afraid. I need fate to be on my side, promising the future I have only hoped for. I've heard enough to know and am beginning to understand, putting the pieces together.

I wake to the sun low in the sky in the east. I push myself up in bed and look out the window to see the waning flowers and hydrangeas of summer, the rosebushes that spill down to the beach and ocean beyond. The twin lighthouses of Cape Ann are in the distance and the sea grasses reflect the golden glow of fall. So many pivotal moments of my life have happened here—and now this is how I feel: different, *transformed,* as if something buried deep within me has been released. The fortress around my heart finally coming down. The sensation of being in the water comes back to me suddenly, the motion of being pulled out and carried in his arms and everything else. Everything he said.

"I can't lose you. I won't ever let you go again, Gabriella."

"Benjamin." My voice sounds so hoarse as I call out his name. I feel bruised everywhere but I want to get downstairs. I have to find him.

I hear Maggie's heavy foot steps as she runs up the wood staircase and bursts into my room.

"Gabriella, you're awake! Oh my goodness, wait a minute." She comes straight for me, her arms outstretched. "Let me help you."

"Maggie, I'm fine." I push myself up and try to sound convincing. "Honestly, I really need to get out of this bed and downstairs. I'm just a little hungry actually."

She claps her hands together. "That sounds much more like my girl."

Maggie wraps her strong arms around my waist and guides me carefully down the staircase and into the glass breakfast area that overlooks the sea. I look out at the surf and feel, once again, the sensation of the water on me, flashes of memory from the night before. My mind wants to edit out the terrifying pull of the water and think only about what had been playing over in my mind since I had awakened. The feeling of being close to Benjamin. His lips on my face.

"I'm going to make you some breakfast." Maggie moves quickly around the kitchen, banging pots, opening and closing drawers and humming to herself. I know she is relieved, busy with taking care of me, but I have other things on my mind.

I slip out of the kitchen when she's not looking and walk toward the windows that face the front of the house. I need to see if there is any sign of Benjamin at all. As I stare out the window, I feel the anxiety rising, the questioning. I don't know what I can trust from my memory. I do know that the bandage around my arm is very real, as is the fact that I am bruised everywhere.

"He's not here, Gabriella."

I turn around and see Maggie standing with a steaming cup of coffee in her hand.

"He was here wasn't he? I didn't dream the whole thing."

"He left very early this morning, but wanted you to have this." Her face is more serious than I can ever remember as she walks toward me and pulls a small envelope out of her apron pocket.

My eyes search hers for any information, anything I can find out about him. "Thank you."

She places the note into my hand, and I hold it for a moment before I tear it open. I want to touch something he had held. I need to tie myself back to his presence in any way that I can.

My Dearest Gabriella,

I am so sorry that I had to leave this morning without saying good-bye to you. I would not have left without the knowledge that you are well and under the watchful eye of Mrs. O Hara.
I have been called away. I know that you will find some of the answers you have been searching for. Everything will be made clear very shortly — it must be.

Until then, know that I am always with you.

—BL

I scan the note and reread the words several times, searching for any interpretations or subtleties that I might have missed. With frustration and a sense of loss that I recognize too well, I crumple to the floor.

"Just tell me, Maggie, tell me that this is real." I hold on to my bandaged arm as I try to convince myself.

She runs over and helps me stand up slowly, pulling me away from the floor. "Oh, my angel, it's been so many years."

I take a step back and look into her eyes. I want her to understand what I'm about to say. "Maggie, I could hear you last night. I heard what you said to him. Everything. You need to tell me how you know these things. *Please,* I need to know."

42

WE WALK INTO THE great room and sit on the couch together. I wait for what I hope are the answers, the understanding I had searched for my whole life. Maggie reaches out for my cold hand and holds it in hers.

"How did you know?" I ask.

"I knew, Gabriella, that this was the way it would be. I have been waiting many years, for a sign, for something to show me that she was right. As she always was."

"I don't understand anything you're saying!"

"I'm so sorry."

"You should have told me."

She laughs, her face filled with an irony I can't understand. "I was waiting—for you to come to me—and you did. Just as she said you would."

I look at her and try to process what she is saying. What I think it all means. "Grandma Sophie?"

She nods. "She told me about him."

"What are you saying?"

"Gabriella, she shared your gift. She wanted me to tell you, to remind you when you were ready to understand. She knew she would not be here to answer your questions."

As we sit together, I know I am on a new threshold. The familiarity of this place disguising a revolution of changes. I turn to look at her and see her eyes, locked on mine. I wait for whatever she will say next.

"Your grandmother's illness—she was terminal."

"What? Papa told me she had been cured."

"He wanted to believe that."

"But she knew the truth? Why didn't she tell him? He's a scientist for God's sake."

"She knew it would destroy him. That it would take him away from his work. She did not want to do that." Maggie takes out her handkerchief and wipes her eyes as I sit stunned, listening to this information. Her warm hand covers mine. "She didn't want to leave you. She knew how much you needed her. So she asked me to wait for the day, this day. When you would find Benjamin, when you would be, well, reunited. I never thought it would happen the way it did, the way she predicted. But it is all as she said."

"What do you mean? Are you saying she knew about *him?*"

Maggie nods slowly. She had said "reunited." I didn't know what else she could possibly say that would shock me more but I brace myself, steel my eyes on the sea ahead, then turn to look into her eyes.

"I have waited for many, many years to tell you this. I was waiting for the time when I felt you were ready to understand. Your parents, your gift, the ability to see and to connect in a way that most cannot. I know you have experienced it, Gabriella. It is what gives you your incredible sensitivity. Abilities and perceptions that make you the intuitive artist that you are."

"Antennae of the race," I whisper the author James Joyce's words.

I'm afraid to hear what else she will say but want to. A clarity that I have been waiting for is now being revealed.

"You are from a long line of mystics, ancient Kabbalists who have an ability to connect to the past, the future, to souls who are here and those who are not."

My parents, my grandmother, those who have come before me, all of them. I was beginning to understand.

"When? When did she tell you these things?"

"Gabriella, I have been with your grandparents for over forty years. What do you think I have been doing all this time?" She finds a moment of humor as she pushes herself up off the sofa. She turns to face me and points her index finger at me. "Wait here, there is something I need to show you."

My mind races as the pieces start to come together.

She comes back into the room carrying a box I have never seen before filled with letters, photographs, sketches, and more of my grandmother's red leather journals. Just like the one my grandfather had given me before I left for New York.

"She wanted you to have these, all of them. When you were ready, she said." Maggie puts the box down gently on the sofa next to me, and I feel her hand on my shoulder. "It's time."

I spend the day slowly going through everything: photographs, newspaper articles, even some of Einstein's letters. Maggie circles back to check on me, occasionally, to see whether I am all right.

The sun is setting when she comes in to light the fire and sit next to me. Finally, I am ready to speak. "Maggie, she knew that Papa wouldn't understand, didn't she?"

She nods. "She wanted to keep it hidden from him, that she wasn't going to live. She believed there was another way. For her to go on."

"It was with Benjamin's help, wasn't it? He was involved?"

She looks right at me, then into the box and pulls out a small album of photographs. She flips through it quickly, then stops and hands an open page to me.

"Look at this."

It is a darkened picture.

"It looks like a party, Maggie, and," I say and hold it closer, "there is Einstein." I turn the photograph over and see a date. "Here, it says 1943."

"Yes." She encourages me with her eyes. "Now look closely. What else do you see?"

I look again. "It's them, together right? The night they met each other, and my great grandparents." I look up at her for acknowledgement.

She nods again. "Anyone else?"

The way she says it makes my skin tingle as her eyes burn into mine. I am afraid to look back down, but I do. It is a large group of people but there it is—the unmistakeable face.

"Benjamin."

I drop the picture and stand up. I back away from the box, from everything she is showing me. From what seems completely impossible.

Insane.

"How can it be? I don't understand, is that really him?"

"Yes, you do. It is in your heart, in what you have always known to be true."

"What are you talking about, Maggie?"

"The theory, the worlds he's been looking for, my darling. They exist. They have always been there. Always." She takes a breath. "Your grandfather never stopped believing. And now he has the proof and he's ready to show the world."

"When?" I know what this will mean, how our lives will change forever.

"At the World Conference in December, Gabriella, you must be ready."

I am completely overwhelmed. I need to separate each concept from the other, slow down the avalanche of emotion and information. I have not taken my eyes away from Benjamin's face in the picture. "He hasn't aged at all. He looks the same."

"Yes."

"It's been over *sixty years* since that night, how can this be?"

"It's the way it works; I remember how your grandmother explained it to me. You are subject to the physical laws of the world you come from. Everything can be the same yet time can move more slowly or quickly, so you don't age the way you do in our world."

"It's him."

"Gabriella." She pauses, knowing that what she will say next will change my life. "What your grandfather has been searching for all these years, the missing link in his theory—it's Benjamin. It is not a mathematical formula, it's him. *He* is the proof."

It was all meant to be, coming together in a crashing inevitability. I could feel it somewhere deep in my heart.

His work with my grandfather, the first day of school, the cathedral, the architecture review, and the incredible evening we shared after. And of course, the unforgettable moment when he saved me from the pull of the water on the beach.

It was destined to be.

I am sure.

"Your grandmother always told me that Einstein would say—"

"Einstein?"

"That things are not always what they seem. She wanted you to know, for me to remind you at this very moment to trust yourself. To trust the things you are seeing and feeling. Do you know what I'm saying?"

"Yes."

"She wanted you to know . . . that you are not alone."

And with those words, she acknowledged what had haunted me my whole life. What I had been afraid to recognize and speak of. That my visions of the future were connected to the mystical tradition I inherited from so many who had come before me. I thought of the many things in my life I had gone through, and now I saw clearly the good, the bad, the terrifying, and the *wonderful* things in my future. I believed everything waited. With Benjamin.

"Maggie, I need to find my grandfather, I need to speak with him. NOW!"

"Gabriella, it's late, he's at MIT. He's giving a talk tonight. You need to stay in bed."

"I have to go." I stand up, pushing myself off the sofa with my uninjured arm.

I see her looking at me as she decides what to do. She looks like she's made up her mind and says, "You're not going alone. I'm coming with you."

43

I AM STUNNED.

Not only from everything that has happened in the last twenty-four hours but the historic and shattering reality of what Maggie has confirmed: that the dream, my grandfather's lifelong quest, which had been relegated merely to theory, might in fact come to be presented, proven, and accepted as fact. I would be able to see it happen, and Benjamin, Benjamin's vital and central contribution, was what made it possible. Maggie and I drive in silence toward Boston. It's as if the information needs time to settle. This is the quiet—the calm—before the storm.

Gloucester, the farthest point on Cape Ann, is a world unto itself, connected to the North Shore and Boston by bridges that many local residents never cross. For people like my grandfather, Gloucester had always provided a welcome refuge from the city and a busy travel schedule. It was a place centered around the physical pleasures and sensations offered by beautiful beaches, sunsets, salted sea air, and endless views. Balancing out the pursuits of the mind.

The weather is the perfect envelope, a welcome shift of clear sky and light dry air. I recognize that in less than thirty miles one can move so completely from one world to another. I take the opportunity during the drive to organize my thoughts and questions. As the road near Boston's Logan airport crests upward and the city comes into view, I see the beautiful Leonard P. Zakim Bunker Hill Bridge, a symbol of the benevolence of the city. The engineering and design of this masterpiece is the perfect combination of art and technology, honoring a humanitarian who had died too young of cancer. The metaphor for the building of bridges is one that aptly represents the accomplishments of the man after whom it was named. Every time I drive across the cable-stayed bridge, suspended in the air, I am reminded of the many values it represents: the minds who had created it and the hands who had built it.

We follow the stream of traffic onto Storrow Drive. We pass the Hatch Shell where the Boston Pops perform every Fourth of July. The canons explode as they play Tchaikovsky's "1812 Overture," an iconic symbol of what our nation's independence means. Turning onto Massachusetts Avenue to cross the bridge over to Cambridge, the great domed building at the center of MIT's campus, the Maclaurin Building, or Building 10 as it is called, comes into view. Visible from the banks of the Charles River, its dome is featured on every publicity shot of the university. It is also the location of many important physics meetings my grandfather has attended over the years, and a place I have come to know well.

"We're almost there," Maggie recognizes that I am deep in thought but tries to encourage me.

I think about MIT's campus as an architectural collage, an irreverent jumble of styles, shapes, and materials that seemed to belie any sort of central planning, so different than the restrained Beaux Arts symmetry of Columbia University. And yet, it seems appropriate as a reflection of the varied talents and theories being investigated there. Discussion, debate, and dissent are always welcomed and encouraged, in a home to many Nobel Laureates.

Maggie parks the car and before we enter the building, we stop to turn and admire the view of the Back Bay of Boston.

"Maggie." I notice that she seems to know exactly where she is going. "You've been here before?"

"Many times." She turns and winks at me. "Come on, let's hurry."

I feel electrified. The mixture of adrenaline, the narcotics of the painkillers, and the thrill and terror of the night before is still in my veins. The range of emotions all centering around Benjamin—still having an effect on me.

218

We enter the lecture hall, and I see the panel of scientists on the stage. The sound reverberates through speakers that surround the room. I hear familiar terms: *wormholes, multiverses,* the *bending of light* and other theoretical topics. As we stand in the back of the room, my eyes scan the space. My grandfather is seated in the center. I recognize his thinning gray hair, the slight curve of his proud shoulders, and a far away look on his face. Just at the moment my eyes lock onto him, he looks up. It's as if he can hear the thoughts screaming in my head.

"Sit down." Maggie grabs the back of my jacket to stop the momentum she can sense that is about to propel me down the stairs and straight for him. "Here, sweetheart." She does not let go of me and points to two seats at the back of the hall.

As I wait in this room full of hundreds of journalists, scholars, and scientists I try to control the thoughts in my mind. I feel dazed, I need to make a plan, decide what I can do or say. The anger grows inside of me, turning into rage. Maggie keeps looking at me; she strokes my arm in a futile effort to calm my frayed emotions. When the lecture concludes, thunderous applause ensue, and the moderator opens the discussion for questions. Hands are immediately thrust into the air as journalists jump out of their seats, shouting questions over each other and snapping photographs with the nonstop motor drive of their lenses.

I can no longer deny the need to confront my grandfather and, although I know this isn't the time or place, I launch myself out of the seat and down the steps of the auditorium. Right to the front of the room.

"Gabriella, come back!" Maggie calls as her hand swipes my back. But I am out of her reach.

I start to run toward him as I take two steps at a time, ignoring Maggie's protective presence a few steps behind me.

Everyone's eyes are on me.

"Though no direct evidence for wormholes has been observed, this could be because they are disguised as black holes . . ." The speaker's voice slows down as he reacts to my presence. I stand in front of the stage and stare at my grandfather. There are murmurs in the room as it becomes quiet with the anticipation of waiting to see what is going to happen.

I face him and finally find words. "Why . . . *why* didn't you tell me?" My voice is filled with anguish.

He looks straight ahead. He has not acknowledged that I am standing in the aisle in front of hundreds of people directing my question to him. This is so completely out of character that even I can't believe what I am doing.

"Answer me, tell me why?" My voice is loud, breaking with the pain I feel, the years of confusion and loneliness. The many nights I had spent lying in bed, wondering why I was different, why I had lost my parents, and the terrible guilt that I should have saved them. How much I still needed and missed my grandmother, the one person who seemed to have the answers.

Two large security officers push down the stairs toward me very quickly just as I feel Maggie's strong arms grip my waist. They shove her aside easily.

"Come on, let's go, kid." Their hands are on me.

I struggle to release myself from their hold that crushes through the bandage of my injured arm.

"Get your hands off of her!" Maggie tries to push them away.

I bend over to absorb the shock of pain and catch my breath. I need to determine my options and act quickly. When I straighten up, I see my grandfather's face.

"Leave her." The authority in his voice makes them release their grip on me instantly. "She's my granddaughter, it's quite all right. Come on, Gabriella, let's go." His face is sad as he looks at me.

"I'm sorry to do this but I *need* to talk to you."

The room is silent. With everyone's eyes on us, we turn and walk up the steps and out of the auditorium.

We emerge from the building, and I inhale the cold air as I try to fill my lungs. I need to feel the life in me, to help gather the courage for whatever is going to happen next. I look at my grandfather. He seems broken—lost, much smaller than I remember. I feel shattered that I am responsible for his pain, that I am putting my own needs in front of his, but I can't stop now. I need to understand. No matter how.

I walk over to him and hand him the photograph from 1943 of Einstein, him, my grandmother, her parents, and Benjamin. He looks down at it.

"Where, where did you get this?" he says, and I know he is furious.

"Maggie?" He turns and looks angrily into her face. "What is this about?"

"It happened, Dr. Vogel, just as Sophie warned me, so many years ago. It was as she told me. He saved her. Gabriella would have *drowned*."

We stand in the great open plaza with the Charles River and the lights of the city behind us.

"What do you mean?" His voice gets louder.

"Gabriella came from New York, and I didn't know. Nobody knew." She twists her hands, covers her heart, tries to explain, to make him understand and see. The inevitable.

"What are you saying? Maggie!"

"And then, Gabriella, she, she went for a swim, *just* as Sophie had warned me. She knew."

He holds the picture I have given him and his hands shake. He stares at it with rage. "Look at this, do you see this, Gabriella? Look at how I've aged—and your grandmother." He points at her beautiful smiling face. "She's *dead!* Gone. She left me."

I stand and look right at him. I look into his face. I know he needs to say these things and I feel each word pierce my heart as I try to absorb the years of frustration and pain.

"Papa, please."

"And look at *him*." He points to Benjamin. "It's been over sixty years—*sixty years!* He hasn't changed at all."

"I don't understand," I whisper as I back away and shake my head. I am afraid of what he will say next as I know he is about to explain this to me.

"He remains subject to the laws of his world as long as he only stays for short periods of time. No one from that world has ever stayed here and *no one* from our world can go there. Your grandmother died trying to go through."

"She knew she was going to die anyway. She knew."

He lets out an anguished cry, and I think that my heart will break from the sound and everything it means. But I can't stop. I'm riding into the momentum that I need to carry me to Benjamin.

"No, Gabriella!"

"I'm going to make it work," I say flatly.

"This will not happen, Sophie did not understand. The consequences." He turns around and faces me, his face distorted with fear and pain. "Gabriella, he will *not* take you too. It cannot happen!"

And then, I remember everything my grandmother had told me. What she made me promise her. That I would choose for myself. That I should trust my heart, what I believed, and that I would *know* when I had found what I was looking for. That's what she said. That I would know.

I turn to my grandfather and say the words I never thought I would feel with the conviction that I did. "Papa, I can choose for myself. I will choose and—I choose him. He is what I want, it's meant to be. I know it."

"No one from that world has ever stayed here, Gabriella. It goes against all the laws of our universe. It cannot happen. I will not have you give up your life." He looks out into the night. "Like she did."

I wait, then slowly take a step toward him and reach out for his hand and say, "She tried to go with him, so she could *live.*"

"It's my fault, all of this. And your parents, that bomb was meant to kill me." He is sobbing softly. "And my beautiful, beloved Sophie—it should have been me. She thought it would work. I should have known, I should have seen her pain. I should have been there to help her."

"She knew what was going to happen. She knew her future, she could see it. Like I can," I say very softly.

"No one knows the future, Gabriella!" His voice thunders across the open plaza. "*No one!*"

I stand there for what seems like an eternity. I look down at the ground as the echo of his words dissipates through the open space. And then, I fight back. I reach into the crush of emotion that has remained behind the dark wall I built in my heart and I find the light. This is a chance I know I need to take, there is no choice. I wait until the silence has settled all around us.

"I can see something, and Benjamin is there. I just know and I need to try, to trust this." I point to my heart as I feel the tears rolling down my cheeks.

"Gabriella." His voice is broken as he says my name and steps toward me.

"Papa, she's here with me and she's with you, too. I can feel her inside. She told me to make my own choices, to trust my heart and I do. Please understand."

He looks at me with eyes that have seen so much, more than I could ever know.

"It's been so many years." He takes my face in his hands. I feel that he wants to make sure I really understand. "And I'm so tired, Gabriella, of the fight and all the doubt."

Maggie walks over to him and puts her hands on his arm as she nods to him in encouragement. "Let her go."

"Gabriella," my grandfather says with resignation. "We took our chances, we had our dream. It's time for you to live yours."

44

I SINK BACK INTO my seat on the train. I want to take this time to balance out the stunning revelations of the last two days. The rocking motion is a welcome predictability in the route I have traveled so many times between Boston and New York City. I keep replaying in my mind everything that happened. The terrifying pull of the sea, what I had learned from Maggie, my grandfather, and, of course, Benjamin. Everything they had said and what they had not. There was also the recognition that I was not alone, my grandfather's confirmation had finally acknowledged what had haunted me my entire life. The visions and dreams I couldn't understand and why my grandmother never came back. The pieces were coming together, and Benjamin was at the center of it all.

I couldn't help myself from feeling, *knowing,* that I was on the edge, the threshold of the beginning of everything in my life. What I had wished for and what had always been beyond my reach. There is also the undeniable sense of dread that I keep trying to push away about my grandfather and our trip. Maybe time with Benjamin will help clarify the many questions I still had and give us time to foster a more conventional progression of our relationship.

Fat chance. *Nothing* about this was conventional.

As sleep finds me, I feel myself clinging to my grandmother's words and Maggie's assurances. The feeling I have deep in my heart that meeting Benjamin is my destiny.

"Good morning, beautiful."

It's Philip.

It feels good to be back in the architecture studio in Avery Hall, safe at my desk, in a world I feel that I have a little bit of control over.

"Heyyy." I try to sound enthusiastic, overriding the exhaustion I feel.

"I got you coffee. You look like you could use one." He notices my eyes, my bandaged arm. "Or something stronger?" He laughs at his own humor and then becomes more serious. "Are you okay?"

"Thanks, it's a little early for the other, but I'll take the coffee." I ignore the question and the concerned look on his face.

"Did you go away for the weekend?" He has his foot on my suitcase thrown on the floor next to the desk.

"Yes, I went home."

He raises one eyebrow, and a devilish grin forms on his face. I can almost see the thoughts formulating in his mind. I know he is trying to engage me in conversation, to figure out what is bothering me.

"A wild weekend I see." He gently strokes the sling that holds my injured arm immobile next to my body. "Are you keeping someone a secret from us, love? That might explain your unwillingness to *socialize* with your close friends?"

If he only knew the secrets I had.

"No. Just visiting my grandfather."

I thought I would leave out the other information such as the almost drowning part, that my family were mystics, and my grandfather was on the verge of proving Einstein's theory that tunnels existed, connecting our universe to other worlds. Oh, and that I thought I had met my soul mate from another world who lived in the most mind-blowing loft in the middle of New York City.

"How is my good friend, the mad, lovable scientist Dokteurrr Vogel?" He says the word doctor with a German accent as he raises his fingers in front of his face. "Let me see if I remember what Ms. Mary Shelley wrote in *Frankenstein*. 'The world was to him a secret which he desired to divine. Curiosity, earnest research to learn the hidden laws of nature, gladness akin to rapture...' Gabriella?"

"Something like that." I laugh at the absurdity of the inference, yet realize that I have always loved those words from the novel. "Well, you got something out of that fancy boarding school you went to. A few memorized lines from classic British literature."

"Quite right, darling."

I turn away and look out the windows.

"Helloooo?" He waves his hand up and down in front of my face. "Anyone home? What's up with you?"

I want to tell him. I want to tell him everything. I need someone to assure me that I am not insane, that my world still has pieces in it that are real, predictable, *normal.*

"Hey, kid." He puts his hand on my shoulder as he looks down at everything on my desk. "How is your project coming?"

I stare at the papers and wood models, layers of computer generated drawings, charcoal sketches, and other works in progress that cover the surface of my desk completely. I see the books and papers that are piled high and squint my eyes to focus on the calendar pinned to the back of my bulletin board. Checking again how many days we have left to complete the semester, numbering the hours before the final critique.

"Fair actually, I'm not sure how I'm going to pull the whole thing together before the end of the semester. I have so much to do."

"You'll be fine. You always are."

"I don't know, Philip. It's been hard for me to concentrate."

He tilts his head. "Maybe what you need is a home-cooked meal. Why don't you come over later. I'll take care of you." He winks. "Given your injury?"

"No, I—"

"Wait, don't tell me." He puts his hand up in front of me in the stop position. "You can't, you have something to do. Let's see, meeting with someone who is about to change the world." He folds his arms in playful resignation.

"Now that's not fair, Philip, eating is low priority," I lie. I can't believe I'm rejecting his tempting offer of a home-cooked meal. "I'll probably just stay here at my desk. There's so much to do to get ready for the final critique."

"Right the *critttttt,* how could I forget?" He nods his head and looks up at the ceiling, tapping his finger on his temple. Remembering back to that day a few weeks before. His ever present sarcasm as he emphasizes and draws out the word *crit.*

He isn't finished. I wait and cross my legs in mock impatience as I tap my foot in the air.

"Go on." I brace myself for more teasing.

"Well, Miss Vogel, the pursuant of the joint degree in painting *and* architecture person. What was it that mystery critic said about you? The physicist I believe it was."

I feel every muscle in my body tighten and my teeth clench together as I try to look at him with nonchalance. I don't want to reveal any reaction at all. What I am really feeling at the mere mention of Benjamin. But he isn't finished.

"Oh, yes, something about your inner creativity. Looking for a *new way* of saying things—or something along those lines." He waves his hand in the air. "Quite the compliment, Gabriella."

The memory of that day washes over me as if it had just happened. "Philip—"

"Yeah, man, he really thought your project was—"

"STOP it!" I yell and hunch over the desk as I try to retreat into myself.

"Gabriella." His voice is soft with concern. "It's *him* isn't it? There's something about him and you? Your grandfather?"

I turn to face him. "Yes."

"What is it?"

"They've been working together."

"And? I know you, there's something else. You can talk to me, Gabriella, please, you can trust me."

"He's found it, Philip." I say it with no emotion. I am numb. "He's going to reveal his proof at the World Conference in a few weeks."

He stares at me dumbfounded, then says, "This is it. Everything is going to change."

"For all of us, for our world."

"I'm calling Emily." Philip picks up his phone. "You need us now. It's time for you to tell us. Everything."

We sit together in a corner booth at our favorite diner on Broadway. It's the first time that I can remember Emily not saying a word. She just sits and listens to what I am saying, shaking her head, tears in her eyes. They are both shocked by everything I am telling them. The truth about who Benjamin is, my grandfather's stunning proof, and what really happened to my grandmother in Switzerland.

Philip slams his hand on the table and everyone in the diner turns to look at us. "I knew it, I *knew* he could do it. This is amazing, historic, it's going to change everything."

Emily reaches across the table and squeezes my hand. "Gabriella." She has finally found her voice. "You need to go find him."

"Oh, Emily, I think he's away. But I don't know."

"This is the most amazing, crazy, romantic thing I've ever heard. It's like a fairy tale."

"Emily is right. You've got to go. Now!"

And in their eyes I recognize for the very first time what these two people are to me. That they have really always been there, to support and love me.

"You're right." I feel my heart accelerating at the thought of what I am about to do. "Thank you, both."

I get up from the table and—I *run*.

45

I WILL GO DOWN to Benjamin's loft. To find him, to tell him, to thank him for saving my life. For saving *me*. The last few days, everything I did, everywhere I went, conjured up images of him and everything I loved about him: the cathedral, the architecture critique, and the way his face had looked at my drawings pinned up on the wall. Then, the night he saved me on the beach, the amazing things I had seen before the pull of the water and everything he had said. This was new territory that I found myself in.

I couldn't believe the absurd, crazy changes that had come over me in the last few months. Within minutes, I am on the subway hurtling through the depths of the city. My preferred means of transportation, I need *speed* to get to him. I cannot be delayed by traffic or other impediments. I feel that I am holding on for dear life, to the safety bar on the rocking subway and to my resolve—that I would never permit myself to feel this way about anyone. To open my heart completely to another.

It is all being discarded.

I can't wait to see him, touch him, and wrap my arms around him. I need to prove to myself that he is *real*, that I haven't simply imagined it all. So much of my life has been lived in the safety of my imagination. Now I question whether I can trust even that.

The screeching wheels of the train brake as we arrive in the midtown station where I will emerge, closer to him. I stand close to the doors and wait for them to open so that I can rush out. My foot touches the platform and I break into a run, bounding up the steps two at a time while I sidestep other passengers.

"Excuse me, sorry."

I force my way through the crowd and out into the night air. Rain hits my face and again I realize how unprepared I am for everything. I have no umbrella to protect myself, not even one of the many Red Sox caps I was known to wear, inviting comment in this city of Yankees. The long avenue seems endless, and I run as fast as I can and turn down his street. I arrive at the door, its simplicity belying the world that I know exists beyond. The last time I was here had been burned permanently into my memory.

Changing my life.

I ring the bell once and then again as I feel myself being pulled forward by exhilaration and hope. I knock, praying he will open the door. Finally, I hear a clicking noise and a buzz. The small camera positioned above the door frame turns slowly and focuses on my face. The lens opens and snaps shut, and I hear the loud release of the door as it disengages from its lock. It swings open slowly, and I walk into the elegant vestibule and stand alone in its silent emptiness.

"Benjamin?" My voice is urgent, I don't understand why he hasn't answered himself. "Are you here?"

Everything seems different, empty and dark. It is all so quiet, so still. The warmth and magic that had pervaded the space the last time I was here with him is gone. I feel a panic that I try to suppress.

"Miss Vogel."

It's a soft male voice. He says my name as if he has known me my whole life. I spin around as I try to regain the sense of balance I seem to be without when I am here. Standing in front of me is a slight, middle-aged man, dressed in black. Some sort of a uniform. I had definitely not seen him the last time I was here. I know this because I had replayed every detail of that night in my mind hundreds of times.

"It is wonderful to have you here, again," he says the words as if delivering a well-rehearsed message. "I work for Dr. Landsman, my name is Max."

"Nice to meet you, but—" I try to stay calm, polite. "Where is he?"

"Unfortunately, he is unavailable, he's on his way to Geneva."

"What? He's not here? I thought he was still in New York." I need to hold myself together. "Please, tell me how I can find him."

"He left here about an hour ago for the airport. He flies out later this evening."

I don't want to acknowledge what he has said. I need to push it away. "No, this can't be. I thought he wasn't leaving for a few more days, I thought—"

"He did leave a message to give to you. He said that there was a possibility you might come here tonight."

I listen carefully, silently questioning why he had not called me himself.

As if my mind is being read he continues, "Miss Vogel, I know that he was planning on calling you from the airport. Dr. Landsman received an important message from CERN and left immediately."

Right away I understood where he was going. It was where my grandfather had been spending so much of his time over the last few years. The European Organization for Nuclear Research, CERN.

"I *need* to see him and speak to him," I plead. "Please, tell me where he is, I will go to Kennedy Airport now. You must have his flight information?"

He looks at me, and I think I detect sympathy in his warm smile. I realize how ridiculous I look, dripping wet from running through the rain. Completely incongruous in the clean elegance of Benjamin's vestibule. I don't care. I have already crossed the line, broken all my rules and I know there is no turning back now. The momentary stillness between us is broken by a subtle buzzing. Max reaches into a small pocket in his shirt and pulls out a phone. With the subtlest of smiles he recognizes the phone number and holds the device to his ear. I turn around quickly to stare at the wall as I attempt to release some of the incredible frustration I feel. I need to stay calm, take advantage of the timely interruption to think, while I consider the few limited options I have.

Silence.

"I see," I finally hear him say.

"Yes, certainly, I will take care of it. Of course, Dr. Landsman. I will tell her."

I stop moving. "Was that *him?*" I know the answer.

"Miss Vogel, the car will take you to where he is."

"No! No, thank you, Max. I can take a cab, a taxi. To Kennedy."

He walks over to me. "Gabriella, he is at a private airfield outside of the city. You would not be admitted if you attempted to enter yourself. We will take you there."

It is not a request but, rather, a statement of fact. I realize what is happening. He puts his hand out to take mine and turns me back toward the entryway. I hear the now familiar click of the front door as it unlocks and swings open, and see a black Range Rover pull up in front of the building. With relief and gratitude I turn to Max and throw my arms around him and hug his thin frame. I feel him stiffen slightly and realize he must be unaccustomed to this sort of display. More than anything else I could have possibly hoped for him to say, he looks at me and points toward the car.

"Gabriella, he will be waiting for you."

46

WE ARE TRAVELING quickly through the night, speeding along the West Side Highway and into the tunnel toward New Jersey.

I have never been to Teterboro Airport but know that my grandfather has often traveled from there on private jets by invitation from corporations, foreign governments, or other wealthy sponsors of his research. I recognize fully that he has become an international figure, and we are all trying to adjust to the overwhelming international media attention. At the same time as certain of his theories are ready to go public, I know he still has many secrets. He never went anywhere without his bodyguards and always seemed to be traveling to an undisclosed location, attending mysterious meetings in foreign countries. There were so many unexplained absences.

It was rare that I would allow myself to think about the terrible, dark ending in what was supposed to have been a beginning. When we all met in Paris. The celebration that never happened—to honor my grandfather's achievements. We had been detained by the French government and flown back to Israel for the funeral. There was endless questioning and a secret investigation. Philip had been with me through all of it, the bond we shared was wrapped inextricably in his accompanying me through those difficult years. I remember the morning he came silently into my dorm room at Oxford. He turned on the European news station to the account of the NATO forces bombings of several international nuclear reactors and accelerators. He wanted me to believe that this was part of the plan to put an end to the terrorist cell who had targeted my family.

"It's over, Gabriella," he had assured me, "just like they said it would be. You need to move forward now."

But I didn't believe it; I knew it wasn't over.

Everything was changing and there were so many things I could no longer count on. So much about my grandfather that I did not know and the many things about myself that I was discovering. There were very few things that I felt sure of at this moment. Except for one.

My world, my life without Benjamin in it, was no longer an option.

The car accelerates as we burst out of the dark tunnel, and I can see by the lit-up odometer that we are well over the speed limit.

"Are we almost there?" I don't know how long this is supposed to take.

"Yes, Miss Vogel." The driver looks at me in the rearview mirror.

"Please, *please*, hurry."

I try to compose myself, plan what I will say. I want to return to where we had left off on the dark beach and the unforgettable night when he pulled me out of the water. I see the flashing red lights of the airport in the distance and put my face close to the window. The car slows as the guard waves us in.

"Where are we going?"

The driver points toward a hangar, and we enter the structure through the giant doors. As the car pulls in and makes a large arc, I see the most magnificent Gulfstream jet shining in the bright overhead lights, a low roar coming from the engines. Our car comes to a complete stop in front of the plane. The jet's staircase lowers silently down to the ground, I push the handle on the door and practically fall out of the car.

I see him standing at the top of the stairs.

I start to walk and then break into a run until I reach the bottom of the steps and look up. He descends toward me, and I think that he is the most beautiful sight I have ever seen. I try desperately to keep my balance and wait until he stops, inches away from me.

I lift my hand to reach out and touch him as my fingers trace the lines of his face. I need to make sure that this is real, that he is not a dream. I try to steady my breathing, heavy from the run, the excitement, and everything I am feeling. With his intense eyes locked on mine, he reaches out and pulls me to him. And finally I am in his arms, kissing him everywhere.

My lips cover his eyes, his cheeks; my fingers are in his hair. I take in every piece of him, breathe him in like oxygen I have been deprived of. As my arms wrap tightly around his neck, he kisses me back with a force I have not felt before, finding his own answers in the moment. I don't stop until I need to tear myself away from him and succumb to the need to breathe. He turns my face up to his and looks into my eyes.

"Gabriella." The sound of his voice saying my name is like music to me. "There are things I cannot explain to you right now."

He seems to anticipate my questions.

"No!" I exclaim, "I need to know, I need to understand."

I let everything go. My words are filled with rage and frustration from years of mystery. The many frightening memories of abandonment and loss. He kisses me deeply and pulls me back to the moment. I realize that this is not about the past, or even the future. It is about the present. Mine. Ours.

"It is better this way."

"I heard you, everything you said on the beach. I remember, I remember all of it." I look right at him and feel the power in my words. "You said that you would never let me go again. Now I'm here, offering myself to you in every way I can. Please, *take* me."

What comes out of my mouth is emerging from my heart, everything I think and feel and believe since the first day we met.

"I couldn't let it happen." He looks so sad as he turns his head away slowly. "I couldn't survive losing you."

I know that this is the moment where everything will change as we determine the course our lives will take.

"You are the one, Benjamin. I know it now. We are meant to be together."

"I know," he says.

"I heard everything, *everything* you said. And Maggie, she told me about my grandmother and you. I saw the picture from 1943—with my grandparents in Jerusalem. And, I have this."

I hold up the amulet. He looks at it, then at me, and staggers back.

"I've loved it my whole life."

"Gabriella—"

"Benjamin, I don't understand any of it, why and where you come from. But I do know one thing. We are meant to be together." Tears stream down my face.

"There are infinite possibilities, infinite choices. I'm sorry, Gabriella."

"I've made my choice." I push away his words and interrupt him. "There is only one choice for me, and it is you." I look into his eyes, knowing that the direction of my life hangs in the balance.

His face is a mask of pain and sadness, but he says nothing.

"Benjamin, I'm coming with you. Nothing matters to me if we are not together."

I didn't know I possessed this reckless side. That I would be willing to walk onto this jet and fly away from everyone and everything—my carefully constructed life. He looks at me as if he is storing this moment away in his heart.

"Gabriella, you don't mean that. So many things matter." He seems to know my thoughts. "But I made a promise to your grandfather."

"You are what matters to me now." I pull him toward me.

"I'm so very sorry. I should never have let this happen. I couldn't help myself." He takes a deep breath. "I just couldn't stay away from you."

"We are supposed to be together. I know it, I want this. I want *you*."

He starts to back away from me. I see the frustration on his face, the sorrow that hangs in the space between us as he says, "We cannot live in the same world. It has never happened, it cannot work."

"What? No!" I yell.

"You don't understand."

I feel a power that I have never had before, a certainty that drives my actions and my words. I have no more fear. I am operating from my heart while trusting it to guide me through this moment. The next thing I say to him is everything I have felt since the truth was revealed to me at the beach. "Benjamin, I have already decided. I can't live in this world without you."

"Please, Gabriella!" He is shouting, frustrated. "Do not say that. You can and you will. You will have a long and wonderful life, right here."

I grip him tightly; my face is in the curve of his neck and my tears are on his skin.

"If I need to die to be with you forever, then I will. That is the choice I will make." I feel like I am going to stop breathing. That I can't take one more second of the uncertainty. "I'll do anything." My voice is a hush, a whisper, a statement of fact.

"Gabriella." He carefully disengages. "I must go now. I will see you in a few weeks and, I promise, you will understand. Everything."

"In a few weeks." I say it out loud and repeat his words, convincing myself. I calculate the distance between that moment and this one. I know I am running out of time with him again. I hear the engines of the jet begin to accelerate, warming up for the inevitable transcontinental flight that will take him away. "Please, tell me. Can we be together?"

We stand for what seems like an eternity, and then he pulls me into him. His lips are on my ear, and I hear him say, "We will find a way."

I breathe in the words from his heart. I am in the present but, amazingly, I can see the future I want, with him. He lifts his hand to the pilot, kisses me deeply, then turns to climb the stairs into the waiting jet.

"I'll be waiting for you," I say.

I'm in the car speeding back into the city and away from Benjamin. I think about everything that has just happened. I have that feeling once again of being on the threshold. Except that this time, I have crossed over. It has happened—everything is already different.

Especially the pieces of my life that I have cautiously relied upon as constants. My relationship with my grandparents, my friends, and even the consideration of my parents and the life they had chosen in pursuit of their work. Elements of my own character and my inability to find love.

Everything is shifting, even the most basic assumptions that I hold about the nature of the universe. It's as if I am really seeing everything I know so well, for the first time. Understanding something so familiar in a new way.

I realize that with the knowledge I have gained, everything in my own life has changed completely. I look out at the millions of lights in the architecture of the city and the stars in the night sky. As the car rockets into the tunnel, I know that this image has been one of the recurring dreams of my childhood.

"Here we are, Miss Vogel."

These are the first words the driver has spoken as we turn the corner onto my block. I was lost so completely in my own thoughts that I hadn't realized that he knew exactly where he was taking me, without asking. I blink my eyes and look out at my building, finding comfort in the familiarity of it all.

"Thank you."

I lift my bag over my shoulder. He opens the car door for me and lowers his head as I walk past him and slowly enter the building. As I stand at the elevator, I can feel his eyes on me, waiting, watching me from the car, ensuring my safe return home. This is a new feeling for me.

A messenger for Benjamin.

I slide the key into the door of my apartment quietly. Exhausted, I collapse on the bed and manage to strip off my clothes. My head sinks into the feathered pillow and I pull the covers up under my chin and stop momentarily to look out at the clear, dark sky. I fight to keep my eyes from closing. I don't want to separate yet from Benjamin and into the next day. The last thing I see before I fall into sleep are the sparkling dots of light that form the familiar pattern of the constellations in the dark black canvas outside my window. Stars, planets, and airplanes moving in the sky.

I think about the one carrying Benjamin away from me. Across the Atlantic.

47

" I T'S SO GOOD TO SEE you, Gabriella," Wallace Gray says as he opens the door to his office.

A welcome change from the pressures of the architecture studio, this is the closest thing I have to my grandfather in New York. Not knowing how else to survive, I try to live in the familiarity of routine. Finding any way to manage my overwhelming desire to be with Benjamin, I push myself forward through the days of the semester to reach the end. I try to concentrate on the significant task of completing the rigorous requirements of school with the prospect of our trip to the World Conference and what it represents right below the center of my consciousness. Things are off balance, but it's a feeling I'm accustomed to.

The weight of history and experience permeates the office. There is an intimacy to the furniture, the walls lined with books, framed art, and articles from his years of teaching and correspondence with students. Signs of gratitude and accomplishment, honoring the past and believing in the future. Everything about being here is a connection to my grandfather: the lack of compromise, the intense quality of exploration, and the desire to shed light on the darkest parts of our world, be it the cosmos or the secrets of the human heart and mind.

Hamilton Hall has been in use for over one hundred years, witness to the turbulent student protests of Vietnam and the Civil Rights Movement. The same wooden desks are here, sat in by those who have passed through these rooms, retaining the vibrations of questioning and intellectual challenge. It was as if the walls had absorbed the potential, the atomic energy that waited to be released by the interaction of professor and student and the workings of their imaginations. Just like the architecture studios.

We are quiet, and I look down at the treasured book in my hands: *Four Quartets*. The same one that had fallen out of my bag in the cathedral. I could relive the moment Benjamin had handed it back to me as he watched me in the most arresting, unforgettable way.

"You're here, Gabriella. Quite amazing isn't it, how time plays with us?"

I notice that it has started to rain and lighting flashes outside his windows. The trees sway violently and mark the empty spaces between our words. He looks down at my small book, recognizing this older out-of-print edition and reaches for it.

"May I?" he asks, looking at me with a certain sadness in his gray eyes.

"Of course."

"You know, Gabriella, I almost thought you had changed your mind about joining us this semester. Students taking my class know about the tradition of the first lecture. I looked for you. Since you were absent, I thought you were not coming."

The memory of the day in Hamilton Hall and what had occurred comes flooding back to me, and I am almost knocked over by the force of it. The first time I met Benjamin and the fateful error in my schedule.

"I had been on my way. I was *intending* to be there, of course, and something very unexpected occurred. I'm so sorry. I still don't know how it happened."

He looks at me and raises his eyebrows as if he wants to respond, but instead, changes the subject. "There are many ideas that we explore, ones that might be helpful to you, Gabriella, in your *other* work. In your life. Your grandparents and I had many debates about this."

His words cling to me, the distant memories they evoke. Their weight anchoring me into the space across from him as the relevance of his teaching to my work and personal life is mentioned.

"I am familiar with the authors we are studying, especially T.S.

242

Eliot. My grandmother loved his poems. She said she could find so much in his words."

"And you? What is it that you are looking for?"

I think for a moment. "Answers?" I continue slowly, taking a deep breath to try to calm my nerves. "The truth, in painting or architecture." I shrug my shoulders. "I really don't know."

"Or a scientific proof as your grandfather might say?"

"I have so many doubts now. Things are becoming *less* clear to me, more confusing."

"Think about T.S. Eliot, Gabriella. He celebrates the courage of which the human spirit is capable. I know you understand; I can see it in you. Courage, then clarity."

I sit in silence and look deeply into the eyes of Professor Gray, feeling the energy of the space we occupy. The years of student's questions that have been investigated right here. The ideas that float like thick clouds in the room. I feel his passion, his desire to address fundamental questions, a force that has driven me to him now. I think about what he said, "Courage then clarity." The words remind me of my family.

"Have you talked to my grandfather lately? I mean, I know you speak to him regularly." This is the reason I've come to his office, to find out what, if anything, he knows.

"Yes, of course, why?"

"I'm worried about him."

He pauses and frowns as he creates a single line of his brows. He chooses his words very carefully. "He is looking forward to the trip with you and the conference, Gabriella. I talked to him about it the other day. He called me from China. You know, he's been waiting a long time for this moment."

I try to convince myself that this is all it is—excitement and anticipation. Presenting his life's work.

"I was just wondering whether he expressed any concerns to you at all. About his safety that is."

He squints his eyes to help them focus and pushes a cup of tea across his old wooden desk toward me. "Your grandfather has taught many people to believe in the pursuit of their deepest dreams. He himself has done it while maintaining a steadfast adherence to his convictions."

"He's taught me that as well."

"It takes great courage, to really look within."

"That's what he's doing."

"And this is what he wants for you."

"Yes," I hear myself say, "I understand."

"The search," he continues. "He is searching for the things that are timeless. Just like you. Remember when we discussed this in class?"

Of course I remembered.

I know that he is referring not only to this conversation, but to a fundamental belief at the heart of his teaching. His own original interpretation of the texts we study line by line. The same way my ancestors studied the Old Testament, analyzing every word while searching for the secrets they held, looking for something new.

"Take *Four Quartets,* Gabriella. The poem is about doubt and resolution. The union of time and the stillness of what is eternal."

Both of my hands rest on top of my legs; my eyes are down. I am afraid to meet his gaze. "What is eternal?"

"Your grandfather's journey."

"He has already accomplished so much and inspired so many."

"Your grandfather is an explorer. This is how T.S. Eliot would have described him. I've told him this many times."

I listen intently and imagine the years of dialogue between these two friends. The scientist and the artist. Slowly, he leans forward, pushes off the arms of his chair, and stands up.

"There *is* something I just remembered."

At the rear wall of his office is a low cabinet that contains many well-used books kept safe behind locked glass doors. He reaches into one of the drawers in his desk and takes out a long brass key and slides it effortlessly into the lock on the cabinet. The latch releases and the door swings open.

"Where is that book?" he asks himself and bends over with effort as his eyes scan the shelves.

These are clearly his special treasures, kept separate from the hundreds of other manuscripts. Safe for private perusal and guarded under lock and key. He continues to talk to himself, muttering, clearly trying to locate something not looked for in a long time. Something remembered.

"Here it is. I've been wanting to pull this out for some time, and now here you sit calling it forth." He looks at me over the top if his glasses. "Incredible."

He hands me a copy of what I recognize clearly as the same slender version of *Four Quartets* that my grandmother had given me, but this text is bound in a leather embossed binding. An original edition.

"It's the same as mine."

"Go on, read," he instructs me. "The pages that are marked."

I open it and see why he wanted me to find these particular passages. They were her favorite parts, the words of the poem my grandmother had often spoken.

We shall not cease from exploration
And the end of all our exploring
Will be to arrive where we started
And know the place for the first time.

Not farewell but fare forward
Voyagers.

I want to understand why these words encourage and yet terrify me at the same time. Why they feel so very personal.

"Endings and beginnings, the nature of time." Concepts that speak directly to me.

"One of his favorites."

"My grandfather?"

"He loves to talk about it. Always looking for new meanings and interpretations in the words. Especially how the poem relates to his work. To what he believes."

"I never knew that about him."

"Now, look inside the front cover, Gabriella," he says deliberately.

I hold the fragile copy in my hands and open it to the first page and immediately recognize the handwriting. It belongs to someone I love deeply, the unmistakeable lettering that had penned so many notes to me, held safe in a small cherished box of my treasures. The handwriting belonged, of course, to my grandmother. As if the prophetic words predicted the moment that I would be in this room holding the book she had given him.

"Go ahead, read what she wrote."

To My Dear Friend Wallace,

May we always remember not to be burdened by the past, nor fear the future.

We have far to travel. Teach this well, to those I love.

SV, 1962

My eyes fill with tears, as if reading the words is like sitting in her presence, feeling her arms around me in encouragement. I look at Professor Gray, realizing that I understand for the first time, so many things I've been told. What she always wanted me to believe. In what she had whispered to me over the years, the many silent messages of my heart. As recently as this day.

"My grandmother gave this to you?" I look carefully at the initials and the date. So long ago, before I was born. And now I am here with him, holding it. Once again the fateful intersections of my life.

"Your grandmother was a true artist, ahead of her time. She would have been very proud of the woman you've become." Then, as if he can hear my thoughts, the endless questions that still remain in my head, he puts his hand over mine in encouragement. "You will find what you're looking for."

"How will I know?"

"You will. The answers are inside of you. They reside within the spacious architecture of your mind. Fare forward, my voyager."

48

"GABRIELLA, THIS IS *ridiculous*. I haven't seen you at all." Emily, as always, is a force to be reckoned with. "And this time, I'm not taking no for an answer!"

There's no use trying to make excuses. I hold the phone several inches from my head to insulate my eardrum from her enthusiastic diatribe. I look out the large window next to my desk at the dark December sky. Another day has passed quickly, bringing me closer to the trip with my grandfather—and Benjamin. I know that everything in my life is about to change, and it is good to be absorbed in my work.

"Where are you right now? Are you still in Avery, in that architecture studio?" I can tell her eyes are rolling by the tone of her voice.

"Yes, Emily, of course I am. We all practically live here."

"Well, I'm coming to get you for dinner."

"The final review is just a few days away. No. But thank you."

"Please? I really miss you. Besides, we have a special surprise for you."

"*We?* Emily what are you talking about?"

"Meet me downstairs. I'll be right there."

The business school was right across the courtyard from Avery Hall, and I knew she was right. We had spent so little time together and with the semester ending and the holidays approaching, we needed to see each other. The marathon of deadlines were taking their toll on everyone and tensions were incredibly high. I was pushing forward, mechanically moving through the motions of my life. Concentrating on each day to not let the overwhelming anticipation stop me completely.

"Please, I really can't do this right now. Em?"

"Gabriella, Philip's coming too." Her voice seems serious. "This is important. Just for once, can you please go with it?"

"Okay, I'm sorry." I look at everything on my desk and then at my watch. "One hour—that's all I have, but I would love to see you. I'll meet you in the lobby in ten minutes."

I start to organize things on my desk. I know that she will want to talk about everything. My concerns about my grandfather and the development of my relationship with Benjamin. If that was what it was. I hope that by articulating my feelings they might become clearer in my own mind as well. Try to assign words to the many things I cannot define.

It is cold and raw outside, and I tuck my goose-down coat under my arm and pull on my hat. I run down the circular stone stairs that wrap around the elevator shaft two at a time. It seems ironic that the inventive design atmosphere that is encouraged at the school is contained within a building defined by its symmetric and classical proportions. The ultimate intersection of old and new. These iconic forms of architecture are clearly understood to express the early American formal values of order, what a historic university campus of importance should look like. However, I know that on the drafting tables and computer screens in the studios above, there is not a single student trying to emulate these classical forms. Nor would that have been encouraged. We were expected to read, absorb, and understand the past. Then reject it all.

As we try to invent the future.

With a blast of ice-cold air, the door opens, and I see Emily, smiling ear to ear as she strides confidently toward me through the lobby. She reaches out and holds me for a few moments. As always, she looks magnificent, dressed in a long belted black wool coat, and perfectly coordinated. Unlike me in my frayed jeans and mismatched outfit. We make quite the odd pair.

I hug her back so tightly I surprise even myself. "I'm so happy you're here."

248

"Let me see you." She takes a step back to look me over. She beams from the warm greeting I've given her while I stand still, eyes at the ceiling, like a child being inspected by a parent. "Actually, I thought you'd look worse—with the hours you claim to be keeping here." She grins as she throws her arm over my shoulder. "You're perfect, sweetie, you could wear a paper bag on your head and still look good. Actually, you're practically glowing."

I laugh, "Em, look at me!"

"It's *love,* Gabriella." She reaches out for me. "It's written all over your beautiful face."

I take her hand and hold it to my cheek as I turn my face away from hers, afraid of what she might see in my eyes.

I feel like time is accelerating, whether I am working, painting, or pushing into my future.

Despite what Einstein said, there does not seem to be any relativity in *my* experience. I am living in the forward unstoppable momentum of my life. Bringing reality closer to the reunion with Benjamin that I have hoped for.

The first semester of architecture school is almost over, and I can feel it ending on a high note. My project for the science institute had been noted as a courageous attempt at a new form of architectural composition. *Different* and *original* they had said. The pieces of my personal life helping to form a foundation on which the design stood. I still marveled at the irony of that first design challenge.

"Gabriella, are you okay, honey?"

"Yes, of course, why?"

"You're lost in thought again, but we're almost there."

Emily leads me down Broadway to one of our favorite local restaurants.

"Hey, girls." Philip runs up from behind and puts an arm around each of us. "Aren't I the lucky guy?"

I love his crooked grin and feel very fortunate to have both of them steering me out of the freezing night into the warmth of the café.

"Three of us." Emily takes charge and points the hostess to a round table by the windows. "That one please."

We sit down, and I look at Emily and Philip.

"I just want to tell you both, you really are the best friends anyone could ask for."

"We know." Emily's eyes are on the menu, but I see her smiling.

Philip looks right at me. "The semester is almost over, are you ready for your trip to the World Conference with your grandfather?"

"I don't know, Philip."

He knows so much, and I can see it reflected in his eyes: concern, excitement, the powerful history we have shared.

"I wish we could go with you," Emily says very seriously.

"I told you," Philip continues, "we will be here for you, no matter what happens. Remember?"

"Yes, I . . ." But, it's happening again, the familiar sensation. I reach for my temples.

"Gabriella, what's the matter?"

"I'm fine," I say slowly, trying to shake off the blurred vision.

"I know her, Philip," Emily says with maternal authority. "She's hungry." She flags down the waiter. "Excuse me? Can you please bring us three martinis—*dirty*—and hurry."

"What about some food." It's Philip's concerned voice. "Gabriella?"

But I am already very far away.

I'm on the top of a dark mountain in the desert. I can see it all; I can feel it. There is sadness here, mixed with a certain peace. An understanding that things are as they were always meant to be. I look up into the night and realize that I have never seen so many stars, so many beautiful lights in the sky. They are infinite. We stand together on top of the flat mountain, this sacred space where the spirits of so many wrap around us, calling to my grandfather. I know that it is happening as she said, my grandmother, in the words she had promised to me. That I would find what I was looking for and that I would *know*. I see her opening her arms for my grandfather, calling him to join her. And Benjamin is there too, he is with me. I feel his strong protective arms wrapped around me and—

"Gabriella?"

They both stare at me.

"Where *were* you honey?" Emily's face is serious. "Are you frightened?"

"No, I'm not afraid anymore. I could see it all but I don't know, if I can trust it."

"Like the night at the bar when you knew that girl was going to—die?" Philip is incredulous.

"Yes, but this was different. It was good. Beautiful." I catch my breath as I realize what I'm saying. "But *not* what I expected."

I decide to keep the details of what I have seen to myself, hoping that the vision of my grandfather saying good-bye to me is wrong.

"Gabriella has always been able to *see* things, Philip. Just like her grandmother."

His face betrays no emotion as he looks at me then downs half his drink. "Paris." Philip's word electrifies the energy between all of us.

"Yes." Emily's voice is soft, gentle, as if she knows this is a subject that needs to be addressed like an open wound. "And the accident with Lily."

"It's all starting to make sense to me now." I hear my own voice. "Everything." I look at my hands.

"You know." Emily reaches across the table. "I may not see it as you do, the future, Gabriella, but I do *remember*. I remember when we were little. The dreams that would wake you up, how much you taught me in our summers together, and so many other things." She lowers her voice. "Like after Lily's accident. It was as if you built a wall around your heart, but I understood why and I waited. When your parents died, I didn't know what would happen—how you would go on. I always believed that this day would come. When you would come out of that dark place into the light, when the wall around your heart would come down." She squeezes my hands together. "And it has."

"Yes."

"Even your grandmother. It's just as she told you isn't it, all of it?"

I realize that Emily was right about so many things. "Thank you, both." I can't think of anything else to say.

"Gabriella." Emily raises her glass to me and looks right into my eyes. "Have a wonderful trip. I know you'll find what you're looking for."

49

"**E**MILY!" PHILIP POINTS to his watch. "We need to go—now!"

"Oh crap, we're going to be late." She grabs my hand and pulls me out of the booth.

"Emily, what are you doing?"

We run out of the restaurant, the incongruous threesome, and back toward the campus. The trees that line College Walk are illuminated with small, white Christmas lights that punctuate the night, the magic brought on by the end of the semester, and the celebration of the season. The beginning in the ending.

"Where are we going?"

They lead me across College Walk toward Amsterdam Avenue, and I feel the magnetic pull of the cathedral in the distance. I have been avoiding this side of campus, choosing to take an alternate route other than the way I went home when Benjamin found me in the darkness of the cathedral. It is too painful to relive that night, when I heard him playing the piano solo. It's taking every ounce of energy I have to stay sane and focused on what I have to accomplish before the end of the semester. I cannot let myself think about any of it—the trip, the Conference, or the reunion that I hope will be.

As we turn toward the eastern edge of campus, the wind picks up and sends a shiver through my exhausted body. Emily is two steps ahead of us, walking quickly, and Philip pulls me forward with determination.

"Philip." I try to disengage my hand from his grip. "You know I don't like surprises. Tell me what is going on!"

"Please, Gabriella, honestly, no questions. We need to walk quickly," he says.

Emily's head is down, concentrating, but smiles as she says. "The things I do for you."

They both stop suddenly and look at each other. "I'll see you there—in a few minutes," Philip says to Emily.

"Go, hurry up!" Emily tells him.

"Philip? Where are you going. Em?"

She smiles affectionately at me and links her arm through mine. "It's okay, Gabriella, you're going to *love* this."

We are, in fact, walking toward the cathedral. Still on the west side of the street, I try to convince myself that we are going to continue by, but Emily looks both ways, and we cross the street and stop right at the bottom of the great steps.

"Emily, why are we stopping here?" I try to conceal the emotion in my voice, my hesitancy to move forward up the steps. This feeling, this place that I had spent so much time in as a child, now holds new meaning for me.

"Emily!" I realize with shock that we are ascending. "I can't go in there right now, please." There is panic in my voice.

"It's okay." She seems genuinely puzzled by my hesitancy to enter the cathedral but encourages me inside as she grabs the handle of the great bronze door with one arm. No small feat—they are eighteen feet high and weigh practically three tons. "Come in." She grins.

Our eyes meet as so much understanding passes between us. In this moment, I feel her love, the history we have shared, and even the promise of our future together. It is so clear. There is simply unconditional love as she delights in her role. Presenting the unexpected event that is about to be revealed to me.

I need to trust her.

We enter the core of the building. The lights are dimmed, but in the distance is a Steinway grand piano. It sits in the center of a circle of chairs that shine in the dim lights of the nave. This is not unusual I remind myself, but as we get closer, I turn and look at Emily as I start to ask a question.

She speaks first. "This is so exciting! Your grandfather knew that you would be completely engrossed at the studio, too busy to even notice that your birthday was coming up. Now you know how I hate to miss a party, so he called me." Her voice reveals the pride in the alliance they have formed for my benefit.

She sits down and pats the chair next to her. I look around at the empty seats under the great domed crossing of the church, and then I hear a familiar voice.

"Gabriella!"

I turn around and see Philip running toward us pushing Lily's wheelchair, both her hands waving as she calls out my name. I look over at Emily and see the tears in her eyes.

"We're all together, just like we said we would be."

I'm amazed that the long, awaited reunion we had hoped for is taking place now, in this place that held so much meaning. A place that contained the many pieces of my past—and my future.

"Hurry, everyone, here sit down." Emily orchestrates our seating arrangements. "They'll be right out."

"This is for you." Lily pulls a small envelope out of her purse that has my name on it. She gently places it into my hands. "Open it," she encourages me, her eyes shining as she leans over and gives me a hug. "Happy birthday, Gabriella."

I had completely forgotten that my birthday was a few days away.

"Twenty-four," Philip breathes the words. "Time for your life to really begin. I hope you're ready."

I open the card and read a printed sheet that outlines all the musical details of the piece we were about to hear. At the top it says,

> *Composed for Gabriella Vogel*
> *on the Occasion of her 24th birthday*
> *with love forever, Papa*

"Your grandfather wanted this special performance to be your birthday gift from him. He said you would understand everything when you heard the music." Lily's voice is low.

I study the information on the card, trying to understand the multitude of variables and moving parts required for this moment to take place. Then, I hear footsteps. Three people whom I have never seen before enter and take seats on the chairs awaiting them. One sits at the piano, the other two pick up the violin and viola. The pianist turns his head and nods in acknowledgement to us, their small mis-matched audience.

I sit between my two lifelong friends and hold onto them as Philip stands behind, his hands resting protectively on my shoulders. When the music begins, I immediately recognize the piece. It's the same composition I heard so many weeks before, the night I met Benjamin in this very place. The haunting melody that stayed with me.

We let the music wash over us, taking in the beauty of the sounds and the space. I think about everything that has brought me to this moment, the last time I heard these notes, the night I had stumbled on Benjamin composing and rehearsing, and the power of art and music to carry messages through time. I remember the conversation we had and the words Benjamin had said to me. "The soul of the artist . . . in his work."

The sound is all around. The music enters my heart, and I recognize everything Benjamin has shown me. The ability I have to feel things I never knew I was capable of. Short of being with him, this is the greatest birthday gift I could have received.

As we leave the cathedral together, Emily puts her arm around me. "He loves you *so* much."

I stop and look at her, not sure what she means.

"Your grandfather," Philip clarifies. "What an amazing gift—to have commissioned this work for you."

"Is that what he told you?" I ask, wondering exactly what, if anything, they have been told.

"Well, yes, he said the piece wasn't finished yet," Emily says with authority. "Still in rehearsals or something like that. But he needed our help to get you here tonight so that you would know that it was a gift—from him—for your birthday. He wanted you to have it now. He didn't want to wait until after your trip."

My eyes move from Emily to Lily, and I notice Lily nodding to me, encouraging me to accept what I am feeling. As if she knows. My head is full of the melody of the music that has been played in my honor as well as the thoughts generated by what has just taken place. There was still so much I did not understand, but, as disoriented as I seemed to be, there were several things I *did* know.

Emily and Philip knew nothing about the night I had first heard the music.

My grandfather did.

I had a terrifying premonition about why he wanted to present this gift to me before our trip together.

50

I HAD TERRIBLE CELL service in the studio but I could hear the panic in Maggie's voice message. She seemed frantic. I need to call her back, understand what is going on. I climb the stairs to the roof of Avery Hall to find a quiet place to sit and think. This is where students go to smoke, relax, and look out over the rooftops of the Upper West Side.

Or anything else they want privacy for.

I try to stay calm, assure myself that there must be a simple explanation for Maggie's urgency, and push away the feeling that something terrible has happened. I clear my mind and look out at the view. I see the Hudson River, and all the way down Broadway. It's raining lightly and the headlights of the cars create ribbons of color on the pavement as they move through the wet dusk. Another day has gone by, and I'm getting closer to the trip with my grandfather and—Benjamin. My cold fingers punch the number into the phone, and I'm immediately connected to her voice at the beach.

"Gabriella?"

"Yes, hi, Maggie, it's me."

"Of course it's you. Oh my goodness, Gabriella, how are you, baby? Are you all right?"

"Why wouldn't I be? I'm fine, would you please tell me what is going on?" I know everything about Maggie, every facial expression and intonation of her voice. She sounds terrified.

"I hate to bother you at school, I know you have your exams and everything." She stops.

"It's okay, what is it, Maggie?"

"I *need* you to come home. Before you leave for your trip, if possible. If you can find any way."

I hear the fear in her voice.

"Well, yes I . . . I'm not sure how I can get there before the end of the week, but I'll find a way to . . ."

It's freezing on the roof. I had rushed up without my jacket and I start to shake—not only from the temperature but from everything she is saying. And what she is leaving out.

"Gabriella, are you there? You know I wouldn't ask you if I didn't think," she breathes the words rapidly. "I mean if I didn't know that—"

"Know what, Maggie?"

"It was important. That you need to know."

"Maggie, please tell me what you're talking about. Where is Papa? Does he know about this?"

I feel two strong arms: Philip. And by the look on his face I know he has heard my side of the conversation.

"No! Gabriella, he doesn't know anything. Please, if you speak to him, don't say anything. I'm so sorry to have to call you about this." Maggie is practically sobbing.

"Listen to me, I'm going to get there as soon as I can. I just need to figure out how."

Philip turns me to face him. He understands what is going on. "I'll take you there, right after our exams. Then I can bring you back to Kennedy Airport."

I look at him and see the care in his eyes, the concern.

"Okay, Maggie." I nod to Philip. "We'll be there as soon as we can."

"Good, that's good. Just don't say anything about this to anyone. Especially your grandfather."

"I won't."

"Fine then. I'll be waiting for you."

51

"Y OU KNOW," I SAY, my head pressed flat against the seat as Philip
accelerates his car into the night, "there *is* a speed limit in this country."

The BMW is flying up Route 128 toward Gloucester. We have
made the trip in record time from New York—just over three hours.

"It's the middle of the night, Gabriella, even your cops are sleeping.
Close your eyes. We'll be there soon, love. You know how emotional Maggie is, always worrying about everything. I'm sure there's a simple explanation."

"I don't know; I hope you're right."

I look out the window at the moonlight on the thin layer of snow.
It is surreal—winter has turned the lush green world that I love into a frozen
landscape. Put it to sleep. It is so quiet and beautiful even without the ra-
diance of the sunlight. Maybe this trip was a good thing. A short break
from the city after the harrowing end of the semester and everything ahead.

"Gabriella?" He concentrates on the road and doesn't turn to look
at me. "Are you sleeping?"

"If I was, I'm not anymore."

"I was just thinking about something."

"What is it?"

"Benjamin."

"Yes, Benjamin." My eyes are closed as I smile and repeat his

261

name.

"If he really *travels* from another place, then there's a way he gets here and goes back, right?"

"Go on."

"And the laws of physics—if they are different there, you know, time and all that, then the theory says that he is subject to those laws right?"

"I suppose."

"I mean think about it. I know that the science talks about tunnels or black holes but what the hell does it all really mean? How does it really work?

"I have no idea, Philip." I open my eyes.

"I think I do. That's why he can't stay here, or why he can only stay for short periods of time. That's why he keeps disappearing!"

I look at him. "What?"

"That's it. The reason! He can only spend a certain amount of time here before he becomes subject to the laws of *our* universe. Maybe that's why he's two hundred years old and still looks so young."

"Philip, please."

"But, I wonder, Gabriella, why he's really here?"

I turn away from him, from the conversation, and from everything I have seen in the premonitions I've had about my grandfather. "I don't know."

"Well, we're going to find out aren't we?"

"Along with the rest of the world," I mutter under my breath.

"Did you ever consider that there may be more than one answer?"

"Philip, more than one answer?"

His hands are off the steering wheel, helping to make his point. "I mean, maybe it's a metaphor for something else, a bigger idea, more than simply a scientific explanation."

"Like?"

"Like your grandmother's book—on mysticism."

"What?"

"Think about the things in there, what they say about time."

The small book is in my bag next to my feet.

"I have it here," I say.

He smiles. "Of course you do."

I reach down and open the book and look for her notes. The paragraphs that have been underlined, circled. The many thoughts in the margins, things she wanted to remember and draw attention to.

"Turn the light on, Gabriella, and read it to me."

I take a deep breath.

Concerning the nature of time, Kabbalah finds evidence in the most recent scientific findings. Physicists tell us that time cannot be separated from space, nor space from time. The speed of a clock is faster when flying in one direction around the earth than it is when flying in the other. Time stands still at the edge of a black hole . . . it comes to a dead stop at the speed of light.

I look up at him. "It's everything Einstein said."

We both sit quietly as we absorb the words I have read.

"Gabriella."

"What is it?"

"I have to tell you something I've been thinking about. Something your grandfather told me when we were in Switzerland with him a few years ago."

"What did he say?"

"That he was going to choose *science,* not the mystical tradition you have inherited. What your parents had devoted their lives to."

His voice softens as he mentions my parents.

"I see."

"He said that the Kabbalists—they were always considered the scientists. And now he wants to find the scientific data to prove what he already knows, what he has always known is true!"

"He told you that?"

"Think about it. Even if Darwin is right and everything evolved randomly, and a series of insane chance events had to occur to allow everything to happen in the correct sequence so that cells could emerge from the primordial soup, then—"

"Philip, slow down."

"Then there was still that moment, Gabriella! The moment when the genetic code was created, the brilliance of each cell to understand that code. There is no way—no way all that happened by chance. Your grandfather knows it, Einstein knew it, and others, too."

I read the last sentence my grandmother wrote in the book I hold:

Science, in its quest to reveal the underlying unity within nature, constantly finds itself returning to the origins of the universe, to the beginning of time. Science and Kabbalah both seem to agree that the idea of time adhering to some vast, universal rhythm is a complete fallacy.

"Einstein again, Gabriella."

As I finish reading the words, I realize that we have arrived at the house. The car turns down the long driveway toward the sea. I am overwhelmed by what I have just read. The description of what I know and what I have experienced.

"Stop, please. I need to get out!"

I burst out of the car and welcome the shock of cold on my skin. I pull the air into my lungs as if I had just emerged from the depths of the sea. I need to get away from the words, away from what I know to be true. That my parents and my grandmother are all still very much with me, close, watching and communicating and sending messages from another place and time. Confirming that my life was beginning to unfold in the way it was always meant to. The force and power of what I thought were random events suddenly make sense. And they all connect back to Benjamin.

"The beginning is the end and the end is the beginning," I whisper under my breath.

"What did you say?"

"It's *Four Quartets*, the poem." My words are barely audible.

"There it is again. The idea, I mean, about time."

"Philip, you remember that night at Columbia, when my grandfather spoke? When you saw us on the terrace of the restaurant?"

"I will never forget that night, you and your grandfather arguing. The way you stormed down the stairs."

"It was one of the worst nights of my life. Except for one thing. I was talking to a colleague of my grandfather's. A brilliant woman I've known for many years."

"Dr. Potter. I know who she is, Gabriella."

"She said something to me then that I couldn't understand. Not until now, that is."

He leads me toward the house, out of the rain, and onto the porch. As we sit quietly for a few minutes in the rocking chairs that overlook the sea, the motion of the drive from New York slips away and the stillness enters.

"Philip?"

He looks out at the twin lighthouses off the coast, beacons that guide so many out to sea and back home. "It's so beautiful here, Gabriella. Timeless."

"I asked Dr. Potter to explain certain things about my grandfather's research, about the different theories. What they mean and how it would work. The last thing she said to me was completely, well, unscientific."

"Unscientific?"

"She said that it all depends on what you *want* to believe and what you're looking for."

Philip leans his head back onto the weathered rocking chair and exhales slowly. He folds his arms across his chest and closes his eyes. "Exactly, Gabriella. That's what I mean. That's exactly what I mean."

52

"JESUS, MARY, AND JOSEPH!"

It's Maggie.

She lapses into her thick Gaelic accent at the shock of Philip and me sleeping in the living room. She runs over and throws her arms around me as she starts to kiss the top of my head.

"When did you get here? I thought I heard the alarm being turned off last night, but I can't believe this."

I'm stretched out on the sofa where I collapsed the night before and I try to lift my head off the pillow to look down at Philip. All you can see are his feet sticking out from the blanket. Teddy, my golden retriever, lies protectively across my body, and I can't move.

"Maggie," I groan, "what time is it?"

"Oh, I can't *believe* this whole thing. I mean, you said you were coming, but I didn't realize it would be in the middle of the night. I've been so exhausted lately, recovering from my jet lag and dealing with the house, your grandfather, and everything that is happening of course." She wrings her hands again, a sure sign that she's anxious about something. "You should have called, my pet."

"Please, slow down. I didn't want to wake you. It was so late."

"Gabriella." It's Philip's groggy voice, very low as he draws out my name in a yawn.

Teddy jumps up and starts to lick him, pulling the blanket away so he can reach Philip's face.

"Oh, Philip." Maggie notices him on the floor. "Hello, dear—nice to see you again." She is all business.

Philip grunts in response.

"I'm going to make breakfast," Maggie says.

This is not a question, whatever we would have said would have been irrelevant.

"Come on." I pull the blanket off of him and throw it over the back of the sofa. "Get up! We need to find out what's going on."

In the kitchen, Maggie moves quickly, and soon the breakfast table is filled with a feast of my favorite foods.

"Coffee." Philip points to the espresso maker, the only word he seems able to speak.

Maggie walks over to help us. "You look good, my pet." Her eyes scan me suspiciously. "Tired—but good." She shakes her head. "As I've always said. Archi*torture*." She seems relatively satisfied that I have survived three months in New York.

"You sounded so worried when you called." I reach across the table to her. "Please tell me what's going on?"

"It's the library, your grandfather's office."

"What do you mean?"

I need to see what Maggie is talking about, to confirm for myself the suspicion I feel that the preparations he's made for this trip are somehow very different. I'm no longer interested in the food and push away from the table to walk down the hall in the direction of the library. Philip and Maggie both jump up to follow me. Maggie talks nonstop, filling the tension with her nervous chatter. "It will be good to take a nice trip, spend some time there with him, I mean. Just the two of you."

"Uh huh."

"Really, sweetheart, I know how hard you've been working since you started school and everything else, I mean everything that's happened."

I look over at her and remember that she knows. *Everything.*

"Yes."

I take long purposeful strides, and she takes two steps for every one of mine. Philip tries to keep up but he can't seem to take his eyes off of the paintings that I walk quickly by without a second glance. His eyes are practically popping out of his head at the changes in my grandparent's art collection.

"Your grandfather." Maggie tries to catch her breath and keep pace with me down the long skylit gallery. "He is really looking forward to this trip with you." She pulls her sweater over her shoulders as she shakes off a chill. "But I have to tell you, he was meticulous about preparing everything before he left."

I stop suddenly. "What do you mean?"

"It's probably nothing, honey, but he spent hours organizing his files and papers. He went down to the bank several times and made sure everything was in order. I know he met with Mr. Sack, his attorney." She takes her handkerchief out of her pocket and dabs her eyes.

"And?"

"Well, it's just that he hasn't seen him in *years,* Gabriella. Why now?" She waves her hands in the air in front of her as if she is pushing away her thought. "He's usually quite organized when he goes away, but this time it feels different. I have never seen his library like this, I don't know what came over him, really."

I feel goosebumps on my skin. The information she has just shared with me shakes me to the core.

Philip puts his hand on my back. "Come on, Gabriella, let's see what Maggie's talking about."

We continue to his library and turn the corner. I stand in the doorway and cannot move. I understand immediately what Maggie means.

The library has never looked like this. Empty—organized, with no trace of his recent presence. The usual disarray of papers, evidence of his rich mind pursuing many ideas at once, is absent. Instead, the desk is wiped clean, nothing but the gleam from the polished wood reflecting back the photograph of him with my grandmother. The books are all put carefully away on the shelves, filed in alphabetical order, the usual backlog of mail and personal items—missing.

"See what I mean, Gabriella?" she says.

"Where is everything? His papers, computers, all of his . . ." I can barely finish my sentence. "His *work?*" I turn to look at Maggie, then at

Philip, and wonder whether they can hear my pounding heart, sense my fear. "When, I mean, who did this?"

I am unable to believe that this is the work of my grandfather. I need information to try to understand the mystery of this completely un-characteristic behavior.

"Well," Maggie begins and tries to steady her voice. "I was away for a few days, you remember don't you? I went to visit my sister in Ireland. Anyway, he was here—in the house, he just insisted I go. I think he had a *visitor* then."

I feel all the blood rushing to my head as I sit down in his chair. "What?"

"I mean, it made me feel better to know that he wasn't alone. You know I hate to leave him when he's here in Gloucester, but I had no choice. Anyway, I came back, and he had already left for the Far East. I found everything in the house as it usually is—except for *this*." She is clearly frightened.

"Yes." I look around the room one more time then back into her eyes. "Now I understand."

In that moment, I realize that Maggie and I are two people who love Sydney Vogel very much, our futures, in different ways, inextricably linked to his.

53

THERE IS NOTHING else to say. Nothing to do at the beach house except worry and wonder what is going on. Why nothing about my life seems familiar anymore. So Philip and I head back to New York for my flight to Tel Aviv.

"Gabriella?" Philip's voice is concerned. "Maybe I should come with you. Your grandfather would like that I'm sure. Right?"

"That's ridiculous. Everything is fine; it's all going to be just fine."

I am going to make it that way. I need to see my grandfather, to reassure myself that he is well and to share the luxury of the many hours alone with him on the flight. This would be a rare opportunity to be uninterrupted—no appointments or cell phones. I couldn't wait to have him all to myself, there was so much we needed to talk about.

"Are you listening?"

"Yes, of course."

"When I fly home to London, I can easily continue on to Tel Aviv. I've talked to my parents about it, and they agree I should go with you. They also said your grandfather is everywhere." His voice drops down. "Front page news."

I feel sick.

"No, Philip, that's not necessary." I reach out for his hand. "But, I've been meaning to tell you something for a while. Everything you have done for me, Philip, it's all too much—more than I deserve. I'm going to be a better friend to you in the future. I promise."

"You are an amazing friend," Philip says.

"No, I'm not."

"You've given me so much, Gabriella, taught me."

"What could I possibly—"

"To really *see* people, and things, in a new way, the many possibilities. Things I could never have imagined."

"Really?"

"Yes, I thought I had it all figured out. That I had all the answers, but now I see how wrong I was."

"You do, you know so much. You are so good at everything—music, architecture."

"No, it's okay, Gabriella. I like it better this way."

"Like what better?"

"To live in a world of infinite possibilities, where anything can happen."

We cross over the bridge and turn toward Kennedy Airport. I see the skyline of New York City in the distance.

"*Anything,*" I whisper as I look out the window of his car.

"That's right."

"So exactly what is it that I've taught you, Philip?"

"Something really simple. It's not always about what's in your mind—what really matters is what's in your heart."

Kennedy Airport. Where one can board an aircraft, sleep, endure the passage of time, and then emerge in another world. Looking around at the variety of passengers, I wonder where people are going, what significance this travel represents to them, and how it might change their lives. Coming here reminded me of the many trips I had made with my parents, flying across the world and into the past.

"There's the TWA Terminal. That Saarinen." Philip whistles. "Now there's an architect with a vision of the future."

His car speeds quickly through the airport and comes to a stop in front of the iconic building.

"You're in the middle of the road, pull over!" I say.

"Just look at that building."

"I know, it's amazing."

"He makes concrete look like wings of a bird in flight." Clearly in awe, he continues, "When he designed this, it was the height of the International Style, but he didn't care. He completely bucked the system—went against all the purists to create a building that expressed new ideas. Optimism."

"I know, architecture with something to say."

"He wasn't trying to fit into the status quo. He used his knowledge of technology to create something new and here it stands. Still."

"Science and art," I say very quietly.

"That's right. Just what I told you, Gabriella, exactly what you're doing." He shifts the car into gear and accelerates away as I look back out the window at the beautiful building. "Let's get you to your grandfather."

54

WE HAD PLANNED TO meet in the business class lounge of EL AL, the Israeli airlines. It seems to be taking longer than usual to pass through the rigorous checks, and I feel as if I'm going to jump out of my skin.

"What's going on here?" I ask the young Israeli security officer who carefully looks through my suitcases.

"I'm the one supposed to be asking the questions," she answers as she eyes me carefully.

"I mean, I haven't traveled on EL AL in a while but it does seem like—" I look quickly around the terminal and see the unmistakeable uniform: sunglasses, blank expressions, young dark men blending into the background but carefully watching every passenger. It's dark outside, no need for sunglasses. "There's a lot more security. Everywhere."

She compares the name on my ticket and passport again, identifying me.

"Someone *important* on the flight tonight." She winks at me.

"Oh."

"Don't worry, we take good care of you. Our pilots are the best."

"I know they are."

"Go ahead, we are done here."

I am glad to complete the security check and find the lounge where I hope my grandfather will be waiting. I walk in and immediately feel better.

Recently renovated, the space reflects the sophistication of the international design community, furnished with icons of modern design, flat-screen televisions, and a large buffet of my favorite Israeli delicacies. I drop my backpack, computer case, and coat on the floor and walk over to the windows that face the runway. I see the blue-and-white 747 parked at the gate and the pilots in the cockpit going through their preflight preparations. To me, it is an amazing sight, all that it represents, the memories, and the many times I had flown on this airline. With my parents.

"Look at it." My father had pointed to the Star of David boldly emblazoned on the tail of the plane, the beautiful aircraft that would carry us across the globe. I stood on my tiptoes, my chin on the window ledge, my small form barely reaching the glass to look out.

"Never forget. *Never* forget what it means, Gabriella."

"I won't."

"That star is a *wish*—it's a promise to you."

"My wish is that we'll always be together."

But that's not what happened.

I remembered the flight that had carried my parents back to Israel after the explosion that had killed them in Paris. Their bodies stored below in the cargo hold while I sat with other passengers above them, clutching my grandmother's hand. So much death was woven into the thread of my own life and my history. I thought of the millions who had died to make the small country I was traveling to a reality, what must have seemed like a completely impossible dream. After thousands of years, we had a land to call our own.

I sit down in an Arne Jacobsen Egg Chair and spin slowly away from everyone in the room and close my eyes. I take the moment to consider everything that is ahead, the beautiful sacred land that I am traveling to that holds so much meaning for me. The irony of my grandfather's life-changing scientific findings being presented there.

"There's my girl."

I feel the chair being turned back to face the interior of the room. It's the voice I have waited to hear. He must have recognized the puddle of my belongings on the floor. I jump up and hug him tightly.

"Papa! It's so good to see you." I wrap my arms around his shoulders in a gesture reminiscent of when I was a child. "When did you get in?"

"My flight from California was early, and the traffic from New Jersey to Kennedy was lighter than I expected. So I've been here talking to my old friend Eyal. He is the head of security in New York now."

"Why?" I try to conceal the concern in my voice.

"Stop worrying. He promised that they will take special care of us on this flight."

"I'm not worried," I lie.

"Hmmm, I can see something in your eyes. What is it?"

"Everything just feels different this time. There is so much more security than I can ever remember. By the way where are your—*friends?*" I look around for his private security detail.

"I don't need them here."

"Still."

"Gabriella, I believe there may be some government representatives on board or other scientists heading to the conference."

"Like you?"

"I'm sure we'll recognize them." He winks at me.

I'm not satisfied. I want the nagging anxiety to go away. I want to believe him, the explanation of why there seems to be so much security present—more than usual. The distinctive appearance and unmistakeable shape of the machine gun outlined by their clothing. I look at him and take in every detail of his face. I search it for evidence of anything unusual and I know he can sense my apprehension.

"Come, sweetheart, let's board now and get settled."

"I'm ready."

We begin the procession down to the gate. He talks about the details of his meetings and lectures in China and the global excitement building in anticipation of the International Physics Conference.

"But mostly, I'm so happy you're with me." He takes my hand.

There are so many questions I have, but they can wait. As we approach the gate, I see the body of the large jet through the windows. We find our seats in the upper deck and settle in to prepare for the long crossing. I lean back into my seat and buckle the seat belt around me as I hear the engines warming. I try to relax, feeling safe next to him, in the cradle of the vehicle that will transport me to everything that waits at the other end. Known and not. I look down at our interlocked hands, their union clearly showing how time has affected him.

"Papa?" I remember something he had said.

I turn to him and see that his eyes are closed, but I believe he has not yet fallen asleep. There are so many things I want to discuss with him, so many questions I know he can help to answer—about myself, my parents, and, specifically, about Benjamin.

"Do you think it's the right time?"

"I don't know."

"Is the world really ready?" I had never asked him that.

"I'm not sure about the world, but *you* are. It's time."

"Yes, I am. I'm ready."

"You will see how everything is connected."

"I understand."

"Your grandmother told you, that you and she were different." His hand tightens on mine as he mentions her name.

"Papa, please, you don't have to—"

"I've spent my whole life looking for the connection. In our family's mystical background and the laws of science."

"And have you found it?"

"I needed to do these things. It was not a choice I made. It was to understand myself, to understand *her,* and find the missing link."

The one that somehow Benjamin was tied up in.

As the plane takes its place in line, the captain's voice comes through the speakers telling us to prepare for takeoff. And then, I remember—something he had said earlier that didn't make any sense.

"Papa, you said you came from New Jersey to meet me here, but you never travel through Newark airport."

He opens his eyes, looks at me, and leans his head back onto the leather headrest, a satisfied smile on his lips. As if he knows that the words he is about to say will reveal a multitude to me. "Not Newark, Gabriella. *Teterboro,* where the private planes are. I flew in with a colleague." He exhales and says the next words slowly but deliberately. "Someone you know quite well I believe."

55

WE ARE FLYING HIGH above the Atlantic Ocean, moving through time. Through *worlds*.

I feel the transformation taking place inside of me. The obligations and responsibilities of my life in New York have been a good distraction the last few weeks. The perfect excuse to avoid what I could no longer deny. In a few hours, we would be landing in Israel and, I prayed, finding out the answers I needed to know about Benjamin. One thing I know for certain, I will never forget everything that has happened—all the things that have brought me to this moment. I am carrying it with me. All that I have lived in this life, the knowledge that I am not alone, and especially that those who are no longer here, are with me.

Lighting my path.

I see the dim overhead light from the galley where the flight attendants are whispering to each other. They keep looking back toward our seats. I get up to stretch my legs and walk toward them as they immediately make themselves busy.

"Hello," I say.

"Everyone is sleeping, you are not tired?" She offers me a glass of water.

"Yes, I am but I can't sleep."

"Is it your first time going to our country?"

"No." I think back to my childhood when I spent most of the year in school in Israel with my parents—counting the days until the summers in Gloucester with my two friends. "I used to live there."

"Ah." She nods. "So you are going to see someone you love."

I look down at the floor. "Yes," I say quietly.

"Beautiful. Our country is a wonderful place—everyone can find what they are looking for. For thousands of years this is where people have ended their journeys." She looks at the other flight attendant then back at me. "You are traveling with him?" She points several rows down to my grandfather's sleeping face. "We know he is very important, to so many. We will take good care of both of you."

"Thank you." I turn around and return to my seat. Very cautiously, I raise the shade on the window. It was closed to keep out the morning light of the continent over which we are flying. The tops of the Swiss Alps emerge from the cloud cover, their majestic presence a reminder of Earth below. I remembered taking this trip as a child, and the wonder of seeing the world from this perspective, from high above. The land reduced to graphic shapes. How different things seem depending on your perspective and where you are in your life.

Relativity.

This time, this trip, *everything* is different.

The angle of the sun is low in the sky, and I know that we are approaching the exact day of the winter solstice. I remembered a discussion with my grandfather on the significance of our planet in its orbit.

"The concept of the solstice is embedded in ancient Greek celestial navigation," he had explained. "Throughout history, we have looked to the heavens to guide our journeys. We are all voyagers aren't we?"

I had agreed. And then I remembered, the kidnapping and executions at CERN, the bodies found at the Café Solstice. I try to push those thoughts away and think back instead to my visit with Wallace Gray. The small, fragile volume he had shown me in his office, given to him as a gift by my grandmother, filled with the prophetic words she had inscribed: "May we always remember not to be burdened by the past, nor fear the future. We have far to travel."

"Nor fear the future," I say softly, reminding myself. "We have far to travel."

"Gabriella, you *will* find your answers, simply trust your heart."
Wallace Gray had spoken her words.

I could see it in his eyes, I had felt my skin tingling, responding to
the layered sensation of memories in the room.

He could see my doubt but continued, "Yes, they reside deep within
the spacious architecture of your mind—fare forward, voyager."

I remembered. How those words encouraged my spirit. Now, I try
to absorb the enormity of everything that was happening. The voyage, the
crossing that I knew I was on.

I lean back into the seat and reach out for my grandfather's warm
hand. I close my eyes to rest and then, time slows down, I am somewhere
else. I know sleep has found me and that I am in a dream.

It is all so clear. I can see her, my grandmother. And the light—the
way it comes in from above. It is dark, it looks like a cave but it is filled
with a warm glow. She is so young, so incredibly beautiful and strong. She
is not afraid. She is talking, answering questions about herself, what she
wants and what she is looking for. I can see his face, the way he looks at
her. His beautiful, familiar face.

It is *him*.

Then everything changes. They are in a white stone house under
the stars. So many stars and candles—everywhere. People and music and
food and happiness. Celebrating. But she needs to get away, something is
drawing her into the garden. A beautiful garden, filled with roses and
trees—twisted, gnarled olive trees—as old as the oldest thing she could see
in the ancient city everywhere around her. She hears their voices, *his* and
Papa's. He is there too, only she doesn't know him yet. She hides in the
shadows—she isn't supposed to be there.

They are gone and it is quiet. She enters the dark house, and he
finds her. He hands her something small, round, and shiny. It is the amulet.
She holds it to her heart and keeps it with her, always. Until she dies. The
house overlooking Jerusalem, the dark garden that smells like rose oil, the
perfume she always wore, the trees that have seen so much. I see it all.

But there is more, much more. The sun is setting and the garden
has changed. It is a different season, a different *time*. There are people
everywhere, happy, celebrating, looking toward a wedding canopy covered

with roses from the garden. A white aisle, petals on the ground, music, and a face. The smiling face with beautiful green eyes that waits for the veil-covered bride as she walks toward him, and he raises his hand to—

"Gabriella?"

I wake suddenly to the clatter of dishes, the smell of coffee, and my grandfather's smile as he looks down at me.

"Good morning, sleepy head." The back of his hand touches my cheek. "You looked like you were having a wonderful dream, hmm?"

I straighten up in my seat, surprised, as well, that sleep had found me. "Where are we?" It feels as if I had just been looking out the window at the mountains moments before.

"I think we have less than two hours until we land, but if there weren't so many clouds we could probably see the islands of Greece."

I lean back in my seat to make a place for him as we both strain to look out the small window and down toward the surface of the earth. We take in the majestic sight. I know this is my chance. I need to talk to him and I don't know how to begin.

"I want to thank you."

"Yes? For what, my dear?"

"My birthday gift—that was very special. Incredible."

"I'm glad you liked it. He is *quite* the musician. Among other things."

"So much has happened in the last few months. I feel so disconnected from you."

He sighs deeply. "Nonsense."

"Every single thing in my life has changed. Even you."

"A lot has happened."

"I just want to understand."

"It's not so complicated, Gabriella. Quite simple, actually. It has always been a goal of mine to use science to find the answers. Maybe simply to confirm what I already knew in my heart was true."

"What do you mean, something you already knew, but why?"

"In a way, similar to what your parents were working to understand. Finding a synthesis of solutions."

I look at his profile, his bent shoulders. "My parents?"

"And then, of course, the greatest gift I could ever have hoped for. Something I could never have anticipated nor expected."

"A gift?"

His voice is very low. "Because I now understand, that I would have lost you too. That night on the beach."

I am incredulous. "Benjamin."

"Yes."

"He changed my fate."

"He changed *all* of our fates. Something he began so many years ago."

"How could it be that you knew him? That you were all together?"

But, my grandfather is not listening to my words; he is not answering my questions. Rather he is talking to himself, as if he needs to hear these things spoken aloud, to believe that they are true. "He has shown me many things and changed so much, especially in my work. But I now realize that I've arrived back to a concept I was taught when I was very young. I am back where I started. Where my parents and their parents were looking, and so many before them."

"I don't understand. Where you started?"

"And as you already know very well, I have found my answers."

"It's him isn't it?" I say it so softly that he does not hear me.

"The missing link in my work." He is not talking to me but says the words as if he still cannot believe it. "The missing piece has always been right in front of me. The tunnels." He has never been this explicit before.

"Benjamin."

"He is living proof that the passages do exist and have been used for thousands of years," he says it simply—as if this would not be history making, altering the way we see our universe forever. I can feel the weight of my body melting into the seat I'm sitting in, as if I am dissolving. Liquefying. I need to stay calm, the shocking reality of what he is confirming raises infinite questions.

"Papa," I say slowly, not sure what reaction I will receive. "I need to know. Can Benjamin and I be together?"

I feel a courage that I am living out the fate that has been written, the many pieces of my life finally coming together. He seems ready to answer my question.

"I realize now that the answer is not up to me. Gabriella, *you* need to search deep into your heart. That is where you will find the answer. Whether he is your destiny."

56

I LOOK UP, DISTRACTED momentarily by the overhead lights that are all suddenly illuminated and the ringing sounds of the alarm system on the aircraft.

I hear the captain's voice. "Attention ladies and gentlemen, please fasten your seat belts. We will be making an unscheduled landing. There is nothing to worry about, we've had strong headwinds and need to take on additional fuel."

Despite what the captain said, anxiety rises quickly in the cabin. Passengers look out the windows and ring call buttons while flight attendants move expertly up and down the aisles to buckle seat belts and calm nerves. The plane banks sharply to the left and begins its steep descent. I try to conceal my fear. A voice comes over the loudspeaker in English, then Hebrew, and informs us that we will be landing briefly in Turkey. That's it, no other information. As we descend toward earth, turbulence shakes the plane, and I grip my grandfather's arm, as if in some way that could counterbalance the force of the winds outside the aircraft.

"Don't worry, my Gabriella. You have a long and wonderful life ahead of you. We are safe in the hands of these pilots."

All the same he reaches over to tighten the seat belt around my shaking body. Just to show me how relaxed he is, he places the headphones I have given him into his ears and settles into the remainder of what is now our premature, terrifying landing.

The giant plane emerges through the cloud cover above Istanbul—our new unplanned destination. We are much lower than I anticipate, and the thickness of the clouds has concealed a terrible rainstorm that we fly into. The jerking motion is making me sick to my stomach, and I try to empty my mind of all thoughts, find the faith that he has, that we are safe. Yet, I am overcome with a sense that all is not right, and it connects directly to his safety. A reason for this unexpected change in plans, I know, I'm sure, has something to do with my grandfather. As I turn to him, I feel the tears streaming down my face.

"I want you to know something; I love you so much, Papa. I am so happy for you and proud of you. Of everything you have done." I grip both his hands in mine as the shapes of the city come into focus out the window. He has a faraway look on his face, and I keep talking. "And the Conference. We will all be there together with you, and then, of course, there *will* be the Nobel Prize."

This would be the last remaining honor that has eluded him all these years. He seems to listen to me, waiting for the shaking and vibrating of the descending flight to stop so that he can respond. Searching for words as a seriousness comes over his face. "Gabriella, if for any reason anything should happen to me, you must know that all that I have is yours. The house, everything in it, my papers, my research, and the studio, of course. These things are for you."

"Why are you saying this? Please, Papa, nothing is going to happen to you. We don't have to talk about this now."

"I have made all the arrangements. You don't have to worry about anything. Ever."

"Why are you telling me this?"

He has never spoken before about my life without him, and I don't want to hear it. Not now, not on the threshold of everything he has worked for. Nothing was going to happen.

"Please remain in your seats." The Captain's tense voice comes through the intercom again as the wheels of the plane slam into the ground. "Do not move until we receive further instructions."

I notice that the men who had been sitting near us—the security guards—have jumped to their feet. One has moved to the exit door, and the other has his back to the cockpit. He is less than five feet away from us. We taxi away from the active landing runway, and it is clear that this is not a routine landing. I see flashing emergency lights—blue, white, and red—circling and lighting up the sky and then, something else. It's the cars on the runway; not first-aid trucks, fire, ambulance, or even refueling tanks. They are military and unmarked security vehicles. The jet comes to a complete stop in the center of a distant runway and I am certain that we are nowhere near the main terminal area. Men with drawn guns run toward the aircraft, wheeling a large staircase toward the door behind where we are sitting. Everyone is silent.

I clearly make out the sound of pounding feet climbing the metal staircase outside the fuselage. I hear banging on the door from the outside. The flight attendant I had spoken to earlier and one of the security agents begin to unlock the door. His fingers are on the trigger of his small submachine gun. There is a knock from outside and a conversation on cell phones in Hebrew. I strain to understand what they are saying, desperate for any information.

"Yes, yes, he is here. We are prepared to move."

The door bursts open and five armed men storm onto the plane and over to where we are sitting.

"Dr. Vogel," one says in perfect English, "please come with us. We have important information regarding your safety. Your security has been compromised—please hurry."

They reach for him and unbuckle the seatbelt, moving quickly, not giving him time to react. I force myself to process the surreal nature of what is happening. We had just been flying thirty thousand feet over this country talking about the future and fate and—

"STOP!" I yell. I grab onto his arm in a tug of war over my grandfather's delicate frame.

He turns to the men in dark glasses and finally speaks. "What about my granddaughter? We are traveling together."

"She will continue with the other passengers. We have made arrangements for her. She will be escorted to a safe location," one of the men responds as he eyes me cautiously, as if he is identifying me from a photograph, confirming. The men speak rapidly into their cell phones.

"She is the most important thing in the world to me," he looks at me as he says the words slowly.

"No, Papa—please." I try to get a grip on my emotions, calm down, believe what they are telling me, put his needs first. "Don't worry about me. Please."

His safety is the only thing that matters at this moment.

"I don't want to leave you," he says.

It is clear that there is no choice, the situation is bigger and more dangerous than either one of us can imagine.

"I will see you in Israel, just like they said." I try to convince myself.

Reluctantly he accepts my answer.

"Dr. Vogel, come with us. Now. Please hurry. There is no time to delay."

He turns and walks toward the open door of the plane, assisted by an agent on either side of him. I am in shock, I cannot believe what has just occurred. I am unable to gather my thoughts, process what all of it means. And then, I hear his voice once again. "Wait, please. I have to tell her something."

I stand up in the aisle of the plane as he returns to me. He takes my face in his hands and holds it firmly, pressing my cheeks as he looks deeply into my eyes. And when he is sure he has my attention, he says the words he had said the day I stood in his library at the beach. The day before school started when he gave me the amulet.

"Remember this, you're never alone. We'll be with you. Always."

I watch as he is led away and know how right he is.

57

F OR THIS LANDING, the view out of the window is very different.
The unplanned detour to Istanbul has delayed our arrival into Tel
Aviv's Ben Gurion International Airport by several hours. Given everything
that has happened, I am relieved to see the coastline of Israel appear as the
easternmost edge of the Mediterranean meets its shores. It is sunset, and I
see the miraculous view, a golden glow cast over the land. The sense of
homecoming and the magical sight has calmed me somewhat. But all I want
to do is get off the plane and try to figure out what to do next. The vacant
seat next to me has been filled by a stone-faced security agent. He stares
straight ahead at the wall either too bored to or under orders not to
converse with me.

"Excuse me." I try to get his attention. "Tell me what's going to
happen when we land?"

"You find out shortly," he answers without even turning his head
to look at me.

"Where are you taking me?"

No response.

I steel myself for whatever is ahead as I try to quiet the range of
thoughts in my mind. I lean against the window and feel my forehead on
the cool plexiglass. The skyline of Tel Aviv comes into view, a city whose
amazing growth has been fueled by the brain power of so many who reside
in this small country. We fly over white beaches and houses and roads as

the jet banks for its final approach.

I feel the buzz of his cell phone as it vibrates on the arm rest between us. He picks it up and listens, nods, and answers a few questions in Hebrew. Then he looks over at me and exhales. "You are architecture student, yes?" He seems annoyed, as if he was told to engage me in conversation.

"Pardon?" He's talking to me now?

"You study architecture, in New York. Our new airport is very beautiful." He is clearly uncomfortable with small talk.

I blink at him in disbelief. "Where is my grandfather, *why* is this happening?"

He turns away as if he has not heard my question. Clearly, he is going to be of no help at all. "When we land, turn on cell phone. You will have message."

With a sudden jolt and screech of wheels, the plane hits the ground, and I hear the familiar cheering from passengers, applauding our arrival. I hold my phone in my palm and wait for the moment when I can turn the power on. Immediately after I do, the phone starts to vibrate.

I have several messages waiting.

The first is from Maggie, the second from Emily, and the third one from my grandfather. He has left a phone number for me to call upon landing and my fingers cannot dial fast enough. I need to hear his voice on the other end. Finally, I get my wish.

"Gabriella." He tries to greet me calmly as if we have not just experienced the most frightening of circumstances together.

"Where *are* you, are you okay?" I try to keep my voice low although every instinct in me wants to scream out with frustration and fear.

"Yes, fine. I promise you. I am completely fine." His voice shakes slightly. "Quite grateful actually to the international intelligence community. I cannot tell you where I am right now, but please know that we will be together soon. I am comfortable and—safe."

I can tell that he is frightened; I can hear it in his voice.

"I've been so worried about you. Papa, I haven't spoken to you about this but I've had the sense for a while now that something might happen. I should never have allowed you to—"

290

"Rubbish, sweetheart, nothing will happen. You need to take care of yourself now, and I will see you very soon. Everything is fine."

I don't believe him. "What about the conference? Will you be able to present your paper?"

"Gabriella, I have been told not to speak specifically over the phone even though this is a secure line."

"But—"

"Please, you must not worry about anything, remember what I promised you."

I have a thousand questions that need answers but I realize he is no longer on the phone. The next voice I hear belongs to someone else. "Ms. Vogel." It's English but covered with a heavy Israeli accent. "I want to apologize to you for this change in plans."

"Who are you, why—" I stop mid sentence as I realize that I am being handed a small device, similar to a cell phone, by the grim-faced passenger who has sat next to me for the last two hours. I am stunned.

"You can be in secure contact with your grandfather with this device," the man on the phone says, as if he knows the exact timing of what has just been placed in my hand. "Please play the message that has been left for you."

For the first time, my eyes meet those of the man to my right, and he points to a small green button on the phone. "Here, press and put on."

I take the headphones he hands me and place them in my ears. The message begins. My grandfather's face appears on the screen. I realize that the recording must have been made moments before the phone call and sent electronically to the device I hold. I look carefully at his face and scan it for any signs of distress. There are none. He seems calm—almost peaceful—as if he was sitting with me in his library at the beach.

"Gabriella, I want you to know that I am completely fine. I am very sorry to have put you through this ordeal. I was advised not to travel by commercial airliner several weeks ago, but I thought if I changed our itinerary you might become alarmed. Clearly, I underestimated the situation and apologize to you for this unexpected event. But all is well. As a precautionary measure, you will be taken to a secure house in Jerusalem where you will be well taken care of. Some new information has been revealed, and it has caused me to—*reconsider*—certain basic assumptions. About my work."

It was a scripted act, and I could see right through it.

I knew he was upset. The screen goes dark and the device shuts itself off. I am left staring at a black screen, stunned by what he has said about his work. I had been so completely focused on the message from him that I didn't notice that everyone has disembarked from the plane, and I am sitting quite alone with my personal security detail to my right, watching and waiting for me.

"Are you ready, Ms. Vogel?" He looks out the window, satisfied that what he seeks is there. "I take you to Jerusalem, as you were told in message."

"Yes." I am too exhausted to protest or question anything further. I get up and walk to the door of the plane with him and down the stairs, into the private car that waits on the runway, my grandfather's ominous words swirling in my head.

58

WE ARE SPEEDING, flying through the Judean Hills on our ascent up to Jerusalem. The familiar road switches back and forth, and I know we are not very far away. I feel completely exhausted—physically, mentally, and emotionally. I try to sleep during the forty-five-minute drive from the airport. My watch says that it's nine o'clock, and I know it's been more than twenty-four hours since we left New York City. There are very few cars on the road, and I am too tired to even worry about where I'm being taken. My only concern at this point seems to be getting some sleep to gather my strength. I know I will need it to deal with everything that waits and that there is no choice other than to trust what my grandfather has told me. That all is well and that I will see him soon.

But I don't believe him.

I am half asleep as the car arrives at a large private home on a hill overlooking the Old City of Jerusalem. When I emerge, I am struck by the feeling I recognize very well, the familiarity of this place. I have seen it before. The wind greets me as I step shakily out of the car and onto the ground. It feels crazy but I *recognize* where I am—everything about it. The limestone walls, the flat roof, and the beautiful black iron gates that I'm sure, lead to a garden of olive trees and roses.

I feel two warm arms around my shoulders as a heavy-set woman silently escorts me up the steps and into the house. She leads me into a large bedroom where she respectfully helps me undress and get ready for sleep.

I lie down in the bed and inhale the delicious lavender scent of the soft white sheets. They feel so cool and refreshing against my weary body. I can't think or question anything anymore. All I want is to move into the world of stillness, cradled by the heavenly down comforter that seems to float all around me.

When I open my eyes, I'm not sure where I am.

Slowly, the memory of the last two days comes back to me. All of it. The state of my grandfather's library in Gloucester, the flight, and the unexpected landing in Turkey. Especially everything my grandfather had said to me—about the possibility of not coming back.

I sit up in the bed and look around the room for the first time. Sweeping views of the Old City of Jerusalem fill the glass wall across from the bed. The power of the sunlight on the golden city is stunning, and I determine that I am near the Mount of Olives as I recognize many landmarks that I know so well. The space is a brilliant combination of contemporary and ancient construction. A curved glass wall wraps around the front of the room and large steel beams hold the cantilevered floor out three stories above the ground below. Typical everywhere in the city, the floors are made almost completely out of ancient building materials, elements that connect every building to the ancient origins of the city. A perfect juxtaposition of old and new—Jerusalem limestone, marble, and slate. The walls are smooth and pure-white plaster in contrast to the uneven surface of the stone. Other than the few remarkable paintings, everything in the room is white. The furniture, the large feathered bed, the magnificent flowers, and the filmy curtains that frame the wall of glass. Hardly the dark remote bunker I had formulated in my mind when told I was being taken to a *secure* location.

And then, there is the music of the city—the sounds of faith and belief: minarets that call worshippers to the mosque to pray and voices that rise in the many markets where negotiating is an art, the continuation of thousands of years of history. The location of the sun in the sky indicates that it must be late morning. I know it's been almost two days since I've left New York, yet it feels like a lifetime.

I find my clothes pressed and hung in the large armoire near my suitcase and choose to dress modestly—a skirt, cashmere sweater, and scarf bought expressly for the trip. I pick up the phone I've been given to communicate with my grandfather, open the door to the bedroom, and emerge into a large hallway filled with art and sculpture. I start down the staircase and stop to look through a large arched window at the view of the city and magnificent garden below. When I arrive at the main level of the home I am overtaken by the incredible familiarity of this place; I have felt it since I arrived. Drawn by a force that I can't explain, I find glass doors that lead outside. I step out into the sunlight and walk into the garden. As I stand in the middle of the space, I see the ancient olive trees and roses blowing in the cool breeze all around me. The earth is ripe. It smells like rosemary, lavender, honey, and memories—layered memories of the centuries that have gone by. I close my eyes and then it hits me, the powerful force of the instant, unmistakeable recognition.

I *know* where I am.

It is the house I have seen in my dreams. Everything is here—the trees, the roses, the stone, and the old wall at the edge of the property. All of it. More than anything else, I feel my grandmother's presence. I know she has stood in this very place. They've all been here, seen the same sky, felt the breeze, and breathed the same air. I lean forward to put my hands down on the low wall and feel its roughness under my fingers, a perfect vantage point to overlook the Old City below. I stand for a moment and close my eyes as I try to understand why I am here, and then, the silence is broken.

"Gabriella." It's my grandfather's voice.

I turn around and realize that he's been watching me for a few moments, his face is shining with pure joy and love. He is calm, peaceful, *safe.*

"Papa, you're here!" I run to him and hold him close for several minutes. I need to reassure myself that we are really together.

"You see, there was nothing to worry about. I told you that I was safe and that we would be together in Jerusalem."

We sit in the garden for hours, the questions I have for him finally surfacing from the dark places I had relegated them to. The ancient and modern city of Jerusalem behind us—our past and future everywhere.

"I can't believe everything that's happened in the last few months."

"But now we're here."

"Together, " I say.

"You know, it was a decision I made. To spend my life searching, looking for answers—and I know how difficult things have been for you, too."

"No, I'm fine, I—"

"I know that you didn't always understand, Gabriella. Especially when you were young."

"Some of your choices."

"My choices and my reasons."

"Your work. I know it was always about your work, Papa."

"We made our choices, whether they were right or wrong. We tried to do our best. I pursued my research and your grandmother, her search was—"

"Different." I finish his sentence.

"Yes." He smiles. "In the undeniable force of her mystical gift."

"That she inherited?"

"That you *both* did." He stops and takes a deep breath, as if what he is about to say is very difficult for him.

"It's all right, we don't have to talk about her now."

"I want to. You deserve to know. I've seen you grow into everything you have been given. Even if you didn't always understand." He takes my hand and looks into my eyes. I understand what he is telling me. "She is still with you, always. You know this don't you? You are beginning to understand many things about yourself and the things you are connected to."

"Yes."

"Good. She knew you would."

"There is something about this house. She was here wasn't she? You all were here together?"

"Many years ago."

"I can feel it."

"This is a very special place. This house is," he says and looks up toward the timeless limestone building, "where I fell in love with your grandmother. That was the beginning, the start of everything in my life."

"I know what you mean, Papa."

"However, I need to tell you something. Things may change."

"Change? In what way?"

"I told you once before, things aren't always what they seem. Sometimes they are— "

"Better?"

"Yes, maybe better. If you're ready."

"I am."

"Gabriella, you are, but the world simply may not be."

"What? What does that mean?"

"I might choose not to."

"Why, after everything, would you stop now?"

"We wouldn't be safe, I mean *you* wouldn't be safe—after. I need to think about the future. Yours and—"

"You have worked so hard for this, your whole life. You can't stop now!"

"I didn't say I would stop. I'm very stubborn as you know."

"I love that about you."

"Just like you. Our convictions have led us through much adversity."

"Despite the criticism of the people who thought you were throwing your life's work away?"

"On dreams and fantasy. *Science fiction*, they called it. Using empirical data to measure and mysticism to find meaning. But, I just don't know. What good has it done? Look at the world—are we in a better place now?"

I try to absorb everything that is happening: the overwhelming sensations I am feeling about what he is telling me and the suggestion that the moment he has worked so hard for might not come to be. The moment I always hoped we would share.

"You have found it."

"As you have, Gabriella."

For the first time, I recognize something in his face. It is a resolve, an acceptance.

I want to feel grateful that, finally, after so many years of questioning he has found what he sought. Like the sculpture in the Cathedral Church of Saint John the Divine, of the divine breath being blown into Adam's nostrils, I feel a new conviction about so many things in my life. The journey that I have been on has led me back to where I started, to my family, and to finding the answers that have always been in my heart.

"Maybe there are things that simply cannot be measured," I whisper.

"You do understand," he says.

59

EVERYTHING IS HAPPENING the way it was intended to.

The sun begins to move farther into the western sky, and I realize we have spent most of the afternoon together, talking and finding a new understanding of each other. The delicious lunch we had been served marking what seems now to be a celebration.

"Things will be as they were meant to. This is a very special time for you, Gabriella."

"And for you, too, Papa." I don't take my eyes away from his as I try to understand the sadness. I know somewhere in my heart the undeniable truth in what he is saying.

"Come here, I want to give you something. I've saved it for a long time. Actually it is not from me—it's from someone else who loved you very much. Someone who told me that this very day would arrive." He shakes his head at the memory and reaches over to lift a silk bag that sits on the chair between us. "Open it."

I reach into the pouch and pull out a small book. I touch the exquisite silver cover and look at the inlaid colored stones. It is the *Song of Songs,* written by King Solomon. I know that this is the book of one hundred and seventeen verses from the Old Testament that speak directly of love and one of the most important texts in the Kabbalah. I remembered clearly reading from this treasured collection with my grandmother as she introduced me to the powerful poetry and the symbolism that defines the importance of spiritual, emotional, and even physical love.

"Go ahead," he encourages me. "There is something I want you to see."

"I remember reading this book with her."

"That's it, the one that is marked," he says and points to a small piece of paper that holds the place. I move the bookmark aside, feeling its roughness under my fingers and begin to read the ancient words.

> *Therefore do worlds love you*
> *one generation after another,*
> *a love transcending lifetimes.*
> *Every soul is connected to every other.*
>
> *Suddenly she knows*
> *or seems to remember something*
> *that she could not possibly have yet experienced.*
> *These memories survive the forgetting*
> *that seems to separate*
> *one lifetime from another.*

I wait to look at him, hoping that the tears in my eyes will not reveal the emotion welling up inside of me. The sheer force of this beautiful excerpt, connecting everything we have spent the last several hours speaking of, overcomes me. The discussion of mysticism and the suggestion of other lifetimes.

Other *worlds*.

Slowly, I turn over the bookmark in my hand and see an embossed image of the symbol that I know so well. It is the same as the amulet I have, the icon of the great mystical tradition of our family.

"It was your grandmother's."

I look up and see him wipe the tears from his eyes. Through these words and this sublime gesture, I know he is giving me the greatest gift I could have ever hoped for: acknowledgement of the special qualities I possess that tie me to my family history and the confirmation that the secrets I have held in my heart are, in fact, grounded in a timeless spiritual tradition that connects me to my past.

And future.

My grandparents, my parents, my friends—we were all looking for our own place in the world, on our own journeys, searching for our purpose.

"Thank you, Papa."

And then, as if scripted by a benevolent divine source, my grandfather looks up and smiles at something behind me. He takes my hand and lifts it in a gesture reminiscent of the bride being presented to the bridegroom.

"Gabriella."

It's the voice I had prayed I would hear.

I turn around slowly, wanting to confirm that this moment is really happening. I am not in a dream but I am awake. *Alive.* I want to savor the reunion I hoped would come in this city. For a moment we stand facing each other as our eyes meet. Mine are filled with tears of gratitude and Benjamin's with the joy and pleasure I have seen before when he looked at me. I run toward him and practically knock him over with the force of my body as I throw my arms around him.

I know I won't let go, ever again. This is a promise I have made to myself.

60

EVEN THOUGH I HAD dreamed of this moment, willed it to happen, the reality of it is better than anything I could have imagined. I want to fill myself completely with everything that is *him*. I close my eyes because I want to feel it, all of it: the cool Jerusalem breeze that swirls around me, my hands wrapped tightly in his, and the presence of my grandfather. All those who stand with us and those who were not here.

"Gabriella." My grandfather's voice finally breaks the silence. "There are so many things I need to tell you, but first, I want to apologize."

I turn to face him. "No—please, there is nothing you need to—"

"Yes, listen to me. I was wrong about many things, and you—you are the one who made me understand. You helped me to see things differently, really for the first time. So much has become clear to me now. Especially things about your grandmother."

"I see," I whisper the words as I look at him, searching his face.

"I blamed so many people for losing her, for her death. But there was really no one to blame, least of all Benjamin. I know we will be together again. Soon."

"What do you mean?"

"You were right about her, and I know why you could understand so clearly. She wanted me to understand this and she told me that I would, one day."

"That you would understand what, Papa?"

"That she was right, especially when I would see the two of you. You and Benjamin. Together," he says the last word slowly and deliberately.

My grandfather holds my face in his hands, his eyes are sparkling with delight. "I will see you in a few days."

"Where are you going?"

I turn around and see that a black car with the United Nations security force emblem on its doors has pulled up in front of the iron gates.

"I've been invited to spend the weekend with several of my colleagues, at the Prime Minister's estate. It is an invitation that I could not refuse." His eyes are shining with his own secret as he looks at me.

"Yes, of course, but—"

"We have waited many years to arrive at this time. In all of our lives." He takes a step closer. "Benjamin?"

I watch them embrace; a deep intimacy in their exchange, that of old friends. The common bond and deep understanding that unites them is beyond the need for words. Despite everything that has happened in the last few months, this is the first time the three of us are together. As they hold each other's gaze, I see an understanding that could only come from the familiarity of many years together. Then, at the same time, they both turn and look at me. These two men whom I love so deeply and so differently.

Benjamin moves to stand behind me, the strength of him supporting me, balancing my trembling. My hands are wrapped protectively inside of his, and I know that this moment is, in the most unexplainable way, the realization of a wish, a dream. I know what my grandfather is giving me. It is the gift of time alone with Benjamin. His *blessing*. The acknowledgement of our being together, made evident by his insistence on leaving and returning to his life.

Leaving me here with Benjamin to begin mine.

61

THINGS SLOW DOWN as peace and rest begin to blanket the golden hills. People prepare for the Sabbath, the time when the holy city stands still. I feel the power of the sacred energy, the changing light in this magical place as it washes over us. The wind carries messages from earlier centuries, and I am sure that I can feel the souls of those who have loved me; confirming, encouraging the path we are on.

Benjamin reaches for my hand and brings it to his mouth and kisses it softly. "The sun will be setting soon; let's go for a walk."

I want to savor every second, what has brought me to this place and more, everything that is ahead. The realization that we have this time alone together. His arm is around me, and I let go. This is everything I have waited for.

We walk through the gates of the house, turn down the steep hill, and enter into the Old City together, taking in the beginning of the Sabbath celebrations. We pass through Dung Gate, the closest access to the Western Wall and approach the heart of the Jewish Quarter. The iconic wall before us is the only remaining architectural element from the Second Temple that had been destroyed by the Romans in 70 CE. The *Kotel* as it is called in Hebrew. We stop in the center of the large plaza that faces the holy space and are swept into the energy and activity of the worshippers. I want to approach the wall; I can feel its magnetic pull.

"Go, touch it, Gabriella."

Reluctantly, I slip my fingers out of Benjamin's hand.

"Wait here—*don't move.* I'll be right back."

"Of course, where else would I be?"

Whenever I have been in Jerusalem in the past, I had always needed to mark my return by coming here. To let the power of this place encircle me, connect to unnameable energies. I look up at the multitude of tiny scraps of paper tucked into every crevice and opening of the wall that contain messages and prayers, the hopes and requests of so many who have stood here, before me, searching for answers. My fingers run across the polished surface, worn from the many thousands of years of loving touch. I lean my forehead against the ancient limestone and close my eyes as I whisper a prayer. "Thank you for bringing me to this moment, for giving me this life, and allowing me to see, understand, and accept what has always been in my heart."

I back away and glance over my shoulder to see Benjamin standing exactly where I had left him. He never takes his eyes off of me, and I try to get back to him as quickly as I can. I navigate through the path of worshippers and finally, when I reach him, I throw my arms around his neck and start to kiss him. I know that unlike many of the other prayers being made on this day, in so many ways, mine have already been answered.

"Gabriella." I feel his mouth brush across mine slowly and sensuously.

He gently disengages himself from the lock I have him in and discretely kisses the inside of each of my wrists.

"What is it?" I am not ready to separate.

"Look around." He laughs at my enthusiastic need for him as he reminds me of where we are.

"Oh." The center of the Orthodox world. "Sorry, I forgot that this sort of public display of affection is not exactly appropriate here."

I look around at the modestly-dressed worshippers. I really don't care anymore what is right or wrong, appropriate or not. I'm having a hard enough time controlling the incredible range of emotions I am feeling.

"Just wait," he laughs.

I feel the most insane electricity coursing through my body. Trying to blend in with the other normal people who have come to the Old City at this sacred time seems impossible.

Normal is one thing I know we are not.

"Benjamin, I want to thank you."

"Really—for what?"

"For the beautiful piece of music you wrote for me—the piano composition. For my birthday." I look at his profile.

"Do you like it?"

"Of course."

"Well, you almost ruined the surprise." I know he is teasing me again.

"What, why?"

"That night you overheard our rehearsal in the cathedral—you were not supposed to be there."

"What do you mean?" I remember the promise I had made to Emily, that I would go straight home and then the overwhelming force that had drawn me into the cathedral as I reversed my direction, a completely out of character move for me.

He takes a step closer and pulls me into him. His eyes become dark. "I thought of you—I thought of *everything* I love about you when I put the notes together. That music is the sound of my heart. My promise to you."

I can't understand what he means, how it could be. "But, we hadn't met yet."

"I wanted to give you something, to store away in your heart and your mind. It's what Einstein said—that he *thought* in music. That it was music that composed his dreams. Remember, no one can ever take that away."

"Benjamin." I reach up for him.

He catches my wrist in his fingers and encircles it, as if he is measuring its size, looking at it from all sides. "I will know every inch of you so I could build you if I needed to. My own private replica."

I look right at him. It's as if I can feel his heart beating inside of me. "I don't understand." I feel confused, overwhelmed by what he is saying. "You have me."

He steps away and points to the limestone ruins of an ancient wall. Changing the conversation. "Look, Gabriella, look at what Herod built."

He takes my hand and turns me around slowly, framing a view back toward the City of David, the many structures on the hill that overlook the area of the Temple Mount and the hills of Jerusalem beyond.

"Are we talking about *architecture* now?" I am incredulous, but the topic of architecture is probably the only thing that can take my mind off of him. For the moment at least.

"The Romans allowed Herod complete autonomy and made him King of Judea. His building projects are seen everywhere across the region," he says it softly as he turns to look at me.

"Well, he was a terrible tyrant."

"Gabriella." He laughs at my frustration at this topic change.

"*Those* are the people who get their projects built." I fold my arms across my chest in dramatic resignation.

"You have everything it takes to be a great architect. You understand what it is that will make something last, the timeless qualities. What is unchanging."

I'm not sure if he's talking about architecture—or something else.

"What do you mean?" I ask.

"Making the world a better place, through your actions. Your choices."

"My choices?"

"Yes."

One of the most fundamental ideas of Kabbalah.

I feel a new power, a courage I never knew that I possessed. I know that I need to trust myself in this moment. The door is open, and I feel myself walking through it, transitioning into everything that has been waiting for me. I want answers from him. "And what about your choices?" I challenge him.

How could I define the multitude of questions I had for him?

"Gabriella." He expertly avoids the directness of my question, moving the discussion back to the story of Jerusalem. "There are other secrets about Herod. Things that are not known."

"Oh, and you know them?" I am frustrated.

He is quiet and looks down at the uneven stones of the street we are walking on. I can see the ruts and marks left from the generations that have crossed through this very place—all on their own very different journeys. I feel that what I said has struck a nerve in him, and a flash of fear that I am conditioned to returns. I want to touch him. I look at the back of his head, the way his hair curls over the top of his collar, the softness of his skin. I am worried that I have said the wrong thing and I stop walking in the middle of the street. He turns to look at me.

"I'm sorry, Benjamin."

"Yes, I do know the secret about Herod," he practically whispers. There is something about the way he says it.

He takes my hand, and we continue to walk in silence. We travel back through the Arab market and toward Jaffa Gate. We cross over the newly built complex by the architect Moshe Safdie and reconnect to the modern city. The project is a brilliant preservation and restoration of historic structures, with the design of new buildings, hotels, and parks. A combination of ancient building materials and contemporary technology, housing stores, restaurants, and outdoor cafés.

"Let's sit down here." He points to a cushioned settee at a busy café, with a view of the wall that circles the Old City, beautifully illuminated for the night.

We have moved out of the traditional religious observant world to the secular one, and I hear live music being played and end-of-week celebrations occurring. His arm is over the back of the seat waiting to hold me, and as I sit down his fingers move through my hair. There is a desire in his eyes that I have not seen before—matching what I am feeling. "We have much to celebrate." He smiles.

"I know." I'm worried that the urgency of my questions might have broken the spell of the evening.

"I have been waiting for this night for a long time."

"So have I."

"Gabriella, I told you that we will have to find a way."

I feel his words in my heart. Wine is brought to our table. He pours me a glass and raises his to me. "To finding your way."

"To finding everything you've been looking for," I whisper.

I want only him. To know everything about him, to be with him. I look out at the view then at Benjamin, wanting to seal this image in my mind. The perfection of it. The evening moves quickly into night, and I feel the cold, the many stars in the sky, and his eyes everywhere on me.

"Dinner is waiting for us." His green eyes shine. "Let's go back."

He doesn't need any reason for me to return to the house with him.

62

WE STAND ON THE terrace of his house together; the light of the moon is on his face, and I remember.

I remember the night he had stood in the doorway of the cathedral, the way he had looked at me, the promise he made.

I know.

I realize that the desperation I have felt, the waiting and hoping and willing this moment to come, is finally over. The answers I have sought my whole life are right in front of me, and Benjamin is at the center. It is all meant to be, an amazing perfect inevitability. I feel it, deep in my heart. I am sure. I am no longer afraid. I know I need answers from him, and so I ask.

"Benjamin, I saw the letter—the one my grandmother wrote so many years ago. She predicted *you*. She said this would happen."

He touches my cheek.

"How could she have known?"

"It's because we have always been together, Gabriella."

"What do you mean?"

"We were together, in another place and time."

"Another place?"

"Yes." He turns away from me suddenly, and I see the pain that distorts his face.

"What is it?"

"I thought I was going to lose you, that night on the beach. I couldn't let it happen, I couldn't—"

"I thought I was going to die," I whisper as the memory of that moment overtakes me. "I thought I had."

"I'm here with you now. We are together. In this world."

"This world," I repeat slowly.

"We were made for each other, Gabriella."

I know that what he is saying is true, that for every person, every soul, there is only one other that completes them—two lost halves created for the singular purpose of being united. We had found each other. Again. It was written in the *Song of Songs* thousands of years before, predicted by my grandmother, and confirmed today in the poem given to me.

"I need to be with you; I only want to live in a world that makes us eternal."

From the very first time I had seen him, to the night when he pulled me out of the icy Gloucester water, this was how I felt. I want to be inside of him, under his skin, in his blood, pushing through his veins toward his heart.

"You are the one, Gabriella. It's always been you." He is so close to me, whispering the words, pouring them into me, filling me. I take them in, drinking in the moment, learning every detail of what he is saying, how he stands, the way he breathes in and out. Loving everything about him.

"No more secrets," I say.

I desperately want to, but do not let myself touch him. I need my eyes to focus on his, but feel his power drawing me in, connecting into me and through me. He pulls me into him. This time it's not in a gentle way but in a passionate crush, as if he has waited a lifetime for this moment. He sweeps his arms under my legs and lifts me, carries me up to the house and into the room I had slept in the night before, now filled everywhere with flowers. As he carefully lays me down on the bed, he stops to look at me.

He waits.

I reach out, I am unwilling to delay any longer the realization of this moment. I need him to join me. He bends down, and I feel his lips cover my skin, as if he is learning every part of me, confirming for himself what he already seems to know, igniting a fire in me I did not know I possessed. And I feel that finally, there are no more mysteries, no more secrets. I have found the truth I had always known somewhere in my heart. A complete and perfect order out of the chaos that I have endured.

I don't take my eyes away from his as he slowly takes off my clothes. He pushes me onto the bed so that I am under him and lifts my arms up over my head and back into the pillows. I feel his mouth drawing slow patterns into the shapes of my body—exploring—as he discovers his way back to my face. He marks my fingers, my elbows, around my shoulders and up into my neck, claiming every part of me.

"I will know all the beautiful space that is inside of you," he says.

"I need you, to be with you. Always."

I surrender completely into him, the incredible sensation of him touching me.

"Gabriella." He stops and looks up at me. "Please—light the candles, now. I want to see your face. I need to see you."

The moonlight is not enough.

And I know that this is the melting of our worlds. I want to stop time, to savor every sensation. The taste of his fingers in my mouth, the way his skin feels pressed against the length of my body. The sounds he makes.

"Benjamin." I need to know that I have his attention, there is something I want him to hear.

"No words now, Gabriella." His powerful, urgent kisses silence me. He covers me with his body, and I feel him everywhere, every part of us intersecting.

But I need to say it, so I do. "I love you." I fill the words with everything I have stored in my heart for this moment and say it again, "I love you—where there is no space or time."

He smiles. "I know."

Then his mouth covers mine as he swallows my words, as he drinks them in.

I feel him everywhere. He uncovers every part of me with his desire. He pulls me over so that I am directly underneath him and undoes me, slowly and deliberately. I use all the strength I have to pull him toward me.

"I believe it now. I believe all of it."

"Gabriella," he exhales as he turns and lifts me. I hang above him, suspended, my hair is in his face, my breath is everywhere on him. His mouth moves up the side of my neck and his lips stop in my ear. "I found you."

I close my eyes and then . . . there is only him. We become one.

In our lovemaking I find everything.

All the answers, my future.

The entire world ahead of us.

The Infinite.

Like the pull of the tide by the moon, the rain pushing through a storm-filled sky, the plates of the earth shifting, this is the pleasure I feel as I submerge into him. It pulls me up as my desire is met with everything he offers. The endless, eternal gift—of him.

Later, I wake to a powerful storm.

The rain slams the shutters against the windows of our room. The candles have all burned down and there is only darkness and him. My face is against his heart, and I wait. For the sound of each beat, the perfect lullaby that I had dreamt of. I reach out and touch him. My fingers trace the line of his nose down to his mouth. We live in each other's arms as we always have, as we always will.

He opens his eyes and looks at me, and I see something I don't expect.

"Is that a tear?" I lift it off his face and into my mouth as I swallow the salt of his body. I need to make sure it's real.

He pulls me onto him. "Yes," he says.

"I love the way you taste. I love everything about you."

"Were you dreaming, Gabriella?"

"I was."

He kisses me again. "I knew you were."

"I could see you, Benjamin. In this house, with my grandmother. She was here that night, when she met my grandfather. You knew him then didn't you, you were all here—with Einstein?"

"Yes."

"Did he know about you, where you were *from*?

He smiles at a distant memory. "They all did."

"And it was that night, wasn't it, that you gave her the amulet?" I know the answer.

"That's right."

"Did you know it would be mine?"

"Of course."

I put my head down on his heart and I wait; I breathe.

"What else did you see?"

"I stopped it; I needed to wake up. I wanted to make sure—that you were still here. That you hadn't left me."

He shakes his head.

"Promise me. *Tell* me, Benjamin."

He slides his hands slowly up my legs as he turns to face me. "I will show you," he says.

I have offered all I am to him, and he has accepted. We have learned everything about each other. The past, the present, and the future. I am addicted to him and I want it all.

This is the only way I will be satisfied.

63

WE STAYED TOGETHER LIKE this for several days, living only in each other.

Even if I had allowed myself, my mind, my heart, the permission to imagine this, I would not have been able to. I would never have let myself hope for what I knew I had found. The sun rises and sets, marking time. The moments, the years we want to create. I marvel at the incredible sequence of events that have led me to the miracle of Benjamin and our relationship. Parts of my life that I had always needed every ounce of courage to face do not scare me any longer. Everything seems clear, as if I am on top of a mountain looking out, having gained the perspective to see things more clearly.

My eyes are closed, but I feel my wakeful consciousness coming back to me. I can sense from the light outside that it is early morning and I have the familiar feeling of being watched. I open my eyes very slowly and see his face. He sits on the bed, smiling at me, and I have to remember to breathe as my eyes focus on him. "Benjamin."

"I love to watch you sleep; sometimes you say incredible things."

I try to turn away to hide my embarrassment, but he leans over and holds me down, pinning my hands into the bed on either side of me.

"How . . . are . . . you . . . this . . . morning?" The words are barely audible as he says them in between kisses, his mouth everywhere on me. He reluctantly releases my hands and pulls the covers away, the electricity

317

in his touch instantly reminds me of everything we have shared.

"I feel wonderful." I try to grab him and pull him back into bed with me. I know we are going to Masada at the end of the day and I want as much time alone with him as possible.

A lifetime would have been about right.

"Are you ready to get up?" He slips away from my grasp. "I have an enormous breakfast—just for you."

His eyes sparkle. The subject of my appetite is now a source of humor between us.

I reach out for him. "No. That's not what I want right now. Come back to bed with me, please?"

He takes my hands and touches the inside of each of my wrists with his mouth then pulls me toward him and into his arms. My head rests on his chest, and I can feel the deep powerful beating of his heart. I don't want this time to end. I have not allowed myself to think about what will happen next.

I notice the silence of the city, the wind outside the balcony, and the aromatic smell of coffee and breakfast coming from somewhere in the house. Benjamin tilts my face up to his. He looks at me as if he is storing the image away, recording every detail, and then, his face changes.

"What is it?"

"Gabriella, I want you to understand something; it is very important that you do."

He has a seriousness about him that I have seen before. I nod slowly, preparing myself for whatever he is going to say.

"Your grandfather has devoted his life to asking the most profound questions about the nature of reality. Some of the answers he already had, just as you do."

"I don't have any answers."

"You do, as did your grandmother."

"Our gift?"

"Yes, and since it is considered to be of the mystical realm, it is not deemed threatening to sources who might not, you might say, *agree*."

I concentrate on his words and remove my instinct to let my emotions, rather than the rational side of my brain be in control.

He stops and looks right at me. "You understand?"

"Yes." But it is clear that there is much more.

"There are very real threats, forces who want access to the information he possesses," he says slowly.

I look straight ahead. "I have had the sense for a while—"

"And others, Gabriella, who are trying to *silence* him."

"Others? I just don't understand why."

"I have tried to warn him." He turns away from me, unable to meet my eyes.

"The last few months, Benjamin, things have not been right with him. He's different—I feel it. Like there's a darkness surrounding him. It's something I haven't felt in a very long time." My mind flashes back to the increased security, the night at the museum with Emily, and especially the state of his library at the beach. I know it's connected to the terrible darkness and the images of the explosion in Paris I've been seeing.

"Yes."

"But this time, it's different, it's a feeling that he is *choosing* something. Going away. And not coming back," I say.

"He has always known that this reality, the one that we can see and feel and comprehend is not the only, let's call it 'truth.' As a scientist, his goal was to find the evidence."

"So, he has spent his life looking for the proof, the existence of other dimensions."

He looks at me cautiously, protectively. "He is completing the task that others before him began."

"Benjamin, I know it's you. You found him when he was young and you helped him. Isn't that right?" I try to retain my composure but feel the tears coming down my face. "And Einstein, right? Who else? How many others have there been? How many others have known?"

He turns to face me. "Many others."

"Then why, why did they not reveal the proof?"

Benjamin looks at me with a sadness I have not seen before. "Gabriella."

"It has something to do with you, doesn't it, Benjamin?"

"Yes."

"Please tell me why; I need to know."

"I was sent here—to stop them."

"What?" I am not expecting this.

"In every generation events happen. Circumstances arise where people are tested. Throughout time we have come and observed how your world would handle these situations. What choices they would make. We needed to see whether your world was ready." He walks over to the wall of windows that overlook the city and stands there, his arms crossed, his back to me.

I climb out of bed and pull his shirt around my bare body. As I come up behind him, I slip my arms through his and step into him. "Benjamin, please."

"Your grandfather planned to continue the work of Einstein and— reveal everything. But he needed to understand, just like Einstein did. We had to tell him why he could not."

"*We?* So there are others, like you?"

"Yes. Our task is to monitor the rules of the universe, the laws of nature you might say. Otherwise." He looks out the windows and shakes his head as if he is remembering a scenario just like the one he is describing. "Otherwise, Gabriella, terrible things happen."

"Do you mean things that we cannot understand? That simply make no sense at all?"

"Some scientists have tried to measure what may not be measurable. Others have looked for reasons to explain things that there simply are no answers for."

"Like natural disasters, tsunamis, the Holocaust."

"Some of those are inflicted by nature but others like the systematic destruction of people are caused by—"

"Man," I say.

"That's right. There is a difference between destruction and death by unavoidable natural occurrences and those that are intentionally committed by human beings against each other. Those are the rules we are talking about, the ones that involve choice."

"Like choosing our fate?"

"Gabriella, I have broken the rules."

"You? How, Benjamin, could you possibly—"

"By changing your fate. And mine." He shakes his head. "I was not supposed to help your grandmother, to take her through."

"My grandmother knew about everything, didn't she?"

"Your grandmother was a very brave woman. She knew everything about his work and she understood about the *ports*."

"She knew she was going to die."

"She wanted to try to cross over, to go through the tunnel with me. So she—"

"Could live in your world."

"Free of illness and subject to very different laws of time."

"But she died."

"Her soul was able to go but not her body, Gabriella."

"He would never have let her go, so he blamed you, but not anymore. You heard what he said. He forgives you; he forgives her. He understands now."

"I knew he would."

"And you, Benjamin?" The question I have been afraid to ask. "What about you?"

There is silence for what seems like an eternity. He strokes my hair, his lips touch the top of my head as he pulls me into him. "Your grandfather always thought that he needed me to help prove his theory. But he does not. He's found the proof, all of the answers, and he's done it on his own. He knows this. But I'm afraid—"

"What is it?"

"If your grandfather chooses to reveal the proof, then I can't stay here. It is impossible."

I need to calm myself, to fight back the panic I am feeling and control my own selfish needs—somehow process the information and consider whatever limited options I have. I look at him and feel as if for the first time in my life, I am pleading. Begging.

"Benjamin, I can't, I won't live in this world without you. If you cannot stay here, then please, *please* let me go with you."

"Our worlds are not meant to intersect. It cannot be."

"Benjamin—"

"No matter what happens, you must always remember how much I love you. Promise me that, Gabriella. Always remember."

"Yes. I will." As the words come out of my mouth, I barely recognize my own voice.

64

I STAND ALONE ON the terrace and look out over the Old City.

I wait for Benjamin to come back with the car and feel a certain resolve. I understand now. Everything has become perfectly clear. I will accept what he has told me, because it is bigger than anything I could have imagined. All the things in my life have led me to this moment: my grandfather's life's work, everything he has sacrificed and worked so hard for. All will now be revealed as it must.

And I will lose Benjamin.

I feel the space between us growing, marked only by the silence. He drives quickly, and we descend over the road on the way out of Jerusalem, down through the Judean Hills toward the Dead Sea. There are no words, only his hand held tightly to my heart, my head turned away as I look out the window. The sun is behind us and lights up the hills that are dotted with vegetation and the occasional Bedouin flock. It is an overwhelmingly beautiful sight, and I lean back onto the headrest of our Jeep, the warm air all around me. I turn my body back toward his and move my hand slowly up his arm and around the back of his head. Even though I try not to, I *need* to look at him. He takes his eyes off the road for a second and, as his eyes meet mine, I feel the power of the connection between us.

"Benjamin." I want to tell him that I feel like I'm going to vanish without him. Dissolve. "I want to remember all of this."

"You will."

"I've decided that it's safer to live in the past."

"No," he says. I can hear the pain in his voice.

I pull my hand away from his. I need to be strong. I look out at the mountains and the Dead Sea. "I used to love to come here with my family when I was a little girl and I want to remember."

"You do remember though."

"I want to *remember* what it felt like when things were simple. When my life approximated some semblance of normalcy."

"Do you know where we are?"

"The lowest place on earth. There." My finger points to a dark opening in the limestone hills. "The caves of Qumran."

"Where the Dead Sea Scrolls were discovered."

I remember the amazing story of how in 1947, a Bedouin shepherd boy was searching for a lost goat near Qumran on the shores of the Dead Sea. He entered a cave and stumbled upon one of the most significant archaeological finds ever made. I know this is where Benjamin met my grandmother.

"This is where you found her isn't it? She was on the archaeological expedition under the British Mandate."

"1943."

"Where were you?" I ask.

"At the top of the mountain. In the cistern."

There is so much more I want to know about that time when they were together, so many years before I was born. I question him as I feel the backs of my fingers brush lightly along his cheek.

"Masada."

"For many generations the story of Masada was considered only legend." He seems relieved to move the conversation to something less intimate.

"When you were with her then, in 1943, it wasn't known yet?" I ask.

"It wasn't until 1963, when the area was excavated by a large international expedition that proved the legend to be fact."

"But *you* knew."

He turns his head to look at me, to make sure that I will understand what he is about to say. "Masada is one of the most enduring examples of the determination of individuals. To be free. To choose their fate through their own actions."

Of course, I knew the story very well, both from visits to the mountain and the incredible legend of the place, the story that was told to me over and over as a child: the mountain that rose in the solitude of the Judean Desert.

"Look, there it is." I point to the flat-topped mountain in the distance. "It's ironic, don't you think? The ancient history that has taken place in this small part of our world and now, the group of scientists gathering to propose the theories that will change all our futures, forever."

"Another link between two thousand years ago and today," Benjamin says quietly.

"For very different reasons."

My eyes move away from his burning gaze to the mountain that is the site of so much bravery and death. I see the ruins of Herod's palace on the north face. The mountain is odd in its architecture—perfect for a fortress and geographically isolated from its surroundings by deep gorges on all sides.

We step out of the car, and I slam the door and wait for him to come around and stand behind me. I need to collect myself. I don't want my grandfather to see me like this.

"They were all here, Gabriella, so many have stood in this very place."

Seventy-five years after Herod died, a group of rebels and their families fled Jerusalem after the destruction of the Second Temple in 70 CE. They established a large camp on the top of the mountain and began their resistance to the Roman Empire. In my mind, this had always been our story of David and Goliath. For two years almost one thousand people survived.

"What is it about this place, Benjamin? Why? Ten Roman camps, unlimited wealth and funding, the greatest army in the world, and they couldn't conquer those few at the top of the mountain. Men, women, and children? It just doesn't make sense."

I knew that in 73 CE the Roman governor, Flavius Silva, led an attack on the mountain with almost fifteen thousand militia. This time, the Romans were determined to quash the rebellion, knowing that escape from the summit was absolutely impossible. With sophisticated weapons and massive fires they broke through the defenses and prepared to take all their prisoners.

"The Romans did not anticipate the spirit and conviction of the defenders up above. Almost one thousand men, women, and children, who had other ideas, ready to face the Roman Empire." He looks at me.

"What do you mean?"

"They decided that rather than being taken alive they would choose their fate. So they took their own lives. They burned everything but left all of their food. They wanted the Romans to know that they had *chosen* this."

I look up again at the northern edge of the steep cliff. I can see terraces connected by rock-cut staircases. I know that above there are living quarters, a small private bathhouse, a synagogue, store rooms, throne rooms, and cisterns to collect and store water. All covered in frescos of multicolored geometric patterns, mosaics, and cut marble. It would have been a remarkable construction project anywhere and at any time. But it was accomplished two thousand years ago, on the top of a mountain, in the middle of a desert.

"The bravery of individuals, to push forward into the unknown."

"To choose freedom," he says.

"To fare forward." The words slip out of my mouth. I remember the poem from *Four Quartets,* and my grandmother's encouragement to *not be burdened by the past, nor fear the future.* Something I needed to keep with me always. A good luck charm and reminder, a link to my own past. "She wrote 'we have far to travel.' My grandmother, so many years ago in the inscription."

"I know." He smiles at me. "She always said that."

"The poem is all about time, the ideas seem illogical, yet—completely coherent. It is so personal, almost prophetic."

"You have done as she predicted."

I can see the new structure that has been built at the base of the mountain. The magnificent museum and visitor center where the reception is being held is completely surrounded by armed guards and security barricades. Soldiers stand still with their weapons at their side, and there are hundreds of press vehicles everywhere.

"Oh my God." I catch my breath at the sight of the massive security. "This is insane."

Benjamin is completely unfazed by the activity in front of us. "Gabriella, there is something else, about the poem. You know the third chapter, the 'Dry Salvages?'"

"Why are we talking about this now?" I don't want to talk anymore; I can't think straight.

"Because, it's named after a group of three rocks that are very close to your home in Gloucester, right off of Cape Ann, where I found you in the water. Did you know that T.S. Eliot wrote his poem there before he left and moved to England?"

"No, actually, I didn't."

He takes both my hands in his. "You are the music, while the music lasts."

I recognize the words from the poem and I don't know what to say; I'm numb.

"Benjamin." I fight back my tears. "Maybe it was enough just to know that the *possibility* of you existed." I turn my head away from him but feel like I can no longer breathe. "When this is over, all I will have left of you—will be words."

"Just promise me, Gabriella, that you will remember what I told you. There were families and children on the top of that mountain, and they had to choose while the Roman soldiers surrounded them. There are moments in history when the correct order of things is so violated that—"

"Fates must change," I cut him off.

"That's right, there are rules."

65

I FEEL THE SACRED MOUNTAIN.
The familiar sensations I have experienced ever since I was small of the unmistakeable energy, a layered knowledge of the souls and hearts of those who have been in this place before. The density of those experiences somehow floating in a zone that I have access to, as if there is no space or time separating that moment from this one. I am sure that it is with my heart that I understand an essential part of my own history and who I have become. The many secrets of my world, all finally being revealed.

I hold tightly to Benjamin's hand as we approach the building. It contains all the modern elements of a comfortable tourist destination. A museum, theatre, reception hall, gift shop, and even a cable car that brings visitors to the summit. I try to imagine this place before any of that existed, two thousand years ago.

"Here, Gabriella, put this on."

Benjamin hands me a laminated badge that has my photograph on it, a barcode, and other numbers and symbols.

"Where did you get this?"

"Always so many questions." He smiles but doesn't answer. "We can go through the other door with this pass. Come this way."

The reception hall is bursting with people, and I hear many languages being spoken. A wall of cameras and international press photograph everyone who comes in through the door in a blinding, continuous burst of flashbulbs. There is the undeniable sense that this group of people is at the forefront of something that will change everything—and my grandfather is at the very center of it.

"Look, there he is."

A large group of reporters surround my grandfather.

"Yes," Benjamin says. "Go to him, Gabriella, I will find you after."

I am relieved to finally see my grandfather. The familiar shape of his shoulders from behind are slightly bent forward. In one hand, he holds a stack of papers and the other hand rests on a colleague's back, steadying himself, allowing him to place his ear close to the speaker's mouth. He never wants to miss a word. His hearing had been declining in the last few months, and this, along with several other physical changes that I had noticed, was disconcerting. I promised myself that we would have him visit his doctor when we returned to New York. Seeing him again in his element helps to alleviate the worry I have felt about his well being since we had been separated on the ground in Istanbul.

I run to greet him.

"Gabriella." He tries to disengage himself from the bear hug I have him in so that he can look at me.

I stand and wonder if he can see the invisible but dramatic changes in every part of me. "I've been so worried about you," I say as his eyes meet mine. He reaches for my hands and kisses them both in the way he has always done since I was small.

"You are a sight for sore eyes." He takes my arm and loops it through his. "Come, I want to talk to you."

We push our way to the back of the room, stopping briefly to acknowledge the many who are attempting to speak with him. The flashing lights of the cameras are making me dizzy, and I feel overwhelmed by everyone pulling at my grandfather. I keep looking around hoping to see Benjamin, but he is nowhere.

"Quite a group," my grandfather whispers into my ear.

Suddenly, a young woman dressed in military fatigues has both her hands on him. "Dr. Vogel, come with us. We need you at the front of the room. Now."

"Yes, yes." He pries her hands off of him. "I will be there in a moment."

He ignores her request and continues to push me in the opposite direction toward the back of the room. Clearly, he wants privacy.

"Papa, where are we going?"

"Look at you, so grown up." He moves a stray hair away from my eyes. "So much is happening more quickly than I ever imagined and now, Benjamin and you."

I feel myself blush deeply, but he continues, "You must listen very carefully to what I'm about to tell you."

There is an urgency to what he is saying. Even though the program for the evening has started, he leads me out the doors and away from the auditorium into the hallway.

"Of course, what is it?" I ask and force myself to push away the growing anxiety I feel. "Shouldn't we go back in? Can this wait?"

"All this." He ignores my questions and points to the other room. "Is very gratifying. However, *you* are the one who has shown me many things."

I look at him as I try to block out the sounds of the applause and the speaker from the other room.

"What do you mean? Tonight is about you, *your* accomplishments. In a few more days everyone will know. You're going to show everyone that you've been right all along."

"Although these ideas have always been more the stuff of science fiction than scientific fact . . ." The speaker has begun his introduction in the auditorium.

"You have taught me one of the most important lessons of my life," my grandfather says.

"Papa, listen, the speaker, they've started. Let's go back. They are talking about you—your work." What could he possibly have learned from me? And then, I remembered what Benjamin had said about my experiences somehow influencing him. I can't understand what he is doing and I try to lead him back, frightened by the tone of our conversation. "We need to get back in there, Papa, now—"

"Gabriella, please stop. *Listen* to me. I want you to know that you have shown me what I always wanted to believe."

"What? No, please, I don't understand."

"The work of Dr. Vogel will finally prove that a truly advanced civilization might be able to circumvent the obstacles associated with these theories . . ." the speaker continues.

"Simply by seeing it—in you."

"Seeing what?"

"That one could find happiness, find everything they are looking for not by looking outward but by looking in. Finding the answers that reside deep in your heart."

And then, I realize what he is saying. I can see it. The acceptance in his eyes, a peacefulness that I have not seen before. "But you've done it! Everything you've worked for your whole life; it's all coming together for you right now."

He shakes his head slowly and smiles at me. "This has been an interesting time. I have had the opportunity to really reflect on things, my own accomplishments and my contributions to the field of science. More important, I have recognized the incredible gift we have been given to be together for so many years and I now really believe what Einstein always said."

"About time?"

"Yes." He pauses. "And that things are not always what they seem."

The speaker in the other room starts to wrap up his introduction. "What has always been the realm of science fiction will now become fact. The very thin line between physics and metaphysics will finally be bridged. This is the proof that humankind has waited for."

There is something about what my grandfather is saying and how he is saying it. I know he is preparing me, saying things that need to be said before there are no more opportunities to do so. I recognize the feeling. I know it well and I know what it is.

It is a farewell.

"So, in preparation for the World Conference next week, where he will present his proof that will change everything we know about our world, please welcome, Dr. Sydney Vogel!"

Just as I am about to respond, he places his index finger over his lips and quiets my objection. "They're calling me, Gabriella." He kisses the top of my head and turns to hurry away. "I'll see you, right after."

"I'll be right here." I try to hold his hand for a few more seconds.

"Think about what I said." He turns and walks away.

When I go back into the auditorium, I see him standing at the podium and hear thundering applause. Hundreds of cameras flash and everyone pushes forward to get a glimpse of the humble scientist who is about to change the world. I stand alone, the crush of people pushing past me toward the front. As I back away to the rear of the room, I look up at my grandfather and notice something very unusual and out of character for him. Rather than greeting the applause with his usual good-natured humor and warm self-conscious smile, he looks down at the floor.

66

WE WALK OUT OF THE hall together and into the night. The stars are unlike any I have ever seen before.

Brighter.

I feel the shift in the air. It's the kind of wind that would rustle the leaves on the trees—if there were any here. I look around and realize that we are quite alone. The scientists have boarded buses and departed for Jerusalem and the various hotels where they are staying, ready to attend the next event on their carefully orchestrated itineraries. All in preparation for the conference—where my grandfather is expected to reveal his proof. I look at him as he turns to face me and remember everything I love about him.

"So many have stood in this place before us, Gabriella, and they will continue to after we're gone. Moses, the Israelites, Herod, Alexander the Great, Caesar, Napoleon—"

"It's as if time is collapsing."

"Yes."

"This place is amazing," I whisper.

"It's a different kind of desert, a different kind of place." He shakes his head.

"Not one of sand and dunes, a desert where the wind leaves its fingerprint. Time is *erased* here."

"Come here, Gabriella." He reaches out for me.

"This is a desert of rock, of presence—of soul."

"You feel like you're close to heaven, don't you?"

"There is something different about tonight. About you, Papa." I try to identify what it is, but he doesn't hear me. He is looking up at the sky. "And yet, some things are the same. The stars are just like ours at the beach."

I hold his hand as we walk toward the railing at the edge of the open plaza. I feel the cold metal under my hands as I grip it firmly and try to find my balance.

"Similar to our beach, but this is different," he says.

"I know, it's special."

"Every place has within it memories of the past, Gabriella. What you now know is how to recognize the things that are truly important, the values and ideas that stand the test of time. How to choose—what to believe."

"To trust and rely on my heart," I whisper my grandmother's words. I put his hand against my cheek; I don't want this time with him to end.

"Yes."

I had forgotten the cold of the desert night and tighten the thin sweater around my shoulders. He puts his arm around me, and we stand there looking out into the sky together. My arms wrap around the front of my body and cover my heart. I feel that it is going to break out of my chest.

"It's so bloody cold when the sun goes down." I hear *her* words come out of my mouth, the exact same words spoken by my grandmother in this very place, so many years ago. I have heard them and seen them. In a dream, a memory.

"You do remember."

"I don't know anymore what I am. Who I am becoming. The past and future they—they blend together. Sometimes I'm not sure if I can tell them apart."

"Gabriella?"

"Maybe my *memories* aren't even mine?" I turn away from him in frustration.

He reaches out for me. "Yes, they are your memories." I know there is something else he wants to tell me.

"What is it?" I ask.

"You must always remember to really see what is around you. The stars, the sky, the earth. Even the invisible, but especially everything that *you* are. "

"Why are you saying all this now?"

"There is so much all around us, and yet, there is so much more."

"More?"

But he doesn't hear me. He seems far away. He is calm, and I wonder whether this is what happens when you have arrived, when you are ready to put it all together, everything you have worked so hard for.

You realize that you have only started.

Suddenly, I hear an unexpected sound. It is the mechanism of the cable car engaging, but I know everything is shut down for the night. The cabin glides into position in front of us and very slowly, the door slides open as if responding to some invisible command.

"Look at this, our own private ride to the top."

"This is crazy! Papa, why would we want to go up now?"

"Come, let's get in."

"No, I really don't think we should—"

He reaches out for me, and we enter into the dark cable car as the doors slide closed behind us and lock. I thought we were alone until I hear a voice.

"Sydney."

I turn around and realize immediately who it is. "Benjamin!"

He reaches out for me, and I run into his arms. I hold onto him tightly as we ascend the side of the steep mountain. No one speaks. We are quiet, lost in our own thoughts as we look out the windows of the shaking cable car.

Finally I find my voice. "What is happening?" I need answers, information. "Can one of you please tell me what's going on?"

The door to the cable car opens slowly as we lock onto the arrival platform at the top of the mountain near the northern face of the plateau. I feel desperate, trying to remain in control of my emotions and the truly unprecedented panic that is beginning to overtake me. Benjamin turns his face away from mine.

"Gabriella." My grandfather's voice is calm.

It reminds me of how he would speak to me when I was a little girl, and he would hold me on his lap in one of the rocking chairs on the porch of our home in Gloucester. I would be in my pajamas wrapped in his arms, and we would look out to the sea together. We would talk late into the night, inventing stories. I had always felt so safe and secure there.

But this night is different. I can feel it.

"There's something about this place isn't there?" I say slowly.

"Yes, you're right." He walks toward me. "And I want to tell you something; I have made a choice." I know that he is preparing me for something I cannot imagine. "I will not be going to the conference next week to present my paper. My proof." His hand lifts my chin so that I will look in his eyes. I am crying, and he reaches into his pocket to pull out a handkerchief and hands it to me.

I shake my head. "No!"

"I understand your disappointment." He is calm and seems already far away. "But, you must know that with the exception of seeing you like this right now, this is truly one of the happiest moments of my life."

I try to absorb the incredible power of his words. "What are you saying?"

I feel Benjamin next to me as he takes my hands in both of his and I turn to look up at him.

"You remember what I told you? That there was a secret about Herod and about this place, don't you?" Benjamin's eyes burn into mine as he reminds me.

"Yes, of course, I remember. "

I remembered every detail of every minute I had ever spent with him. I committed them all to a visual record that I could draw upon when I needed to play them over in my mind, in case they would be all I would have left—the solitary moments with him. As if I had learned to love a ghost.

"As you know, it is Benjamin who has shown me the proof, helping me to find the last pieces of the equations," my grandfather says. "You see, the tunnels Einstein suggested do, in fact, exist and have been used for thousands of years."

"They connect to other worlds." It is Benjamin's voice.

"These worlds are similar yet different from ours in critical ways." My grandfather pauses. "Many of the things we take for granted in this world are different there."

"Like the laws of physics, " I say.

"Yes. And specifically," Benjamin says and looks right at me, "that we can exist and experience time in a different way than your world does."

"We? You mean you, Benjamin."

"Everything could be the same but time is different," my grandfather says. "They could be farther ahead or even behind us."

I knew what it meant and ask, "Where are they—the tunnels? The way in?"

"There are several locations. CERN is one, as your grandmother knew. But there are others. Some of the ports change over time. They can open up when . . ." Benjamin pauses. "When they need to."

I listen to what they are saying and try to understand. I think of my grandmother, the way she held me and what she said.

Remember, Gabriella, things are not always what they seem.

"When they need to? You mean when the rules of the universe are broken?" I ask.

"Like the shifting cycles of the solar systems that make up the universe, changing the relationship of the planets and stars to each other, the tunnels do not remain in a static location. The ports of entry, the points of *access,* change. This is why the portals have always been so elusive, so difficult to find."

He points to the very spot we are standing in.

"Here?"

"Yes." Benjamin smiles.

I stand still, afraid to breathe as I wait for more.

Benjamin continues, "Herod had in his consultants many of the most brilliant advisors in the Roman Empire, astronomers and mathematicians, who knew that Masada was one of the ports. That is why he built his palace here. However, despite his attempts to gain access, he failed."

I am stunned. "This is a way into one of the tunnels?"

"The nine hundred and sixty people who appeared to have died in this very spot almost two thousand years ago did know. They were successful where Herod failed. They knew that the port would open and that they could leave their bodies behind and find a life of freedom in another place. Together with those they loved."

"And when the Romans burned the barricades and arrived at the top of Masada?" I hear my own voice repeat the story I knew so well.

"They found what they thought was a mass suicide—nine hundred and sixty bodies. But as you now understand, that is not what happened."

"How? How could they have known this?" I ask, unable to imagine a people from two thousand years earlier who could understand the physics of a concept that was only going to be revealed in this generation.

"They were told." Benjamin says as he kisses my hand.

67

THE WIND HAS QUIETED, and I look up at the velvet blanket of sky. The stars are winking, beckoning—whispering of other possibilities, so incredibly close.

"This is so much bigger than all of us." My grandfather is calm.

"But your work, Papa, all these years! You were right."

"I know, but it's time to choose, to trust what my heart is telling me."

"Please, please don't do this. Not for me. You've worked your whole life for this." I pull my hand out of Benjamin's grasp and turn away.

"Gabriella." My grandfather's voice is soft. "It has been decided."

"What do you mean?"

"It's time to tell her, Benjamin; she deserves to know the truth."

"Come here." Benjamin takes my hand.

The three of us walk away from the northern plateau past the ruins of a Byzantine church, several small structures, and the makeshift sun shelters set up for the tourists who come to explore this place. The moon lights up the hills of Jordan, and I see its distorted reflection on the Dead Sea. Benjamin leads me with purpose a little further then down a steep staircase, and we descend into what seems to be a cave.

"Where are we?" I ask, yet there is something very familiar about where we have arrived.

"Gabriella, this is where I first met your grandmother. Right here in this place, in this very cistern."

I know that what Benjamin is telling me is true, that this is where he had found her while she was searching in these ruins. I had seen it before.

"I, I know."

"Of course you do—and your grandmother." He smiles at a distant memory. "She was quite persuasive, like *you* I might say. But, she wanted answers and she found them. She understood the science—she realized that it could be a way for her to live. She convinced me, she asked me to take her, to bring her through. I did not want to see her die and so, I did. Sydney knows this now, he understands."

"But, how could you? That went against everything. You violated the correct order of things?" I ask.

"That's right. As I told you, I did break the rules. I was warned that it could never happen again. No individual from your world could ever be brought through unless—"

"You don't need to tell me this. You don't ever need to explain your reasons to me."

"I do, though; I want you to know. I was told that if it ever happened again, the ports would be forever closed. To me that is."

"Benjamin, I understand. You can't stay. I don't want you to give up your world, your timeless existence. Not for me."

"Gabriella, I've already decided. It's all right here. Everything I've always wanted, everything I have always searched for—and it is you."

"No, you can't."

"Many years before you were born, Albert Einstein and I were together, and he told me something." He narrows his gaze then closes his eyes as he breathes in the distant memory. Then he repeats word for word what the great scientist had told him. "He said that 'one cannot help but be in awe, as one contemplates the mysteries of eternity, of life, and the marvelous structures of reality.'"

"This makes no sense, I don't—"

"Don't you see? It's you. He was talking about you."

"Gabriella." I turn to my grandfather's voice. "Even though you do not know why, you understand some of the mysteries of this world. You have chosen life and understood death. Even your architecture, 'building the marvelous structures of reality,' just as Einstein said."

I need to listen to him, to everything he has to tell me. To both of them.

"No, please, Benjamin, Papa! Please don't do this for me."

"This is the way—the way it is supposed to be, Gabriella." My grandfather's eyes encourage me.

"But, your work, if it's not for your work, everything you have been waiting to prove, then what is it for?"

"Gabriella." Benjamin waits until my breathing has slowed. "It's for love. That's what we're here for. All of us. And love is bigger and more powerful than anything—any scientific theory, any one individual's will, and sometimes even the rules of the universe. Love is more powerful than time itself."

Suddenly, my grandfather falls to the ground. I run to his side and put my hands under his head. I bend down to hold him and kiss him.

"Papa, what is happening?" His breathing becomes shallow and he closes his eyes. "Benjamin! Please help him! Please talk to me, Papa, are you—in pain?"

But he already seems far away.

"Gabriella, you believe everything we told you tonight about this place don't you? About the ports?" Benjamin says.

"Yes, yes, of course, I believe you." I search his eyes for anything else.

"Now look." Benjamin gently takes my face and turns it away from his down toward my grandfather's. I look into his eyes; they are open. He is calm, quiet, and peaceful.

"Gabriella," my grandfather says, his words slightly labored, "I'm not afraid and I don't want you to be. It is so . . . beautiful." He looks up past me, and I follow his eyes. I see the moon through the opening of the cistern. "I can see her. Sophie is here, she's with us. She wants you to remember; she wants me to remind you that you are not alone. Those who love you are always with you. When you feel the breeze kissing your cheeks, remember. When you see the sun rise, remember. When answers to your questions are being whispered into your heart—remember."

"Yes, I will."

"I was not ready to go forward until I knew, but now I'm sure. It's your turn now, Gabriella. You have both found what you've been searching for." He looks at Benjamin. "You have found your soul mate." Then he closes his eyes and says the last words he'll say on this earth. "Now it's time for me to return to mine."

68

I LEAN BACK INTO the deep leather seat and wrap my arm through Benjamin's as I look past his beautiful sleeping face and out the small window of the jet. I see the surface of the earth below and the stars in the sky above and feel myself slipping through time.

Traversing worlds.

We had buried my grandfather in our family plot in Israel, and I was overwhelmed by the worldwide outpouring of sentiment, letters, calls, and e-mails about his legacy and life. The vision and courage of a small man who had inspired so many. It was an incredible story, widely featured in the international news. The great scientist who died suddenly at the top of the mountain—days before presenting the findings of his life's work.

But I knew different.

I remembered everything about that night on the mountain and the incredible days before with Benjamin. I put together what had seemed like disparate pieces of my life—random occurrences—and realize, *know* that they are not. I have found the clarity that can only come from looking at things afterward. Fate, destiny, or whatever the many forces could be called, all played a part in what led me to him. I realize that so many people who loved me knew all along that it would happen.

And I know that our being together is the only way it could ever be.

I was beginning to accept the idea that my grandfather was in another place, one that he had always believed existed, one he had finally found. He had proven in every way what he had always known in his heart to be true while teaching me to believe and trust in what my heart was telling me as well. I understood for the first time how it all might work. That the soul can exist in many forms, in different *worlds*. And I knew that the tunnels my grandfather and Einstein had found were impassable physically to those from this world.

At least for now.

And then, there was Benjamin. It was as if everything in my life had led me to him. The unstoppable inevitability of our finding each other and my understanding that the rules of the universe were very different for him. He had chosen to stay in this world—with me—and had given up his ability to travel through the tunnels and his timeless existence. We would be together, and he would stay here where we would age and be subject to the same laws of time.

He said that this was the way it was always meant to be.

I realized that the connections I had always found in the many parts of my life—literature, architecture, science, and even ancient mysticism, all pointed to the same thing: the idea that everything exists for a purpose, that things happen for a reason, and that through our choices, the power and freedom we have been given, we can change our lives and the world.

I finally understand what it means to find the beginning in the end.

FARE FORWARD,
A NOVEL

BY WENDY DUBOW POLINS

A Reader's Guide

READING GROUP QUESTIONS AND
TOPICS FOR DISCUSSION

Q: What is the meaning of "The power to choose your own fate?"
Do you think one can actually choose?

Q: Einstein said, "Everything is connected." What does that mean to you?

Q: What is special about the relationship between Lily and Gabriella?
Have you ever felt that same relationship with a friend?

Q: The book tells us that "Art and science are asking the same question—
what, if anything is eternal?" Do you agree? Can you think of any
examples?

Q: Gabriella and her grandmother have premonitions. They know or feel
things before they happen. Do you know anyone with that gift or power?

Q: Gabriella's grandmother, Sophie, wrote, "Only art education can improve
quality of life, understanding and knowledge." What do you think she
meant by this? Do you agree?

Q: The book deals with destiny and fate and whether we can change things.
Do you believe that "What did not happen might still remain possible,
if we could go back in time and choose differently?"

Q: The book proposes that art is a legacy for the future and a way to live on
into time. Can you think of other ways to live on, to leave your mark,
your legacy, after your death?

Q: The book is in the first person, the voice of Gabriella. Would it have been as effective in the third person?

Q: The scientific community believes that everything will be ultimately explained through the "Theory of Everything." Do you agree or do you think there are mysteries in the universe that will never be explained?

Q: Einstein proposed that there may be wormholes that connect to other universes and might allow people to live longer and age differently. Do you believe these wormholes, connections through space and time, exist? Why or why not?

Q: What is the connection between the mystical tradition of Gabriella's parents and the theoretical physics of her grandfather?

Q: Do you believe, as the book suggests, that there is ONE person destined for you in the universe, one that completes you? Or do you think that many people could fill that role?

Q: Sophie often quotes T.S. Eliot's poem *Four Quartets*, found on page 245, from which the book title comes. What do you think is the meaning of this poem?

Q: Many times in the book Gabriella says she has so many questions. Do you think she is imitating the way we, as readers, as fellow travelers, feel?

Q: Benjamin suggests that LOVE is more powerful than any rules of the universe. Do you agree? Why or why not?

A special thank you to Renee Nadel, for her help in crafting these questions.